The Belial Search

A Belial Series Novel

R.D. Brady

Scottish Seoul Publishing

"Sooner or later everyone sits down to a banquet of consequences."
Robert Louis Stevenson

"The day science begins to study non-physical phenomena, it will make more progress in one decade than in all the previous centuries of its existence."
Nikola Tesla

PROLOGUE

Shoreham, Long Island
1902

James Franklin II looked out the window as his driver pulled to a stop. It had taken hours to get here from Manhattan. Thank God he had been able to borrow Mr. Morgan's Curved Dash Oldsmobile and driver. But his bum was still sore from the bumpy ride.

Irritated, he pulled out his handkerchief and wiped his face. This was lunacy to begin with. He couldn't understand why a man of Mr. Morgan's intellect would have bought into it. Thank goodness he'd finally seen the light.

Smoothing down his coat, James picked up his bowler hat from the seat next to him as the driver hustled to open the door.

He stepped out, looking around with distaste at WardneClyffe Tower—a metal skeleton that rose 186 feet in the air before ending in a metal dome. To Franklin, it looked like a giant mushroom. *Wireless electricity for the east coast. Ridiculous notion.*

Some people claimed Nikola Tesla was a genius who was in tune with a knowledge greater than that of mere mortals. Even his birth was something out of a story: a ferocious lightning storm was said to have hit the night Tesla was born. The midwife had thought it was an omen and claimed he would be a child of darkness. His mother had retorted, "No. He will be a child of light."

1

James had also heard that the man had a peculiar fondness for pigeons and a complete fear of germs. The man was insane.

"You, boy," he called to a dark-skinned figure kneeling on the ground and banging something. The boy turned, and James realized he was much older than James had assumed, closer to James's own age of fifty. Not that he apologized.

The man got to his feet, removed his cap, and held it in front of him. "Yes, sir?"

"Where is Mr. Tesla?"

The man pointed to the building. "He's in his lab. Do you know the way?"

"Yes, yes of course." James paused, glancing at the building warily. "Is he conducting an experiment?"

James had seen more than enough of Tesla's demonstrations. Tesla could stand in the middle of balls of electricity—have them shooting out of his hands, in fact. James wasn't sure how he did it without killing himself, or someone else.

The man smiled. "No. Just writing something."

"Very well." With a determined stride, James headed across the barren lawn to the building. He rapped sharply on the door before pulling it open. "Mr. Tesla?"

Inside, two men stopped their conversation to stare at him. Nikola Tesla, with his dark hair and mustache, pierced him with his blue eyes. He had this uncanny ability to look as if he was staring right through a person. The man next to him had bushy white hair and wore a white suit with pinstripes.

James's eyes grew large. "Mr. Clemens, I'm sorry I didn't realize you were here."

Samuel Clemens turned to Tesla. "Who's this, Nikola?"

"The money," Nikola said dryly.

"Ah, well, that's my exit cue then. Next week in Manhattan?"

Nikola nodded. "I'll be there."

2

Samuel nodded at James as he departed.

James watched him go. He'd heard that the two were on friendly terms, but he had no idea the great writer would be here today.

"Could you shut the door? You're letting the flies in," Nikola said from behind him.

"Right." James hastily reached for the handle and shut the door. He turned. "Mr. Tesla—" Tesla was nowhere to be seen. "Mr. Tesla?" But the man did not appear.

James stalked forward. "Mr. Tesla?" He wandered through the rows of tables and piles of metal, making his way toward the office in the back. A light was on, and Tesla sat behind his desk.

James shook his head as he stormed up. "Mr. Tesla, I need to speak with you."

Tesla did not look up. "Then speak."

James ground his teeth. "Right, fine. Well, Mr. Morgan has decided to cut extraneous expenses due to the downturn of the market."

Tesla continued making notes on the schematic in front of him.

"He won't be able to continue funding your project," James said.

Tesla's pencil stilled, and James gave a satisfied smile. Finally, the man was paying attention.

Tesla looked up, his eyes narrowed. "What did you say?"

James swallowed and took an involuntary step back. "Mr. Morgan has been a generous supporter of your work. But now—"

"Do you have any idea what I am doing here? I could control the weather. Reduce the impact of storms. I will make it possible for people to have electricity without having any wires. Do you get what that could mean for mankind? What this could lead to?"

"Yes, well, Mr. Morgan is not convinced the project will be successful. Nothing like this has even been done before."

Tesla stood up and stalked around the desk. "Yes it has. But you people are too blind to see it. *I* have seen it. I *know* it will work."

James was rethinking not having his driver come in with him. He knew Tesla was viewed by some as being only a hair's breadth from crazy. The man claimed that he could envision entire machines, mold and change them in his mind.

But James knew that was not how inventions happened. They didn't magically appear. And nowhere in human history had mankind been able to control the weather, for goodness' sakes.

"Nevertheless, Mr. Morgan will not be funding the project any further," James said.

"Then Morgan is a fool."

"Good day, Mr. Tesla." James backed out of the office, keeping an eye on Tesla. But Tesla was staring off into space, caught up in something in his own mind. James quickly made his way back through the lab and toward the door. The man was crazy.

A few minutes later, James was being driven quickly away. He stared out the window at the metal skeleton Tesla had erected, and scoffed.

Control the weather. What hubris. That is God's work, not man's.

4

CHAPTER 1

Washington, DC
Today

Delaney McPhearson pushed through the heavy hotel room door. "Jake?"

"In here," Jake Rogan called from the living room.

Laney steeled herself as she made her way down the marble-lined hallway. It had been good to get away, but the last few months of stress couldn't be completely erased.

She shoved her concerns aside and instead focused on the luxurious hotel room she was in. She remembered the days when a hotel room meant two double beds and, if she was lucky, a working ice machine down the hall. Now, she was staying in a suite that had a bedroom, kitchen, living room, and a bathroom that was larger than her bedroom growing up. Times sure had changed.

But although the hotel had been a nice perk, after two weeks, she was sick of it. She wanted nothing more than to head home to her little cottage in Baltimore. Of course, if there were any more meetings like the one this morning, that wouldn't happen for a while.

Laney turned into the living room. Jake's dark brown eyes lit up, and her heart squeezed. Getting away had been good for him, too, even if it meant meeting after meeting. He had been injured six months ago, and it had taken a long time to regain the muscle that he'd lost while recuperating. He still had some loss of motor function, but the doctors assured them that in another few weeks he'd be back to what he was before.

Jake started to get up from the pale green couch.

She waved him down. "No. I'll sit with you." She took a seat next to him.

He took her hand. "You need to stop worrying about me."

Laney knew he was right. But she'd seen him shot twice, and neither time was something she was likely to forget. The idea of losing him was just too terrifying to contemplate. After this most recent incident, the first few months had been the worst. Jake had wasted away, unable to eat much. Now he was back to his normal workouts, which, shallow as it was, Laney really loved watching him do. There was something about a sweaty muscular man that was infinitely appealing.

"How was your day?" she asked.

Jake groaned. "Oh, great. My subcommittee was made up of senators from the heartland. Each was more interested in grandstanding than listening to the answers to the questions they posed. One guy made this long-winded speech before finally getting around to the question, and as soon as I started to speak, he got up and left. Who the hell elected these guys?"

Laney laughed. "Sounds like we met with the same people." Although Laney had met some incredible people in her time in DC, most of them were not elected officials. The elected ones were too concerned with how everything was perceived rather than the truth. She sighed. *And they're the ones I need to convince that everything is fine.*

The problem was, she wasn't convinced herself.

"Matt called a few minutes ago," Jake said.

Matt was Special Agent Matthew Clark of the Special Investigative Agency, an offshoot of the Department of Defense. For a long time, the department had been unknown to the majority of people in Washington, DC, including those within the intelligence community. But the last few months had thrown all of that secrecy out the window.

6

"Do I even want to know what he had to say?" Laney asked, pulling away from Jake to look at his face.

"There was another incident."

Laney groaned even though she had known what Jake was going to say. "Okay, tell me."

"Better yet, I can show you. Here." He leaned over to the iPad that was on the coffee table, turned it toward her, and hit play.

Onscreen, a huge waterfall roared. A few boats bounced along, keeping well away from the onrush of water.

"Is that Niagara Falls?" Laney asked.

Jake nodded. "Yeah. This video was taken by a tourist yesterday afternoon. Watch the top of the falls on the left."

Excited utterings came from the iPad's speaker, and then the camera operator zoomed in. At the edge of the falls, two men stood as if waiting to make sure people saw them—which Laney was sure was exactly what they were doing. After a few seconds, the men dove over the edge into the raging water.

"Goddamn it," Laney muttered.

The men's act was met with stunned exclamations and concern. The video zoomed in to where the men had gone under. A few seconds later, they popped back up and swam for shore. They pulled themselves up on the bank and then sprinted out of view.

"Son of a bitch." Laney sank deeper into the couch. "How many hits has this gotten?"

"Enough," Jake said, his voice grim.

Weariness settled over Laney. Another Fallen incident. "How long was this video up?" Laney asked.

"Thirty minutes."

Laney closed her eyes. Thirty minutes on the internet was a lifetime. "What's the response?"

"Most think it's a hoax. The rest are split between CGI and special suits. Only a very few are suggesting it's like some of the other incidents that have hit the web. I already have Dom trying to figure out a plausible explanation for how two individuals could survive such a fall."

Laney shook her head. The one person who might be loving the Fallen popping up as much as they were was Dom. So far, he'd spun stories about doppelgangers and electromagnetic energy, among other things. In response to one spectacularly fast sprint by a Fallen through the crowd in front of the Vatican, he'd even blamed drones.

"Matt's spinning this one," Jake said.

Laney knew that by now Matt's people had infiltrated the online discussions and started an onrush of comments downplaying the possibility of it being real. The SIA had a public relations arm whose entire job was to spin Fallen incidents. And lately, that division had been working overtime. The Fallen incidents around the globe had exploded. Henry and the Chandler Group had even had to start pitching in. It was beginning to take up all their time.

And Laney still couldn't figure out why. The Fallen had been around for thousands of years, reincarnated time and time again. Yet they had always stayed in the shadows and out of the spotlight. Until now. Now, it seemed like they *wanted* the world to know about them.

An image of Victoria flashed through Laney's mind, along with a wave of grief. Victoria had stopped them from achieving immortality at the cost of her own life. Laney knew that had something to do with the change in the Fallen's behavior, but she couldn't figure out what.

And Victoria hadn't been the only casualty. Laney's and Jake's relationship had taken a hit as well. When she had first returned from China, she had spent all her time with Jake and Henry as they recovered, but after two months, with more and more Fallen incidents popping up, she had known she needed to get back in the field.

Jake and Henry had been in no shape to do the same. And Jake had not handled it well.

8

Jake pulled her into his shoulder and Laney laid her head there. "We'll figure it out. We always do," he said.

Laney leaned up and kissed him softly on the lips, then leaned her head back on his shoulder. "Still no sign of Elisabeta?"

Jake shook his head. "No. And Matt has everybody looking. I'm pretty sure he's also commandeered more than a few international databases to run facial recognition. But she hasn't poked her head out."

Laney frowned. Where was Elisabeta? Her minions were popping up all over the place like some international game of whack-a-mole, yet the queen bee had stayed hidden. The only news on her lately had to do with her latest philanthropic donations; and Laney was pretty sure the leader of the Fallen angels hadn't turned over a new leaf.

Laney wasn't sure what made her more nervous—all the Fallen popping up or Elisabeta quietly maneuvering behind the scenes.

Her cell rang and she read the caller ID with a frown before answering. "Hey, Matt. What's going on?"

"Laney, there's been a threat."

"Where?"

"The Capitol building."

"Fallen?" Laney asked, keeping her eyes on Jake.

"Not sure yet. But if it is…" Matt said.

Laney nodded. "I'm on my way. Call Jen?" Jen was Jen Witt, Laney's best friend and a nephilim.

Jake stood up and strode across the room.

"Will do," Matt said.

"Any other agents in the area?" Laney asked.

Matt blew out a breath. "No. With everything happening, we're spread pretty thin."

"Okay. I'll be there in five."

Laney stood, and Jake turned to face her, his arms across his chest. "A Fallen incident?"

"Maybe. I'm heading to the Capitol."

9

Jake said nothing just gave her an abrupt nod.

Laney wanted to say something, but she had no idea what magical mix of words would get Jake to understand that she had to do this. She felt the last two weeks of peace slipping away. "I'll call you when I'm done."

"Sure," Jake said.

Laney started toward the front door, wishing she could slam it behind her. Instead, she pictured how much hell she was going to unleash on the Fallen who had created this tension between her and Jake.

CHAPTER 2

Captain Hank Reinhardt of the Capitol Police had a barrel chest and a bald head that made him look like a villain from a seventies James Bond film. Laney tilted her head back to study him. *He needs an eye patch,* she thought. *Or maybe a cigar.*

Using his towering frame to his advantage, he stood way too close to Laney, staring down at her. Her multiple attempts to put more space between them failed, so she gave up the fight. Apparently he was one of those people who simply didn't understand the appropriate distance between strangers.

"Agent McPhearson, discretion is the most critical factor here," Reinhardt said. "We have foreign dignitaries, school kids, tourists, senators. You name an important position, and they or a member of their staff is somewhere in that building. I don't think I have to remind you this needs to be handled as delicately as possible."

"And yet here you are reminding me," Laney drawled.

He glared, and she could swear he moved even closer. "My men have the suspect's picture."

"And they know to not approach him, right?"

Captain Reinhardt's eyes narrowed. "Yes."

"Okay, well, guess I'll go help look."

Laney headed into the crowd making its way into the Capitol. Matt had wanted to evacuate the building but he'd been shouted down by Homeland Security, who argued that without a definitive threat they would not panic the American public.

The suspect was the son of a known Fallen. The SIA knew the father had abilities, but they weren't sure about the son. Still, Capitol Police were told that if they sighted him, they were to contact the SIA agent on scene.

Laney wandered through the crowd, her eyes scanning everyone who passed. Matt had sent her a picture of their suspected Fallen—actually, nephilim. Rico Fuenes was nineteen, with long curly light brown hair he wore in a ponytail, dark eyes, and a scrawny beard. Slim in the picture Laney had seen, he could appear as a college student or tourist.

He'd tripped the SIA alarms when he'd gotten off the metro today at the Capitol South Metro Station. They'd been able to track him to outside the Capitol building but they still hadn't found him. Honestly, the kid could be anywhere.

"I might have him on the second floor," a voice over the radio said.

"Hold until the SIA arrives," another voice responded. And Laney realized with a shock that the second voice was Jake. Where the hell had he come from?

"He's going for something in his pocket. Could be a gun. I'm going in."

Shit. Laney sprinted for the stairs. Yells and screams sounded from the second floor, and a wave of people rushed down the stairs. Laney struggled to get past them, momentarily contemplating firing into the air to get everyone out of the way. But at last the crowd thinned and she dodged past them to the second floor.

An officer lay on the ground, blood seeping from a wound in his shoulder. He was conscious, but he was out of the fight. His gun lay a few feet from him. Rico Fuenes stood another thirty feet away. He looked at Laney with big eyes, blood still dripping from the knife in his hand.

12

She walked slowly toward him. And she felt nothing—no tingle of electricity. She smiled. *Not a Fallen. Well, this is a nice change of pace.*

Laney held up her hands. "Hey there, Rico. Why don't you put down that knife?"

"Capitalist pig."

Laney shrugged. "My pitiful wardrobe begs to differ."

The scuff of a shoe behind her caused her to turn. A man lunged at her, a knife in his hand as well.

Damn it. Laney barely leaped out of the way in time. He lunged again, and she stepped to the side and simultaneously sent a front kick to the man's groin. He screamed. She stepped toward him, placed her left hand on his knife arm, and turned his chin away from her. Then she kicked out his leg, still holding on to the knife hand.

He crashed to the ground, his arm contorted behind him. Laney stepped on his shoulder and yanked the arm back, dislocating the shoulder. He screamed again, and she quickly stripped the knife from his hand.

The man now lay crying in between her and Rico. Rico stared, his jaw slack, his eyes big.

Laney moved around the man, her attention now completely on Rico. "Like I said, put down the knife."

Rico glared. "No."

"Your choice." She stepped forward, but Rico opened his coat. Underneath, he wore a suicide vest. "Now you'll do what I—"

Laney moved before he could finish his thought. She kicked out his knee and turned his shoulders so his torso was twisted, his head turned to the side. Then, placing one hand on the back of his head and one on the front, she twisted hard.

Rico's eyes bulged, and then he went still. Laney caught him and lowered him to the ground.

"There's a bomb. Evacuate the building," Laney yelled into her mike.

"Laney, get out of there," Jake yelled into her ear.

13

"No time. This thing's beeping." She grabbed Rico's knife and sliced through the straps on the vest. She sprinted for the window, pausing only to grab the officer's gun and fire at the glass. She emptied the magazine, but the window didn't break.

Shit. She looked around. She might be able to break the glass by flinging a heavy bench at it, but she would have a tough time explaining that. She had a better idea. She turned back to the window. *Okay, let's see how much my practice has worked.*

She stepped to the side, her focus on the sky above. Clouds rolled in. Thunder clapped. Two bolts of lightning struck the glass, shattering it.

Laney threw the bag out the window. The swirling wind grabbed it and dragged it upward. Seconds later, the explosion ripped through the sky. Laney dove to the side as the concussive blast rolled through the open window and shook the building.

Car alarms went off outside. Laney got to her feet and peeked out the window. People were gaping up at the sky.

Laney turned around with a sigh. *Well, I hope that was discreet enough for the captain.*

14

CHAPTER 3

Baltimore, Maryland

Yoni Benjamin swung a right hook at Laney's head. Laney ducked under it, aiming her own hook at his ribs. Then, grabbing his shoulders, she kicked him in the back of his knee and aimed a knife hand at the front of his throat, stopping an inch before making contact. She placed the palm of her hand under his chin and pushed it up, adding a kidney shot to his back with her other hand.

He crashed to the ground. She stepped back, breathing hard.

After the bombing, Laney had gotten a nice long chewing-out by the captain. Jake had taken the opposite approach, and had given her the silent treatment all the way home. As a result, Laney was in a bad mood. She had saved hundreds of people's lives, yet she was being treated like a misbehaving child. The only good thing to come out of this— well, besides saving those hundreds of lives, she reminded herself—was that due to security concerns, all the hearings they had scheduled with Congress for the week had been canceled.

So as soon as they got back from the Capitol, Laney had hopped in her truck to visit Cleo and let off some steam. Luckily, Yoni had been at the school and in the mood for a good workout.

He was probably reconsidering that right now.

Yoni stood up, eyeing her. He was technically a Chandler operative, but he was so much more than that. Israeli by birth, standing at five foot three with a completely bald dome, he'd served with Jake in the Navy SEALs. These days, though, he spent most of his time helping run the Chandler School. And he said he'd never been busier in his life.

"I know with Jake out of commission you need a sparring partner, but do you think you could save my male pride a little and let me win once in a while?"

"What? You took me down a few times."

"Twice. And each time I was thankful I wore protection." He paused. "You okay?"

Laney shrugged and turned away. "Yeah. Just working some stuff off."

Yoni was quiet for a moment. "Look, Jake just needs a little time. It's tough not being able to do the stuff he used to do. To not be—"

"Him," Laney said.

"Yeah."

Laney walked over to her bag, pulled out her water bottle, and took a long drink. Everybody told her she needed to give Jake time. But what about her? She was still struggling with Victoria's and Ralph's deaths, not to mention missing Kati, Max, and Maddox. And honestly? She was now annoyed. He needed to snap out of it. He would get better; it was just a matter of time. He was already in PT, and his strength was almost back. It was only his mobility that was a little hampered. And life went on. She couldn't just sit by his side until he could get back in the field.

Laney twisted the cap onto her water bottle with a little more force than was necessary. *Men and their stupid ideas of what makes them men.*

"Lanes, I have to get going. I promised Sonya and Bear that we'd go out to dinner."

Laney composed her face before turning around. "That sounds great. Have fun."

16

"You're sure you're okay?"

"Yeah, I'm good. Now get going. That little boy of yours is practically changing by the minute."

A smile spread across Yoni's face. "Tell me about it. See you later."

Laney waited until Yoni was out of the gym before turning back to her bag and grabbing her MMA gloves. Cleo looked up from her spot in the corner. Cleo was a Javan leopard—a giant one. She stood four feet tall at the shoulders and was almost ten feet long. She was completely black, and when you got close to her you noticed even darker black spots on her coat.

I'm okay.

Cleo gave her a look suggesting she didn't even slightly believe her.

"How the hell did we get here, Cleo?" Laney wanted nothing more than to head home and make everything right. But if she went back to the cottage right now, she'd probably end up in a fight with Jake.

But she knew how they'd gotten here. Both of them had taken hits, and neither of them was whole. Jake's injuries were just a little easier to see.

Laney pictured Victoria's face. "Some things must happen in a certain way." Laney couldn't see why things had had to go *this* way though. She took a trembling breath. *I should have saved her. I should have found a way.*

She was heading to the heavy bag when her cell phone rang. She hesitated, considered ignoring the call. But she knew she needed to at least check and see who it was. When she glanced at the screen, surprise filtered through her. Mikio Lachowski, the stepdad of one of the children she'd helped saved from the Grand Canyon last year. Mikio and his wife, Sheila, had responded well to James's nature, even if they were a little shocked. But they loved their kids, and they were even helping some of the other families deal with the changes in their own kids.

Ripping off her gloves, Laney took a seat on a bench and answered the call. "Hi, Mikio. How are you doing?"

Mikio's words came out in a frantic rush. "Laney, thank God."

"What's wrong? Is it James?" James was nine years old, with dark hair and a serious persona. He loved to read and play video games. And one day, he would develop the abilities of a nephilim.

Mikio's usually reserved tone was choked in panic. "No, it's Sheila. She's missing."

"What do you mean, missing?"

"I got a call from the doctor. She missed an appointment with the pediatrician for Jillian. I called, but got no answer. I rushed home. I knew something was wrong."

"Okay, Mikio, I need you to calm down and tell me what happened."

Mikio's voice was shaking. "I could hear Jillian screaming from the car. The front door was unlocked. I saw the kitchen right away. Plates were broken on the floor. And her car's gone. Someone took her, Laney."

"Have you called the police?"

"Yes, but they don't think she's missing. They think she just walked away. Please, Laney, you know she wouldn't just disappear. She wouldn't leave Jillian all alone. Something's happened."

Laney knew Mikio was right—Sheila loved her family fiercely. Even if for some reason she wanted to leave them, she would never do it this way.

"Give me her cell phone. I'll track her."

Laney scribbled down the number as Mikio rattled it off.

"You'll look for her?" Mikio asked.

"Yes, I'll look for her. I'll call you when I know something."

She sent a quick text to an analyst to have them track the phone and check if Sheila's car had GPS. Then she shoved her issues with Jake into the back corner of her mind and hurried out of the gym. Sheila Lachowski was missing. And right now, that took precedence over her difficult love life.

CHAPTER 4

Laney called Henry from the school to let him know what was happening. Then she managed the twenty-minute drive to the estate in fifteen minutes with Yoni next to her and Cleo in the back. The whole way she told herself there was a rational explanation for Sheila going missing. But she didn't believe that.

The guards opened the gates as soon as they saw Laney coming down the road. She barreled past and pulled up to the main house a few minutes later.

Yoni jumped out at the main house. "I'll get the chopper ready." Yoni had volunteered as soon as he had learned of Sheila's disappearance. Laney knew he was trying to spend more time away from the action, but Sheila was part of the Chandler family.

Laney watched him run off and hoped they would soon have somewhere to take the chopper.

"Come on, girl." Laney leapt from the car and Cleo slunk out behind her.

As she sprinted up the stairs to the main house, she thought about how many times she had done exactly this— learned of horrible news and rushed to see if there was something she could do to prevent something even worse from happening.

She pictured Sheila Lachowski. She'd just had her daughter four months ago. Sheila loved being a mom the second time round. Laney and Jen had gone to her baby shower, and Laney had seen no signs of post partum depression, no signs that Sheila had been anything but happy about the birth of her daughter. Sheila had even managed to maintain her trips with James to the Chandler School for Children.

And now she was missing.

Laney burst through the doors of the Chandler main house with Cleo at her side. When she'd first arrived at Chandler, the sight of the three-story round entryway had blown her mind. Now she sprinted up the spiral stairs without a thought to the perfectly restored historic home.

She strode into Henry's office. "What have we got?"

Jake looked up from the conference table. "She went missing about two hours ago, according to the police files. The back door was broken into, and there were signs of a struggle."

Laney ignored the lurch of her heart at Jake's cool face and kept her focus on Sheila. "Why wouldn't the police consider her a missing persons case?"

"I don't know," Jake said.

"Any history of problems we don't know about?"

Jake shook his head. "Nope. Nothing in the neighborhood or the town that suggests a serial. And there's no information on anyone specifically targeting them."

"So there's nothing?"

"Danny's running a trace."

Henry Chandler, Laney's brother, walked in. Standing seven-foot-two, he towered above Laney's five-foot-four frame, and with dark hair and violet eyes, he looked nothing like her. But Laney saw Victoria in his eyes. "Yoni's got the helicopter warmed up and ready. Danny will patch you any info as he gets it on the trace. Jen's en route. She'll be about twenty minutes behind you."

Sheila and Mikio lived in Virginia—only about forty minutes away by chopper.

Jake sat at the table with his arms crossed, his face expressionless. Laney tensed, but all he said was, "Be careful."

"I will," she said and then took off at a run, Cleo on her heels. *Hold on, Sheila. I'm coming.*

CHAPTER 5

Norton, Virginia

Laney scanned the ground below her, looking for any sign of movement, but the tree coverage and the fading sunlight were making it impossible. They had tracked the GPS on Sheila's SUV to this area before it had cut out. Danny thought someone had disabled it. Laney leaned a little farther out. *Come on. Come on.*

"Anything?" Yoni asked from the pilot seat.

"No, but there could be a dozen people down there and I still wouldn't be able to see them. There are too many shadows."

"Only another minute and we'll be at the park."

"And don't you even think about going in there until you have backup," Jen Witt ordered over Laney's headset.

Laney shook her head. "Jen, you're ten minutes away. Sheila doesn't have ten minutes."

"Damn it, Laney. You don't know that. It'll take Yoni time to shut down the chopper. He won't be able to go in with you right away. You don't have any backup."

Cleo raised her head in the back of the chopper and Laney grinned. "Yeah I do."

Jen cursed over the radio.

"Hey, my virgin ears," Yoni complained.

"Sorry, Yoni," Jen said, not sounding even slightly contrite. "But you need to make her wait."

"Sure, no problem. See you in a few." Yoni snapped off the radio.

Laney raised an eyebrow. "You going to try to get me to wait for backup?"

"Will you wait for backup?"

"No."

Yoni shrugged. "Well, I can honestly say I tried. Just do me a favor and don't get killed. Jake will be really mad at me."

"I promise."

"Ten seconds. We're going to come in hard."

Laney held on as the chopper veered toward the ground. They were above an old park that had been closed due to too many kids getting into some old mines. The place had been closed for decades and the trees and shrubs had overtaken it.

"Yoni, look!" Laney pointed to a silver SUV that had been left halfway into the trees. She tensed. "That's Sheila's car."

"There's nowhere to land here, Laney. The nearest clearing is a mile away."

"Just get me over it." Laney looked at Cleo. "You coming?"

Cleo stretched her back as she stood. Laney climbed into the back of the chopper.

Yoni hovered thirty feet off the ground. "This is as close as I can get," he said. "After you drop, I'll go park this thing and double-time it over to you."

"No problem." Laney slid open the side of the chopper. "Let's go, girl."

Laney hesitated for only a second. *Oh, I hate this part.* Then she stepped out into nothingness.

After a toe-curling plunge, she called on the wind to buffer her and Cleo. An updraft caught her, stopping both her descent and Cleo's next to her. Then she began a controlled fall

24

as the wind reduced its power. They landed softly on the ground only twenty feet from the SUV.

Laney couldn't sense anyone around, but she pulled her Beretta from her holster anyway as she heard the chopper recede in the distance.

Silently, she moved up to the truck. Cleo slunk around the other side, but Laney got no sense of danger from her. She looked in the back window. No one. She moved to the side, peeked in, and blanched. She tapped her mic. "I've got Sheila's car. There's blood. Lots of it."

Next to her, Cleo sniffed the air and went still.

"Cleo's got a scent."

"Do not go anywhere until Yoni reaches you," Jen ordered.

Go, Cleo. Laney sprinted behind her. "No time."

"Laney—" Jen warned.

"There's too much blood, Jen. If Sheila's here, we need to reach her *now*."

Jen paused. "Be careful."

"Will do," Laney said as she sprinted through the trees after Cleo. She frowned as she pictured the map she'd seen of the park. She knew there was an old mine three hundred yards away.

Anyone? she asked Cleo.

No.

Laney picked up her pace, trusting Cleo to warn her of danger. Together, they ran through the trees and up a small rocky incline. Ahead, Laney could see the entrance to the mine. But there were no people. There was nothing.

A sweat broke out on her brow. *We're too late.*

Cleo let out a roar. And Laney's heart nearly stopped.

Blood.

Cleo could smell it, and now Laney, too, could make out the barest scent of copper in the air.

They raced to the mine entrance, but an old gate blocked the way. Through the gate's slats, Laney could see candles burning low, nestled into the nooks in the rock walls. Wax spilled over the sides. *Cleo, anyone?*

No.

Laney grabbed her Beretta and shot out the lock. She kicked the gate open.

Inside, it was as silent as a tomb. The light flickered along the rock walls casting moving shadows along the ground. Laney's heart began to pound even faster as they reached a turn in the tunnel. Beyond, she could see the glow of even more light.

Laney stepped around the turn and gasped. Cleo stopped next to her and let out a hiss.

Sheila Lachowski, age thirty-two, mother of James and Jillian, wife of Mikio, lay flat on a raised stone slab, her blue eyes staring at nothing, her blond hair falling over the side, matted with blood. More blood dripped from her wrists, but slowly. On the wet floor, more blood had puddled. Far too much blood.

Laney curled her fist. Sheila taught third grade and Sunday school on weekends. And she loved to do puzzles. *I'm so sorry, Sheila. You didn't deserve this.*

Laney grabbed her radio. "I've found her."

"Should I send the paramedics?" Jen asked.

Laney looked at what was left of Sheila. Her clothes were a bloody mess. Her chest was caved in as if something had been plunged into it. And there were cuts on the backs of Sheila's wrists and knees—spots that would hasten blood loss.

Laney swallowed down the lunch that threatened to re-emerge. "No. She's way beyond that now."

CHAPTER 6

Laney watched from the bottom of the hill as the emergency crews removed Sheila's body. She closed her eyes, picturing Sheila's family. Her son, James—or Jimmy, as everyone called him—was already too serious for his age. But that seriousness had been a boon when he'd been kidnapped by Grayston last year. He'd been one of the kids who'd helped keep the other ones together. One day, Laney knew he'd be a force for good in the world—if this tragedy didn't derail him.

Jimmy was a nephilim, although he'd received that ability from his father, not Sheila. In fact, Sheila had been completely unaware of Jimmy's father's abilities; he had disappeared shortly after she became pregnant. It had been only Sheila and Jimmy for six years, and then she'd met Mikio. Last year, they'd had their daughter, Jillian. From what Laney knew, they were a happy family.

And now they would be a devastated one.

The officers carried the stretcher carrying Sheila—zipped inside a body bag—down the hill. Laney and Yoni had tried to keep the scene preserved for the SIA, but the locals had pushed back, claiming jurisdiction.

Laney wanted the case. There was no Fallen element, no link to anything that they were currently working on. But Sheila, Jimmy—they were part of the Chandler family. And

Laney would make sure that whatever monster brought this pain to Sheila's family was caught and punished.

Now she just had to wait until the SIA did their bureaucratic mumbo-jumbo and got control of the scene.

Yoni was currently being questioned. Jen was keeping the rest of the SIA agents away until the jurisdiction issues were worked out. Laney had sent Cleo off into the woods to hunt and stay away from the humans. It was hard enough explaining her own presence here, never mind the presence of her giant black leopard.

The tall detective in charge turned from watching the body bags progress to head over to Laney. Laney braced herself. She didn't think the detective was a bad sort, but she got the impression her higher-ups were pressuring her to control the scene.

"So, Agent McPhearson, care to tell me what the SIA, an agency I've never heard of by the way, was doing out here?" Detective Theresa Ventrudo was tall with blond hair, strong cheekbones, and bright blue eyes. *She looks a lot like Sheila*, Laney thought with a pang.

Laney nodded toward the stretcher. "Trying to find her. Her disappearance is part of an ongoing case." It was a bit of a stretch as far as logic went. But as far as Laney was concerned, Sheila's murder was part of the ongoing case of her disappearance.

The detective blanched. "Care to explain exactly what case that is?"

Laney shook her head. "Afraid I can't."

The detective crossed her arms over her chest. "And why's that?"

Laney nodded to the group of men just emerging from the trees. "They won't let me."

A tall Egyptian man with dark hair and eyes, Mustafa Massri, separated from the others and made his way over. He nodded at the detective before turning to Laney. "My apologies for taking so long, Agent McPhearson. I had to wake up a judge."

"Did you get it?" Laney asked.

Mustafa pulled a folded paper from his blazer pocket and handed it to Detective Ventrudo. "I believe you will find everything in order. The SIA now has complete jurisdiction over this crime scene."

The detective flicked on her flashlight to read the paper. She looked up when she was done. "So it seems. Well, I guess that's it for us." She started to walk away and then turned. "Look, no bruised egos here. Don't tell my bosses, but to be honest, I'm happy to have this one off my plate. My nightmares are going to bad enough after seeing that scene without having to live with it while tracking down the asshole that did that."

Laney knew what she meant. She was having a tough time keeping the image of Sheila out of her mind as well.

"Besides, this is way out of my league. We have a couple of assaults at most per year, and never anything like this. I don't want to see anything like this ever again. I don't know who she was, but even if she was Jack the Ripper, she didn't deserve that. Promise me you'll find who did this and make them pay."

Laney pictured Sheila again and clenched her fists. A clap of thunder rang out across the park, startling the detective and causing almost everyone to look up—everyone except Laney and the SIA agents.

Laney met the detective's gaze. "Oh, I assure you, whoever did this will pay."

CHAPTER 7

Two hours later, Laney climbed into an SUV Jen had acquired from somewhere. Laney didn't know where and she didn't care. Cleo hopped in the back, curled up, and promptly went to sleep.

The local police were gone, and the SIA agents were finishing up at scene. There was nothing for Laney and Jen to do there. They were needed somewhere else.

"You okay?" Jen's dark eyes looked even darker with only the light from the dashboard to illuminate them.

Laney and Jen had been friends long before any of the Fallen craziness had begun. Laney had never known Jen was a nephilim and Jen didn't know Laney was the ring bearer. But that early friendship had been a glue that had helped both of them once their individual destinies had come to light. And Laney was so very thankful to have a friend she didn't have to hide anything from.

Laney leaned her head back against the headrest. "No, not even close. Sheila was a good mom. I mean, a lot of the parents were terrified when they learned what their children would be capable of one day, but not Sheila. She just hugged Jimmy, told him she loved him, and that they would deal with things as they came."

"We'll have to let the kids at the school know. It's going to be tough on them."

30

Laney felt even more tired at the thought. She had been thinking the same thing and dreaded having to do it. Part of Sheila's plan to help Jimmy had been to bring him to the school every month to get used to being around other kids who were going to develop powers one day, or who already had powers. She wanted Jimmy to have a peer group in place to support him.

In fact, Sheila had arranged for all the kids from the Grand Canyon to be brought in for long weekends. It had been a great addition to the school. It gave some of the other teenagers a chance to give back and help kids who would one day struggle just like they had. Sheila had arranged different activities: movie night, potato sack races, even Lego competitions. The kids had loved those weekends, and they had all really taken to Sheila as well. These kids had lost so much, and now they had lost one more person who had been in their corner.

Laney's cell rang. She checked the caller ID and answered wearily. "Hey, Mustafa. What's going on?"

"We are still analyzing the scene. But there are a few things I can tell you, if you want to hear them."

Laney pictured Sheila's body and didn't want to hear any more details. But she owed Sheila and her family her best. She hit the speakerphone button. "Okay, you're on speaker— Jen's here. Tell us what you found."

"The ME believes the death was due to blood loss. Almost her entire blood content was in the cave."

Laney had figured that.

"But there was an anomaly that did not make sense. Near the body there were charred remains."

Laney frowned. She hadn't noticed that. Of course, after the first check to make sure Sheila wasn't alive, she really hadn't looked too closely at anything else.

"Further testing will need to be done, but the ME believes that Sheila's heart may have been removed and then burned."

Laney felt her jaw fall open. She had no idea what to say to that.

Next to her, Jen gasped. "Are they sure?"

"No, but the heart is missing from the chest cavity, so it seems a natural assumption."

"Anything else?" Laney asked, hoping the answer was no.

"That is it, until a full autopsy can be completed. It will be done as soon as the body arrives at our facility."

Laney nodded. "Okay. Thanks, Mustafa."

Mustafa hesitated. "I am sorry for your loss. I hear she was a good woman."

Laney blinked back tears. "Yeah, she was."

"I will send the autopsy results as soon as I have them." Mustafa disconnected the call. Jen and Laney drove in silence for a while, neither seeming to know what to say.

Finally, Jen spoke. "What kind of freak does that?" she asked angrily.

Laney shook her head. "I don't know."

But Laney's mind had shifted on to the possibilities. The clinical analysis of the case was like a lifeline right now, one that kept her from the sadness that was slowly seeping through her.

"I suppose it depends," Laney said. "Could be someone in the middle of a delusion, could have some sort of religious or psychological significance. Could be part of some serial killer's MO. Jeffrey Dahmer kept body parts in his fridge and a large vat in his living room. Dennis Nilsen and John Wayne Gacy kept whole bodies in their homes. Ed Gein made death masks out of his victims' faces. I mean, trophies, rituals, and killers are a cliché for a reason."

Jen stared at her before turning her attention back to the road. "I keep forgetting you were a criminologist in your past life."

"Yeah, me too," Laney said. "Remember my whole plan to finish up my second doctorate in archaeology?"

"Before your life took a radical shift to the right?"

"I think it's safer to say it completely left the tracks." She shook her head. "Do you think there's any chance we'll one day have normal concerns again? Annoying co-workers? Stresses over taxes rather than life-and-death situations?"

"Well, I find some of Chandler employees really annoying."

Laney laughed. "Well, at least there's that."

Jen turned onto a residential street and the small moment of levity disappeared.

Laney looked at the middle class homes as they passed. Playgrounds were tucked in the back of most of them. Basketball hoops on driveways, a few bikes here and there that someone had forgotten to put away at the end of the day. Yards were well kept but not professionally manicured. It looked like a nice place to raise a kid.

Jen pulled up in front of a ranch house with sunflowers towering along the side. A white picket fence enclosed the yard.

Laney looked at the happy little house. When she was a kid, she had always wanted to live in a house like this—a house that screamed "happy family." She'd thought happy families were somehow protected from the cruelties of the world.

Now she opened the car door and prepared to shatter the world of the Lachowskis. *Apparently, no one's protected from the cruelties of this world.*

CHAPTER 8

Baltimore, Maryland

Laney and Jen arrived back in Baltimore just before dawn. They'd sent Yoni ahead in the chopper and elected to drive back. They didn't say much in the car ride to the Chandler estate. After all, what was there to say? That it sucked that two children were going to grow up without a mother? That life wasn't fair? That Sheila had deserved so much better than that?

All these things were true and none of them mattered. Questioning didn't change anything. Beating themselves up didn't change anything. Dead was gone. And right now, all Laney felt was tired and sad.

Jen pulled up to Laney's cottage. Laney mumbled a thanks and headed inside after releasing Cleo from the back of the car. Cleo headed immediately for the trees. Laney knew she'd hunt for a while before heading to the cottage.

Laney went inside, stopping at the stairs before changing her mind and heading for the kitchen. She opened the refrigerator. She was starving, but at the same time, she didn't want to eat. And nothing in the fridge was calling out to her. Finally she grabbed a strawberry yogurt. Pulling a spoon from a drawer, she leaned against the counter and started to eat, her mind numb.

She heard Jake on the stairs and tensed. *Not yet. Just a few more minutes,* she begged. But Jake appeared in the doorway. "Hey."

"Hey," she said.

"Tough night, huh?"

Laney nodded. "Yup."

An uncomfortable silence fell between them. "I know what you're going to say. I should have waited for backup."

"Yeah, you should have."

Laney shook her head. "Jake, she could have been alive. I couldn't wait."

"Laney, none of us is immortal. We can all be hurt. You need to be more cautious."

Laney sighed. Ever since Jake's injuries at the hands of Cain and his slow recovery, he had been incredibly protective. "Let's not fight about this, please?" her voice cracked. "It's been a really lousy night and I'm exhausted."

"I know. I'm sorry. Why don't you get some sleep?"

Laney nodded, tossing her yogurt container in the trash and the spoon in the sink. "Yeah."

She headed upstairs, and Jake made no move to stop her. It was like their small reprieve in DC had never happened.

These last few months had taken a toll on them. Jake was no longer the soldier leading the charge. He was behind the computer now, and neither of them had adapted to his new role very well. Laney knew he was just trying to look out for her, but she resented him thinking he knew better. And he resented her for not listening to him, seeing as he'd been a soldier a lot longer than she had.

As she reached the top of the stairs, she realized he hadn't tried to comfort her. And she hadn't reached for him either.

Feeling even more tired than before, she made her way to her bed, praying that she would sleep and dream. Because in her dreams, she and Jake were the same as they had been before he'd been injured. She lay down and felt the tears running down her cheeks. And she knew these tears weren't for Sheila and her family. These were for the love she felt for Jake slipping away.

CHAPTER 9

Laney stared at the ceiling. She could tell by the sun peeking through the blinds that she'd slept through the morning. All was quiet; Jake would have left for the main house long ago. With the reprieve from the congressional hearing, he was probably back to his new mission: working with the team that was tracking down Fallen incidents across the globe and sending out operatives to help cover up their antics. They were also trying to find any sign of Elisabeta, but so far, she had stayed hidden even while her troops became more and more visible.

Laney's stomach growled, reminding her it had been a while since her last meal. Cleo stepped onto the bed and curled up next to her, laying her head on Laney's chest. Laney ran her hand through Cleo's pelt. "Hey, girl. I missed you."

Cleo closed her eyes and sighed. Laney had planned on bringing Cleo back to the school because she knew she'd most likely be leaving the estate to run down leads. But she'd needed a little Cleo time. Laney lay next to her, content to not think, just to breathe with Cleo for a little while.

Then her stomach growled again.

Cleo rubbed her face on Laney's stomach in answer. Laney smiled. "Yeah, I'm hungry too."

But Laney made no move to get up. The image of Sheila's body flashed through her mind, causing her to shudder. And remembering Sheila's family's reaction only caused her to feel more tired. Some days, it was all just too much.

Her phone lay on the side table and she pulled it over, not really wanting to see what was there. She had twelve texts. She scrolled through them to see if there was anything she couldn't put off until tomorrow. At the end, she found one she could not avoid. It was from Jake:

Got the ME report. Meet us at the office.

Laney closed her eyes, wishing she could just pull the covers back over her head and pretend she hadn't seen the message. But duty called. And each time she thought of shirking, she remembered Victoria's sacrifice. *No—sacrifices.*

She sat up. "Okay girl, let me grab a shower and we'll see what the next crisis is."

Thirty minutes later, Laney had managed a shower and was heading downstairs to the smell of bacon. She frowned. Jake should be at the office. But part of her felt a small kernel of hope. *Maybe he wants to talk.*

A smile beginning to spread across her face, she stepped into the kitchen.

A tall man with red hair turned his blue eyes to her, two plates in his hands. "Morning, sweetheart."

Her smile dimmed, and the hope that had bloomed in her chest died. But she tried to hide it from her uncle. "Morning, Uncle Patrick."

Father Patrick Delaney, the man who had raised Laney since she was eight, placed the plates on the table. "I thought you could use a good breakfast."

Her stomach growled in response. "I definitely could." She took a seat before glancing around. "Where's Cleo?"

"I let her out."

Laney placed a napkin on her lap and picked up her fork. "This looks delicious. Thanks."

His eyes twinkled. "Anytime."

38

They ate in silence, for which Laney was thankful. Finally, she leaned back from the table, her coffee mug clasped in her hands. "I really needed that."

Patrick watched her over the rim of his own mug. "I heard about last night. How are you doing?"

Laney shrugged. "Okay. What about the kids at the school? How are they handling it?"

Patrick sighed. "It's hard to tell. But Sheila had a really good impact on all of them. I've planned a talk tonight."

"Shouldn't you be there?"

He watched her for a moment. "I thought someone else might need me a little more right now."

She felt tears press against the back of her eyes. "Thank you."

"So tell me how you're *really* doing."

The image of Sheila's blank stare came back to her. It was an image that had played through her dreams all night long, along with visions of Victoria, Henry, and Jake.

Her uncle sat waiting patiently for her to speak. And she knew he would sit there waiting patiently until she gave him an honest answer. *Patiently. In our family that's also known as stubbornly.*

She sighed, feeling Sheila's loss and hearing the anguished cry of her husband again in her mind as if for the first time. Her shoulders fell, and she felt the failure of last night all over again. "I couldn't save her. I wasn't fast enough. I failed her."

"Laney, no." He reached out to take her hand, but she pulled it away.

He shook his head. "You need to stop thinking like this. You can't save the world. It's not possible."

"But I'm the ring bearer—isn't that my job?" she asked with more than a little bitterness. *A job I seem to be failing at more and more.*

Patrick said nothing, and Laney looked over at him in surprise. Usually he fired right back at her. He sat with his arms crossed, his lips pressed tightly together.

She frowned. "Uncle Patrick?"

He threw his napkin on the table. "That's it. I'm done."

"What?"

"You have been beating yourself up since Victoria died, since Henry and Jake were hurt. Your ego is running out of bounds."

"My—my *ego*? What are talking about? I don't think I have any ego left."

"Really? Because as far as I can see, you're blaming yourself for every horrible thing that happens in the world. Because you think you—and *only* you—are responsible for fighting back the bad of this world."

"But—"

"Victoria has lived time and time again. She had a job, too. You are the ring bearer. She is the mother of humanity. Your job does not surpass hers. She did her duty the same way you do yours—with full commitment. And Henry and Jake were injured to allow her to do hers and you to do yours. You are not in this alone. You are part of a team. You need to start remembering that."

"But Sheila—"

Patrick's voice softened and Laney saw the sadness in his eyes. "Her death is horrible. But it is *not* your fault. The same way Victoria's wasn't. You need to let all that go. It's making everything too hard for you. And it's not fair. Not to you, and not to the people you're trying to help."

Laney looked at her uncle. He had told her this before. But today his anger was making the words resonate in a way they hadn't before.

"You are the ring bearer, and that comes with huge responsibilities. But not every move the other side makes is yours to counter. That's too big a task for any one person to take on. Measured against that expectation, you are doomed to

40

failure. But you are doing everything you can, Laney. You found out about Sheila going missing, and you put everything into finding her. And you came closer than anyone else."

"It wasn't enough to save her."

"No, but it will be enough to find those responsible for her. And I have no doubt you will find them."

Laney looked away from his knowing gaze. Finally she let out a laugh. "I am kind of my own pity party lately, aren't I?"

He gave a small laugh. "You could say that. I know these last few months have been difficult. But I won't let you beat yourself up over things that are beyond your control. It serves no purpose other than to make your life more difficult."

"Thanks, Uncle Patrick."

He glanced around. "Speaking of difficult, where is Jake?"

Laney groaned.

"What?" Patrick asked.

When Laney and Jake had started having problems, Patrick had stayed out of it. But over the last few months he had become more and more annoyed at Jake. And he was making no attempts to hide it.

"Look, Jake—"

"Needs a good kick in the ass," Patrick said.

"Uncle Patrick—"

Patrick put up his hand. "I won't say anything to him, but you two are so much alike it's scary. You both think you're responsible for other people's safety. You think you're responsible for the world's safety, and Jake thinks he's responsible for yours."

Laney had never thought of it that way. "That's probably true."

"So. Are you heading over to the office?" Patrick asked.

Laney looked at her uncle. A few more grays had worked their way into his red hair, and the wrinkles at the

41

corners of his eyes had gotten a little deeper. With a pang, she realized she would one day lose him too. She'd seen very little of him these last few months. He'd thrown himself into his work at the school and she'd thrown herself into her work tracking down the Fallen. And she'd missed him.

Laney shook her head. "Nope. I've got some time. Tell me what's happening with you."

Patrick smiled. "All right."

CHAPTER 10

Taipei, Taiwan

Maura Katz gasped as she stepped out of her back door and onto the lanai. She and her husband had flown in late last night. It had been too dark to see the garden, and she had been too tired. But as soon as the light hit her windows, she made her way outside.

A single lotus flower had begun to bloom sometime while they were away. Its bright pink petals had unfurled to reveal an exquisite yellow center.

Almost in a trance, she stepped over to the flower, as if pulled by an invisible string. She sank into the grass and stared at it, unable to believe its beauty. It had sprung up from the small memorial in the garden. Her four-year-old daughter Aiko's face smiled back at her from the picture she had placed there, carefully wrapped in airtight hard plastic to protect it from the elements. Aiko had shared her father's dark hair and had her mother's hazel eyes.

Maura traced the outline of her daughter's face. "Good morning, beautiful."

A weed had begun to encroach on Aiko's space. With a frown, Maura yanked it from the ground. Then she closed her eyes, picturing the lotus in her mind as she focused on her breathing. *In and out. In and out.* She tuned out all noises, all scents. There was only the image of the lotus and the rhythm of her own breathing.

She stayed focused, deep in her meditation for fifteen minutes, before she opened her eyes again, feeling renewed. The earth felt centered under her feet, and she felt connected to all of it.

"You've seen it."

Maura got to her feet with a smile and looked behind her at the tall man walking over to her. Even now, almost thirty years after they had met, Derek was still the most handsome man she had ever laid her eyes on. Tall, with dark hair and dark eyes, he maintained his athletic build with daily workouts.

He stopped next to her, kissing her lightly before wrapping his arm around her shoulder. "She approves."

The lotus had bloomed every year since Aiko's death.

But it had never been so radiant, so drenched in color and life. Aiko had been one of the thousands killed in the 2011 Japanese tsunami. The family had gone to Japan for a vacation. Derek's grandparents had lived in Japan, and Maura's grandfather had once been stationed there, and they wanted to show Aiko this piece of her history. But while they were at the seashore, an earthquake struck out in the Pacific, sending a wave over a hundred feet tall racing toward the eastern shores of Japan.

Aiko was swept away by the raging floodwaters, yanked right out of Maura's arms. Both Maura and Derek leapt in after her, but it was too late. Although, Maura supposed, in a way they were among the lucky ones—they at least had found their daughter's body.

The years since had been a blur. But then Maura had received her mission, and it had given her a reason to go on. She knew what she was doing was right—for her, for Aiko, for all the other children who lived in this dying world.

She turned to look at the lotus once more. This bloom was a sign. Aiko approved of what they were doing.

In the dark of night, she had wrestled with her doubts. But in the bright light of day, her doubts had been chased away, as they always were.

44

Gently, Derek turned her to face him, speaking as if he could read her mind. "You know there is no other way. The world is reaching a tipping point. If we do not turn the tide, you know how many more deaths will follow. You know how many more parents will lose their children. Families will be wiped out in wave after wave."

Maura closed her eyes and leaned against Derek's chest. He wrapped his arms around her and she felt his warmth, his strength. "I know," she said softly.

"You have a good heart. It is one of the many reasons why I love you. But you must harden it. You must remember that they are the reason for all of this. Without them, the world would not be at this point. Without them, Aiko—" his voice cracked.

"Aiko would still be with us," she finished for him.

"Mankind's greed and their refusal to learn has pushed us to this action. And we must follow it through."

She rested her head on his chest. Neither spoke for a few moments. Maura finally broke the silence. "Have the teams found the next one?"

Derek nodded. "They will move into place shortly."

She pictured Sheila Lachowski, how she had begged them to spare her for her children's sake. The woman deserved to die, but it had been difficult. "It's not another mother, is it?"

"No." Derek's voice was filled with loathing. "It's one of *them.*"

Maura looked up. "Really?"

"Yes. He is alone. We'll take him tonight."

Anger burned in her. *One of them. The seeds of humanity's destruction.* "Good."

CHAPTER 11

Baltimore, Maryland

Henry Chandler stood up from his desk and winced as pain shot through his leg. He sucked in a breath. He kept forgetting about it.

"You okay?" Jake asked.

Henry grabbed his cane. "Yeah. Just forgot for a moment."

"Yeah, I know what you mean." Jake turned his attention back to the monitor in front of him.

Henry knew Jake was having trouble accepting the limits his injury had placed on him. Henry understood Jake's frustration—Jake had been a soldier for the last twenty years. It wasn't just a job. It was who he was. And now that he wasn't, he was having a lot of trouble figuring out who that made him.

Henry, on the other hand, enjoyed his injury in a weird sort of way. It was completely new to him. He had come into his nephilim powers as a teenager, and ever since he had always healed from any injury in mere minutes. Now, strangely, it was kind of nice to feel what every other normal human felt. It made him feel more human.

He headed for the coffee machine and poured himself a mug. *And more human is something I'm okay with.*

Laney appeared in the doorway. Henry smiled, put down his coffee, and wrapped her in his arms. "Hey. How you doing?"

Laney sighed and hugged him tightly. "Better now, thanks. Anything new with Sheila's killer?"

"No. The SIA still don't have any leads. No old grudges, no video. They're coming up dry."

"Maybe we should look into it."

"Laney, Sheila's death is horrible, but we need to let the SIA handle this one. We have too many other things going on. And we don't even know if there's a link to the Fallen."

She sighed. "I know. I just—I saw her, Henry. No one should die that way."

"Where's Cleo?"

"My uncle took her back to the school. I figured I'd probably be off the grounds depending on what we find. And I thought she might help some of the kids."

Henry looked down at her. He didn't like how pale she looked, didn't like the dark circles under her eyes. He frowned. "You need more sleep. Why don't you go get some? Nothing here needs your attention that badly."

She stepped away from him. "Jake said the ME's report was in."

Henry shot Jake a look. He loved Jake like a brother, but he didn't like how he had been behaving around Laney lately. "I see."

Laney took his arm. "It's all right. *We're* all right. It's just—a rough patch."

Henry nodded. "Okay." They walked over to Jake together.

"Hey," Laney said lightly.

Jake looked up with a brief smile. "How was your sleep?"

"Deep," Laney said, sinking into a chair two away from him.

The exchange was perfectly polite, and it made Henry want to throttle the two of them. They loved each other—more than anything. And right now, they were acting so polite that it was as if they were strangers.

47

Henry took one of the other seats. "Laney said the ME's report was in."

Jake hit a few buttons on his keyboard. The screen above the conference table came to life. Then he tossed two copies of the report on the table.

Henry picked one up and scanned it. He'd already seen the crime scene photos, which he knew he would be unable to forget any time soon.

"Any surprises?" Laney asked.

"Yeah, the cause of death," Jake said.

Henry scanned the form. *That can't be right.* "She drowned?"

Jake nodded. "Her lungs were full of water. They're testing to see if the water can tell us anything. But it seems she was drowned before the bloodletting and before her heart was removed."

"I'd say that was good news, except I hear that it's a horrible way to die," Henry said, looking up. Laney sat silently, her face pale. "Lanes?"

"Uh, nothing. It's, um, nothing. Is this my file?" Laney pointed to the second copy of the report.

"Yeah," Jake said.

Laney picked it up. "I'll go through it and see if anything jumps out. See you later."

She walked out of the room with her shoulders slumped. Henry watched her go, wishing he could do something to help her. He noticed Jake watch her as well, but he didn't say anything either. He just turned back to the table when she was out of view.

And that was it for Henry. As soon as the door closed behind Laney, Henry whirled on Jake. "What the hell are you doing?"

48

CHAPTER 12

Her knees curled up to her chest, Lou sat in Cleo's cage watching Cleo prowl around the outside. Sheila, Jimmy's mom, had been killed. Lou shook her head. It was so wrong. Jimmy and Jillian were without their mom.

Just like me. Lou's grandmother was gone, and she'd lost her sister Charlotte just last year. She'd never known her dad. At least Jimmy and Jillian still had their dad.

Her gaze strayed to the Chandler School for Children. It was a brick monster of a building that even had turrets. It had been a high-end boarding school before it had fallen on tough times. Now it was Lou's home.

For a while there, Lou and her sister had been barely getting by, but now here she sat, at a school that looked like a smaller version of Hogwarts. She even had a private room with a window seat and velvet curtains. She spent her days going to school, in self-defense training, and hanging out with friends.

I should be doing more. She'd been thinking this for months, but Sheila's death had really brought the feeling home. Lou had abilities. She could help. And she knew the Fallen were causing more and more problems. Even though she was young, there must be something she could do.

Besides, the adults were basically being sidelined right now by the government. They'd spent the last few weeks in

Washington, DC, taking meeting after meeting to justify their actions with the Fallen for the last two years.

Lou shook her head. By her count, Laney, Henry, and Jake had saved thousands of people at this point. And instead of being thanked, they were being interrogated. And that was on top of Laney and Henry losing their mother.

And here I am sitting on my butt, wondering what TV show I'm going to watch tonight. It's not right.

Cleo came over and laid her head in Lou's lap.

Lou told herself she had come outside for Cleo's sake, but right now, she wasn't sure. She lowered her head to Cleo's. "Hey, girl. How come you always know when I'm down?"

The giant cat seemed to have a sixth sense when it came to people's moods. Whenever Lou felt out of sorts, Cleo would stand next to Lou or rub up against her. Lou thought of it as a Cleo hug.

Cleo looked up, and Lou stared into her eyes. They were undeniably leopard eyes. They were round, yellow, and never seemed to blink. But at the same time, there was something almost human in them. When Cleo looked at you, you felt like she really *understood.*

Cleo put her head down again and gave a little sigh. Lou ran her hand through the cat's coat. Lou knew that Cleo was lonely these days. With Laney away, she'd had to spend most of her days in the cage, unless she went back to headquarters and stayed at Dom's. But Laney wanted her at the school while they were out of town. Lou, Rolly, Danny, and Zach all tried to spend as much time with her as possible. But between classes and everything else, Lou didn't think it was enough. Besides, Cleo needed someone who understood her. She needed another leopard. The problem was, she wasn't like any other leopard out there.

Lou hugged Cleo around the neck and whispered, "You're one of a kind, girl. And I'm really sorry about that."

CHAPTER 13

Henry stood up, towering over Jake. "Are you actually trying to make this harder for her?"

Jake sat back, his mouth falling open. "What are you talking about?"

Henry gestured to the door. "You, Laney. You're acting like an ass."

Jake clamped his mouth shut. "Gee, thanks, Henry."

"Look, you got hurt. I know. But you have got to stop treating her like this. It's not her fault you got hurt."

"Stay out of it, Henry."

Henry threw up his hands. "I would love to. Except it's in my face every day. And I care about both of you. And I've never seen you act this way with anyone. You are so damn polite, it's sickening."

"Henry—"

"Jake, she's grieving. She lost her mother. She nearly lost the two of us. You are destroying your relationship. You—"

"I know!" Jake yelled, running through his hair. "I know," he said more quietly. "I don't know what it is. She's the last person in the world I want to hurt and yet, I hear myself when I talk to her. I hate how I'm talking to her, but I can't seem to get myself to shut up."

Henry watched his best friend and saw the struggle on his face. "It's not her fault you were hurt," he said again.

Jake ran a hand through his hair. He looked like he wanted to tear it out. "I know. But I think I blame her anyway. I mean, she goes through hell, and comes out without a scratch. We face Cain and come out almost dead."

Henry watched his best friend. He knew how hard these last few months were for him. But Jake needed to snap out of it. "You know she's not uninjured. Each time she goes into one of these things, she comes out changed. She loses something. And we might be the triad, but the biggest burden is on her. She needs us to help her, not make it harder."

"Do you think I don't know that?" Jake shook his head. "I'm just so angry. I hate that I can't help her fight. That I can't—" Jake went quiet.

"That you can't keep her safe."

Jake nodded abruptly but didn't speak.

"You need to trust her to protect herself. She's smart. She's tough. She doesn't need us to keep her safe all the time. But she does need us to have her back."

"I have her back. I always have her back."

Henry paused. "Do you really? Because I don't think she believes that. I mean, have you even talked to her about what she went through last night?"

Jake met his gaze and then looked away. "No."

"Jake, she put everything on hold when you got hurt. But she had to get back to her mission. No one can do what she does. But she needs *you* too—because no one else can fill your role in her life. And each time you act like a polite stranger to her, it hurts her."

Jake let out a breath, and Henry could sense the helplessness in him. "I know. But I don't know what to do. It kills me each time she goes on a mission without me. Because, you know her, she will lay down her life for someone else without a thought. And I can't lose her."

Henry nodded, feeling his gut clench because Jake was right. Laney would lay down her life without a thought, just like their mother did. Apparently it was encoded in their DNA. He studied the proud man in front of him. "Would you do any different? Wasn't that exactly what you did when you shot Cain? You and I both knew there was every chance we would not survive that."

Jake looked at him for a long moment before turning away. "I don't know."

"Jake, you need to stop pushing her away. Death isn't the only thing that can take her away from you. And if you keep this up, you really are going to lose her."

CHAPTER 14

Laney took a seat on the back veranda of the main house. She pictured Jake this morning. *Perfectly polite—and perfectly unlike Jake.*

She flipped through the stack of papers Jake had handed her, trying to focus.

My secret talent—being able to sneak up on pretty girls.

The memory slipped into her mind. It was her first day at Chandler. And it was the first time, even with all the craziness surrounding them, that she knew there was something between her and Jake.

And now what is there? She still loved him. She would always love him. It was just so hard to be around him right now. It seemed like she had to weigh every word. *How did we get here?*

But she knew the answer to that question. Too much death, too much hurt, and her damn destiny always snapping at their heels.

She shook her head. *Enough.* She had turned her and Jake's relationship over in her mind time and time again. And it never made a difference. Until Jake let her in, it never would.

Laney glanced at the SIA report in the stack. Steeling herself, she read through it. Lots of blood—she knew that. The

SIA criminalists had confirmed that the burned item Mustafa had mentioned was indeed Sheila's heart.

Laney shuddered. It was like some horrible B movie.

She scanned through the rest of the form, stopping at the cause of death: drowning. *How the hell does someone drown on land? That must be a mistake.*

Her phone rang. Laney checked the screen before answering. "Hey, Matt. How's it going?"

"Good. Just calling with an update."

Laney grimaced. A few months back, Matt had started calling her with weekly updates. Although she liked to know what was happening, there were times, like today, when she would rather not know. "Okay, hit me," she said.

"Well, we've had seventeen more Fallen-related incidents, including the one in DC."

"Seventeen? In a week?"

"Yes. Most were easily explained and we managed to get control of the scenes that were more public. The Niagara Falls incident was the most challenging."

"Anything we should be especially concerned about?"

"I'm not sure. There's something unusual about these cases. It's not the troublemakers. Take for example the case two days ago in Minneapolis. There were reports of an extremely fast man who was the target of an attempted murder. The man managed to escape. We don't know who the perpetrators were—the whole report was kind of sketchy."

"Are you sure it was even a Fallen or nephilim who was the target?"

"That we are sure of. He was one of the ones we keep an eye on. But he's never caused any trouble. Just lives his life quietly."

Laney frowned. "So why go after him? Was it other Fallen?"

"I don't know that either. I have some agents interviewing him today. We should know more soon, but I just wanted to give you a heads-up."

"Thanks." Laney went silent.

"Everything all right?"

Laney sighed. "It's been a rough night."

"I heard. Want to talk about it?"

Laney hesitated. But then she thought, maybe Matt knew of some expert somewhere who might be able to help. "We lost the mom of one of the Grand Canyon kids last night." She told him about the phone call and about tracking Sheila down too late. "I just read over the crime scene report, and they burned her heart. But that's not even the weirdest part. The *weirdest* part is—"

"—is that she drowned," Matt finished for her.

Shock took Laney's voice for a moment. "How do you know that?"

"I know that because she's *not* the first victim of that killer."

"Not the first? How many have there been?"

Matt was silent.

Laney's alarm grew. "Matt? How many?"

"Thirty-four."

CHAPTER 15

Laney couldn't process it. "Thirty-four murders?" All she could picture was the scene of Sheila's death. Someone had done that almost three dozen times? "Wait, why do you know about this?"

"We keep track of unusual murders. It's part of our record-keeping."

Right, because keeping a list of ritualistic killings is all in a day's work. Laney knew, though, that that was possible. After all, VICAP kept track of all violent crimes, allowing law enforcement to determine connections between different offenses across states. Interpol allowed for the same to be done on a global level.

"Okay. But I can't imagine why you personally would know about this one, unless there was—" Laney paused. "There's a link to the Fallen, isn't there?"

"Yes."

That one word had the force of a shotgun blast. *Damn it.* "What's the connection?"

"All the people killed, are closely tied, either by blood or friendship, to a Fallen. We're calling them the companion murders."

Laney's mouth dropped open. *Closely tied.* Like Sheila—the mother of a nephilim. "Are you saying you *knew* someone was going after the people related to the Fallen and you didn't tell me?"

"There's so much going on, I didn't want to bother—"

"*Bother* me? Sheila Lachowski is dead. Her children have lost their mother. I could have warned her!" Laney forced herself to calm down even as she wanted to reach through the phone and strangle Matt. Sheila was gone, but others might still be at risk. She needed to help them first, kill Matt later. "Tell me what you know."

"Hold on, let me pull up the files." Matt was quiet for a few moments. "Okay. There's been a murder every two weeks or so for the last eighteen months. The murders always occur at sunset. About half of them correspond to the full moon."

"The full moon?"

"Yes. My people think there's some group, a cult even, that may be responsible."

Laney closed her eyes. *A cult. As if this isn't all horrible enough.* "And the murders? They're always the same?"

"Yes. The victim is drowned, then their blood is drained, and finally their heart is removed."

Matt said it all so coolly, so clinically. But Sheila's death was too fresh for Laney, and each description made her shudder.

"How long before the murder are they grabbed?"

"Not long. Usually only a few hours."

"Which means whoever is doing this is organized and prepared."

"Yes. And the victims—they stretch across the globe. We didn't even make the link until last month."

Laney's voice was cool. "You should have told me."

"I'm sorry, Laney. I thought with everything else, that you had enough on your plate."

"*That* was not your call to make. I need you to send me everything you have on these cases."

"Consider it done."

58

Laney disconnected the call without another word. Gathering her papers, she turned and strode toward the main house, her mind already churning through the list of what she needed to do. She needed to get security in place for the families of all the kids they knew of and warnings out to the police departments in the areas where they lived. Her mind flitted from one detail to the next. *All the people killed are closely tied, either by blood or friendship, to a Fallen*—the number of those who could fit that description was overwhelming.

She needed to improve security at the school. And Cleo would need to stay there longer to serve as a little extra protection. *Hell, maybe I'll move there for a little while. It'll be more peaceful than staying with Jake.*

More and more of the people she needed to warn raced through her mind. There were literally hundreds of them. And fear sliced through her as one more truth hit home.

I can't protect them all.

CHAPTER 16

Henry pushed back from his desk, staring at all the files Matt had emailed over. He'd had copies made immediately. He had a team going over them with a fine-toothed comb. But he still couldn't believe the number.

Thirty-four murders? How the hell hadn't they known about this? Laney was down in the communications room, arranging to warn everyone she could think of who might need to be protected. Henry knew how angry she was that the SIA agent had kept this from her. *What the hell was Matt thinking? And what else is he hiding?*

Henry looked up from his desk as Jen stepped in. Henry smiled, his spirits lifting at the sight of her in spite of the worry now weighing him down. Unlike Jake and Laney, Henry had found that his injuries had only brought him and Jen closer. And despite everything, he couldn't remember a time when he was happier.

Jen leaned over the desk and kissed him softly on the lips. "Hi."

"Hi," Henry said, looking into her deep brown eyes. He would never get tired of that particular view. "How's everything at the school?"

"Not good. All the kids really liked Sheila. Patrick's putting together a candlelight vigil tonight, and they're arranging a formal memorial service for her tomorrow. Mikio's going to bring Jimmy and Jillian down."

"I didn't think you'd be able to get here today."

"I didn't either, but Lou wanted to make sure Danny was okay. And she and Rolly wanted to talk to Tiffany about the memorial."

Henry nodded. Tiffany was Tiffany Richards, the event planner for the Chandler Group. "She'll take care of them."

"I know. I just hate that they have to deal with another loss. They've all lost so much already."

All the kids at the school came from tough backgrounds. Most of them were orphans, although a few had parents who had kicked them out as soon as their powers developed. As a result, everyone associated with the school had gone out of their way to create an environment where the kids felt accepted and supported. And protected. Sheila's death was going to shake that feeling of security.

"Well, I'm afraid it gets worse," Henry said.

Jen's eyes narrowed. "*How* can it get worse?"

"Sheila's wasn't the first murder. She wasn't even one of the first dozen."

"What?"

Henry explained about the series of murders and what the SIA knew. He gestured to his desk. "These are all the case files they have so far. I'm starting to go through them while Laney and Jake arrange for extra security for just about everyone we can think of."

"The kids at school—they'll have to be on lockdown."

Henry nodded. "I'm sorry, but yes. I've already arranged for extra guards, and Laney said Cleo will stay there for the duration."

Jen closed her eyes. "These kids just can't catch a break."

"I know. But we'll figure out a way to make it bearable. Maybe they can take small trips off campus a few at a time with guards."

"Yeah. We'll have to do something." Jen looked down at the crime scene photos. "May I?"

Henry nodded. "Help yourself. But be warned, they're pretty graphic."

Jen studied a few of the photos and then looked back at him. "Do you have more of these?"

"Too many." Henry handed her another dozen.

She quickly flipped through them, her frown deepening with each one. And Henry had the distinct impression it wasn't just the subject that was causing it. "What is it?" he asked.

"Where are the rest?"

Henry pulled out the remaining pictures and handed them over. "What do you see?"

Jen shook her head and walked over to the whiteboard that had been set up. Henry followed. Jen walked along the board, stopping at a series of dates. She pointed to it. "These are the dates of the murders."

Henry nodded.

"About half have been killed on the full moon," she said softly.

"Yeah. How did you know that?"

"When I was a kid, my mom always kept track of the phases of the moon. I do the same thing. It's just a habit."

Surprised filtered through him. She rarely mentioned her mother. Her mom had disappeared when Jen was seven, and Jen had been thrown into the foster care system after that— which had not been easy. And although she said very little about her time with her mom, Henry had the distinct impression that it hadn't been easy either.

"It's a ritual," Jen whispered. She walked back to the desk and laid the pictures out, one next to the other, until the desk was covered. "Look." She pointed to the spot underneath the body on one of the pictures, and then went through the rest of them, pointing at the same spot in each photo.

"It's an altar," Henry said with surprise. He hadn't picked up on it.

62

Jen nodded. "But it's more than that. They're taking the heart, the life force of the body. Their using water—a purifier—as is fire. These weren't just killings. These were offerings."

"But to who? Why?"

"I don't know. But the next full moon is in two weeks."

"Then so is the next murder."

CHAPTER 17

Laney sat on the grass flipping through the crime scene photos and the accompanying documents. Phone calls were going out to warn everyone they could think of about the danger. But Laney had needed to get away from that for a little while and get some fresh air. And she needed to spend some time with Cleo before she sent her back to the school. Jen had brought Cleo with her as extra protection when she'd brought Rolly and Lou over.

Cleo was sprawled out on the ground. Laney reached down and rubbed her belly. "I hate sending you back there, girl, but I need the kids to be safe."

Cleo stretched and let one of her paws fall over Laney's arm. Laney smiled, not for the first time wondering exactly what had been done to create Cleo. It was more than just growth hormone. Laney had planned on looking into Cleo's background when she got back from DC, but now with these murders, she knew that research was going to have to take a back seat. *Maybe I can get one of the analysts to do some preliminary work.*

Laney pulled out her legal pad and started writing notes. Henry had texted her about Jen's idea. And it made sense, in a completely horrible way.

She frowned. She knew that ritual human sacrifice had a long history, especially in Central America. Captured warriors and children were common sacrifices. In fact, in some cultures, children were groomed from birth to be sacrifices.

The Aztecs presented the most well-known example of human sacrificial culture, as they had engaged in it on a truly horrifying scale; thousands had been put to death, their still-beating hearts ripped from their chests in some cases. But Laney knew they weren't the only ones, not by a long shot, nor was the practice limited to Central America. The Incans, Celts, Mongols, Scythians, Mayans, Toltecs, Egyptians—they had all engaged in the practice.

One group, the Olmecs, was said to have engaged in the practice as early as 1500 BC. The Olmecs were a mysterious group that appeared out of nowhere in Mexico. With them they brought science, literature, and law. But they left little behind except for the massive stone heads with African features. A group that history said had been nowhere near South America at that time.

Laney had once taken some of the older kids from the school to an Olmecs exhibit at the American Museum of Natural History. In the exhibit, the Olmecs were described as Mexico's earliest civilization.

But regardless of which culture you referred to, the sacrifices only came about when things had gone wrong— terribly wrong. And in the so-called "Ring of Fire," disaster was never far away.

The Ring of Fire was a 25,000-mile stretch that rimmed the Pacific Ocean. It horseshoed from the southern tip of South America, up the coast of North America, across the Bering Strait, and down through Japan and New Zealand. And within that area were over 452 volcanoes. So no matter how prepared they were, anyone living in the Ring of Fire would be exposed to extreme natural disasters—savage flooding, volcanoes, earthquakes, tsunamis.

And in times of stress, those groups historically turned to religion as a way to cope. For the older cultures along the eastern portion of the ring, humans were sacrificed to the gods.

They believed that once the gods were appeased, the world would calm down again.

"Hey."

Laney's head snapped up in surprise. Jake stood only a few feet away.

"Oh, hey," Laney said, not sure how to react. "I didn't hear you."

"Glad to see my skills are still intact."

Laney's heart gave a painful lurch.

"You look a little lost in thought," Jake said.

"Yeah, um, just trying to make some sense of all this."

Next to her, Cleo rolled to her feet and walked up to Jake. She bumped him none too gently with her head before disappearing into the trees. When everything had started getting uncomfortable with Jake, Cleo had made it clear whose side she was on.

Jake rubbed his chest with a wince. "She always gets me in the same spot."

Laney tried not to smile. She had to admit, she kind of liked Cleo's snub of Jake. At least someone was telling Jake he was acting like an idiot. "I don't think she's very happy with you right now."

"Yeah, I get that." He paused. "I don't think you are either."

"Jake, I—"

He put up his hand and walked over, then took a seat on the ground next to her. "Let me just say this, okay?"

Laney nodded.

"I'm sorry. I've been acting like a complete idiot. I've been injured before, but never like this. It's never taken me so long to come back. And I'm not handling it well."

"Well, that's a bit of understatement," Laney muttered.

Jake let out a laugh. "True. It's just—I've been a soldier for the majority of my life. And now I'm not, so I guess I don't really know who exactly I am these days."

66

"Jake, you've never been just a guy who throws punches and shoots guns. You're still a soldier, you're just fighting a different way right now."

"I know. It's just in my head. I'm stronger than my body actually is and—"

Laney took his hands. "Jake, you and Henry took on Cain knowing how devastating your injuries were going to be. You risked your lives to save us. And that's not physical strength—that's so much more. *You're* so much more. I don't love you because you can fire a gun and beat up guys. Sometimes I love you in spite of it."

Jake went still. "Do you? Still love me?"

Laney felt a catch at the back of her throat. "Against my better judgment, yes."

He smiled, regret in his voice. "I'm sorry, Laney. I know you've been going through so much with Victoria, and now the Fallen popping up everywhere, and trying to keep the world safe. And I haven't been making that any easier on you. But I promise I will from this point forward."

Laney looked into his eyes, wanting more than anything to believe him. She wanted her Jake back, not this angry man she'd been seeing for the last few months.

"Promise?" she asked.

He nodded. "Promise."

Laney wanted to believe him, but she knew it wasn't going to be as easy as a few words and everything was solved. "You can't keep making me feel guilty when I go out in the field. It's my job."

"I know. It's just—when Henry and I got hurt, it clarified how fragile we are. And it made me realize just how easily you could get hurt, too." Jake shook his head. "I don't know that I could stand that."

"Jake, if I get hurt, then I get hurt. It's not your responsibility. This is the life we lead, and it's not a safe one. But I can't keep fighting you and then going out there to fight the Fallen. I need peace somewhere. And I'm pretty sure the Fallen aren't going to offer it."

"I can't promise I won't be worried. I can't promise I won't want to be by your side when you go out. But I can promise that I will support you. I know what you can do. I know how strong you are. It's just difficult being the one left behind."

"You're not left behind, Jake. You're always right there with me."

He wrapped his arms around her.

Laney closed her eyes and leaned into him. She felt the heat and familiarity of his embrace, and she realized just how much she had missed him even though he had been near her this whole time. Tears sprang to her eyes, and she clutched him to her.

"I'm so sorry, Laney," he whispered in her ear.

And Laney let go of her doubts and her fears and decided to trust. Because whatever the future held, it held it for both of them. Jake had her heart and would always have it.

"I love you, Laney."

"I love you too," Laney whispered, and she hoped that the song was wrong, and that sometimes love was enough.

CHAPTER 18

Laney and Jake had stayed out in the field for a while, lying next to each other, their hands entwined. And Laney could not remember a time in the last few months that had been better, not even DC. She and Jake being off-kilter had sent everything off-kilter. But now her life was back in its proper orbit. Still difficult, still stressful, but being on the same page with Jake made all the rest of it seem surmountable.

She just really hoped it lasted.

Hand in hand, they walked into Henry's office as darkness fell. Jen looked up from the couch and noted their hands. "Well, about damn time."

Laney smiled. "Our thoughts exactly."

She let go of Jake's hand and took a seat across from Jen. "Anything new?"

Jen shook her head. "From what I can tell, this ritual is not one that's been recorded in history. Someone seems to be blending previous rituals together."

Jen's words triggered the niggle of a memory in the back of Laney's brain. Something about the blending of rituals and Cayce.

"Any parts of the world where they seem to borrow from?" Jake asked.

"The Yucatan, although honestly we can't be sure," Jen said.

"That's it," Laney said.

"What's it?" Jake asked as he took a seat next to Laney.

"The blending of rituals. When the people of Atlantis left after the final destruction, they took their rituals with them. Eventually, their rituals were blended into the structure of other rituals."

"But we don't know this has anything to do with Atlantis," Jake said. "I mean, just because it's Fallen-related doesn't mean it's Atlantis-related."

"I suppose," Laney said.

Henry walked in and nodded toward the conference table. "I may have something."

The screen lowered, and an image appeared—one drawn in blood. It looked like a small series of mountains with a lake.

"What's this?" Jen asked.

"At each of the abduction sites, this image is placed somewhere," Henry said. "This one was found in Sheila's kitchen. Mikio didn't notice it in his rush to find Sheila, but one of our guys did when they went over the scene."

"It looks like a mountain range," Laney said.

Henry nodded. "I thought the same. I had an analyst try to run it and see if they could get a cartographic match. We came up empty. It doesn't mean that it's not a mountain, it just means that until we know the scale, we probably won't be able to match it."

"But there must be a reason why they left it," Jen said.

Jake stepped forward, tilting his head to the side as he looked at the picture. "Henry, can you rotate the picture?"

The image shifted ninety degrees.

"One more." Jake said.

Henry rotated it again.

"There," Jake said. "Doesn't that look familiar?"

70

On screen, the mountain range had morphed into the profile of a man with a long straight nose, closely set eyes, and a straight forehead. And there *was* something familiar about it.

"It's one of the heads from Easter Island," Jake said.

Laney started. Although technically a province of Chile, Easter Island was almost four thousand miles west of the South American mainland. And the island itself was tiny—a triangular-shaped piece of land only a little over sixty square miles. You could easily walk across it in a day. It was beyond barren with few trees and lots of wind.

It was also a footnote to the dangers of exploited natural resources. Apparently at one point, it had been a fertile piece of land with a strong forest. But natives had hacked away at the trees and overused the soil. As a result, the land now yielded very little. When early explorers first came across the island, they described its people as among the poorest on the planet, barely subsisting.

Yet the tiny, poor little island was still a place of mystery—the biggest being the moai, the giant heads that were found across the island.

Laney turned to Jen, who had specialized in Pacific civilizations in grad school. "What do you know about Easter Island?"

"It was first reported in 1687 as being a large landmass, but by 1722, on a second visit, only the small island was left, and the rest of the land was believed to have submerged. And it has a sad history."

"How so?" Henry asked.

"In 1862, twelve Peruvian slave ships arrived on the island's shores looking for slaves to mine guano deposits in the Chincho Islands. They kidnapped over a thousand islanders. The few remaining survivors fought off the slavers and managed to steal a ship. They sailed to Tahiti to tell the French court of the barbarity of the Peruvian slavers, and the Peruvian government ordered the slavers to return the islanders. But while more than a thousand had been taken, maltreatment,

71

disease, and devastation had greatly shrunk those numbers. Only fifteen of the original group survived the trip back to the island; and worse, they brought smallpox with them. By the time the disease had worked its way through the island, there were only one hundred and eleven islanders left."

Laney shuddered. The island was in the middle of the Pacific Ocean. Its closest neighbor was Pitcairn Island, over a thousand miles away. She couldn't imagine watching the numbers of your people dropping and knowing there was no chance of help coming. How helpless they must have felt.

"And of course, Easter Island is famous for its moai statues," Jen said. "There are more than nine hundred of them scattered across the island, and no one knows where they came from. The natives say their ancestors did not create them."

Laney pictured the moai. Each one depicted the head and shoulders of a man. They ranged in size from fifteen feet to seventy feet. Each weighed hundreds of tons.

"Have they ever figured out who or how those statues were created or how they were erected?" Henry asked.

Jen shook her head. "No. But of course there are rumors."

"Of course there are," Jake muttered.

"According to the legends, the moai walked into their positions."

"Walked?" Henry asked.

"Yup," Jen said. "Of course, other reports say they were moved into position through mental powers."

"Isn't there a more traditional explanation?" Jake asked, eyebrows raised.

"Well, there is the age-old theory that says they rolled the statues into place on logs," Jen said, her voice indicating her thoughts on that particular theory.

"Let me guess—the terrain makes that likelihood very slim?" Laney asked.

"Yup—very rocky terrain. And some of the moai are in rather difficult to reach locations. Rolling a hundred-ton statute into one of those locations would be highly unlikely."

"Were they once an advanced civilization?" Jake asked.

"Not recently. In fact, most explorers were struck by how poor the citizens were, how isolated. Today, there's only five thousand or so people. But it does get fifty thousand visitors every year," Jen said.

"But there must have been some evidence of an advanced civilization somewhere in their history," Laney said. "I mean, someone had to have built the moai."

Jen nodded. "There's the rongo rongo script that was found in 1864 by Eugène Eyraud. He found twenty-six wooden tablets in various huts around the island. Each tablet was covered in symbols that looked like hieroglyphs. The script has never been translated, but it bears an uncanny resemblance to the script used by the Cuna Indians in Panama and the script used in Mohenjo-daro that dates to 4000 BCE."

Laney started at the mention of Mohenjo-daro, an ancient city in Pakistan built somewhere between four and five thousand BC. The city had been laid out on a grid. It had a sophisticated sewage system, including manhole covers and public latrines on every block. It also had the Great Bath, which was believed to be used as a purification pool.

But what Mohenjo-daro was most known for was the skeletons found strewn throughout the streets, some holding hands. Some believe the city had been the site of a nuclear blast in the ancient world.

"Is there any link between the island and the Fallen?" Henry asked.

"No," Jen said, "not directly. But Easter Island does have some legends surrounding it that have some familiar themes. Its origin myth speaks of a King Hout-Matua, who arrived with his people after the submersion of their homeland.

But according to the legends there were already people on the island—very tall, redheaded individuals."

Laney groaned. *More tall redheaded giants.* "Why are they always redheaded?"

Henry smiled. "I'm sure it's nothing personal."

"Okay, so Easter Island may or may not have some links to Atlantis, but we do see pictures of moais at each of the crime scenes," Jake said.

Jen nodded.

"So if I'm understanding this correctly," Jake said, "we have a group kidnapping individuals who have some sort of link with the Fallen, sacrificing them, and leaving behind a pictures of the statues from Easter Island which were allegedly created by the descendants of an advanced civilization?"

Laney nodded. "Yup."

Jake flopped down onto the couch. "Oh well, it must be Tuesday."

74

CHAPTER 19

Laney had spent the rest of the afternoon looking through all the files that Matt had sent on the companion murders. At five she had called a halt, and she, Henry, Jake, and Jen went to the school to meet with students and attend the candlelit vigil. She knew they needed to track down Sheila's killer but the search could do without them for while. And the kids at the schools needed to be reassured.

Then this morning, they had attended the memorial service. Lou and Rolly did a really beautiful job setting it up. Still, it had been rough. The kids had looked so lost. And Mikio clinging to his two children looking completely shattered was not an image that Laney would be able to shake any time soon.

But it was back to business now. Danny had stayed at the school to be with his friends while Henry, Jake, Laney, and Jen headed back to the estate.

When they arrived, Henry and Jake headed right for the office. But neither Jen nor Laney could stomach looking at any crime scene photos—not after the rawness of this morning. So they went for a run to clear their heads. Eight miles later, Laney knew they had put off work as long as they could.

Laney shifted from a run to a jog as they approached the gates of the Chandler estate. Jen matched her pace. "Feel better?"

"A little. You?"

Jen sighed. "A little."

They shifted to a walk as they reached the gates and waved at the guards in the booth. They continued on to Sharecropper Lane. And just like that, all the murders and questions popped back into Laney's mind. How on earth could there be a link between an island over five thousand miles away and Sheila's murder? And was any of this linked to Cayce and Atlantis, or were they just assuming there was a link because there always seemed to be a link?

Laney sighed. *Yet another moment when I wish Victoria was here.* Before her death, this would be just the type of question Laney would bring to her. And Victoria would answer, albeit in her own cryptic way.

"Laney?"

She looked over at Jen. "Sorry. Got a little lost there."

"Victoria?"

Laney nodded. Jen knew her too well. "Yeah."

"She would be kind of perfect to talk to about this."

"That's what I was just thinking."

Jen hesitated. "Have you thought about finding her?"

"Of course. I've started to a hundred times, and then I always stop."

"Why?"

Laney paused, trying to figure it out herself. "Victoria has lived time and time again. But one thing in common during all those lifetimes is that for the first twelve years she has no memory of her previous lives, of her mission. She gets to just be a child. If I found her, if any of us found her, we could rob her of that. And I think a few years of innocence is the least she deserves. Besides, she may not even have been born yet."

"But right now, all that knowledge of hers would come in pretty handy. What about Drake?"

Drake was an archangel who had helped Laney find the resting place of the tree of life. He also headlined a hugely popular magic act in Las Vegas.

76

Laney shook her head. "I called him yesterday, to warn him. I asked him about the murders. He said he didn't know anything."

"Do you believe him?"

"I don't know. Drake has his own set of rules. I think he would help if he could, unless he felt it went against his mission. Either way, he's no help. Although he did invite us down for a weekend in Las Vegas."

Jen laughed. "Oh, sure. Let's just put everything on hold and go carousing with an archangel."

Laney smiled. It had actually been fun hanging out with Drake for those few hours in Vegas. And then he had been the one who had taken her home after Victoria. She would always be grateful for that. Whatever flash the archangel had on the outside, there was definitely some substance underneath.

"So I guess that means we have nothing," Jen said.

"Unless you can think of someone else still living who knows as much Victoria did."

An image of Cain flashed through her mind. He knew as much as Victoria had, without any gaps where he was an innocent child. He might know something. If, of course, they knew where he was and could get him to cooperate. He had disappeared after going into a river in India. The SIA had searched for him but had found no sign. And he hadn't popped up anywhere since then.

"We still think Cain's dead, right?" Jen asked.

"I think we're not that lucky. He's probably just lying low, like Elisabeta. Besides, even if he is alive, I don't think he'll be rushing to our defense."

"So you're saying we have nothing."

Laney sighed. "Yes. Right now we have nothing."

CHAPTER 20

Lou sat on her window seat, trying to read. She had her Ethics class tomorrow and she needed to get through the Thomas Aquinas reading Father Patrick had assigned, but she couldn't seem to focus. Sheila's death was too recent and had brought up a lot of feelings she didn't want to face. Outside, the sky was darkening as storm clouds moved in.

Cleo was lying in the enclosure created for her, her back pressed against the metal bars. She had looked so listless lately since she'd been locked up. She'd even turned down bacon earlier today when Lou had snuck out to visit her. And Lou had never known Cleo to turn down bacon.

"Earth to Lou," Rolly Escabi called from where he was sprawled on her bed, finishing up his trigonometry. He raised an eyebrow above his pale green eyes—a striking combination with his mocha-colored skin.

She looked over at him. "Huh? What?"

"What's with you? Every time I look up, you're doing everything *but* homework. You're supposed to be the studious one. There's only room for one slacker in this relationship, young lady, and I have already filled that position quite nicely. Fabulously, in fact."

Lou laughed. "True. Sorry, but it just looks like it's going to rain."

Rolly crossed the room and sat next to her, peering out her window at the enclosure across the courtyard below. "Cleo's got a roof. She'll be all right."

"I know. I mean, she's an animal, right? She's supposed to be outside. But I just worry."

"Look, leopards are solitary creatures. She's fine."

Lou raised her eyebrows. "Where did you learn that?"

Rolly looked away. A blush spread across his cheeks. "I, uh, looked it up."

She poked him in the side. "Because you're worried about her too."

"Okay, fine, yes. I was worried. But like I said, leopards are solitary, so she probably prefers to be on her own."

"But she's not exactly a normal leopard, is she? Leopards are also supposed to be nocturnal, and Cleo's not. She's not like other leopards."

Lou looked at Rolly. *Just like we're not like other humans.* The words were unspoken but hung in the air between them.

She checked on Cleo again through the window. She still lay in the same spot, unmoving. "With Laney looking into Sheila's murder, Cleo will barely spend any time outside that thing. I think it's really getting to her."

Lou knew that some of the other kids at the school had complained about being scared of Cleo. It was because of them that Cleo was locked up.

The wind picked up, and Cleo barely moved as a tree branch smacked against her cage. "That's it." Lou stood up and headed for the door.

"What are you doing?" Rolly caught up with her, a grin spreading across his face.

"Exactly what you *think* I'm doing."

Rolly grabbed her arm as she reached for the door handle.

Lou looked up at him in surprise. "You don't want to help?"

"Oh, I do. I just think we should recruit a couple more helpers as well."

CHAPTER 21

Addison, West Virginia

Matt walked down the long pale gray cement hall, entered the elevator, and pushed the button for the SIA detention center's lowest level. The center was over twenty thousand square feet, and only about two thousand square feet were the offices for the SIA agents who worked there. The remaining space was dedicated to the facilities' main mission: housing and holding prisoners that no other prison on the planet could contain.

Currently there were fourteen residents, and most were housed in the first two floors of the building. All of them were either nephilim or a Fallen.

With one exception.

An electric charge ran over Matt's skin as the elevator doors slid open. He stepped out and walked the hundred yards down the hallway to the only cell on this level—fifty feet under the first floor.

Matt nodded at Hanz Friederich, who stood in front of the hallway leading to the special prisoner. The tall blond guard nodded back. "Director, good to see you."

"You as well, Hanz. How'd Lady do this weekend?"

A smile broke across the usual dour Hanz's face. Lady, Hanz's black and white border collie, was Hanz's true joy in life. "Great. She finished first in her division. Fastest time yet."

Matt grinned. Lady was a champion at obstacle courses. Matt had even gone to see her compete a few times. It was pretty incredible. But what was even more incredible was how she could transform Hanz into an absolute softy.

It's amazing what one good relationship can do. When Matt first met Hanz years ago, Matt wasn't sure he'd be able to fit in with the SIA. He was cold and standoffish, and most of the agents had doubts that he was completely on their side. But then Hanz started training dogs, and all of a sudden the anger that had seemed a perpetual part of him began to wane. He still might not smile much, but in the last ten years, he'd proven himself to be loyal. And Matt knew it was the dogs in his life that gave him that grounding, that sense of home.

"How's the prisoner doing today?" Matt asked.

The smile disappeared from Hanz's face. "No different." He pulled the door open for Matt. "He was sedated an hour ago. He should be just waking up. "

Matt stepped through. "Thanks."

He walked down the long hall. There were no guards in here and only one cell, located at the end of the hundred-foot-long hallway. A glass wall stood there, and beyond it were a bed, desk, a small bathroom, and some books. And that was it.

Matt stepped up to the glass and inspected the dark figure curled up on the bed. Above the bed, two air vents stood closed. Before anyone entered the cell, the vents would open and fill the room with a strong sedative, knocking the occupant out. Only once the prisoner was out cold was anyone allowed in the room.

Even with that precaution, the inmate had still proven himself dangerous. Two of Matt's men had been hurt due to carelessness—they hadn't paid attention to the clock and so hadn't realized the prisoner was coming to. So Matt had instituted a new safety procedure: one additional person was now placed on each team whose sole job was to pay attention to the time. Of course, that hadn't stopped the injuries to his agents. But those agents had volunteered for the risks.

82

Matt glanced at his watch; the sedation should have worn off by now. But he also knew the prisoner spent most of his time sleeping. It wasn't his surroundings, but his grief, that kept him unmoving.

"What do you want?" the man on the bed asked without turning.

"A situation has developed."

The figure on the bed let out a sigh, rolled over, and sat on the edge of the bed. His dark hair hung nearly to his waist, and his dark pajamas were wrinkled, but it was his stocking feet that always struck Matt as unreal. One of the most powerful men in history, and he was tucked away shoeless and in pajamas in the hills of West Virginia.

"Why should I care?" Cain asked, looking up, his black eyes focused on Matt.

"Because the ring bearer cares."

Cain raised an eyebrow, the first hint of interest Matt had seen from him in months.

Taking it as a good sign, Matt plowed on. "Over the last two years, there has been a series of thirty-four similar ritualistic-style murders. Each of the bodies has been displayed on an altar, the heart removed and burned. But the individuals were drowned before their heart was removed."

"And each death occurred at sunset, many of them on the day of the full moon."

Matt nodded slowly. He wasn't overly surprised that Cain knew of the murders. Matt had a feeling there was something building, what with the Fallen increasing their appearances, these strange murders, and Victoria being gone. It was like all these events were leading to something. And Matt had a feeling that whatever it was, it was not going to be good for mankind.

He eyed Cain for a moment. Cain had said little to nothing in his time here; now he was engaging in conversation. And that made Matt even more worried. He spoke slowly. "You know who's doing these."

Cain shrugged. "Perhaps. But I can't see any benefit to me in sharing that information with you."

Matt snorted. "Right. So what do you want?"

Cain paused. "I'd like a TV—and a window. I miss the sunlight. And I'd like some time outside, guarded of course."

Matt pretended to consider his requests, then shook his head. He'd known Cain would ask for concessions. And Matt had already decided what he would agree to. "The TV is possible, and the window. But the outside time is out of the question."

Cain narrowed his eyes, but nodded. "Well then, you have a deal."

"Okay, so who—"

Cain shook his head. "Oh, and one more little point—I won't answer your questions."

"But you just—"

"I'll answer the questions of the ring bearer. If she wants to know, then she will have to come to me."

CHAPTER 22

Baltimore, Maryland

Lou and Rolly ran from the courtyard to the building as fast as they could manage. Behind them, Cleo blended into the shadows.

The windows that lined the courtyard were almost all dark. "Do you think anyone saw us?" Lou asked.

Rolly shrugged. "I don't know."

"Okay. Let's go." She opened the door to the hallway and slipped inside. They just needed to get down this long hallway and up the main stairs, and then they'd be home free.

Lou started to creep down the hall when she heard voices. She grabbed Rolly and pushed him against the wall. Cleo flattened herself against the wall, too.

"What?" Rolly asked.

"Listen."

"Zach? What are you doing?" Yoni asked.

"Oh, um, I was just heading to the library. I think I may have forgotten a book there."

"Okay. It's close to lights out though, so make it quick."

"Um, sure. I will."

Yoni's footsteps turned in their direction. *Damn it.* Zach was supposed to head off anyone coming this way, but he was just not very good at lying.

Eyes wide, Lou looked back at Rolly, who threw up his hands. *I don't know,* he mouthed.

Cleo walked over to the pillar across from them. She stepped behind it just as Yoni rounded the corner.

Surprise flashed across Yoni's face. "Oh, hi guys."

"Heeeey, Yoni," Rolly drawled out, and Lou could have smacked him. He couldn't have sounded more unnatural if he tried.

"Yeah, hey Yoni," Lou rushed out. "How's it going?"

"Good, *Lou.* How's it going with you?"

"Good. Well, see you." Lou grabbed Rolly's arm and pulled him toward Zach.

"Oh, guys?" Yoni called.

Lou winced and turned back around, slapping an innocent expression on her face.

Yoni leaned against the pillar directly across from Cleo. From her vantage point, Lou could see that Cleo was standing on her back paws to stay hidden. Lou forced her eyes back to Yoni. "Yeah?"

"Funny thing—the security cameras are out this way." Yoni paused. "But only in this hallway, right where you guys are. Weird, huh?"

Lou nodded.

"Totally weird," Rolly said. "Well, gotta go."

"Yup. Almost past my bedtime," Lou added.

"Whatever you're up to," Yoni said, "don't get me in trouble for it."

"We're not—" Rolly said.

Yoni put up a hand and Rolly went silent. "Just be careful." Yoni walked away.

As soon as Yoni had turned the corner, Lou released the breath she'd been holding and motioned for Cleo to come.

Cleo dropped silently back down to all fours and padded over to them. They caught up with Zach, who grinned. Together the four made their way up the stairs to Lou's room.

Luckily, they didn't run into anyone else. Lou hustled everyone into her room and closed the door quickly.

Rolly pulled out his phone and typed a quick message before shoving it in his back pocket. "Danny set the security cameras back to normal," he said. "He'll be up in a few minutes."

Cleo nudged Zach's hand. Zach ran a hand through her fur. "You're welcome, girl."

Cleo went around and rubbed against each of them before curling up next to Lou. The big cat looked much better than she had for the last couple of hours.

An hour later, the boys had left and it was just Lou and Cleo. Lou crawled under her covers and turned off the lights. "Night, Cleo."

Cleo padded over, sat right next to the bed, and stared at Lou. Lou could feel Cleo's breath on her face. She reached up and rubbed behind the cat's ears. "You're a good girl, Cleo."

Cleo watched her for a few more moments, then lay down next to the bed. Lou closed her eyes and tried to sleep, but she couldn't get the look in Cleo's eyes out of her mind. She looked so sad.

Cleo let out a large sigh. Lou ignored it.

But after fifteen minutes of Cleo's sighs and getting up to stare at Lou, Lou knew this wasn't going to work. "Okay, okay, you win."

Lou grabbed her pillow and blanket and hopped off the bed. She placed them on the floor next to Cleo. She lay down and closed her eyes.

Cleo inched over until her back was touching Lou's.

Lou smiled and adjusted the blanket so it covered both of them. "Goodnight, Cleo."

Cleo let out another sigh—this one much more contented.

CHAPTER 23

Laney spent the next day reading everything she could find on human sacrifice, which was about as much fun as a root canal. She knew water was a purifier and that the Children of the Law of One had used it to wash away sins. In Catholicism, water was used in baptism for the same purpose. In fact, water as a purifier was common across many religions. But she hadn't found any rituals that combined water, fire, and blood loss.

And she simply couldn't read another page on ritualistic killings. She'd read too many crime reports on murders that were believed to be ritualized in nature, and the only thing they had in common was that "ritualized killings" seemed to be code for "extremely brutal."

So she called it a day, telling everyone that if they found anything to call her. She decided to head home and make dinner—something she hadn't done in months.

The front door rang just as she was putting the garlic on the ciabatta bread. She frowned. No one used the doorbell. Most people did a quick knock before walking in.

She wiped her hands on a towel and made her way to the front door. Glancing through the glass next to the door, she was surprised at who was standing there. She pulled the door open. "Hey, Matt."

Matt stood uncertainly in the doorway. "Hey. I'm sorry to interrupt."

Laney couldn't say she was happy to see him, not with their last conversation still on her mind. But they had to work together, and she supposed she needed to bury the hatchet.

"No interruption. But I am surprised. I didn't realize you were in town." She waved him toward the kitchen as she started to the back. "I was just getting dinner started. Jake will be back in about a half hour. Care to join us?"

Matt followed her. "Maybe some other time."

Laney sighed, placing the pan she had just pulled out of the cupboard on the counter. "So I guess this is not a social call."

"I'm afraid not. There's something I need to tell you, and I wanted to do it in person."

"Is it about the murders?"

"Not exactly." Matt gestured to the table. "Can we sit?"

Laney debated for a moment. She had wanted just one quiet dinner for her and Jake without any stress. Things had been so much better between them after their little talk. And tonight, she had wanted to pretend they were just a normal couple, sitting down with some wine and a nice meal after a workday.

Laney sighed. She took a seat at the table and gestured for Matt to take a seat as well. *Well, maybe tomorrow we can play let's pretend.* "Okay, so you look like you just got caught with your hand in the cookie jar. What's going on?"

Matt stared at the tabletop before looking up at Laney. "You remember when Cain went into the river in India?"

Laney looked at him for a moment and said dryly, "Yes, that sounds vaguely familiar."

Matt nodded, appearing not to notice her tone. He stared at the countertop. "As director of the SIA, it is my responsibility to hold some cards close to the vest for security and strategic reasons."

89

Laney frowned. "Matt, what's going on?"

Matt made eye contact. "In the aftermath of the incident in India, we recovered a valuable asset, who we have been holding in our West Virginia facility ever since."

Laney stared back at him. "Since India? Who—" She went still. *No. He said he was dead.* "You have Cain."

"Yes."

Laney was floored. He had Cain—the man who had nearly killed both Henry and Jake. The man who had orchestrated the abductions of both Victoria and Max—the abductions that had let the Fallen know Victoria was around.

Laney rolled her hands into fists. "But I asked you *specifically* about Cain. You *lied* to me."

"Laney, I had to decide—"

"What, Matt? What exactly did you have to decide? That the general of the army of the good should be kept in the dark? This is the second time in two days that I've learned you've been keeping something from me."

"Laney, you have to understand, you—"

Laney stood up. All the anger and impotence she'd been feeling since Victoria's death raged through her. "I am the ring bearer! I am the one who has been chosen time and time again to push back against the Fallen. I am the one who has put her life on the line I don't know how many times in the last few years. I am the one who has had to lose people I love to this stupid war. Don't tell me what I have to understand! I have a very good understanding of the stakes. I don't need a lecture from you on bureaucratic policy."

She stepped away from the table and tried to calm down. He had lied right to her face. He had kept Cain's existence from her for months. She had worried about Cain finding Max, Maddox, and Kati, had lost sleep over it. And that had all been for nothing. She curled her fists. *Goddamn it.*

"Laney, I'm sorry. I chose what I felt was the best course of action at the time."

90

Laney whirled on him. "No. You chose to hide a critical piece of information from me. What happened to the whole 'the government might pay me, but I consider you to be in charge' line you fed me?"

"I still believe that. But sometimes subordinates have to keep leaders in the dark to protect them."

"Protect me? I'm the only one Cain can't hurt. I don't need—" She narrowed her eyes. "What have you been doing to him?"

Matt wouldn't meet her gaze. "Questioning him, analyzing him. Trying to see what biological processes underlie his abilities."

Laney stared at him in shock. As part of Cain's curse, anyone who tried to touch him would receive the injury back sevenfold—except for Laney. "And each time you probe him, one of your people must be harmed."

Matt nodded.

"My God, you placed them all in terrible danger. And for what? Did you learn anything?"

Matt shook his head. "No. The medical tests did not reveal any abnormalities. In fact, if we didn't know what he was capable of, we would never be able to tell from the tests."

"And the questioning?"

"He won't tell us anything."

All Laney could think about was the research on torture. A CIA report to Congress demonstrated that the CIA had misled the public about its tactics and oversold the effectiveness of its techniques. In fact, their enhanced interrogations had led to no actionable intelligence—and worse, had led to false leads that had taken agents away from other possible avenues of investigation. While conventionally the belief may have been that torture resulted in useful intelligence, psychologists for years had warned that subjects would say anything merely to make the torture cease.

And now Matt's been torturing Cain for months. She shook her head. Like there's any chance he'd willingly help them now, after months of torture. "What were you thinking?'

"I was thinking this was one burden you didn't have to bear. That I could handle this one for you."

Laney closed her eyes. She'd had it with men trying to protect her. It wasn't their damn job, and she wasn't some damsel in distress.

She opened her eyes again, and Matt met her gaze. She knew he had done what he thought was best. But she knew it wasn't what was best for her. And she wasn't sure where to go from here. First, he'd kept the murders from her. Now he had kept Cain from her.

She studied the agent. It had taken her a while to trust Matt, but eventually, she had. And apparently she had been a fool to do so. "Why are telling me this now?"

"It's about these murder cases. I think Cain may have some answers."

"And he won't tell you."

"No. But he says he'll tell *you*. Will you talk to him?"

Cain, the man who had ushered murder into the world.

The man whose actions had led to Victoria's death and to Max going into hiding.

The man who had caused this wall to come between her and Jake.

She didn't know if she could trust herself to face him. But she pictured Sheila's family: the devastation on Mikio's face when she'd told him the news; how he'd held his son and daughter at the memorial service. She closed her eyes. She didn't want to see any other family destroyed like that.

She nodded. "I'll speak with him."

CHAPTER 24

Addison, West Virginia

The next day, Laney walked down a long hallway in the SIA facility between Matt and Mustafa. She'd been here before, but she still wasn't sure what she thought of the place. It was designed to hold the Fallen and nephilim. No normal prison was equipped to handle them.

But there was also no trial, no judge, and no sentence. The Fallen were just locked up, and that was it—because the world at large wasn't allowed to know that they existed.

But the moral ambiguity of the facility's mission wasn't her focus today. Cain was. And she was still coming to grips with the fact that Matt had had Cain in his custody for six months without breathing a word of it to her. Laney wasn't sure what to make of the agent now. If he had kept this from her, what else was he hiding? To say the air was uncomfortable between them would be an understatement.

Henry and Jake had been beyond angry when she had told them. Actually, angry was an understatement. Livid was probably more accurate. She'd found herself in the odd position of having to calm *them* down. They had both wanted to come with her. But Laney didn't want their anger getting in the way of what needed to be done. It would be hard enough to keep her own anger in check.

"It's right up ahead," Mustafa said.

Mustafa had apologized over and over again for not telling Laney about Cain, and Laney had forgiven him. She knew it hadn't been either his call or his choice—it was Matt's—and she could tell Mustafa still felt horrible about the deception.

Now Laney made her way toward the world's first murderer. She wasn't sure how she felt about Cain. He had hurt both Henry and Jake, but in many ways, Cain, like Mustafa, had had no choice. Anyone who tried to harm him would be harmed sevenfold. He couldn't help that, couldn't prevent the damage caused to those who attacked him. That was a result of the curse placed upon him after he was banished from God's sight for slaying his brother. And even that murder was not strictly intentional. At the time Cain had killed Abel, he had thought humans were immortal. He had thought his brother would live.

Even Cain's abduction of Victoria and Max was, in a weird sort of way, meant to protect Victoria. He wanted Laney, Jake, and Henry to defeat Elisabeta so that Victoria would not have to sacrifice herself. In his flawed way, it was his love for Victoria that made him do what he did.

Victoria was a big part of the reason Laney was so confused as she walked down the cold hallway. There had been a bond between Victoria and this man, a bond that wasn't just about the fact that they had both lived so long. They had a real concern for each other. Laney didn't understand it entirely, but the fact that Victoria had cared in some way for this man made her own feelings toward him confusing.

And how strange is it that I feel more compassion for Cain right now than I do Matt?

"He was moved from his other cell to this one, at his request," Mustafa said as they approached the end of the hall.

Laney could see the glass wall but not the cell's inhabitant. The cell was similar to what she had seen the other inmates in. As she came closer, she saw a figure sitting on the

94

bed. Mustafa and Matt stopped twenty feet away, but Laney stepped right up to the glass divider.

Cain immediately stood, his hands behind his back, his long hair pulled back into a ponytail. He wore dark pajamas and slippers.

Laney struggled not to gasp. It wasn't his clothing that was the issue, but his face. There were dark bags under his eyes and he was extremely pale. *He's almost as pale as me*, she realized with disbelief. His warm olive complexion was nowhere to be seen. *What have they done to him?*

Laney bit her lip to keep from yelling at Matt. Instead, she inclined her head to Cain. "Jor—" She paused. "What do you want me to call you?"

"I'd prefer Cain. It's been too long since I had my original name, and there's no need to hide it."

She nodded. "All right, Cain, thank you for agreeing to help."

"Well, I was given two out of my three requests, so…" He shrugged.

"What was your third request?" Laney asked.

"To go outside," he said.

Laney turned to Matt. "I think we can arrange that."

Matt shook his head. "Laney—he can't be trusted outside. If he gets loose—"

"*I* will take full responsibility for him. Besides, I'm pretty sure in a fistfight, I would win."

From the corner of her eye, she saw Cain smile.

"Very well," Matt said reluctantly. "When he's told you—"

"No, I think we'll have our chat outside," Laney said.

Matt nodded stiffly.

Laney turned back to the glass wall. "Cain, would you care to take a walk with me?"

CHAPTER 25

Mykonos, Greece

Gerard Thompson walked down the dirt street in Mykonos. Lights shone from the two-story white stucco homes as he passed. Up ahead, a group of kids played soccer by streetlight. An errant ball came flying toward him. Gerard trapped it quickly and sent it back to the kids.

Stavros, age ten, ran up to him with a big smile. "Hi, Giorgio. Want to play?"

Gerard smiled down at him. "Not tonight, my little friend. I have to put these away before they spoil." He indicated the brown bag of groceries in his hands.

"Okay. Tomorrow?"

"Tomorrow," Gerard agreed.

With another smile, Stavros headed back to his friends. Gerard watched them play for a moment before continuing on his way. He had been in Greece for six months. He had first gone to his old village, outside present-day Thessaloniki in the north, where he had lived with Kaya and his children. He had found the spot of their graves and wept for them again.

He had planned on leaving right away, knowing that Thessaloniki would be the first place Elisabeta would look for him. But while he had left the area where he and his family had lived, he could not seem to make himself leave the country. Even though it had changed greatly in the centuries since he had been here, there were parts that were so like yesterday, he almost expected to see Peter and Arya run over a hill to greet him. So he had traveled around the country, feeling at home like he hadn't for centuries.

Finally, four months ago, he had settled on Mykonos.

The island, with its white buildings, its hilly land, and its blue waters, was like a little slice of heaven. He had found a small cottage for himself and begun work as a carpenter, doing repairs and creating furniture. A year ago, he would have scoffed at the idea of him doing manual labor to make a living. But now, he would be happy to do this for the rest of his life.

Up ahead, his cottage stood perched on a cliff overlooking the Aegean Sea. It was small—only one room plus a bathroom. But Gerard had started a vegetable garden and had turned his bed so that when he woke up every morning, he saw the sun rising over the blue waters. He was a mile outside town, but he liked the isolation. He could walk into town when he wanted companionship, but he could also be on his own.

He pushed open the rickety wooden gate, which was slowly decaying after years of neglect. He had plans to replace the gate and the fence next month when he had some more money. For now, he liked the old thing. It was something to look forward to—the next repair.

The moon shone brightly up ahead. Gerard planned out his day tomorrow as he followed the path to the door. Mrs. Helios wanted new planters for her windows. He could get that done in the morning, which would leave him time to start the chicken coop for—

His head whipped up as the wind shifted. Cologne.

He dove for the ground as a dart hit the door ahead of him. He rolled to his feet. Three figures approached from the front, all of them carrying weapons.

The door behind him was flung open and two more men appeared. A dart stung him in his side. Gerard yanked it out and kicked one of the men in the chest. The man flew backward and slammed into his companion, and they both disappeared through the doorway.

Gerard could already feel his thoughts growing sluggish. Two more darts penetrated his body, one in his arm and the other in his neck, and he yanked them out as well. One of the men ran at him, but Gerard managed to sweep out the man's leg, knocking him down.

Using the last of his strength, he ran for the cliff edge.

"Stop him!" one of the men yelled behind him.

Gerard stumbled as he neared the edge, and crashed to his knees. He couldn't stand. He rolled himself onto his side, then rolled again and again... until there was nothing solid beneath him.

He dropped off the cliff edge.

He hit the water, and it swallowed him. He tried to work up the energy to swim, but he didn't have any. He watched the moon as he sank deeper and deeper.

All these months he'd been waiting for the Fallen to find him. He had been on constant guard for the telltale signal that one of his brethren was near. But he hadn't felt that tingle of recognition.

Not that he should be surprised. After all, his attackers were human.

CHAPTER 26

Laney and Cain walked side by side down the long hallway. She had already had them clear the corridors on the way to the enclosed courtyard where she and Cain would speak; she wanted no one to be within Cain's reach.

Ahead, sunlight shone through the glass in the doors. Cain picked up his pace just slightly at the sight. Laney pushed open the doors, and the two of them stepped out.

Cain stopped just past the doors and stood, his face turned toward the sun, his eyes closed. A sigh escaped him.

Laney let him have his moment. Finally he turned to her. "Thank you. We can speak now."

Laney shook her head. "Why don't we walk a bit first?"

Surprise flashed across Cain's face before he nodded. "All right."

Together, the two of them walked around the perimeter of the yard, not saying a word. Laney was happy to let him walk as long as he wanted. There was nowhere for him to go, and a half hour one way or another would make no difference right now.

And there was something different about Cain now compared to when she'd last seen him. His anger was gone. He was not defeated exactly, but he was...

Lost. He's lost, she realized.

"You're a lot like her," Cain said quietly.

Laney looked up in surprise. "Victoria?"

He nodded. "Yes—your compassion. She has—had the same strain of it running through her. You could have demanded answers from me. You could have tortured me and I would not have been able to stop you. Instead, you chose to grant me a wish." He gave a rueful smile and then turned away, but not before Laney saw the flash of tears in his eyes. "She was the same way."

He's grieving her, she realized with shock.

"Do you know how she died?" Laney asked softly.

He nodded. "I knew what was coming long before you did. I've seen it before."

"She wasn't alone," Laney said, surprised by the emotion in her voice. When she decided to speak with Cain, she had never envisioned the conversation heading in this direction.

Cain nodded but didn't speak. They walked on in silence, but there was the beginning of a bond between the two of them, a closeness that Laney wasn't sure what to do with.

They took another lap around the courtyard before Laney gestured to one of the picnic benches. The staff sometimes ate lunch out here. It was a nice spot: the building surrounded them on four sides and towered four stories above them, but the courtyard was large enough for a few benches, and well-manicured flowers and bushes lined the area.

Laney and Cain sat on opposite sides of one of the tables. Cain folded his hands on the tabletop. "What do you want to know?"

"Do you know who is committing the murders?"

"The actual person, no. But I can tell you *why* they're committing them."

"Okay."

"A long time ago, there was a culture that revered the world; they believed in the purity of the world, the goodness. But sometimes members strayed from the path. This group

100

didn't believe in punishing the offender, however. Instead, they performed a purification ritual. The individual would lie on a stone altar and be bathed to wash away the evils of this world—their greed, self-interest, and self-indulgences. When completed, they were considered purified and were returned to their community with open arms."

There were similarities, but that sounded awfully peaceful compared to the recent murders. "The cases I'm looking into are a bit more violent than that," Laney said.

Cain nodded. "I'm sure they are. But your murders started with this other culture. The culture expanded across the globe, sending emissaries throughout the Americas and into Asia and Africa. Eventually, the original culture was swallowed by the sea, but its traditions were then combined with the native cultures that had received their emissaries. The ritual you are now seeing dates back to before the Aztecs."

"The human sacrifice rituals of the Olmecs."

"Yes."

"But why the drowning? The burning of the heart?"

"Those are modifications, if you will, of the purification ceremony."

"Has this happened before?"

"Yes. Which is why you need to stop it. If the ceremony is being conducted, it is because the purveyors of the art believe the world has tilted toward wickedness. The purification ritual is their attempt to right the scales—to bring the world back to goodness. And there are more of these rituals than you think."

"More?"

"Clark said you think they are happening around twice a month. That is not the case. Those are only the ones they are letting you know about. They want you to be aware of their activities."

"But why?"

"To get you to help them."

101

Whatever she had expected Cain to say, it was not this. "*Help* them?" Laney pictured Sheila. "They want us to *help* them kill innocent people?"

"You—the rest of the world. They want you to turn from wickedness. In their mind, their victims are not innocent. They are the ones responsible for the downfall of the world."

Laney stared at him, trying to determine how much she could reveal. But really, who was he going to tell? "They're going after people who have had dealings with the Fallen— wives, husbands, mothers, fathers, friends."

Cain nodded. "Yes—in their eyes the Fallen are the personification of evil. They believe the victims are enabling the Fallen to continue their work, or worse, to bring more evil into the world."

Laney blanched, picturing the children from the Chandler School. None of the children were evil. Each was just a child whose experiences in this life would push them to one side or the other—just like with any other child.

"But you are wrong," Cain said, breaking into Laney's thoughts. "It's not just the associates of the Fallen they are going after. They are going after the Fallen themselves as well."

Laney looked at him in surprise. "The Fallen?"

Cain nodded. "I can guarantee it."

Laney glanced over her shoulder toward the doors. Did Matt know about that as well?

She shook her head. Cain's earlier words came back to her. *Eventually, the original culture was swallowed by the sea, but its traditions were then combined with the native cultures that had received their emissaries.* "Yet again, Atlantis rears its ugly head."

Cain frowned. "Atlantis? What do you mean?"

Laney looked at him in confusion. "You said that the ritual came from the first civilization that spread across the world before they were swallowed by the sea."

"Yes. But that's not Atlantis."

102

Laney stared at him. Atlantis was the earliest theorized civilization, and of course it was swallowed by the sea. "Then what civilization are you talking about?"

"Atlantis *was* an early civilization, but it wasn't the earliest. It was an outgrowth of another civilization that predated it by thousands of years."

Laney thought for a moment. "According to Plato, Atlantis was created by Poseidon, a series of artificial islands."

Cain waved her on.

"And Poseidon must have come from somewhere, prior to Atlantis."

"Exactly."

"So what was the name of this previous civilization?"

Cain smiled. "Oh, they were more than just a previous civilization. They were the motherland of *all* civilizations, the first true civilization on the planet: Lemuria. But you probably know it by a different name."

"Mu," Laney said softly. *Another legendary civilization that's cloaked in mystery.*

She had heard of Mu, of course, but she wasn't as familiar with it as she was with Atlantis. Mu was believed to have stretched across the Pacific. But she had thought that it was a contemporary of Atlantis, or possibly even came after. She had never heard of it as the precursor. "You think someone is borrowing ancient rituals from Lemuria?"

Cain shook his head, his dark eyes intense. "I believe it is the descendants of Mu themselves who are committing these acts."

CHAPTER 27

Baltimore, Maryland

Lou stepped back from the computer in Danny's office. "Okay, I need a break."

She had looked for everything she could find on leopards, but they all suggested they were solitary creatures. They met up for mating, but otherwise didn't socialize—except that oddly, when not hunting, they seemed to get along with antelopes. Still, none of the sites could explain why Cleo seemed to crave companionship.

Rolly raised one eyelid from his position on the couch. "Some of us were already enjoying a break."

Lou rolled her eyes. "So sorry, Your Majesty."

Rolly gave an imperious wave with his hand. "You are forgiven this time. Next time I may not be so lenient."

Lou ignored him and looked at Danny and Zach, who'd shown up just a few minutes earlier. "You guys want to go see Cleo?"

Zach nodded and nudged Danny. "Earth to Danny. Break time."

Danny looked up slowly, his eyes taking a moment to focus. "Huh? What?"

Lou laughed, grabbed his arm, and pulled him out of his chair. "Come on, Einstein. Fresh air."

Together, they headed for the large courtyard at the back of the school—after first stopping by the kitchen for some bacon. The cook always prepared three pounds of it for Cleo's afternoon snack.

Danny's black shepherd mix, Moxy, scampered ahead as the door to the courtyard came into view. She jumped around, her excitement contagious.

Lou smiled as Rolly pushed open the door. "Go get her."

Moxy sprinted across the lawn. Cleo, who had been sprawled out lazily in the sun, jumped to attention. Cleo and Moxy raced each other up and down the length of Cleo's enclosure.

Lou shook her head. "I still don't get how those two ended up being such good friends."

Danny walked to the gate and unlocked it. Cleo slunk through the door, stopping only long enough to rub her head against Danny's chest before running for Moxy. Moxy leaped at Cleo, who obligingly rolled onto her back, trying to swipe at Moxy with her giant paws.

Lou watched in amazement. Even with Cleo's immense size, she never hurt Moxy, never even accidentally. Her control was incredible.

Zach stood next to Rolly. "How *did* she get so big?"

"Amar the horrible added growth hormone to her littermates when she was in utero," Rolly said. Amar Patel was a Fallen who had contracted with some lab to create a litter of Javan leopards. Cleo was the only one of the litter still alive.

"Laney said some of the other guys in her litter were even bigger," Lou said.

Zach shook his head. "I can't imagine that."

"What I can't figure out is where her intelligence comes from," Lou said. "I mean, the growth hormones wouldn't have done that, would they?"

"Uh, actually I think that's because Amar had them mix his blood in with the mixture," Danny said.

"Seriously?" Zach asked.

Danny nodded. "I keep hoping I'll find the formula they used."

"Why?" Lou asked.

"Because I don't want anyone else to use it. Can you imagine if someone else figured out how to make a super predator like Cleo? I mean, Cleo's great, but that's only because Laney got to her first and then introduced the rest of us to her. Could you imagine what would happen if Laney hadn't? If Cleo had managed to escape?"

Lou swallowed. She'd seen Cleo in action and had been really happy that the cat had been on their side. If she hadn't been, there would have been nothing Lou could have done to stop Cleo.

"But all her littermates were killed by Amar, right?" Rolly asked.

After a quick glance to make sure Cleo was still playing with Moxy, Danny lowered his voice and said, "Yeah. Apparently he liked to hunt them down and kill them."

"Seriously, that guy gets scummier and scummier each time I hear about him," Rolly muttered.

Lou caught that pensive look on Danny's face that meant he was wrestling with a problem. Danny's gaze turned to where Moxy and Cleo were playing. His look grew even more despondent. Lou frowned, looking between Cleo and Danny. *What is he thinking?*

Later, they were headed back inside when Zach glanced at his watch. "Oh, man, we've got to get going, Rolly."

"Where are you guys going?" Lou asked.

Rolly rolled his eyes. "We've got a group project for history. As if school isn't tough enough without forcing us to work with one another."

Lou smiled. "Somehow I think you'll struggle through."

Rolly put his hand to his chest. "It's true—I am very resilient. It's just one of my many amazing qualities."

106

Zach shook his head and yanked on Rolly's sleeve, pulling him down the hallway. "Okay, amazing one. Let's go."

Lou laughed as she watched them go.

She turned back to see Danny looking lost in thought and frowning once again. She walked up to him. "Okay, what's going on?"

"What?"

"You've got that 'I'm thinking of something earth-shattering' look on your face."

"Nothing. It's just work."

"Really, it doesn't have anything to do with Cleo?"

"Sh," Danny said as two kids from Lou's math class passed by.

"What?"

Danny pulled her into an empty classroom.

"Okay, what the hell is going on?" Lou asked.

"I think I found something about Cleo. Well, sort of."

"Okay, what?"

Danny just looked away.

"Come on, if it's about Cleo, I want to know. I have a right to know."

Danny hesitated and finally shook his head. "Cleo was never supposed to be as big as she is. And you've seen her. She's gotten bigger since you first met her. She's still growing."

Lou nodded, knowing Cleo had gotten at least a few inches taller. "Yeah, but she's what, three? That's still—"

"No. In the wild, leopards are ready to have cubs at age two. She should be done growing."

"So why is she still growing then?"

"I don't know. In humans, unusual growth rates are often the result of a tumor in the pituitary gland."

"But if she has that, it can be treated, right?"

"Yes, with medication."

"That's good. We scan, treat her, problem solved."

107

Danny shook his head. "No. Bodies are designed within certain parameters, kind of like with cars or planes. You can't just add a ton of weight to a car and expect it to handle the way it did at the lighter weight. In animals, the heart is set to pump a certain amount. Cleo's heart has to pump much harder."

"So she has a strong heart."

"In humans, a heart that has to work too hard usually results in a shortened life span."

Lou felt shock ripple through her. Danny thought Cleo was dying. "But you don't know that for sure. I mean, we don't know how Cleo was created."

"No, we don't." He looked Lou in the eyes. "But I really think we need to find out."

CHAPTER 28

The descendants of Mu are committing these murders. Laney stared at Cain. "How the hell can the descendants of an ancient civilization, the first civilization, one which must have died out thousands of years ago, be responsible for the current murders?"

"Life is often more complex than we realize."

Laney stared at him. "Are you kidding? Is this a joke?"

"Laney, with everything you have learned since you accepted your destiny, can you really say this is impossible?" Cain held out his arms. "After all, I was just a literary device to you until a year ago."

Laney could admit to herself that he was right. In the last two years, she had learned that fallen angels and nephilim walked among us, that her biological father was one of the most powerful angels ever, that her mother was Lilith—who was not the evil witch the Bible made her out to be—and that an ancient library had been hidden away by the followers of Atlantis and was now safely tucked away under the Chandler Group's watchful eye.

She ran her thumb over the ring of Solomon, which bestowed on her multiple abilities including an ability to control the Fallen, the weather, and animals. "I guess you're right. But there must be more you can tell me about the descendants of Mu."

Cain smiled. "I have enjoyed our talk, ring bearer. But I cannot give away everything for free. We will talk again when I have made some arrangements."

"What do you want?" Laney asked.

"I want to feel the sun on my face and the grass between my toes." He gestured around. "I want more of this."

"I'll make it happen."

Cain shook his head, his gaze holding hers. "I have no doubt *you* will. But Clark I do not trust, and you will get nothing more out of me until those things have been arranged."

Laney studied Cain's sallow cheeks, which had the beginning of color on them. She wanted to press him, wanted to demand he tell her what he knew. But she knew he would only dig in his heels. *Damn you, Clark,* she thought. If he hadn't treated Cain the way he had, maybe they would have been able to get more out of him.

"Besides," Cain said. "There is no rush. You should have some time. I look forward to our next chat."

"But—"

Cain shook his head and stood. "I would like some time to enjoy my new accommodations. After all, this information is my only leverage, and I do not trust Clark to keep his word once you have gotten everything you need. I've given you enough to get you started, don't you think?"

Laney stared at him in disbelief. "Right. All we have to do is find the descendants of the world's first civilization. How hard can it be?"

Cain grinned. "That's the spirit."

CHAPTER 29

Taipei City, Taiwan

Maura shook her head as she read over the latest blog for their website at her kitchen table. She was supposed to be looking only for grammatical errors, but she couldn't help but be angered once again by the topic—the disappearance of thousands of species of animals from the planet every year.

Her eyes scanned the post, finding her favorite paragraphs.

Each year between one thousand and ten thousand animals species are lost to the world. They will never again grace this planet. At the current rate, it is estimated that between thirty and fifty percent of all animals in existence today will become extinct by 2050.

And what is the reason for this mass extinction? In one word: humans. Human activities have caused the natural extinction rates to balloon to one thousand times the normal level. And while animals are decreasing in number, humans are only increasing. There are now seven billion humans in the world, with an additional eighty million being added annually. But we're not paying enough attention to the damage we are causing.

We cannot continue to take from the earth and not expect there to be consequences.

She sat back, staring at the words. Did they have enough of a pop? She had placed pictures of the world's favorite endangered species on the same page: cuddly pandas, beautiful polar bears, and impressive tigers. Other animals that were more critical to the earth's ecosystem were also becoming endangered, but Save the Spiders didn't have quite the same impact as Save the Panda.

Her eyes strayed though to the black Java leopard featured prominently at the top of the article. At last report, there were only 250 Javan leopards left, and Maura had no doubt that that number would soon be reduced. After all, it was only in 1990 that Javan tigers had become extinct due to humans pushing their way into the tigers' territory.

Even the Mother's own guardians are in danger, Maura thought as she glanced at the picture of the Great Mother above her desk. In the picture, the Mother sat on her throne draped in fabric, a crown on her head. By her sides were her two guardians: one lion and one leopard. *They didn't even respect you*, Maura thought, trying to tamp down her anger.

Maura finished reviewing the rest of the piece and made a few quick changes before publishing it. Then she pushed away from the desk, knowing that her words would have little chance of making any difference. She had started the blog years ago, hoping she could help organize people toward change, hoping that she could get people to understand the critical point that mankind was now approaching at an alarming speed.

But her words had fallen on deaf ears. Now, she still wrote her pieces, even though she knew they wouldn't change anything. She still needed to pay the bills.

But there were other ways to change the world. And she had been blessed with a new mission. *Everything happens for a reason*, she thought.

She walked down the hall to her office. Everything in the office was bright white—the walls, the furniture, the carpet, the drapes—everything except for her bright red desk chair and red desk accessories. She loved this room.

Humming a tune, she sat down at the desk and pulled out the file in the red folder in the bottom left drawer. Placing it on the desk, she booted up her desktop computer.

She smiled when she checked her email. She opened the email from "lotus friend" and read the five lines quickly. Pulling out a sheet of paper, she jotted down the name from the email. Then she crossed off the name right above it. She smiled and hummed as her pen crossed through the name of Sheila Lachowski.

CHAPTER 30

Lemuria, the motherland of all civilizations.

Laney sat in the back of the Chandler helicopter, her mind awash with everything she knew of the fabled civilization. Compared to Atlantis, very little was known about Lemuria, or Mu as it was more commonly called.

Laney had always thought of it as Atlantis's sister archipelago; whereas Atlantis was found in the Atlantic, Lemuria was alleged to have been located in the Pacific. And, like Atlantis, Mu was not a single landmass, but was instead a string of islands. It began off the coast of South America and extending deep into the ocean.

And just as the survivors of Atlantis were believed to have settled along the countries lining the Atlantic, the survivors of Mu were believed to have settled along the shores of the Pacific, including in the regions that would become modern-day California and Mexico.

Laney also knew the Lemurs in Madagascar were named after the fabled continent. The name Lemuria, in fact, originated with zoologist Phillip Sclater in 1864 to explain why lemurs were found on Madagascar and India but nowhere else. Sclater proposed that there must have been a continent or landmass stretching from India to Madagascar that, by the time of his writing, had sunk to the ocean floor. Sclater hypothesized that lemurs must have once lived on this ancient continent of Lemuria and had been separated when the continent sank.

Madame Blavatsky, the twentieth-century theosophist, had mentioned Lemuria as well. She said that Lemuria was a lost spiritual homeland. Then again, Blavatsky and her followers also said Lemurians were telepathic giants who had dinosaurs for pets, so Laney wasn't sure how much stock she should put in the Russian psychic's reports.

The most cited source when it came to Lemuria, though, was James Churchward.

The story goes that a priest in a library in India showed Churchward some texts in an ancient, forgotten language. The priest was worried that once he passed, there would be no one left who knew about the ancient works. Churchward then spent eight years learning the ancient language, allegedly the world's first language, in order to translate the texts. He eventually came out with six books on the topic, in which he spoke of a technologically advanced civilization that was based on the principle that all people should be kind to one another—as crazy as that idea might sound to the modern world. Churchward maintained that the island civilization once held sixty-four million people, and that at the time of its destruction it was two hundred thousand years old.

Even Cayce mentioned Lemuria in his readings— although sparingly, and those mentions were often cited by Cayce's critics as being proof of his unreliability. But in 1932, he spoke of the location of the ancient civilization, and later, science discovered that there had indeed once been a land that had stretched off the coast of South America and into the Pacific. Parts of it were believed to have remained above water until the end of the last ice age.

Laney couldn't remember much more than that, but she knew Jen had studied the myths of Lemuria as part of her doctoral studies, and had given her a call. Jen had promised to do some quick research, and she would be waiting with Henry and Jake when Laney returned.

115

Jen also promised to get her Uncle Patrick over from the school for the conversation as well. He had been consumed with Edgar Cayce since their first run-in with the psychic's predictions during their search for the Belial Stone. If anyone had additional knowledge on Lemuria, it would be him.

Laney leaned her head against the window of the chopper and stared down at the ground, her concern growing. For the last three years, Atlantis had been a specter in the back of all the danger she had faced. In one way or another, the former island kingdom had reached into modern times and caused all sorts of violence.

And now Cain was suggesting that it wasn't just Atlantis they needed to concern themselves with, but Lemuria as well—a second ancient civilization, one that predated Atlantis by thousands of years. And if Cain was right, it was the mother of *all* civilizations.

Her head began to ache and she closed her eyes. *Another ancient civilization causing trouble. This is not going to be good.*

CHAPTER 31

Lou, Danny, and Rolly sat in Henry's office with Cleo. It had taken some talking to get Yoni to agree to let them come to the estate, but some of the guards were heading back anyway, and seeing as they had Cleo as well, they were able to convince Yoni it would be safe.

Danny and the others knew Laney had asked one of the analysts to look into Cleo's background, and they had decided to try the straightforward method of getting answers: they were going to ask Laney what she had learned. But they weren't sure when Laney would be back, and Danny wasn't sure which analyst Laney had asked. Lou and Rolly wanted Danny to hack into some files and find out, but Danny wasn't quite ready to violate Laney's privacy that way. He did, however, take a quick peek at her calendar and saw that she had a meeting with someone about Cleo scheduled for today. So here they were.

All three heads turned at the brief knock in the door.

A slim, balding man stepped in with a nod, holding a file. "Hey, Danny."

"Hey, Jim," Danny said. "This is Lou and Rolly."

"Nice to meet you," Jim said as he scanned the room.

"I'm looking for—" Cleo raised her head, and Jim's eyes grew wide.

Lou patted Cleo. "It's okay. She won't hurt you."

"Um, right," Jim said, not taking his eyes off Cleo. "Have you seen Laney?"

"Something came up—an emergency," Danny said. "Can I help you with anything?"

Jim shifted the file in his hand from one hand to the other. "No, I don't think so. It's just a little research she had me do."

"You want us to hold on to that for you?" Lou asked.

Jim looked at the four of them and shook his head. "I'm sure it can wait. I'll send her an email and let her know. Nice meeting you all."

"You too," Lou called, trying not to smile as Jim hurried out of the room. Then she turned to Cleo. "Don't worry, baby. We know what a sweetheart you are."

Cleo rolled back on her side and swatted a paw at Lou, who laughed before rubbing her belly.

"Well, I guess we know who's been looking into Cleo's history," Rolly said.

Cleo rolled onto her stomach and sat up, tilting her head as if she was listening.

"Yeah, but he didn't give us the file," Danny said.

"Well, now that we know who it is, I'm pretty sure you can figure out a way to look at that file, can't you?" Rolly asked.

"How? He took the file with him," Danny said.

Cleo walked over and sat directly in front of Danny, staring at him.

"Uh, hey, Cleo," Danny said.

"I think she wants you to find out what's going on," Lou said with a smile.

"Why me?" Danny asked.

"Probably because you're the only one with the skills necessary to hack into Jim boy's computer and find out what's on that file," Rolly said.

"Yeah, but how does *she* know that?" Danny asked.

118

"She is wise in many ways, our Cleo," Lou said. "Now, come on. Let's see what's in the file."

Danny groaned, then headed for the conference table. Lou, Rolly, and Cleo followed. They sat around Danny staring at him expectantly.

"Could you all look somewhere else? This is going to take a little bit," Danny grouched.

"Sorry." Lou turned to Rolly. "You finish Father Patrick's ethics paper yet?"

"Finish? Don't you mean start? It's not due until tomorrow."

Lou shook her head. "Seriously? You need to start—"

"Okay, I'm in," Danny said.

Rolly raised his eyebrows. "I though you said it would take a little bit."

Danny frowned. "It did."

Lou laughed. "Okay, okay. What does it say?"

Danny scanned a document on the screen. "It looks like Laney asked Jim to find out where Cleo came from."

"Really?" Lou rolled her chair so she was right next to Danny and could read the screen as well.

Rolly rolled up on his other side. "What did he find?"

"He traced her back to a lab in New Mexico."

"Does Cleo have any littermates?" Lou asked.

Danny shook his head. "No—not anymore."

Lou winced and reached out, running a hand through Cleo's pelt. "Sorry, girl. Looks like you're an orphan just like us."

Danny pointed to the bottom of the report. "Jim went through some of Amar's files. He traced Cleo's... I guess 'creation' back to a doctor named Anthony Ruggio. He has an MD and a PhD in biological engineering. He owns the genetics lab out in New Mexico. But from what Jim has here, the place is on the up and up."

Lou looked at Cleo. The idea of her being created in a lab seemed so cold, so uncaring. She reached out and hugged her.

"We should go talk to Dom," Rolly said.

"Dom?" Lou asked. "Why?"

Rolly smiled. "Because if Ruggio is some evil scientist, who would be more likely to know than Dom?"

CHAPTER 32

Cleo was waiting for Laney on her porch when the car pulled up. "Thanks. Have a good night," Laney said to the driver as she let herself out.

"You too, " he called.

Cleo rubbed against Laney's side as she made her way to the porch. "Hey girl," Laney said with a smile. "Where is everybody?"

Back.

She frowned. "And what are you doing here? I thought you were at the school."

A vision of Lou, Danny, and Rolly sitting in Henry's office popped into Laney's mind.

Laney nodded. "Ah. Well, do me a favor and stay with them, okay?"

Cleo rubbed against Laney one more time before turning toward the main house. Her tail swished behind her as she disappeared through the bushes.

Laney headed inside, dropped her bag by the bottom of the stairs, and made her way through the kitchen to the back yard.

"There she is." Her Uncle Patrick stood to give her a hug.

"Hey there." Laney returned the hug and smiled over his shoulder at Jen and Henry.

Jake walked up, kissed her on the cheek, and took her hand. Laney grasped his hand with another smile.

"You okay?" he asked as they headed over to where Jen and Henry sat.

Laney took a seat on the couch across from Henry and Jen. "Yeah. It was actually, in a weird sort of way, nice."

"Really?" Jake asked.

Laney shrugged, not wanting to go into the interaction with Cain right now. They had more pressing concerns.

"So, Mu, huh?" Jen asked.

"Mu," Laney agreed, moving a throw pillow from behind her back to get more comfortable. "All I really know about it is that it was alleged to have been an archipelago off the North and South American coasts."

"According to what I could find," Jen began, "it was huge. It extended off the coast of Peru for almost three hundred miles, then it turned and went on for another three hundred fifty miles, right toward Easter Island."

"According to who?" Jake asked. "I mean, is there actual proof of a sunken archipelago?"

"Actually, there is," Jen said. "In the 1990s, two ridges were found under the Pacific. The Nazca Ridge runs in an almost straight line for 275 miles from Nazca, Peru to the Sala Y Gomez Ridge, which in turn extends for 350 miles west to Easter Island. Both were above water before the last ice age. So yes, an archipelago stretching that far is definitely possible."

Patrick nodded. "And recent years have uncovered more and more land under the Pacific that at one point was above the water. There are numerous groups that maintain their existence dates back to a people who escaped a great dangerous flood in the Pacific. Japan, Australia, even North American Indians talk about a great flood. The Hawaiians also mentioned the flood to Captain James Cook when he first traveled there on one of his three trips to the island."

122

"Yeah, well, he was killed on one of those trips," Jake said. "Are we suggesting the descendants of the peace-loving Children of the Law of One killed him?"

Jen put up her hands. "No—just suggesting that there's a similarity in tales across both sides of the Pacific."

"So what about Easter Island?" Henry asked. "What is its connection to Mu?"

"Well, Easter Island is at the tail end of the alleged archipelago," Jen said.

Laney remembered what Jen had said about Easter Island before: that when King Hout-Matua arrived, the island was already populated by tall redheads. History seemed to be littered with tales of ancient tall redheads bringing civilization to the world. Viracocha with the Incas, many of the mummies found in China, even Eric Eriksen and Christopher Columbus were allegedly redheads, although it was safe to say that spreading peaceful tidings was not exactly their forte.

"Mu was flooded, like Atlantis?" Jake asked.

Patrick shook his head. "Not exactly. The submersion of Mu was gradual, allowing the people time to escape."

"Cain said Mu was the motherland of civilization," Laney said.

Patrick nodded. "According to Cayce, Mu was the predecessor of Atlantis. It was in full swing at least fifty thousand years ago."

Jake's eyes grew large. "Okay, that's just not possible,"

Laney smiled. "And yet every time one of us says that, we find out it is indeed possible. And discoveries like the Ipiutak Site bolster that possibility."

Jake groaned. "The Ipiutak Site? Do I even want to know?"

Laney smiled. "It's found 130 miles north of the Artic Circle. Some argue it's the oldest site of human civilization."

Henry raised his eyebrows. "*North* of the Arctic Circle? That's tough living."

123

"Maybe. It's a series of lodges, eight hundred or so, enough to house eight thousand people. It's the largest settlement found that existed prior to the arrival of Europeans. In fact, none of the settlements nearby ever achieved anything remotely close to its size."

"You said it was the oldest. How old?"

"Well, that's the problem. There are no artifacts to date. The site was used by more recent cultures, which muddles the history. But they know it's at least three thousand years old."

"That's it? You said it was potentially the oldest."

"Well, like I said, it's muddled. The site is *at least* three thousand years old. But if you look at the last time when that part of the world was livable, you're talking fifty thousand years ago."

"But that's—I mean that's—" Jake said.

"That's the same time that Mu was alleged to exist. And it is in the right area," Laney said.

"Okay, but besides legends, is there any proof of a Pacific civilization?" Jake asked.

"Well, it depends on how much stock you put in legends," Patrick said. "Take the moai statues. There are nine hundred of them, all made from basalt. That seems like an awfully difficult achievement for anything less than an advanced civilization. And I can't imagine they'd do all that work for mere ornamentation, either."

"So what was their purpose?" Henry asked.

Jen shrugged. "I looked into that after Jake told us about the moai left at the murder scenes. Apparently there are some who believe that the moai were able to keep the ocean at bay through some form of resonance."

"Resonance?" Laney asked, a chill falling over her. The Belial Stone had used resonance. It had been the power source of Atlantis.

Jen continued. "The story goes that when the poles shifted, the power was lost, and they become merely statues."

124

Laney knew the last major pole shift was over eight hundred thousand years ago. They couldn't be *that* old. An extreme weather incident was more likely. They had been known to move the poles thousand of miles, and that would be enough to throw off any sort of technology relying upon them.

"How long ago was Lemuria supposed to be in existence?" Henry asked.

"Well, its first destruction was said to have occurred around 12,000 BC," Jen said.

"Is there anything besides rumors to support that?" Jake asked.

"There is proof that there was a worldwide event that occurred around that time," Jen said. "That was at the tail end of the ice age, and there were three sudden ice melts that caused the sea level to rise sixty-six feet. Low-lying and coastal areas were inundated. It's believed that there was a series of great earthquakes, which would have triggered huge tsunamis."

"But Mu survived that," Jake said. "So what finally destroyed it?"

"One theory is that shrapnel from an exploding star came close to Earth's orbit. The shrapnel from the explosion shot by the planet, with small particles breaking off around 3800 BC and crashing to the Earth. In 2800 BC, the shrapnel returned. Then in 1680 BC was the final submersion."

Everyone was quiet. Laney was picturing the tail of destruction such an event would cause and the horror of the people knowing there was nothing they could do to stop it.

Patrick spoke. "There are also many underwater ruins being uncovered in the Pacific, which strongly suggest that an advanced civilization once thrived there. Like the Yonaguni Monument found near Okinawa."

"That's the underwater monoliths they found, right? I thought they were supposed to be natural formations," Henry said.

125

"The jury is still out on that," Jen said. "You've got well-credentialed people on both sides of the debate adamantly claiming it is or is not a man-made formation."

Laney knew the claims well. She had been equally fascinated by the find when it hit the news wire. In 1996, a diver contacted Masaaki Kimura, a marine geologist at the University of the Ryukyus in Japan, about an incredible underwater structure he had found off the coast of Yonaguni, one of the westernmost inhabited islands of Japan. It had tall step pyramids, with right angles, archways, even quarry marks on the stones. The structure sank beneath the waves thousands of years ago. The largest structure was a step pyramid 150 meters long, but there were at least an additional ten structures surrounding the pyramid.

The sinking of such a site was not unbelievable due to the incredible tsunamis that had been reported in that area of the world. In 2011, a 128-foot tsunami had devastated Japan and killed over fifteen thousand people. In 1771, an even larger tsunami was recorded in the same area.

"And remember," Patrick said, "that site is near currently populated areas. We're talking about an empire that existed across the ocean. I mean, we've barely scratched the surface of exploring the oceans of this planet. We know more about the Moon than we do about our oceans. There could be literally hundreds of sites that are just waiting to be discovered under the Pacific."

Laney knew this was true. Every once in a while a crew would find some incredible site accidentally, like the underwater city of Dwarka in the Bay of Cambay, India. For years, the Indian people had claimed that a fantastic civilization had once existed there. Western archaeologists had scoffed at the idea. Then a city almost ten thousand years old was found, submerged under the waves. Amazing architecture and even human remains had since been found within the city.

"Then there are all those myths that stretch along Asia about people who escaped a great flood and began civilization," Jen said.

"So was Mu just like Atlantis?" Jake asked.

Patrick shook his head. "No. In fact, it would be safe to say it was the exact opposite."

Laney frowned. "How so?"

"Atlantis was militaristic, materialistic, and technologically advanced," he said. "They built cities and conquered lands. Mu was the opposite: they were pacifists, not interested in material wealth. They were more concerned with the richness of the spirit than the body."

"Like the Children of the Law of One," Laney said quietly.

Jen nodded. "Yes. Allegedly, Lemuria had no crime, no laws. Just a priestess who was more of a guide, kind of like the Dalai Lama and a council of advisors."

"No crime? How's that possible?" Jake asked.

"Well, apparently anyone who went against the lifestyle of the Lemurians was subjected to further spiritual training, even a purification ritual. If that didn't work, they were exiled."

"A purification ritual," Laney said. "Cain mentioned that."

"The exiling is kind of harsh," Henry said.

Patrick shook his head. "No, not really. You have to understand that, for Lemurians, it was all about being a good person. Their world revolved around that. In fact, they supposedly looked with both disdain and fear at the Atlanteans' materialism and military aggression. The Atlanteans in turn thought of the Lemurians as a blind race."

"So the Lemurians were a bunch of peace-loving hippies?" Jake asked.

"Without the drugs, yes," Patrick said, with the first smile he'd given Jake in weeks.

"Now why exactly are we talking about another ancient civilization?" Henry asked. "Aren't we supposed to be finding out who killed Sheila? And a peace-loving, non-violent group doesn't exactly sound like it would be connected. So what's the link?"

"The link is Cain," Laney said. "He said that the murders were tied to the descendants of Mu."

Everyone stared back at Laney. Finally Jake spoke. "You must be joking."

Laney shrugged. "That's what he said."

Jen raised an eyebrow. "Yeah, but he's *Cain*. You know, cursed by God, all-around not nice person?"

Laney sighed. "I know, but he's also been around since, well, forever. He's seen the world repeat its mistakes time and time again. And honestly, what else do we have to go on? Do we have any other leads?"

Jake and Henry shook their heads.

"I'm not saying we drop everything to follow Cain's idea. But I am saying we should investigate it like we would anything else," Laney said.

"Do you trust him?" Patrick asked.

Laney paused. "Trust him? No. But I don't think he's lying about this."

"So did he give us a place to start at least?" Jake asked.

Laney shook her head. "I'm afraid not. So, anyone have any idea where some modern Lemurians might be holing up?"

Once again, everyone stared back at her.

She sighed, feeling the impossibility of the task ahead of them. Lemuria had been wiped out thousand of years ago. How were they supposed to trace someone's lineage back through a flood-deluged history that spread out from the middle of the Pacific to both the Eastern coasts of Asia and the western coasts of both North and South America? *Maybe we should just ignore what Cain said and rely on a good old-fashioned criminal investigation for this one.*

She glanced around the group, but no one had any suggestions. Then her Uncle Patrick sat back in his chair, his hand upon his chin, and a tingle of possibility began to nudge away the feeling of defeat in Laney's mind. "Uncle Patrick?"

His blue eyes stared into hers. "I *may* have an idea."

CHAPTER 33

After lunch, Lou Rolly, and Danny headed out of the main building and down to Dom's bomb shelter. They had wanted to talk to him earlier, but he was working all morning. Cleo found them when they were halfway there and joined them.

They made their way through the levels of security before stepping into Dom's front foyer. It was blue with white wainscoting halfway up the wall. Lou always liked how it made the bomb shelter feel like an actual house, and not the full time panic room for a genius agoraphobe.

The steel door slammed shut behind them. *Well, almost like a real house.*

"Back here," Dom yelled from the main room.

As soon as Lou cleared the hallway, Cleo rushed past her, knocking her into Rolly. She grabbed onto him with a yell.

Across the room, Dom let out his own yell. He teetered on a ladder, and Cleo sprinted up to stabilize it before Dom could crash. Shaky Dom looked down at Cleo, who now held the ladder firmly in her paws. "Thanks, Cleo." He climbed down and gave her a long pat.

Lou shook her head as they made their way over. "What were you doing?"

"I set up a sensor for carbon dioxide levels. I needed to check it."

"Carbon dioxide? Is there something you want to tell us?" Rolly looked around, worried.

"No, why?" Dom asked.

Danny smiled. "Don't worry. Dom created a new plant that requires less water and may produce more oxygen. He's seeing how it does in a normal environment."

"Normal, right," Rolly said.

Lou hugged Dom. "Please, be careful in the future."

Dom ducked his head as Lou released him. "I will." His cheeks bloomed red.

Rolly took a seat on the giant leather sectional. "So, Doc, we have some questions for you."

Dom grinned as he took a seat as well. "What about? Is it about the water they've found on Mars? Because I have a theory that life there might be seasonal. And when it warms—"

Lou quickly cut in before Dom could go off on Martian life. She knew from experience how hard it would be to get him to focus on something after his mind went wandering down a rabbit hole. "Um, no. We actually wanted to ask you about a doctor named Anthony Ruggio."

Dom leaned back. "Anthony Ruggio, Anthony Ruggio. It sounds familiar. Where have I heard—" He blanched. "Oh."

"Well, that's not a good sign," Rolly muttered.

"Who is he?" Lou asked.

"He used to work at Plum Island." Dom stared at them expectantly.

"Really?" Danny's eyes grew large.

"Um, what's Plum Island?" Lou asked.

"Plum Island is a Homeland Security site in the Long Island Sound," Danny said. "Originally, it was a USDA research facility back in WWII. It's the highest-level biological research facility outside of the CDC. Its mission is to cure animal ailments like hoof and mouth disease."

Dom scoffed. "Right. Cure animal diseases."

Rolly leaned forward. "So what's the real story?"

"In the 1950s, Plum Island's research turned to offensive weapons. It was all part of Operation Paperclip," Dom said.

"Wait—you mean the Nazi scientists who came to work for the US?" Lou asked. They'd just discussed this last month in one of her classes. After World War II, the United States brought over hundreds of German scientists, engineers, and technicians to work for the United States. A large part of the success of America's early space program had been attributed to the ingenuity of the project.

Dom nodded. "The very same. They were attempting to create ways to carry disease to the enemy's livestock."

"Yeah, but that was the fifties. I mean, we know biological warfare research is happening," Danny said.

"Right, then explain the Lyme disease outbreak in 1975," Dom said. "It first occurred in Old Lyme, Connecticut, which coincidentally happens to be about ten miles from Plum Island. In fact, the highest incidence of Lyme disease occurs in Eastern Long Island, right near Plum Island. And there was a 1978 memo which proved that Plum Island was looking at ticks as a means of carrying disease."

Lou sat back. "You think they *created* Lyme disease?"

"Yes, I do. And I think they found a way to disperse it. I don't know if it was a test run or an accident, but it can't be a mere coincidence that they were researching it and then, lo and behold, there's an outbreak nearby."

Danny shook his head. "But that's just—"

Dom cut him off. "Then there's the West Nile virus. Ten thousand birds and twenty-six people died in the 1999 outbreak—once again near Plum Island. A tourist from Africa was blamed, but the virus isn't transferred from human to human, and certainly not from human to bird."

"Okay, but what does this have to do with this Ruggio guy?" Rolly asked.

"Anthony Ruggio's specialty is genetic and animal physiology. He was on the forefront of animal hybridization experiments for years," Dom said.

"Let me guess. At Plum Island?" Lou said.

"Yup." Dom pulled his tablet over from the middle of the coffee table. "Where is it?" he muttered, and his fingers flew across the screen. "Ah, there it is." He turned the screen around for Lou and Rolly to see.

"That cannot be real," Rolly said, his tone incredulous.

Lou just stared at the image in mute fascination. On screen was a hairless animal. It had the body of a dog, but the face had a beak with sharp teeth, and the paws were sort of like hands, except they had extremely long claws that looked almost like talons.

"It's real," Dom said. "It washed up on a Montauk beach back in 2008. In fact, it was the third unusual specimen to wash up in the previous two years. The fourth was said to be more humanoid in appearance, with long fingers. All of the animals disappeared right before animal control showed up."

"You think Ruggio was involved in that?" Lou asked.

Dom shrugged. "I don't know. He left Plum Island just before it closed, which coincidentally was right after the last creature washed ashore. Why are you asking about him? Is this about Cleo?"

Lou looked up, surprised. "Yeah. We're trying to figure Cleo out a little bit more."

"How do *you* think Cleo was created?" Rolly asked.

Dom sat back. "Well, I ran her blood after she arrived. We know she was given HGH, human growth hormone, while she was in utero. It accounts for her size—mostly. And I scanned her after Danny expressed concerns about her pituitary. No tumor, by the way." Dom paused.

"But there's more, right?" Lou asked.

Dom nodded. "Cleo is intelligent—more so than any cat naturally would be. She's also domesticated—which is unusual. It takes generations to domesticate a species."

133

"But isn't that because of Laney? I mean, she controls Cleo," Rolly said.

Dom shook his head. "I talked to Laney about her relationship with Cleo. She doesn't control her every minute of every day. Cleo understands that Laney doesn't want her to hurt any of you guys at the school or here. But you've seen Cleo in a fight—she does more than that. She distinguishes between the good guys and the bad guys. That's intelligence."

"How does she do it?"

"I'm not entirely sure. It may have to do with the structure of her brain. Proportional to their body size, most animal's brains are smaller than a human's. Cleo's brain-to-body ratio is actually about equal to, if not slightly larger than, a human's."

"So, what? She's more domesticated because she has a larger brain?" Rolly asked.

Dom hesitated.

"Dom?" Lou prodded.

Dom began speaking quickly. "I think it's more than that. The science is already there. I mean, they have created animals like her before, but of course they've destroyed them almost immediately. But if you found a doctor who was less concerned about the moral and ethical implications and only focused on the science, like Ruggio... Well. It would be possible."

"*What* would be possible?" Rolly asked.

But Lou knew even before the words left Dom's lips.

"I think Cleo has a human brain."

134

CHAPTER 34

"You know where the descendants of Mu are living?" Jen asked in disbelief.

Patrick put up his hands. "Not for certain. First let me explain a little bit about where the people of Mu were alleged to have gone."

Laney tried to bite back her smile. Her uncle did love to give a good lecture.

"According to Cayce, Mu was made up of all races. And when it began to submerge, a mass exodus occurred. Forgive my political incorrectness, but using Cayce's terms, the 'white-skinned' individuals went everywhere, the 'brown-skinned' individuals went to Polynesia and South America, and the 'black-skinned' individuals went to Melanesia and Mexico."

"The Olmecs," Laney said softly.

"That's what I thought too," Patrick replied. "The giant heads that archaeologists have not been able to explain because they depict individuals of African descent, when no one with that physiological makeup was supposed to be anyone near there."

"And then there's the uniqueness of the Melanesians," Laney said. "While it's true their skin is dark, many are born with white-blond hair. And it's not the result of European influence—it's an actual unique genetic trait. It's somewhat odd that it would happen to occur in the places where the Mu descendants allegedly went."

"Even if Cayce is right about where everyone went," Jake said, "we're talking what—ten thousand years? I don't think they're all still hanging around together."

"Actually, they might be," Patrick said, before taking a sip of his tea. Everyone watched him.

Laney struggled to not yell at him. "Okay, suspense successfully built. Where do you think they are?"

Patrick laughed. "Hawaii. Specifically, I think they may be the Honu Keiki, on Malama Island."

Laney's eyebrows rose. "Honu Keiki, the cult?"

Honu Keiki was a secretive cult that existed on a small island off the western shores of Maui. There were alleged to be about five hundred members, although there was no accurate head count. They had owned the land for hundreds of years and let very few outsiders in. In fact, the only outsiders Laney knew to have been allowed in were new members to the cult, and even those were very rare.

Patrick nodded. "It's said that the Honu Keiki were run off of their sacred island generations ago. They then settled on Malama, and have kept to themselves ever since. Around two hundred years ago, the group came into money, and they bought the entire island to ensure no one else could lay claim. And that's where they've lived ever since. They are quite literally rolling in money. But they live as simply now as they did before all of this. We know little about them; visitors are not allowed, and the leader refuses requests for interviews. The tiny bit we do know comes from individuals who have been exiled from the group. And even then, only one or two will talk."

"Why would you think the Honu Keiki are the descendants of the Mu?" Henry asked.

Patrick leaned back. "Their name, for one. Honu means turtle. Keiki means children. Their story is that a great turtle

136

brought them to their sacred island—the one they lived on before Malama—when their homeland was submerged."

Laney and Jen exchanged a look.

"What?" Henry asked.

"In a number of flood myths, they speak of a giant turtle that saved people from the flood and carried them to land," Laney said.

Jen nodded. "And in Asia, a turtle is said to unify both heaven and earth—the shell representing heaven, the body earth. Indians have a legend that says the world is supported by four elephants standing on a giant turtle."

"There's even a Japanese fairy tale about a man who protects a turtle from some boys who were bothering it," Laney added. "As a reward, the turtle takes the man to meet the King of the Ocean, and the man marries the king's beautiful water sprite daughter."

"Okay, I grant you that there a lot of legends about turtles," Jake said. "But there has to be more than that. I mean just because their name is 'children of the turtle' or 'turtle children' isn't exactly ironclad proof."

Patrick nodded. "True. But then there is also the name of the island where they now live. They named it Malama Island. The word 'malama' is common in Hawaii. Malama pono means to be careful. Malama mālama ia Hawai'i means to take care of Hawaii. 'Malama,' in essence, means to care for. And the few reports that have come out of Honu Keiki suggest that caring is the group's primary focus. Their days are spent in oneness with nature. There is no crime. Children are raised collectively. Each day begins and ends with a group meditation."

"It sounds like paradise," Henry said.

"Still, is there anything else about the cult that makes you think they could be descendants? I mean, no offense, but it could be any sort of cult," Jake said.

Patrick nodded. "Their symbol is the lotus flower, which signifies an awakening. And their lifestyle seems to

137

mirror what Mu would have been like. And there are one or two other factors about the group which suggest they could very well be the descendants."

Laney frowned at his choice of words—one or two other factors. What was he holding back? But before she could question him, Henry spoke.

"How do you know all this? About Mu, that is."

"When everything started to happen," Patrick said, "I knew I would not have the physical abilities of the rest of you. So I thought the best way I could contribute was by learning everything I could about anything that might be related to the Fallen. And Mu, it seems, may be related."

"Is there anything else we should know?" Jen asked.

"Mu doesn't figure much into Cayce's readings. He was asked once about its absence, and he said that the people of Mu had less karmic debt and, therefore, were less likely to be reborn," Patrick said.

"But if they're the good ones, we shouldn't have much to worry about, right?" Jen asked. "I mean, we *are* taking this on the word of the world's first murderer."

Laney pictured Cain's face when he spoke. He could be a very good liar, but there was no gain for him in lying to her. "Maybe. But honestly, do we have anything else to go on?"

No one said a word.

Jake sighed. "Great. So let's go see what we can find about the turtle kids."

CHAPTER 35

Rolly's arms were crossed over his chest, and everything from his body language to his facial expression suggested he thought Dom had finally lost it. "Cleo has a human brain. Those *are* the words that just came out of your mouth, right?"

"You're not serious," Lou said.

Dom put up his hands. "I know it *sounds* crazy. But believe it or not, human-animal and animal-animal hybrids have been around for over a decade."

Rolly looked around. "Is there a camera on us? Are we being punked?"

"Hold on." Dom typed something on his tablet and then turned it around for them to see. "Look at this."

On screen was a small white mouse with what was undeniably a human ear growing out of its back.

"What the hell is that?" Rolly asked.

"It's the Vacanti mouse," Dom said. "They added cow cartilage to its back to form a human ear. It was one of the first steps in demonstrating that animals could be used to provide tissues and organs for humans."

Lou stared at the image in both horror and awe. "That's amazingly creepy."

"Actually," Danny said quietly, "even more advanced experiments have been conducted. There are entire herds of cows that provide milk that's almost identical to human breast milk. "

    "How?" Rolly asked.

    "*Why* seems like a better question," Lou muttered.

    "To aid humans," Danny said. "As to how: a human gene was inserted into the cows' genetic profile, causing the cows' mammary glands to produce high amounts of lysozyme, the critical component of breast milk."

    "Um, yuck?" Rolly said.

    But Lou couldn't say anything—all she could picture was a field full of cows with giant breasts. "That's just—" she shook her head, not even sure *what* that was.

    "And that's just one example," Dom said. "Science has been creating animal-human hybrids since 2003. Human cells have been mixed with rabbits, pigs, cows. The Mayo Clinic even created pigs with human blood."

    "Okay, fine. But it's still a pretty big leap from that to 'Cleo has a human brain,'" Rolly said.

    "Actually, Stanford already created a mouse with a basically human brain. The mouse was substantially smarter than the non-enhanced mice," Danny said.

    "Why would they do that?" Lou asked.

    "For medical research," Danny said. "If they can make the subject more 'human,' then any tests they perform on the subject will be more generalizable to humans. In drug research, that's huge."

    "And don't forget spare parts," Dom said.

    Lou stared. "Spare parts?"

    "Sure," Dom said. "There's a herd of cows in Wisconsin that has partially human livers, hearts, brains, and other organs."

    "Why the hell have I never heard of this?" Rolly asked.

    Dom shrugged. "It's not publicized much."

    "What do they do with the animals after the research?" Lou asked.

    "Kill them," Dom said.

140

"But they're creating whole new species. That's got to be illegal," Rolly said.

Danny shook his head. "They're not breaking any laws. It's legal. Horrible, but legal."

"But why then wouldn't there be more creatures out there like Cleo?" Lou asked.

"Well, that's an ethical question, not a legal one," Danny said. "Most people view the creation of a whole new species as wrong. But not everyone."

"There's a professor at Harvard who wants to cross Neanderthal DNA with a human fetus to create a hybrid," Dom said with a frown. "He's having some trouble finding a female volunteer though."

"Gee, you think?" Rolly muttered.

"It's still a giant leap from mice to leopards," Lou argued.

"It *is* a leap," Dom agreed. "But it's not a scientific one—it's an ethical one. The ability to create animals with human brains has been around for years. I mean, the things we can do now are astounding. They've even started working on regenerating limbs. They've taken monkeys limbs down to their cells and managed to grow them back using monkey or human DNA."

"That's—that's just wrong," Rolly said.

Dom shook his head. "No—it's just different. Humans have always looked to animals to provide for them. We domesticated dogs so they'd provide us security and companionship. We corralled farm animals so they'd provide us with food. And Amar wanted a challenge—a beast that would be worthy of his abilities. Creating Cleo and her littermates was what fit that bill."

All Lou could think about was the behaviors Cleo had demonstrated—behaviors that didn't fit with a wild animal, but *did* fit with a human.

"Think about it," Dom said, his eyes bright. "Cleo thinks like a human, but she's not. So what is she? She's not a leopard. She's not a human. She's a brand new species."

Lou sat back, dumbfounded.

"Science has reached a point where they can create new species with relative ease. But the question is, should they? In Cleo's case, no one asked that question. They just did it."

Everyone stared at Dom. Lou felt sick. Amar had created a new species just to kill it.

"It's got to be lonely for her," Lou said softly. "Being the only of her kind left."

The other boys nodded back at her, looking as dumbstruck by Dom's revelation as she was.

But Dom shook his head. "Oh, she's not the only one of her kind."

Jaws dropped around the table.

"What do you mean?" Rolly asked.

Dom looked surprised by their response. "Well, Amar had no intention of being killed, which means he probably arranged for future litters."

Lou stared in disbelief. "There are more leopards out there like Cleo?"

"Well, I assume. I mean, there's a chance that they were destroyed after Amar was killed, but I doubt it."

"So where are they?" Rolly asked.

Dom shrugged, but his eyes were troubled. "I don't know."

Lou looked around the table. "I think we should find out."

142

CHAPTER 36

Lou and Rolly waited outside Henry's office. Danny had had to rush off to a meeting, but he'd made them promise to ask Henry about Cleo before they returned to the school. Cleo had headed off to stretch her legs.

They had been waiting outside Henry's office for about a half hour, and were just about to leave when Henry finally stepped onto the landing. "Hey, Danny said you guys were looking for me."

"Um, yeah, but we know you're busy with the investigation and all, so…"

"It's fine. Come on in." Henry walked past them and into his office.

With a resigned sigh, Lou and Rolly stepped into the office. Their preference was to go ahead and conduct the research and *then* talk to Laney and Henry about what they'd found, but Danny had insisted they make sure Laney and Henry were okay with it before they even started.

When they stepped into the office, Henry was already seated at his desk, staring at his computer screen, a frown on his face.

Rolly leaned down to whisper in Lou's ear. "Maybe this isn't a good time. We should come back."

"Yeah," Lou said, and started to turn.

"You two," Henry called, "what's going on?"

Lou walked over slowly. "Um, nothing. You look busy. We can come back."

Henry gave her a tight smile. "I'm *usually* busy, but I can always make time for you guys. So tell me what's going on. Everything okay at the school?"

"Yeah," Rolly said. "It's good. I mean, I still think my room service idea requires further examination, but besides that…"

Henry laughed. "Keep dreaming, Rolly. But seriously, what's up?"

Lou took a seat. "Um, we know Laney was planning on looking into Cleo's background."

Henry narrowed his eyes. "How do you know that?"

"We sort of ran into the analyst that was looking into it for her," Rolly said.

Henry raised his eyebrows. "Really? What a coincidence that was."

"Yeah. And we looked at the file," Lou said, rushing on before Henry could ask how they looked at the file. "But we were just concerned about Cleo."

Henry shrugged. "It wasn't really a secret."

"Well, are you guys going to keep looking?" Lou asked.

Henry sighed. "I know Laney had planned to, but then all this came up."

Lou nodded, trying not to look at the whiteboard with the information on the murders. She thought about Jimmy, Sheila's son. He was a nice kid. The whole family had been nice. She couldn't imagine what they were going through now. "Yeah, we know."

"But when things calm down, Cleo's background will become a priority," Henry said.

"We were thinking maybe we could help you with that," Rolly said.

Henry narrowed his eyes. "How?"

144

Rolly put up his hands. "Nothing dangerous. We just thought we could maybe look into the doctor and his research. That's all."

Lou's words came out in a rush. "It's just—we're worried about Cleo."

"Why?" Henry asked.

"When Laney's away, she's so depressed. And she has to be locked up. She just, I don't know, she seems lonely."

Henry sighed. "I know. Laney's worried about her too. I know she hates leaving her." Henry studied the two of them. "Okay. You two—no, I'm guessing there are three of you. Unless you've roped Zach in as well?"

"Um, sort of."

"Of course you have. All right, you four can look into Cleo. But research only, okay?"

Lou grinned. "Of course."

"Seriously guys, nothing dangerous, just boring data collection."

Rolly stood. "Of course. We'd never think of doing anything dangerous."

CHAPTER 37

Everyone else had headed back to the main building, but Laney decided to stay at the cottage and work outside. Jake was reaching out to different law enforcement groups to have them send over anything they had on the cult. Henry was going to attempt to reach Honu Keiki directly through some contacts that had had dealings with the cult. It was a long shot, but right now they really didn't have any other avenues to take. Patrick was gathering more data on Honu Keiki, and Jen was seeing what else she could dig up on Mu.

Which left Laney with the murders. She reviewed all the victims' files, trying to find something that connected them. The victims were all unknown to one another. They lived in different states and even different countries. They were different ages, races, genders, and occupations. If there was a link, it wasn't showing up.

After an hour, Laney needed to grab a shower. The conversation, the prison, the murders—it all left her feeling dirty.

Walking downstairs after a ridiculously scalding shower, she finally felt clean and refreshed. It was amazing what a really long shower could do for a person's mood. She stepped into the kitchen, checked her computer, and frowned. She'd missed six Skype calls today, the last one while she was showering. Each was from a different number. That was odd.

She turned to grab a glass of water when her computer beeped to let her know that yet another Skype call was coming in. Taking a seat at the island, she hit connect.

Laney let out a gasp as a familiar face appeared on her screen. "Gerard."

Gerard Thompson inclined his head toward her. He was tanned, and his blond hair was a little longer than she remembered, lending some warmth to his cool Scandinavian look. "Ring bearer."

I really need to figure out a way for the Fallen to quit calling me at home. She surreptitiously pulled out her phone and typed a message to Jake out of sight of her computer's camera: `Gerard on my computer. Trace call.`

"So, are you calling to turn yourself in? Or better yet, turn Elisabeta in?" Laney asked.

"Elisabeta and I have parted ways for the moment."

Laney raised an eyebrow. So the rumors were true. Victoria had told her that Gerard had protected Max the best he could while they were kidnapped. And she had heard rumors that Elisabeta had been searching for Gerard. *Interesting.*

"Then I guess you're calling just to catch up," Laney said.

Gerard laughed. "Not exactly. It seems you and I may have a similar purpose at the moment."

"Really? Do tell."

"I recently avoided an attempt to abduct me at my new home."

"Abduct? Not kill?"

"No—abduct." He grimaced. "They would have been able to kill me if that had been their goal."

"Getting a little rusty, are we?"

Gerard glared back at her.

"So I guess Elisabeta is really not happy with you."

"It was *not* Elisabeta. The entire force was humans."

Laney shrugged. "She could have used humans to avoid you detecting them."

"True, but this group moved differently, worked differently." He shook his head. "I know how Elisabeta operates and how her people operate. She did not send them."

"I'm not sure I see how this is relevant to me. Unless of course, you wanted to turn yourself over for protective custody? I'm sure the SIA has a lovely cell that would keep you nice and safe."

Gerard smiled. "Tempting, but no. And the reason this is of interest to you is that I believe this attempt was made by the people responsible for the killings you're looking into."

Laney narrowed her eyes. "How do you know about that?"

"I have been at this game a long time, ring bearer. And I still have my sources. I believe you're calling them 'the companion killings.' Cute name by the way."

"What do you know about the killings?"

"I know they happen every couple of weeks. I know they're going after people affiliated with the Fallen."

Laney hesitated. Gerard was being awfully forthcoming. Of course, if they were in fact after him, it would be in his best interest to be cooperative. The enemy of my enemy and all that. But why would he think it was the same people? "Yes, we think they're selecting these particular targets because they interact with the Fallen. But beyond that, we don't really know why, or more importantly, how they're choosing them. We've found no connection. And I fail to see how you've found a connection to your attack."

"Oh, it's not just my attack. I'm sure if you look, you'll see I'm not the only Fallen who has been targeted. Although, if history is repeating itself, I'm sure not all of the others were as successful at avoiding their pursuers."

Laney paused. Cain had mentioned that Fallen were also being targeted, but Laney had actually forgotten about that until just now. She figured she could be forgiven for the oversight, seeing as she was busy dealing with the whole "there's another ancient civilization that is going to wreak havoc with people's lives" angle that Cain had also mentioned.

"Again, I don't see how this is connected to the companion murders," Laney said.

"Well, ring bearer, after spending time with your mother, let's just say that I can now see a lot more than I used to."

Frustration rolled through Laney. "I have no idea what that means."

"But I do. So suffice it to say, there *is* a connection."

"Well, gee, thanks for that whole bit of non-information. Now if you don't mind, I have work to do."

"What if I told you I know how they find their victims?"

Laney studied him, her mind working furiously trying to figure out Gerard's angle. Was he trying to throw her off the search by feeding her false information? What would be the point of that, unless he was covering for someone? And if he really was on the outs with Elisabeta, he wouldn't have a lot of people to turn to for help. But even so, what was the likelihood that the people who had gone after Gerard were the same people who went after the companions?

Laney shook her head. "Look, Gerard, I have enough on my plate. And I just can't see how the companion killers went after you."

"Even so, I am willing to tell you what I know. Because *I* believe they are connected."

Laney wasn't sure what to say to that. He wasn't asking for anything. He was… *offering* something. It was at least worth listening to what he had to say. It probably wasn't related, but if it was…

She sighed. "Okay. I'm listening. You said you have an idea about how they're finding their victims?"

"I'm very good at my what I do. I know when someone is watching me. And due to Elisabeta's interest in my well-being, I have been even more vigilant since India. No one has been watching me."

"Great. What does that mean?"

"It means they found me without surveying me first."

Laney frowned. "Have you left an electronic trail?"

Gerard laughed. "Oh, please. I'm the one Elisabeta sent to track people down; I know how to hide. I did not slip up. I believe they found me by a more," he paused, "*unconventional* method."

Laney's frustration tolerance was about at its end. "What does *that* mean?"

"It *means* that I believe that I, my Fallen brothers, and the companion victims were all found by the same means."

"And what means is that?"

"Psychics."

CHAPTER 38

Laney stared at Gerard. She wasn't sure if she should groan, disconnect the call, or worry about the Fallen's mental health. "Psychics? Seriously?"

Gerard's voice was dry. "Yes, ring bearer, this Fallen angel is telling you that psychics may be in the mix."

Laney shrugged. *Well, when you put it that way.* "Any idea who the psychics are?"

Gerard smiled. "I need to leave you with *something* to do on your own," he said, and the screen went blank.

Laney sat back, her hand on her chin. *Psychics. What the hell?*

Her phone beeped and she read the new text. Couldn't trace it. You okay?

I'm good. I'll tell you about it later.

She stood up and shook her head. Apparently Gerard had taken a turn into crazy town. She headed for the fridge to grab a bottle of water while she chewed over the idea. Psychics. Was that even possible?

Part of her rebelled at the thought, but another part of her observed the hypocrisy of that view. After all, Edgar Cayce was a huge part of almost every event she had been involved in since everything began, and he was an incredibly powerful psychic. And she knew that psychic ability wasn't limited to the ability to tell the future; it ran the gamut from mediums to remote viewing to intuits to all sorts of other skills.

If psychics were real, was someone seeing the victims and then targeting them?

If so, how the hell was she supposed to stop them?

And now she was, what—taking the word of Gerard? Elisabeta's right hand man and the man who had kidnapped Max?

She realized that she now had *two* of her former enemies appearing to help her. If this kept up, she'd soon get an invite from Elisabeta to meet for dinner and a movie.

Patrick knocked on the doorframe, pulling Laney from her thoughts. "Hey," she said, closing her laptop.

"You look rather far away," he said, taking a seat across from her.

"I was. I thought you were heading back to the school."

Patrick shook his head. "There's some books here I want to go through before I head back. Are you all right?"

She paused, debating what to tell him. "I just got a call from Gerard Thompson."

"What?"

"He said the companion murder victims are being found through psychics." She told him about the rest of their conversation.

When she finished, Patrick rested his hand on his chin. "Huh."

Laney watched him. "Yet again, you do not look as surprised as you should."

Patrick gave her a small smile.

Laney tried not to groan. "Out with it."

"Remember how I said there were one or two other factors that led me to believe the Honu Keiki could be the descendants of Mu?"

Laney nodded.

152

"Well, one of the stranger rumors that has circulated about the Honu Keiki is that they have psychic abilities."

Laney wondered for a moment if she was dreaming. *First Gerard, now psychics. Although if it's a dream, it needs fewer Fallen and more Chippendales.*

"I don't get it. What does that have to do with Mu?" Laney asked.

"As Jen explained, the people of Mu were much more concerned with their inner life than their outer one. Deep meditations were a daily part of life. As a result, the legends say the people of Mu developed psychic abilities. Highly developed psychic abilities."

Laney wasn't sure what to say. *It's not that she didn't believe in the possibility of psychic abilities. I mean, she was the ring bearer, and Henry and Jen were nephilim.* But the truth was, despite everything she'd been through, whenever she thought about psychics, her first thought was of some woman in a turban trying to make a buck, or a con man who had information whispered into his ear by the man behind the curtain. Hucksters and charlatans.

Yet it had been Laney's dreams of her past lives that had led her to the ring of Solomon. She had first-hand experience with real psychic ability. So why was she so instinctively skeptical?

For some reason, a quote attributed to Nikola Tesla popped into her mind: *The day science begins to study non-physical phenomena, it will make more progress in one decade than in all the previous centuries of its existence.*

Even one of the greatest minds of the twentieth century recognized that the physical world was not all there was to know. Even with regard to his own intellect, Tesla acknowledged an outside force at work. He had visions of machines that were perfect in their clarity. He could move them around almost like a hologram. His concentration was said to be complete and intense.

Almost like a trance, Laney thought.

153

Cayce had said his information came from the Akashic Record—an accounting of all that had happened and would happen. And Cayce accessed this information only when in a deep trance.

Was what her uncle was saying all that different from what those incredible men had experienced? Were other people also able to access information outside of themselves, from the greater universe?

So many things had happened in the last two years that on paper shouldn't be possible. And yet...

Then, of course, there were the tales about the children who had incredible abilities, like the superkids of China. Was it possible? Were the test subjects of the lab experiments that failed to generate positive results just the wrong subjects? Were the real psychics staying as far away from scientists as they could? After all, there was no upside for them to be tested. If they proved themselves, the scientists would just try to devise a more difficult test to prove they were wrong. And if their abilities were not working well that day, then they'd be labeled con artists.

Laney looked at her uncle. "What do you think about that claim—that they have psychic abilities? Do you think it's possible?"

Patrick was silent for a moment. "I can't help but think of all the similarities in the ancient stories. They all talk about these great monuments being lifted through mental powers. None of them say they magically appeared. They all say someone moved them into place."

"Like Viracocha or Merlin," Laney said.

Patrick nodded. "Exactly. And I can't help but think of how egotistical we are in the modern age, thinking we're the pinnacle of evolution. Yet there is all this evidence telling us there were far greater civilizations in our distant past—and people who had a knowledge that we're only just now beginning to tap into. Are psychic abilities possible? I can't say for sure, but I certainly can't rule them out."

154

Laney nodded, agreeing with everything he'd said. But it still seemed so impossible. Laney felt a headache building yet again. Psychic abilities? They were really going there?

"I can't believe we're seriously talking about a secret cult with psychic abilities," she muttered. "I'm still trying to wrap my head around the idea of a second ancient civilization, one even less well known than Atlantis. I mean, are we even sure yet that the Lemurians existed?"

Patrick smiled. "Cayce spoke about the descendants of Mu. One of the places he said they went was to the Gobi Desert, back when it was lush. Of course, everyone scoffed, because everyone knew the Gobi Desert was a barren wasteland and was never lush."

Laney knew where he was going. "Until the twentieth century, when archeologists realized the Gobi Desert had at one point been fertile. In fact, it's turned into a treasure trove of fossils. Dinosaurs, mammals, and lizards."

"And then there's the possible discovery of the Uighur capital."

"Not to mention the blond and redheaded mummies," Laney said.

Patrick smiled. "Them as well."

In 1934 a Bronze Age cemetery was uncovered by a team of Swedish archaeologists. The cemetery held two hundred mummies carefully buried in upside-down boats. The mummies were at least four thousand years old, but their clothes were relatively modern in style. In fact, one mummy was buried with ten hats of differing designs. The mummification process was amazing; the mummies were all in pristine shape, considering their age. In fact one mummy still had long thick auburn hair. She was dubbed "the beauty of Loulan."

The problem was that the mummies were located on the western edge of China, and yet they were all very obviously Caucasian. They should not have existed in China at that time.

155

But there they were. Yet another discovery daring history to explain it.

Laney sighed. "I don't know why I keep fighting these revelations. Every time something new pops up, I tell myself it isn't true."

"Laney, with each new revelation the ground shifts more under our feet. Everything we thought we could count on gets turned upside down. It's human nature to want things to remain the same, to be sure in our knowledge. But unfortunately, the more we learn, the more we realize how little we know."

Laney glanced up to see Patrick with a frown covering his face. "What is it?"

"The Children of the Law of One were deceived and killed by the sons of Belial. And from the readings of Cayce, it seems the sons, and the Fallen's greed, are what doomed Atlantis. I can't help but wonder..." He went quiet.

"Can't help but wonder what?"

"We're in an age of almost gluttonous consumption, without concern for the impact it has on the world around us or on those suffering to create those goods. If the people behind the murders are the descendants of the children of Mu, is it at all possible that they've remained untainted? And if so, what must they think about the rest of us?"

"They probably think we're wasteful, sinful."

"Yes," Patrick said softly. "And is it that much of a stretch to think that some of them may think the world would be better off without us, especially those of us that are viewed as helping the Fallen?"

156

CHAPTER 39

That night, Lou, Rolly, Danny, and Zach were in one of the computer labs back at the school. They were looking for everything they could find on animal hybridization experiments, Anthony Ruggio, and his lab, GenDynamics.

Lou stared at her screen, wishing she had gotten something other than animal hybridization to research. Right now she was staring at a mouse covered in tumors. Literally every pore of the poor thing's body had been infected with tumors. She wasn't sure why they had done it to the poor little guy, but she couldn't think of any reason that could justify it.

"Hey. I think I have something," Zach said.

Lou moved over to stare at Zach's screen, hoping for a break from the cruelty she'd been finding on her own screen. She didn't get one. A man with a gun sat hunched proudly over a giant leopard, blood pooled on the ground next to it. The cat looked an awful lot like Cleo.

Zach nodded at the image. "That guy is Harran Guilding, Russian millionaire. Like, just a few million away from a billionaire. He killed that leopard on his ranch in Australia."

"Do they even have Javan leopards in Australia?" Rolly asked.

Zach shook his head. "No. Guilding is part of a special sportsman club that specializes in exotic kills. They'll bring in the animal of your choice and let you track it down."

"It would be more sporting if they let the animals have weapons too," Lou grumbled. She squinted. "How big is the cat?"

"Big. Stands four and a half feet at the shoulders."

That was huge; even the tallest of ordinary leopards stood only thirty-one inches at the shoulder. In fact, leopards were the smallest of the large cat breeds. "So," Lou said, "you think this is one of Cleo's relatives?"

"I don't know," Zach said. "But it seems like a good bet."

Danny stared at the screen for a moment before tapping Zach on the shoulder. "Can I get in there for minute?"

"Uh, sure." Zach stood up and Danny quickly sat down. His fingers flew over the keyboard. Data box after data box appeared on the monitor too quickly for Lou to read. A few seconds later, Danny nodded at the monitor. "The cat was provided by the Halligan Corporation."

"Did you just hack that guy's financials in like ten seconds?" Rolly asked.

Danny nodded. "Yeah, why?"

"Uh, no reason," Rolly said.

"Who are they?" Lou asked.

"Hold on." Danny's fingers flew again, then he said, "Get this. Halligan is one of the investors in Anthony Ruggio's lab."

"What have you found out about the lab?" Lou asked Rolly.

"Not much," Rolly said. "It's right on the western edge of New Mexico. The website says they do high-level genetic testing and specialized private research."

"What does that mean?" Lou asked.

"That they're available to anyone who can pay," Danny replied.

158

"So do we think these guys actually have more giant cats?" Zach asked.

"I don't know. But I think we should find out," Lou said.

"Okay, how?"

Lou smiled. "Let's go pay them a visit."

"You want to go there ourselves?" Zach's eyes were large.

"Are you kidding?" Danny asked. "There's no way we're going to be allowed to do that."

"I wasn't planning on asking permission," Lou said.

Zach shook his head. "No way. I caused enough trouble when I got here. I can't—"

Rolly put an arm around Zach's shoulder. "Hey, it's okay. No one is going anywhere."

"Who else is going to do it?" Lou asked. "Laney, Henry, Jen, and Jake are all tied up in these murders, and everybody else is on some sort of security detail. There's no one else to track theses guys down. And this is for Cleo. Besides, Henry said we could do research."

"Even *if* we went there on our own," Danny said, "how exactly would we go about it?" Danny asked. "It's not like we can call them up and make an appointment."

Lou shrugged. "I was thinking maybe we'd just knock on the front door."

"And if that doesn't work—because you know, we're teenagers…" Rolly said dryly, "then what?"

"Then we break in."

They all stared at her like she'd lost her mind. And maybe she had. But damn it, Cleo was lonely. It wasn't right.

"Look, Cleo is our friend. And now that we know more about who she is, don't you think we owe it to her to try and at least find out if there are more out there like her?" Lou asked.

"Well, it's not like we're going up against the Fallen," Rolly mused. "I mean, these guys are probably just humans, right?"

159

"Exactly," Lou said. "We can just go, check out the lab, and then call in the cavalry if we actually find the litter. We're just gathering data, like we said we would."

"Henry also said not to do anything dangerous," Danny reminded her.

Lou grinned. "It's a lab. And we're just going to look. What could possibly be dangerous about that?"

CHAPTER 40

As Laney walked to the main house, she pulled out her phone. Matt picked up almost immediately. "Hey, Laney."

"Matt, I just got a call from Gerard Thompson. He says the Fallen are being targeted by the companion killers. Cain said the same thing. What do you know?"

"Uh, I mean, the Fallen do get attacked, but no one's red-flagged anything or even mentioned a connection between the attacks. I told you about that one report a few days ago."

Laney shook her head. "That's right. With everything else going on, I forgot. Can you take the aspects of the companion murders and run them against Fallen killings? See if there's anything?"

"Sure. I'll call you as soon as I have anything."

As Laney pocketed her phone, she still wasn't sure this wasn't a complete waste of time. Was Gerard just trying to get her to focus on his abduction as a way of getting her help?

But if someone was targeting the companions of the Fallen, it wasn't that much of a stretch to think they would target the Fallen as well—at least, if they could. Killing a Fallen wasn't exactly easy. The heart had to be completely shredded. Decapitation might also work; Laney remembered Yoni suggesting that back in Montana years ago.

She walked slowly, deciding to take the long way to the main house. All the facts they had gathered rolled through her mind as she searched for connections. Assuming Gerard was right, psychics would enable someone to target the Fallen and their companions without being detected. She had to admit, such an ability would increase the chances that a human could outmaneuver a Fallen.

She frowned. But it couldn't be *a* person; it would have to be far more than one. It would have to be an entire network, seeing as the murders were strewn across the globe. And an undertaking that large would require organization, commitment, and, above all, money.

Her phone rang. It was Matt, and only ten minutes had passed. "Matt?"

"They are being targeted," Matt said without preamble.

Laney stopped walking. "How many?"

"We only had a chance to do a quick search. But I got a dozen hits. We tracked the Fallen's movements and their deaths, and I put in the characteristics from the companion murders. Some details popped up that suggest a connection."

"What popped in particular?"

"The heart being removed."

"Well, but that would be the only way to kill them." Laney knew they could recover from drowning and bloodletting. But heart removal would end them. "Is the heart burned?"

"No, but I think that may have more to with the situations. The Fallen deaths all attracted some attention. I don't think they had the chance to burn the heart. But they did keep it. The heart was missing from every crime scene."

"Well, that's lovely."

"Most crime scenes weren't as private as those of the companion murders, so perhaps they just didn't have time to complete the ritual, at least there. There were even some eyewitnesses, who all report that the victims were assaulted by a group of people, not just one individual."

"Well, that jibes with what I've been thinking. Can I speak with some of the witnesses?"

162

"I can do you one better—one of the targets escaped. I'm going to give him a call, but I'm sure he'll speak with you."

Laney had reached the main house and pulled open the door. "Send me the address and all the case files."

"Consider it done."

Laney pocketed her phone. She felt tired at the mere thought of going through a whole new batch of gruesome crime scenes photos.

Her steps were heavy as she made her way up to Henry's office. She pushed open the door, and Henry, Jake, and Jen looked up from the coffee table near Henry's desk, where they were all working.

Laney took a seat next to Jen on the couch. "So, I have some news."

Jen pushed away the file of papers in front of her. "Good. Because I would like to sleep again, and these photos are not going to help with that."

Laney told them about the phone call from Gerard, Patrick's ideas about psychic abilities among the Honu Keiki, and Matt's information on the Fallen being targeted.

"Matt's information does line up with what Cain said," Jen admitted grudgingly.

Jake shook his head. "I'm not sure I buy that these are connected. I mean, I realize they're happening at the same time, but—"

"It's the same MO though," Laney said. "Or at least as close as you can get with a Fallen."

"True," Jake said.

"So, should we reach out to Honu Keiki? See what they know?" Jen asked.

Henry shook his head. "It's not enough. My contacts say it's incredibly difficult to communicate with the group. We need something very solid before we even attempt it, because I have the feeling we'll only get one attempt."

Laney nodded. "I agree. I mean, yes, they sound like they could be the group. But honestly, any new age cult would be described almost identically. If we go to them with what we have now, they'll just laugh at us. We need more."

Her phone beeped, and she looked at the text. It was an address from Matt in Ann Arbor, Michigan.

"I'll keep digging," Henry said. "See if there's any leverage we can use to get them to speak with us."

Laney turned to Jake. "Could you look into the psychic angle?

"Me?" he asked.

"Well, you're the least likely to believe what you read. I think that kind of skepticism is what we need."

Jake grimaced. "Great. Sounds like fun."

"Thanks. And Jen—how do you feel about taking a little visit to Ann Arbor?" Laney asked.

"I'm always up for a road trip. But what are we going to do?"

"Visit with a Fallen," Laney said, her eyes on Jake.

Jake's jaw tightened. Catching Laney's gaze, though, he just shrugged. "Sorry. Have fun. Or whatever the correct sentiment is for this kind of trip. And try not to get into too much trouble."

"Trouble? Us?" Jen asked, her eyes wide.

Henry laughed. "I'll let the accountants know there may be some property damage we'll have to cover down there."

"Where's the faith?" Laney grumbled.

164

CHAPTER 41

Ann Arbor, Michigan

The GPS beeped to let them know they had arrived. Laney pulled over to the side of the street behind an old blue minivan. She stared out the window across the street.

"This can't possibly be right," Jen said.

Laney pulled out her phone and double-checked the address. The building was brown brick with large tinted windows. Double doors were located next to a sign that read "Temple Beth-El."

Matt had sent them to a synagogue.

Laney laughed and shook her head.

"What?" Jen asked.

She gestured across the street. "I keep making assumptions, and they keep getting turned on their head. I mean we know Fallen come in all size and shapes; why not denominations?"

"Well, let's go meet *this* Fallen," Jen said.

They got out of the car, and Laney looked around. The synagogue was bookended by a florist and a bank. Across the street was a diner. There was no one around on foot, but a steady flow of cars drove along the street.

Running her thumb over the ring on her finger, she started to cross the street. An electric tingle rolled over her skin, and she stilled, her eyes raking the scene. "Jen."

Jen went from unconcerned to on guard in a moment.

Laney scanned the church grounds and the street, but didn't see anyone.

"Lanes?" Jen asked.

Laney didn't look back at her, keeping her attention on the area around them. Matt had said the Fallen was a good guy, but experience warned Laney to keep her guard up. "There's a Fallen here somewhere, but I'm not sure exactly where."

"Do you think he's inside?"

Something told her the Fallen wasn't inside the church but next to it. She nodded to the side of the building. They crossed the street, and Jen fell in step next to Laney as she followed a path around the side of the building.

They came upon a white-haired man kneeling in a small garden, pulling weeds. He wore a large straw hat, and a basket of garden tools sat next to him. He turned quickly and sized Laney and Jen up in a second, but his gaze focused on Jen. As a Fallen, he knew what Jen was; he'd view her as the bigger threat.

Laney tensed, and Jen did the same, pulling back her jacket to place her hand on the gun there and reveal her badge.

The man rose to his feet, a nervous smile on his face as he pulled off his gloves. His eyes shifted between Laney and Jen. "Dr. McPhearson?"

Laney nodded. "That's me."

"I'm Xavier Alejandro."

Xavier was about five foot six with skin tanned and wrinkled from the sun. He squinted, but his eyes showed a warmth and compassion that was both comforting and disconcerting. He was not at all what Laney had expected.

Xavier extended his hand. "Agent Clark told me you'd be coming."

Laney hesitated, then shook his hand. "Uh, this is my associate, Dr. Jennifer Witt."

Xavier looked at Jen but didn't offer his hand—no doubt due to Jen's expression, which suggested she'd rather shoot him than befriend him. Xavier gestured behind him.

166

"There's a gazebo with a table out back. Perhaps we could talk there?"

"Lead the way," Laney said.

Xavier walked to the back, and they followed. Ahead was a gazebo, just as Xavier said.

Jen tugged on Laney's sleeve. "I'm going to stay here, keep an eye out."

"Okay. " Laney continued to the gazebo and took a seat across from Xavier. He nodded to his thermos. "I have some iced tea, if you'd like."

"No, I'm fine."

Xavier clasped his hands in front of him. "Agent Clark said you had some questions for me."

Laney nodded. "Yes. But first, tell me how you know Agent Clark."

Xavier placed his hat on the bench next to him, then poured himself a glass. His bright eyes and tanned skin made him appear younger, but up close Laney thought he was probably closer to seventy than sixty. He took a long drink and wiped his mouth with the back of his hand. "Sorry. Been out in the sun for a while. You sure I can't offer you some?"

"No, I'm fine. But thank you."

Xavier leaned back, eyeing her. "You know what I am?"

Laney nodded. "Yes, I am well acquainted with people with your skills."

He let out a small laugh, one filled with more bitterness than warmth. "My skills. A diplomatic choice of words." He fell silent and looked away.

"Agent Clark?" she prodded.

His gaze shifted back to her, his head nodding in apology. "Yes, Agent Clark. I only met him about ten years or so ago, although I came to the attention of the SIA almost fifty years ago. I was living in Palo Alto. At the time, I was in college and working construction to pay tuition. There was an accident on the site. A crane fell. It landed on the trailer where

167

my boss and a few of my friends were meeting. They were trapped. I pushed the crane off. No one at the site ever realized it was me."

"But when the SIA showed up, *they* knew it was you."

"Yes. You know how it works? The sense?"

She nodded, realizing Xavier didn't know her role in everything. He thought she was an agent without abilities.

"Well, an agent came out, and he sensed me as soon as he stepped onto the construction site. I sensed him too."

"Did you know who, or rather what, you were?"

He shook his head. "No. I grew up knowing what I could do. I thought God had blessed me. My family, we are very religious. And I'd never come across anyone else like me."

"What did the agent do?"

"He asked me about my life, spoke with different people about me. Checked me out to see what kind of person I was."

"Did he tell you what you were?"

"Not at first. He told me that his agency was responsible for watching people with abilities. He said they didn't know why people had them, but that it was important it be kept secret."

"So when did you find out?"

He sighed and looked away. "About six or seven years later, I was getting married. I had kept in touch with the agent and sent him an invitation to the wedding. He arrived on my doorstep the next day. He explained what I really was and what my children could be."

"What did you do?"

He clasped his mug tightly, his eyes downcast. "I broke the heart of the woman I loved. The agent explained that other people might come for me. That not only could I be in danger, but so could Angela, or our future children, if anyone learned what I could do. If anyone even *sensed* what I could do." He shook his head. "I loved Angela too much. I couldn't risk it. I couldn't risk her."

"You left her?"

He nodded. "The agent arranged for me to leave. I moved across the country to Indianapolis. I worked for a church there until two weeks ago."

"A church?"

Xavier nodded. "I thought about becoming a priest, but it felt wrong, being who I am."

Laney wasn't so sure of that. The man sitting in front of her seemed to be the picture of redemption. He kind of reminded her of her uncle. "How did you end up here? Did the SIA help you?"

"No. The church did."

Laney reared back in surprise. "Did the church know who you were?"

"I didn't think so. But after I was attacked, they arranged for me to work here. They must have known."

Laney filed that away. The church had actively hidden a Fallen for decades, and somehow convinced a synagogue to do the same. That was interesting—but it was a fact to focus on at another time. "What can you tell me about the attack?"

Xavier shook his head. "I don't know why they came after me. I had gone into the city; there was a flower market that I liked. I was just picking up supplies, like any other day. I had finished and was packing up my truck. Then I walked to the diner I always went to when I was in that part of town. They came at me when I crossed under the train tracks. I'd never seen any of them before."

"Were they Fallen? Nephilim?"

"No. They were human. Eight of them. They came at me fast. I had no warning. I managed to leap to the platform. I didn't want to hurt them. I didn't think they knew what I could do to them. It's a bad neighborhood, and I just thought they were gang members or something. But there were more of them on the platform. One got me with a knife—a woman with a stroller. When I first got onto the platform, I had yelled at her to run, even shielded her when they came up the stairs. That's when I saw the stroller was empty. She got me in the back. If I had been," he paused, stumbling over the word, "human, I would have been dead. I threw myself from the platform onto a train. It spirited me away, and by the time I reached the next stop, I had healed enough to run. So I did."

"Did your attackers say anything?"

He shook his head. "Not a word."

"Is there anything else you can tell me?"

"The woman, when she stabbed me, the sleeve of her shirt pulled up, and I saw a tattoo."

"What did it look like?"

Xavier reached into his back pocket and pulled out his wallet. He removed a folded piece of paper and handed it to Laney. On it was three stripes with what looked like vines wrapped around them. In the center was a flower with large petals and an intricate stigma.

"I looked it up," Xavier said. "I think it's a lotus blossom."

"Signifying rebirth or awakening," Laney said softly.

Xavier's eyebrows rose. "You're familiar with it?"

Laney thought of the description of the Buddha-like figure that was alleged to have been in the cave in the Grand Canyon where's she'd rescued the children not that long ago. *There are always connections.* "I've come across it before."

"Do you know if it's important?"

She shook her head. "No. But I plan on finding out."

CHAPTER 42

Malama Island, Hawaii

Palm trees lined the meditation space. Aaliyah sat in the square, surrounded by over a hundred people. They all sat in the lotus position on colorful mats: legs crossed, feet resting on opposite thighs, hands on knees. A light wind blew, and the sky was blue overhead.

Aaliyah focused on her breathing, envisioning each breath filling her lungs, reaching through her body to give energy to every portion.

At the front of the square a gong rang out, and Aaliyah opened her eyes. She looked around, amazed at how fast the thirty minutes had gone.

Next to her, Ioane turned and smiled. He had been one of Aaliyah's favorite teachers when she was younger. Over the years, she'd often found herself using his techniques when she taught. She hoped she had his kindness. Even now, when his eyesight had begun to fade, that kindness still shone in his deep brown eyes.

She dipped her head to him and returned the smile. He started to stand, struggling a bit. Of course, seeing as he was one hundred and two, that wasn't really surprising.

Aaliyah placed her hand under his arm to help him up, then reached down and rolled up his mat for him. Handing it over, she said, "Have a wonderful morning, Ioane."

"Thank you, Aaliyah. And you as well." Ioane wandered off with the crowd heading for the docks. She knew he liked to feed the birds and fish in the morning.

What an amazing man. No one would guess his age. It was only in the last year that he had begun to have problems with his joints. Even then, he swore the group meditations helped with that.

And they probably did. Aaliyah had often been amazed at how refreshed she felt after a session of meditation, and the effect was more pronounced with the group session. Only now was the outside world beginning to recognize the benefits of meditation in reducing blood pressure, improving immune systems, reducing stress, and reducing the impact of negative life events. But Aaliyah's people had known about these benefits for a long time. Every morning and evening, the Honu Keiki engaged in group meditation. Everyone who could attend did—although it was not unusual to find someone meditating alone up in the hills that surrounded the island.

Created from a volcano thousands of years ago, Malama was essentially the crater of a long-dead volcano. Lush vegetation covered the island year round, and most people were drawn to meditate at least once a day in that outdoor beauty. The island was thirty square miles, and the residences only took up about half of that, leaving the rest gloriously untamed.

Aaliyah, however, preferred the group meditations. There was a power within the group that enhanced her ability to focus.

Not to mention how well it enhanced her other ability.

Aaliyah was rolling up her own mat when she heard her name being called.

Eighteen-year-old Noriko made her way through the crowd. The sun highlighted the light brown streaks in her dark hair. Her pale eyes were unusual on the island; most people had the traditional dark hair and dark eyes. But her eyes were not what made Noriko stand out. She exuded energy, and she had a smile for everyone she passed.

Aaliyah couldn't help but smile as well. Aaliyah had raised Noriko since she was a baby. At Honu Keiki, children were raised by teachers, not biological parents. Due to her commitments with the Naacal, Aaliyah had been allowed only one child to raise. Noriko had come to her when she was only three months old, and Aaliyah could not have loved her more even if she had been born to her.

"I'm coming," Aaliyah said. Noriko would be teaching some of the children today, and Aaliyah knew she was excited about it. Aaliyah was, too. Noriko was a natural with children. To be honest, she was a natural with everyone.

The sound of running feet caused her to turn toward the temple. Located in the center of the island, it was a step pyramid over a hundred feet high. It was the meeting place for the Naacal, and also where the priestess spent most of her time, although she had another residence among the houses of Honu Keiki.

Aaliyah saw a dozen men and women of the Guard running in formation from the temple toward the docks. She quickly stepped to the side, her heart pounding. The Guard's dark clothes stood in stark contrast to the lighter styles of the rest of the inhabitants. Violence and crime were not a common part of the landscape, but the Guard was there for the rare moments when they occurred. Despite the infrequent call for them, the size of the Guard had swelled in recent years.

Aaliyah bowed her head as the Guard went past. *Off on another mission.* People rarely left the island, and certainly not in numbers. In fact, there were some, like Ioane, who had never left. But lately, there had been more and more urgency in the Guard, and it was not unusual for them to leave for days at a time.

Something was going on. As a member of the Naacal, Aaliyah should have been privy to it. But none of the Naacal save the priestess knew what the Guard was up to.

Aaliyah raised her head again as the rear of the muscular group passed. They carried their usual staff weapons, but she noted that most also had guns in holsters. Aaliyah's mouth fell open. *Guns? Since when do the Guard use guns?*

Shaken, Aaliyah turned to watch them head for the wharf. Most of the citizens had stopped to do the same. Whatever was going on was dangerous. Why else would they send the Guard out with guns?

A wind blew across the square, and clouds floated in front of the sun. Even as she told herself it was just a coincidence that the sky darkened at that moment, it still felt like an omen.

Aaliyah wrapped her arms around herself. Change was coming, and she didn't think it was going to be for the better.

CHAPTER 43

Ann Arbor, Michigan

Laney and Jen were back in their car heading for the airport.

"So what do you think?" Jen asked.

Laney sighed. "I think he's a nice man who's been targeted for what he is, not who he is."

"Do you think Gerard was telling the truth?"

"I don't know. I mean, it's Gerard. But at the same time, I can't see any connection between Xavier and Gerard. They've never met, and they don't exactly seem like bowling buddies."

Jen was quiet for a moment. "Whenever I think of the Fallen, I think of them as evil. And that, when we come across one, we need to be ready to fight. It's disconcerting when they turn out to be decent people. At the same time, I think of Lou or the other kids at the school. I don't think of them in those terms. They're just kids."

Laney's mind drifted back to Cain and his attitude toward her. There had been nothing hostile in it. He had been decent. "It's all sorts of gray these days, isn't it?"

Jen nodded. "Yeah. I liked it better when things were black and white. It definitely made things easier. So—what do we do now?"

"I don't know. I sent Henry the tattoo. He'll run a search. But that's a pretty common flower in that part of the world."

"Henry, not Jake?"

Laney shrugged.

"How are you two doing?"

Laney smiled. "Better. We talked. I mean, we're not back to where we were exactly, but we're heading there."

"Well, you've both been through a lot."

We still are, Laney thought, but she kept silent. "You know, Xavier said he thought the church knew what he was. They arranged for him to move almost as soon as she reported the attack."

Jen raised her eyebrows. "The church *knows*? Has Patrick said anything to them?"

"I'm not sure. I mean, he's worked as the liaison at the Montana site. But the SIA arranged for Xavier to work at a church in Indianapolis forty years ago—which means they've known about the SIA for decades."

"It's not really a surprise the church knows, though, is it? I mean, as an organization, they're full of secrets. The Vatican vaults alone could probably answer questions that have been plaguing mankind for generations."

Laney knew Jen was probably right. Conspiracy theorists had long held that the Vatican archives should be opened for the benefit of mankind. Everything from information on extraterrestrial visits to the fountain of youth had been theorized to exist in the bowels of the Vatican. And even without those extreme possibilities, the Vatican archives certainly held enough verified documents to keep people enthralled, including records on the Knights Templar, the Inquisition, Pope Joan, and the list went on and on.

"Are we going to launch an offensive against the Roman Catholic Church to see what they know?" Jen asked.

Laney laughed. "How about we save that for next week? We have enough on our plate this week."

Laney had meant the words in a lighthearted way, but the truth of them crashed into her. By next week, they would

176

have either saved someone from death or failed. "We need to win, Jen."

Jen paused. "It won't be your fault if we don't."

"I know that, rationally, but—"

"Victoria's death wasn't your fault either."

"Why bring her up?"

"Because she's never far from our thoughts. I've seen you struggle these last few months. I know you're putting on a show to make everyone think you're fine. But I see what's going on behind the curtain."

Laney turned to look out the window. She took a stuttering breath. "It just hurts," she said quietly.

Jen reached over and squeezed Laney's hand. "And it should. It shows how much you care. But it still doesn't mean it's your fault. Place the blame where it belongs: on Samyaza and her group."

Victoria's words drifted through her mind. *Each time we meet, I am amazed by your strength and your desire to fight the good fight, no matter the odds. Your heart is your strongest weapon. Never forget that.*

Laney's heart clenched. She missed her. She had wanted the chance to know her better. Victoria had been so strong. She had faced lifetime after lifetime of combating the Fallen. She had a strength Laney couldn't even begin to fathom.

You have the same strength. You are my daughter.

Laney stilled. She'd heard the words in Victoria's voice, even though Laney knew it was only her imagination. But it was something Victoria would have said.

"So, what's the next step?" Jen asked, forcing some levity into her tone.

"We head back to the boys and hope they can find something about that tattoo," Laney said.

"And if they can't?"

Laney shook her head. "Then I have no idea."

CHAPTER 44

Baltimore, Maryland

Jen dropped Laney off at the estate before heading over to the Chandler School. Jen had a standing dinner date with Lou once a week.

Laney stopped by Jake's office to see what he had learned. She paused at the door. Jake was bent over his desk, his hair falling forward. It was longer than she'd ever seen it before, and she liked it. He frowned and then looked up.

She raised her eyebrows. "So, psychics?"

He grinned. "You're really enjoying me doing this particular line of research, aren't you?"

She smiled as she took a seat in one of the chairs in front of his desk. "I really am."

"How'd it go?"

"Good." Laney pictured Xavier. As she was leaving, he had told her that if she needed any help, to give him a call and he'd do all he could. "He's actually a nice guy."

"No problems?"

"Nope—no gunfire, no ninjas, all in all incredibly boring. And the lack of fighting means I'll still have to go for a run later." She paused. "You're handling it pretty well."

"I'm trying, Lanes. I'm always going to worry. But I'm trying to be a little less…"

"Neurotic?" She offered.

"I was going to say concerned."

She shrugged. "Well, tomay-to tomah-to. Anyway, back to psychics. What did you find out about psychic abilities?"

Jake grimaced. "Pretty much what I expected to find—very little by way of scientific verification. They never seem to be able to pass any kind of laboratory experiment. There always seem to be a couple of high profile individuals in the news and making the rounds on the talk show circuit, but eventually, those guys all seem to be exposed as fakes. And of course there are the more well-known psychics—Ingo Swann, Joseph McMoneagle, Edgar Cayce, and a few others. But I just can't find anyone that's been fully vetted and supported."

"So there's nothing?"

"I wouldn't say that. We know Cayce was right more than he was wrong. And there's certainly been no lack of government testing."

"Testing?"

Jake nodded. "Many government agencies have tested the efficacy of psychic abilities, particularly remote viewing. The Russians' program was probably the worst kept secret, but it wasn't just them. In the 1970s, the CIA sponsored a program at Stanford called the Stargate Project. There were hits, but no one could demonstrate that it wasn't just dumb luck. And in the 1940s, the Canadian government did ESP tests on aboriginal children between the ages of six and twenty. The poor kids had already been ripped from their families and forced into a boarding school."

Laney cringed thinking of the same types of schools in the United States—re-education schools for Native American children designed to remove the taint of their native lifestyles from them. The creator of one of the first schools, Richard Pratt, succinctly summed up the goal of the schools: "Kill the Indian in him, and save the man." The United States government operated over a hundred of the schools beginning in the 1870s. Abuse and a complete denigration of the Native American life were hallmarks of the curriculum.

"Did any of these government tests uncover evidence of psychic abilities?" Laney asked.

"Nothing solid, no, but of course they're not the only ones researching. One article has suggested that psychic abilities are actually the result of a neurological condition called synesthesia. Basically, the brain is cross-wired, resulting in a different way of viewing the world. It can be caused by head injury or it may be inherited. But there are also some who suggest that you can, in essence, re-wire your brain through deep meditation."

"Deep meditation, like Uncle Patrick thinks the Lemurians and the Honu Keiki folks engage in."

Jake nodded. "Yup."

Laney knew that a person's brain patterns could be changed through actions or thoughts. While most people tended to think of our brains as hardwired, the reality was that they had a great deal of plasticity to them. The brain reacts to stimuli and the environment, and those reactions had been demonstrated to literally change the pathways within the brain.

"So, overall, what do you think?" Laney asked.

Jake paused. "I think the world and humans are incredibly complex. And I think not everything can be easily replicated in a lab. So I think psychic abilities are possible. I mean, after the Cayce links we've found, and your abilities with Cleo, I don't see how there's any way to doubt it."

Laney stood up. "Well, okay. I don't know if that helps or not, but if you're not ruling it out, I guess the rest of us can't either. I have to go talk to Henry."

"Hold on a sec," Jake said, walking around the desk.

Laney paused at the door.

Jake placed his hand around her waist and pulled her close. "I'm glad you're back and in one piece." He leaned his head down and kissed her.

Laney wrapped her arms around him and leaned into the kiss. Finally, she broke away, trying to remember where she was going.

180

Jake pushed her toward the door. "Go see Henry."

She smiled as she walked down the hall toward Henry's office. She knocked on the door, still feeling the warmth of Jake's kiss.

Henry looked up from his desk. "Hey. How'd it go?"

"Uh, good," she said, giving him a quick run-down. "Did you manage to link the tattoo with the cult?"

Henry shook his head. "No. But honestly, there's just so little out there on the group. They don't even have a website. Most of the what we 'know' is actually just guesswork on the part of journalists trying to figure them out."

"So what do we 'know' about the Honu Keiki?"

"We know they are run by a priestess who is chosen by the group and given a lifetime appointment. She has six supporters, and together they make up the Naacal."

"Seven again," Laney murmured.

"What do you mean?" Henry asked.

"Churchward spoke of a Council of Seven leading the Lemurians. And ancient teachers all seemed to come in a group of seven. Even the cave in Ecuador had a table with seven chairs. The Shuar down in Ecuador had spoken of seven ships that arrived with seven teachers. There were seven gods in Greek mythology. In India, seven helpers. The advanced peoples of a myriad of myths and legends always seem to come in the number seven."

"It's possible they just copied the style of governance from an ancient group."

Laney nodded. "That's true. It's just interesting. What else do you have?"

"As you know, they have virtually no contact with the outside world, other than the occasional boat that runs supplies to and from the island. And, rarely, a member is banished."

"Do we know the reasons for the banishments?"

"No. The former members are incredibly close-lipped. Some have speculated they have family back on the island that they may be worried about. Others say they're just hoping to be allowed back in."

"Well, that's not much help."

"I do have one more thing." Henry nodded at his screen. "One journalist managed to sneak in. He was caught pretty quickly, but he did manage to smuggle out some pictures. Before he got the chance to go public with them, he was smacked with one lawsuit after the next. It was made clear his life would be a living hell if he let these pictures get out. But..." He grinned. "I managed to get a copy."

Laney walked around the desk and stood on his side. "And how'd you manage that?"

"I have my ways."

Laney laughed. "Fine, keep your secrets, big brother."

She leaned forward to get a better look at the images on the screen. Nothing really stood out—they were just pictures of strangers standing together, smiling, walking around. It was like looking at someone else's vacation photos. They were pretty but had no real meaning.

But what she could tell was that Honu Keiki's property was gorgeous—giant palm trees, trails cutting through lush foliage. The houses reminded Laney of what she'd seen the one time she'd been to Maui for a conference. Most were one level with a lanai outback. Some had a few steps leading to the front door, but for most that wasn't necessary. Big windows adorned the front of most of the homes, which were primarily white, blue, or tan—no dark colors. Honestly, it looked like any other Hawaiian neighborhood except there were no roads and no garages. Apparently cars weren't part of daily life. Everyone was in sandals or flip-flops and casual clothes, and no one looked unhappy. It looked like a corporate retreat.

She scanned through the photos, growing more and more frustrated. *There's nothing here.*

"There's an awful lot of cats," Henry muttered.

"That's not surprising," Laney murmured, still looking for something that might tie this group to the attacks.

"Why not?"

"Huh?" she asked.

Henry gestured to the screen. "The cats?"

"Cats were revered in the many ancient civilizations. For instance, the Egyptian goddess Bastet had feline features. She was the protector of the home, protector against evil and disease." Laney paused. "Actually, now that I think about it, those civilizations were all along the Pacific Rim—Japan, China, India. All places where the descendants of Mu allegedly went."

"So you think this is proof?"

Laney smiled. "I think it's interesting. Proof is a different story."

Henry raised an eyebrow. "Seems there's a lot about them that's interesting."

"So there is. And maybe enough interesting facts can turn into some proof."

She turned her attention back to the images. There had to be a way to—

Her gaze flew back to a picture on the left of the screen. She sucked in a breath and pointed. "Can you zoom in on that one?"

Henry clicked on the picture, and the image expanded until it took up half the screen. It was a shot of a man, a woman, and a child standing in front of a sign, with a large palm tree overhead and a bloom of flowers. The man was blond, the woman had dark hair, and the girl had light brown. One might think they were a family, but they didn't look alike.

"Do you recognize someone?" Henry asked.

Laney shook her head. "Not someone—something." She pointed to the sign. The people were blocking any lettering, but most of an image was still visible: three green stripes on a white background, with what looked like vines encircling each stripe, and on the left, a pink lotus flower.

The sign was exactly the same as the tattoo that Xavier Alejandro had seen on one of his attackers.

183

"Well, I'd say that's a definite connection," Henry said.

Laney stared at the photo. "Let's set up a phone call. It's time to see what they have to say."

CHAPTER 45

It took Henry three days to arrange a phone conversation with Honu Keiki. Henry's name tended to get doors opened, but getting in touch with Honu Keiki proved difficult even for him. He had to have over six individuals call the group and vouch for him. Laney knew he wasn't used to that, but he took it in stride.

Laney, however, had begun debating whether it would be worth it to just drop in on the Honu Keiki and hope for the best, even with the long plane ride to get there. But finally, Henry called to say he'd arranged the call for the following morning.

Unfortunately, Laney woke to the news that there had been a new murder. They weren't sure what the connection was yet, but the elements of the crime scene were familiar: altar, burned heart, lots of blood. This time the victim had been a man in his sixties. The body had been found in Ukrainian Pioneer Home, in the Astotin Lake Area of Elk Island National Park in Alberta, Canada. Jake immediately flew out to meet with Canadian officials and see what he could find out. The SIA were on the ground as well.

Jake said he'd call when he had something, but all morning, Laney's phone was silent. She hoped the victim didn't have any family; with the image of the Lachowskis still in her mind, she hated the idea of any other family going through that.

And she worried what it meant. This murder had come pretty fast on the heels of Sheila's murder. Was the timetable speeding up? And if so, why? Laney had no answer for that. But she was more determined than ever to get to the bottom of everything.

She pushed those thoughts aside as she walked into Henry's office. She needed to focus on the phone call with Honu Keiki. Because she had the impression one shot was all they were going to get.

"Any minute," Henry said from his desk.

Laney nodded and made her way over to the couch near his desk. "Where do you want me?"

"I'll set the call up at the conference table. Why don't you sit next to me?"

"You sure it won't be better if it's just you?"

Henry shook his head. "No. If they're matriarchal, as I believe they are, it would be beneficial if you were seen onscreen."

"Matriarchal?" Laney asked. Interesting. And consistent with what Laney knew of Atlantis and Mu. Both were allegedly matriarchal societies.

"Yes. One thing I did manage to dig up on the group was that that they are followers of the Great Mother."

"As in the cult of Magna Mater?" Laney took a seat.

Henry gave her a surprised look. "Yes. I'd never heard of it before this. What do you know of it?"

"The cult of Magna Mater, or the Great Mother, could be argued to be the world's oldest religion," Laney explained. "It predates Christianity. It's even mentioned in the Old Testament by Ezekiel. Earliest mentions go back six thousand years. The cult flourished in ancient times although it eventually gave way to other religions. The Great Mother was adopted into Roman life as Cybele. In all, though, she is viewed as…" Laney paused.

186

Henry sat down next to her with a frown. "What?"

"Did you know the Great Mother was supposed to have helped develop medicines, and she healed both humans and supernatural beings? In fact, in the Western world, God is male, but in the ancient world she was female. She was the mother of all."

Henry went pale. "You don't think—"

"That the great mother was our *actual* mother? It does kind of fit, doesn't it? And she *was* the one who led the fight against the Belial who resisted their influence."

Laney thought back to the photos of the Honu Keiki. One had depicted a black cat sitting on a step. "The Great Mother was often depicted with her two guardians: a lion and a leopard."

Henry paused for a moment. "Cats. That's some coincidence."

Is it? Laney thought about the rumors that the ancient civilizations had been ruled by women and not men. "Remember when we talked about the Iroquois?"

"You mean how Cayce said the noble class of the Iroquois were the pure Atlanteans?"

Laney nodded. "Exactly. I did some reading on Native American cultures after that."

"Of course you did," Henry muttered.

Laney shrugged. "I couldn't sleep one night. And the power structure within Native American cultures actually inspired the women's suffrage movement in the United States."

"Seriously?"

Laney nodded. "Yes. In Native American cultures women had essentially equal status with men. In some ways, they were even elevated above men. For example, in the Mohawk clan, of which suffragette Matilda Gage was an adopted member, only women were able to nominate candidates for the position of chief. In fact, all the big names in the United States women's suffrage movement—Gage,

187

Stanton, Anthony—claimed Native American groups as their inspiration."

And Mom may have ben the inspiration for all of it, Laney thought with a chill. Victoria had such a lasting influence, and no one even knew.

Henry reached for the screen to initiate the call. "It's time. You ready?"

Laney nodded, trying to focus on the conversation ahead and not the weird connections her mother might or might not have to the world's oldest religion and Native American culture.

"Okay, here we go." Henry keyed in the number and hit send.

Laney was surprised at the nervousness that flowed through her. She reached up and wrapped her hand around the ring on the chain around her neck. *It's just a phone call.* But she had the feeling this phone call was a lot more than that.

A few seconds later, a woman appeared on the screen. She looked to be in her early forties, with dark hair and eyes, and a Polynesian look. She inclined her head. "Mr. Rogan, I am Vanessa, head of security for Honu Keiki." Laney didn't expect a last name. She had learned that much of the group—they didn't identify as families, and therefore no one had a last name.

Vanessa frowned as her eyes fell on Laney. "Who is this?"

"Dr. Laney McPhearson, my sister."

Vanessa sized Laney up in a glance before nodding her head. "Dr. McPhearson. So what is this urgent phone call about?"

Laney leaned forward slightly. "We have reason to believe that a string of violent crimes may be connected in some way to Honu Keiki."

Vanessa raised her eyebrows but showed no other interest. "Indeed. And what exactly is the basis of that belief?"

188

"One of the attackers had a tattoo on his arm. It was three lines encircled by vines behind a lotus flower," Laney said.

Vanessa shrugged. "I don't see what that has to do with us."

"We know this is a symbol associated with your group," Henry said.

"You are mistaken. We do not use symbols to identify ourselves." Vanessa narrowed her eyes. "What exactly is the nature of the crimes these people have committed?"

Laney spoke carefully. "Murder."

Vanessa's eyes grew large. "Well, I'm sure you know we are a pacifist society. There has to my knowledge never been a murder in Honu."

"There are aspects of the crime scene that refer back to ancient customs that we believe your group may be familiar with," Laney said.

Vanessa's eyes narrowed. "What kind of customs?"

"A purifying of the body with water and fire, and the removal of the heart of the victim."

The woman was cool, but Laney caught a slight widening in her eyes. "I believe you are mistaken. The citizens of Honu Keiki, whether present or former, do not engage in such acts, as I have already said. It is an insult to even suggest it."

"Could you at least provide us with a list of the people who have left your group?"

"No. We value their privacy even if they are no longer members of Honu Keiki."

Henry nodded. "We understand. But if we could perhaps speak with the priestess, perhaps—"

"She does not speak with outsiders. But I will pass along your request." The screen went black.

Laney sat back. "Well, she's lovely."

Henry gave a small laugh. "She won't be winning any personality contests, but did you catch her reaction when she heard the description of the crime scenes?"

Laney nodded. "She tried very hard to make sure we didn't see it."

"So what do you think?"

Laney stared at the black screen for a moment. "I think Vanessa is not being entirely forthcoming. But I don't think we can pin our hopes on them calling us back with information. We need to speak with one of the exiles."

Henry nodded. "I'll make it happen."

CHAPTER 46

Malama Island, Hawaii

Aaliyah flipped through the papers in front of her. They were convened in the Council Room, the main room in the Temple of Mu. Large basalt blocks had been taken from the quarry and used to create the temple when her people had first arrived on Malama. Slits within the rock walls allowed light in. There were no adornments, and no electricity either—an homage to their ancestors' ways of doing things.

Aaliyah looked around the high table. The Naacal—the seven priests that formed the ruling body of Honu Keiki—sat on either side of the table. They were composed of three women and three men, plus the priestess. All wore the white robes that marked them as Naacal. Gold bands were wrapped around their forearms, each ending with the face of a roaring cat, its teeth exposed.

The priestess sat at the head of the table, her guards behind her. The priestess had once been called Xia, but unlike some priestesses in the past, she would now answer only to her title. She had called this meeting because she had arranged to purchase another piece of land—this one in Australia. Ostensibly she needed the Naacal's approval for such an action, but more and more, that approval seemed to be assumed.

Aaliyah observed the priestess. Her dark hair stood in a tall bun on top of her head, and her dark eyes were lined in heavy eyeliner. On anyone else, this would look cartoonish; but the priestess looked like Cleopatra come to life. The priestess was only two years younger than Aaliyah, but they had never been friends. The priestess initiated only those friendships that benefited her—though, Aaliyah thought, few seemed to be able to see that. She was good at getting people to believe they wanted to do what *she* wanted them to do.

The prior priestess, a woman named Adele, had been much respected. Under her tenure, the Naacal had adhered to the old ways: little governance, and much support for the people and their way of life. But then, fourteen years ago, she died unexpectedly, in an incident that still did not sit well with Aaliyah. According to a witness, Adele was last seen walking along the boardwalk. It was generally believed that she fell in, perhaps hitting her head and drowning. Her body washed up the next morning.

Xia was appointed as the new priestess a week later, and soon after, things had begun to change.

Aaliyah had been part of the Naacal since she turned twenty-three, eighteen years ago. There was only one member of the Naacal who had been there longer: Kai, Aaliyah's closest friend. The rest of the Naacal had all been replaced within the last five years—an incredibly quick turnover. Two of the former members had been exiled and two had elected to step down. Aaliyah knew her days were numbered as well, although she wasn't sure what form her exit would take.

Standing beside the priestess was Enzo. At twenty-two, he was the youngest member of the Naacal. His dark hair was neatly cut, his dark eyes focused on the priestess. "And that concludes my presentation," he said. He took his seat, glancing at the priestess like a puppy looking for a treat.

Aaliyah tried to roll back her distaste. Enzo had been reporting on the additional lands he had arranged to purchase in Australia. How had they come to this? Buying land like it was board game? What would their ancestors think of this materialism?

192

The priestess smiled at Enzo like the prized pet he was. "Very good. Very good indeed."

Enzo puffed up his rather small chest. Aaliyah kept her expression neutral, bowing her head to Enzo as if in accord. But inside, she seethed. The priestess had lined the Naacal with yes men who never questioned her, who took everything she said as if her words had been spoken by the Holy Mother herself.

At the head of the table, the sunlight glinted off the gold that draped the priestess's arms. Jewelry had been passed down from generation to generation for as long as their history spanned. The bands on Aaliyah's own arms were over five hundred years old, and each piece was lovingly crafted and bestowed with the affection of the people. But the bracelets on the priestess's arms were not among these treasured gifts. These were new, shining in gold and diamonds. In private, the priestess had taken to flaunting her possessions—while at the same time, Aaliyah had seen some of their people going hungry, had seen the worn clothing they wore.

Aaliyah cast her eyes to the tabletop in case the anger and disgust in them gave her away.

A messenger slid up to the priestess and whispered in her ear. The priestess waved him away. "Send her in."

The double doors at the back of the room were thrown open, and Vanessa strode across the room. Forty-nine years old, Vanessa had a body that been honed by years of training. Her dark hair was pulled back into a severe bun and her dark eyes missed nothing.

Once again, Aaliyah tried to hide her loathing and her fear. Vanessa was head of the Guard. A Guard that had swelled to a size never seen in their history. They were often leaving the island for "missions" that no one knew the nature of. In the past, leaving the island was rare; now it was practically a weekly event.

And then there was the brutality. Guards would trip the poorest among them; would take fruit from merchants without

193

a word; and all under the watchful and approving eye of Vanessa. And they had taken to wearing their weapons on their belt at all times. Another example of how far they had fallen.

Vanessa ignored the Naacal, her eyes only on the priestess. She bowed low. "Priestess."

The priestess waved her hand at the Naacal without even looking at them. "Leave us."

The priests stood and began to file out the door. Aaliyah took her time, being the last to leave.

Behind her, Vanessa began to speak. "The call was completed. They are worried about the murders."

A chill ran through Aaliyah. Murders? She stopped outside the doors and stood to the side, out of view of the room. One of the other priests glanced back at her, so she opened her notebook as if checking for something.

"Will Chandler be a problem?" the priestess asked.

"No. They know nothing. They're merely fishing," Vanessa said.

"But the Chandler Group has a habit of being diligent in their projects."

Vanessa nodded. "True. But they have been shut out. They have nothing that links us or any of our former members."

"Very well. See to that other matter."

"Yes, priestess."

Aaliyah quickly hurried down the hall. Murders? And an outside group believed the Honu Keiki knew something about it? Aaliyah felt the weight of the knowledge on her. But she didn't know what to do.

She stepped out of the temple and into the sunshine. She drank in the peace of her home. Her eyes strayed to the guards standing at attention on either side of the temple entrance.

But it's not as peaceful as it once was.

CHAPTER 47

Addison, West Virginia

Laney walked down the hall of the SIA facility, accompanied only by Mustafa this time. After the call with the Honu Keiki, she had felt she was just spinning her wheels back at the estate. Henry had found an exile, but he wouldn't be back in town until tomorrow. She hoped that maybe a visit with Cain might shake loose some additional information.

"How has he been?" she asked.

"Good. He's much improved. He's even been heard laughing. I think his new cell agrees with him."

"Well, I suppose that's good. And he's been going outside?"

Mustafa nodded. "His cell adjoins a small courtyard which had been sealed off from the rest of the facility. It can only be entered from his cell, and the door is only opened to allow him entrance three times a day, depending on the weather."

"And he will remain in this cell after the conversation today?"

"I believe that is the case, yes."

"Good." She paused. "If Matt tries to move him, will you contact me?"

Mustafa nodded slowly. "Yes."

They turned a corner, and the same guard who had guarded the hallway to Cain's last cell stood waiting.

Mustafa nodded at him. "Hanz."

"Mustafa." Hanz glanced at Laney. "The prisoner is in his courtyard."

Laney hefted the bag she'd brought. "Great. Could you open the door?"

Hanz hesitated.

"Hanz," Mustafa said quietly. "Dr. McPhearson asked you to open the door."

Hanz nodded, his lips tight. Laney stepped through as soon as the door was open, and Hanz shut it quickly behind her.

The new cell was much brighter than the old one. It contained a bed and small divider to provide him privacy in the bathroom. A TV was embedded in one wall, covered in a clear plastic. On another wall a glass door stood open, and beyond it she could make out grass.

Laney stepped outside into a small courtyard, only about thirty square feet. A plastic table with two chairs stood in the middle. The furniture was made of a light plastic—she'd gotten Max a similar set when he was three. There were no metal parts—nothing, Laney noted, that Cain could use as a weapon.

Laney also noted the four snipers on the roof. Matt was taking no chances.

"Ah, Delaney. Lovely to see you again," Cain said, stepping from the shade.

Laney was stunned by his transformation. His hair was neatly combed back into a ponytail, and his skin had regained its former healthy color.

"You look good," Laney said.

"It seems the outdoors agrees with me." He gestured to the table. "Would you care to sit?"

"Thanks." Laney placed her bag on the table, unzipped it, and pulled out a few boxes. She slid one across the table to Cain. "For you."

196

Cain opened it and smiled. "Sushi. Oh, I have missed it. Chopsticks?"

Laney shook her head. "Afraid not."

"Ah, well, when in Rome." He picked up the salmon roll, placed it in his mouth, and swallowed it quickly. "Now that is lovely."

Laney let herself relax a little. Strange, spending time with Cain was the most relaxed she'd been in months. *And that's not worrisome.*

"So, have you learned anything new about your killers?" Cain asked.

"They seem to be speeding up their timeline." Laney shared with him what she knew. "You said they were descendants of Mu. Care to expand upon that?"

"I'd be delighted. But first, have you discovered where those descendants are?"

"Honu Keiki."

Cain smiled broadly. "I knew you'd figure it out."

"It wasn't me. It was my uncle."

Cain nodded. "Victoria mentioned him. She had a great deal of respect for him."

"And him for her."

"Well, your uncle is correct. Honu are the children."

"How is that possible? I mean, it's been thousands of years."

"Well, as you know, Mu, like Atlantis, was destroyed in a cataclysm. But unlike Atlantis, Mu's decline was more gradual. They knew their archipelago was going to go under. It gave them time to organize—to prepare. So their descendants scattered across the globe, setting up different communities."

"Where?"

"All over the place. Easter Island, Japan—where they were called the Ainu by the way—Ecuador of course, India, China."

"I thought it was the Atlanteans who went far and wide."

197

"They did. But whenever you hear about beneficent people coming to the shores to teach people, you are most likely hearing of the Lemurians. The Lemurians and Atlanteans couldn't have been more different. The Atlanteans were a materialistic group, with a strong military and a focus on technology. The Lemurians were pacifists, interested in inner strength and peace, not outer. They had no military, no real police. Atlanteans viewed them as odd, to say the least."

"That's what we figured."

"Unfortunately, their pacifist ways marked them as targets. In most areas they were eventually killed, overrun by the baser elements of human nature."

"Like on Easter Island."

Cain nodded. "Yes."

"So how did the Honu survive?"

"They isolated themselves on islands, surrounded by rock. No one was interested in them there."

Laney frowned. "But they're in Hawaii. It's beautiful. Even the ugly little houses on some of the islands go for a million dollars."

"Yes, but Hawaii is not where they first settled. After they left Mu, they settled across the islands of the Pacific: Pohnpei, the Philippines, Okinawa, Easter Island, Australia."

"How did they end up at Hawaii?"

"They were forced there from different lands. Remember, they were pacifists; they wouldn't raise a hand to protect themselves. They were an easy mark." He shrugged. "But when they were pushed from their homeland, they learned their lesson. And one of their tenets fell by the wayside."

"Which tenet?"

"Pacifism. They learned to defend themselves."

"So... they're dangerous?"

"I wouldn't call them dangerous, exactly. My sources say violence is only used in defense, and even then extremely rarely. But you would be wise to be careful. From what I have

198

heard, the current priestess is somewhat different from her forbears."

"How?"

"I can't say. I only know that she is not quite what she seems. Be careful, Laney."

Laney looked up into Cain's dark eyes. She saw concern there. But was it real? And why would he be concerned for her?

But she didn't say any of that. Instead, she nodded. "I will."

They lapsed into silence, each alone with their own thoughts while they ate. Laney finally spoke. "If this former pacifist group is committing these murders, what's the end goal? Is it revenge?"

Cain shook his head and wiped his hands on a napkin. "No. In fact, from their perspective, they are engaging in these egregious acts for the most noble of reasons."

Laney pictured the crime scenes she had been wading through since they all began. "There's nothing noble in this."

"Well, I suppose in this case, nobility is in the eye of the beholder."

"Okay. If not revenge, then why are they doing this?"

He paused. "To save the world."

"By sacrificing people?"

Cain nodded. "Yes."

Laney shook her head. "Any idea why they would start accelerating the murders? They've broken the two-week pattern."

Cain's hand stilled. Laney would have missed it if she hadn't been watching. "Hm."

"What do you mean, 'hm'?"

"Well, as I said, they think they're saving the world."

Laney didn't understand. "What does that have to do with them speeding up?"

"I'm guessing they think they need to save it faster."

CHAPTER 48

Taipei, Taiwan

Anger rolled through Maura as she read over her words. How could they not see what they were doing? Was it not obvious to all of them yet?

And yet, she knew it wasn't. But each time she wrote, she grew more and more angry at their refusal to see what was coming. Had they learned nothing from the past?

The world is reaching ever faster toward a doom that we have created. There is still time to act, but it must come soon. A recent report by Loyola Marymount University and the Massachusetts Institute of Technology has found that large portions of the Persian Gulf will be completely uninhabitable by 2100. And this time it is not the encroaching sea that is to blame, but the heat itself.

The critical metric in the study is the wet bulb temperature. The wet bulb addresses how much water is in the hot air. Less humid areas allow human bodies to sweat and receive relief from the heat through that process. As humidity increases, that relief decreases. Therefore, the drier the air, the easier it is for humans to cool down. Currently, in areas around the Persian Gulf, the wet bulb temperature only reaches 88 degrees Fahrenheit on the hottest of days and never reaches 95 degrees, which would be lethal for humans.

By 2100, that will not be the case. On an average day, the temperature will break through the lethal threshold on a

200

daily basis. Humans will not be able to survive living there at that time. Other locations will see an increase in heat as well, but without the increase in humidity, those locations will be survivable, if not comfortable. For example, Kuwait City is expected to reach temperatures of 140 degrees, but it will still be livable, because the air will remain sufficiently dry.

Regardless, the ever-increasing temperature of our planet is a recipe for disaster. We need to make changes, and we need to make them now—before it is too late.

Maura hit publish after one last read-through. It was already too late for them; Maura knew that. But she would do what she could to give humanity a fighting chance.

Even if they didn't deserve it.

CHAPTER 49

Malama Island, Hawaii

Aaliyah walked through the garden tucked behind the temple. Red gingers, purple anthuriums, yellow hibiscuses, pink oleanders, white Tahitian gardenias, and dozens of other flowers bloomed around her. It was beautiful, and it usually brought her peace, but she couldn't get the priestess and Vanessa's conversation out of her mind.

Murder? It must be a mistake. Our people could never do something like that, even those who were exiled. To kill in cold blood? She shook her head. No. It just wasn't possible.

The gong rang out three times. Aaliyah went still, her breath catching. A banishment—the second one this month. *What is happening?* Aaliyah hustled down the garden path around the temple and toward the square.

Vanessa stood on the platform usually reserved for whoever led the meditation. Her dark eyes scanned the crowd impatiently. Over two hundred people had gathered. A low murmur rang throughout the open space.

"Attention," Vanessa called. The crowd quieted at once. "Maia and her infant daughter have been banished as of this morning."

Aaliyah gasped. Maia was only twenty years old. She had given birth just three months ago, and they'd had the naming ceremony for the child three days ago. Aaliyah knew Maia was having difficulty accepting the idea that someone else would raise her child; Aaliyah had even interceded with the Guard to allow her extra time. She had been hoping perhaps she could convince the priestess to make an exception in her case.

Around her, the crowd began to murmur loudly. A yell sounded to her right. A young man pushed through the crowd. "Where are they?" he yelled. It was Hanale, the father of the exiled child.

Oh, no. Aaliyah moved quickly to Hanale's side.

Vanessa looked down at Hanale with a small smile. "That information will not be released. They will be well provided for. That is all." Then she turned her back on the crowd and walked off.

Hanale started to follow, but Aaliyah grabbed his arm. "No. It will be worse for you, and them, if you cause trouble."

Hanale looked up at her, his eyes wild. "I didn't know. I would have gone with them. How can they have sent them away?"

Aaliyah noted two members of the Guard paying a little too much attention to them. She turned Hanale away and ushered him onto the path. "Do not do anything foolish. If you are exiled, it will not be to the same place."

Hanale clutched her hand. "I have to find them."

Aaliyah nodded, knowing he wouldn't rest until he did. Hanale and Maia had been inseparable since they were young. No one was surprised when they declared for each other. "Leave it to me."

Hope filled his face. "You can find them?"

She nodded. "But you must not cause any trouble. Let me find them first. Then we can decide what to do."

"But—"

She squeezed his hand. "You must think of them first. Any time you think of saying or doing something that will draw attention to you, remember that it increases your chances of never seeing them again. I know you want to do something, but for right now, the best thing you can do for them is nothing."

He looked away, a tremor in his chin. "Okay. But you will find them soon?"

"It is my only priority."

"Thank you, Aaliyah."

She watched as he walked off, his shoulders low, his walk slow. How had they come to this? This was not what Honu Keiki was supposed to be.

"Aaliyah?" a tear-filled voice called.

Aaliyah turned to see Noriko hurrying down the path, tears dripping down her cheeks. Aaliyah opened her arms and Noriko burrowed into them. Maia had been one of Noriko's closest friends.

"How can they do this?" Noriko cried.

Aaliyah turned Noriko toward their home. "You need to calm down. People are watching."

Noriko wiped her cheeks and ducked her head as they walked. A few minutes later, Aaliyah opened the door to their home and nudged Noriko inside. Noriko took a trembling breath. "It's not right. Maia only wanted to be with her child. How can that be wrong?"

Aaliyah sighed, placing her arm around Noriko's shoulders and leading her over to their couch. "It is not our way."

"But separating a mother from her child, separating Maia from her people, how is that right?"

"It's not. But you must keep these views to yourself, and you must hide your feelings even more. They are too close to the surface and will only cause you problems."

"I know... but it is hard. How can we sit back and let them be alone?"

"They won't be alone," Aaliyah said quietly.

"What do you mean?"

"There are resources at play outside that will protect them, that will help them."

204

"You're sure?"

"Yes. But that doesn't change the need for you to be careful." Aaliyah bit her lip. "I cannot lose you."

"I'm sorry."

"I know. You have a good heart. Never lose that."

Noriko leaned into Aaliyah. "Why does it have to be this way? This can't be the way it's supposed to be."

"It's not. Originally children were raised by the whole village. All took part in a child's upbringing as an aid to the parents, and to make sure the child felt welcomed and loved. That is where the tradition comes from. But it was never meant to pull families apart."

Noriko smiled. "The original children."

Aaliyah nodded. "Yes. They were pure. They were enlightened. They were good. They were our ancestors. We have fallen from their straight path."

"Can we get back on that path?"

"Of course. All it takes is a few brave souls to do the right thing. And then we will be the true children." Aaliyah knew the words weren't just for Noriko. She needed the reminder herself.

Noriko nodded. But Aaliyah still saw tears in her eyes. She pulled her in for another hug. She would find out where Maia had been sent, and she would learn more about the murders. Because as much as it pained her to admit it, Honu Keiki was changing, morphing into a place she didn't recognize.

And it's my duty to help get it back.

CHAPTER 50

The last time she flew home from seeing Cain, Laney had been too overwhelmed to do anything more than stare out the window. This time, she didn't have that luxury.

She looked over her notes on the Children of the Law of One. She'd researched them before of course, but this time she was looking for a link with the Mu. According to the book of Enoch, the world had split into two groups: the Children of the Law of One and the Sons of Belial. The Children were interested in protecting this world, enriching the soul, and in general being good people. The Sons, on the other hand, were motivated by greed, selfishness, and power. They were violent and aggressive, while the Children sometimes wouldn't even raise a hand to protect themselves. According to the War Scroll, the Children and the Sons would come to a final battle at the end of days. And from reading between the lines, Laney got the impression the Lemurians were the Children of the Law of One.

Of course, she couldn't help but wonder how this could possibly be relevant. They were talking thousands and thousand of years ago. It couldn't extend into modern day.

Then again, the Council existed until the modern day. The Council was a high-powered group that was searching for the remnants of Atlantis. Using haplotypes to determine their claims to being Atlanteans, they had amassed a fortune over the centuries. But even the Council hadn't existed as a single group since the time of Atlantis, like the Honu Keiki allegedly did.

When they landed, Laney quickly ducked under the chopper blades and hopped into the golf cart Jen had driven to meet her.

"Okay, so what's up?" Jen said as soon as the noise from the chopper died away.

"Cain still thinks the Children of the Law of One are behind the murders."

Jen stared at her.

"There's no punch line, if you're waiting," Laney said.

Jen shook her head. "I just don't get that. Aren't they supposed to be the good guys?"

Laney nodded as they headed to the main house. "Yup."

"Did he tell you anything helpful?"

"He said they came from different islands in the Pacific: the Philippines, Okinawa, Pohnpei—"

"Pohnpei? Really?"

Laney looked at her in surprise. There were over two hundred fifty islands in the Pacific; she wouldn't have expected Jen to know them all. "You've *heard* of it?"

Jen nodded. "And so have you. Its nickname is the Venice of the Pacific."

Laney stopped short. "It's where Nan Madol is."

Nan Madol was a mysterious ruin that had been built on a coral reef. No one knew exactly who had created it, but experts agreed it was an incredible undertaking. As far as they could tell, Nan Madol was the earliest artificial island ever created.

Jen nodded. "Yup—the island of Pohnpei is part of the United Federation of Micronesia. Nan Madol can be found on the eastern shore of Pohnpei. Its ninety-two islands created on top of a coral reef. All the buildings were made out of basalt logs, and each weighs somewhere between five and forty tons."

Laney knew the logs had been placed on each other like Lincoln logs, with no ornamentation, but no one knew what the purpose of the ruins was. "And there are canals that were created to connect the buildings, and even underwater tunnels, right?"

Jen nodded. "The whole thing was encircled by a rock wall, over three thousand feet long. The site measures out at one and a half square miles. Some of the walls are twelve feet deep."

"Deep, not high?"

"Deep," Jen said. "The site is beginning to be swallowed by the land, but it's believed that the walls once towered forty feet high."

"And let me guess, the structure is beyond the capability of the island's inhabitants."

"That's right. Some of the bases of the stone platform are buried in in the ground. There's one stone platform that has a sixty-ton log balancing on it. By modern estimates, the entire structure would have required between twenty and fifty thousand workers to construct. The island could never have supported that type of a work force. I mean, today it only has about thirty-five thousand people living there. And the current population makes no claim to its creation anyway."

"When was it created?"

"Again, no one is sure, but going by the canals, which are at different heights, they believe it was around the beginning of the last ice age and has been built on since then."

Laney had been expecting that answer. Honestly, if anyone had told her that one of the sites related to some horrific threat was built within the last two hundred years, she'd be shocked.

But an artificial island created in antiquity? She didn't think that was possible. Artificial islands had been created in the modern day, but they were huge undertakings. China had created some artificial islands in the China Sea to extend its borders. They weren't yet recognized by the United States as being Chinese territory, and they had led to some tense international incidents in recent years.

But islands had also been created for less ominous reasons, like the ones created by Dubai to replicate the world map. These private islands were intended as a getaway for the rich and famous. Unfortunately, they had already begun to sink back into the sea.

Yet this ancient man-made island was only just now beginning to be reclaimed by the jungle.

"So how was it created?" Laney asked.

"According to legend, two brothers named Olishipa and Olsohpa created the site by levitating the logs in the air. They then placed them with the aid of a flying dragon. The brothers came from an advanced Pacific kingdom called Kanamwayso, which dropped into the ocean as a result of falling stars and earthquakes. Olsohpa was the origin of the Saudelers' dynasty, which ruled the island until the arrival of modern Pohnpeians. Apparently, the Saudelers were easy to defeat, as they had no military, nor any interest in military affairs."

Like the Lemurian pacifists, Laney thought.

"And Japanese archaeologists even found some ancient bones at Nan Madol which indicate that this former civilization was much taller and more robust than the current Pohnpeians."

"Why create an artificial island though?" Laney asked. "Especially there."

Jen shrugged. "No one knows. It's in the middle of nowhere. It's not even close to sea lanes or trading routes. It's way off the beaten track."

Laney pictured a lonely island in the middle of the Pacific. There must have been a reason to build the structure there, but what?

"So," Jen said, "is that it? Did Cain tell you anything we can use?"

"I think he knows more, but he's worried that as soon as he tells us everything we know, he'll be tossed back in a windowless cell. And Matt... well, Matt hasn't exactly been treating him well."

Jen studied her. "Are you feeling *bad* for him?"

"I'm feeling..." Laney frowned, not sure what to say, "confused. I thought I knew what I thought about Cain, but I don't. Like everything else since Victoria, it's changed."

"I don't get it. Why is Cain helping us? I thought he only did things that benefited him."

"He does. And I think us finding them *does* benefit him. I think he wants us to know what's going on; he wants us to stop it. There was something I saw in his eyes..."

"What?"

Laney paused, picturing the ancient man. "Fear."

CHAPTER 51

Aaliyah slipped into the communications room. Outside she could hear Kai regaling the technician with tales of his last fishing trip. She hurried over to the computer and scanned the screen. She was relieved to find that the technician hadn't initiated any security protocols when he'd stepped out of the room. *Thank goodness we're all so honest,* she thought wryly.

She quickly found the log for the video call and inserted her flash drive. As the file began to copy, she opened a screen for the exiles.

"Where are you?" she muttered. The files had no identifiable names, so she sorted them by date and opened the most recent. *Yes.* Maia Terranova and her daughter, Kaylee, had been dropped ashore in Okinawa.

She shut down the data box and watched the progress bar as the file copied over, willing it to move faster. Her eyes constantly strayed to the door; if anyone found her, she would have no defense for being here. She would be exiled immediately, probably by the guards who found her. She wouldn't even be offered a chance to say goodbye.

The progress bar finally reached 100 percent. She ejected the drive and slipped it into her pocket. Then she peeked out the door.

For only a second, Kai caught her eye. The technician's back was still to her. She slipped out the door, dashed over the porch railing, and disappeared around the side of the building before he could turn. Stepping onto the path, she struggled to put a serene expression on her face despite her pounding heart. She nodded to a man and woman who walked toward her.

Once they had passed, she quickened her steps. She made it back to her home without seeing anyone else.

"Noriko?" she called as she stepped inside. But only silence greeted her.

She made her way into her bedroom, where she closed the door behind her and pulled the shutters closed. Counting the floorboards, she pulled up the eighth one from the wall and pulled out a laptop wrapped in plastic.

Computers were used on Malama, but their use was strictly controlled. No inhabitants were allowed a personal computer in their home. But Kai and Aaliyah had realized how important it would be to have one—especially with the priestess's increasingly rigid rules—so a year ago, Kai had smuggled in laptops for them both.

As she booted it up, Aaliyah said a small thanks that it still had power. She inserted the flash drive and brought up the video call.

The screen showed a man with dark hair and violet eyes. Next to him sat a beautiful auburn-haired woman. She could tell the pair were close, but she did not think they were husband and wife.

She listened to the conversation, and her heart almost stopped at the description of the murders. Not because they sounded brutal, but because they sounded familiar.

No. It couldn't be. She put a hand over her mouth. *They couldn't be bringing back the old ritual, could they?*

And this was happening outside their land. Was it connected? But how? The exiles? Who else would know the details?

A chill fell over her. Vanessa should have recognized the description of the murders. The priestess would have

212

undeniably recognized it. Why had she denied them help? Aaliyah knew the priestess had made them even more isolated than they had been in the past, but the Honu Keiki could investigate it on their own. What was going on?

Her eyes strayed back to the couple on the screen. Why were these two looking into it? They weren't law enforcement or the government. Even Aaliyah had heard of the Chandler Group. What was their interest?

She reached up to turn off the computer when her hand stilled and she squinted at the screen. There was something familiar about the necklace the woman wore.

Aaliyah zoomed in on the charm on the chain. As she brought it into clearer resolution, a gasp escaped her lips. It was a ring, made from a dark metal. On its square face were two entwined triangles, and a small gem winked at each corner.

She stared in disbelief, then zoomed back out to get a better look at the woman's face. For a moment, all thoughts left her as she stared at the woman's deep green eyes. Then reality slammed back into her.

By the Holy Mother, she's the ring bearer.

CHAPTER 52

Laney and Jake pulled up to the Alexandria bookstore owned by Abe Hanley, former resident of Honu Keiki. The large picture window held an antique chair in red velvet beside a little table. A Tiffany lamp gave off a soft yellow glow, with a wall of bookshelves behind it. The words "Antique and Rare Books Bought and Sold" were printed across the glass in yellow outlined in red.

The whole scene invited you in to read. It exuded a feeling of age, as if the store had been there forever, when in fact it had opened only fifteen years ago. Before that, it had been a cafe.

And it was a great location, right in the middle of King Street, with its red brick sidewalks and cobblestone streets filled with foot traffic.

"I like it," Laney said.

Jake smiled. "I'm not surprised."

Laney smiled back, her heart giving a little leap. That smile was the old Jake.

"Shall we?" he said.

"Yes." She opened the car door and climbed out. Together they crossed the street, dodging through cars. On the opposite sidewalk, a steady line of pedestrians passed, some with briefcases, some shopping bags, some strollers or a combination of all.

Laney paused next to the store.

"Anything?" Jake asked.

"No spider tingles. How about you?"

Jake stepped next to her to whisper in her ear, looking to the world like an attentive partner. "There's a camera above the door that covers the sidewalk, and two more on the light poles, covering the street."

"Private cameras?"

"Nope. Those are government-issue police cameras."

Laney laced her hands on his waist with a smile. "Then I suppose we should smile."

"Oh, we can do better than that." He leaned down and kissed her.

Laney's heart pounded and ached at the same time. She'd missed this. Missed him. But she shoved her feelings aside. *Focus on the mission.* "Well, let's go chat with Mr. Hanley."

Hand in hand, they walked to the store. A bell above the door jingled as Jake pushed it open. Inside, bookshelves lined the walls, and more shelves created narrow aisles. A small couch with two chairs flanked a fireplace on the right. The light was dim, but there was enough light to read the titles, and brighter lights were available near the comfortable chairs strewn through the store. A sign indicated that there were more books both downstairs and upstairs.

Laney itched to wander the aisles and see what she could find. But the job came first.

They made their way toward the back. A woman with salt and pepper hair sat at an ancient scarred wooden desk, her hand resting on her chin. A pair of glasses was perched on the end of her pointed nose, and her blue-gray eyes were firmly fixed on the book in front of her. She didn't look up as they approached.

"Excuse me?" Jake said.

The woman didn't move.

He tried again. "Ma'am?"

Still nothing. He stepped to the side and put a hand on the desk.

The woman gasped and leaned back in her chair, her hand on her heart. That's when Laney noticed the earbuds and the wire connected to an iPod.

The woman quickly pulled out the buds. "Oh, I'm so sorry. We were quiet, so I thought I'd get some reading in." Laney could hear the strains of Beethoven coming from the earbuds. "I'm re-reading *Pride and Prejudice*. Listening to music makes it seem like it has a soundtrack." The woman hastily pushed the book aside. "How can I help you?"

Laney smiled in spite of herself. She completely understood getting lost in a book. "We called earlier. I'm Dr. Delaney McPhearson. This is Jake Rogan. We're with the Chandler Group."

"Oh, of course. Abe said you'd be coming by. He just got back about an hour ago. I'll take you to him." She pushed away from the desk and grabbed a cane. She waved them toward the back.

Laney fell in step behind her. Jake followed. They had to proceed between the shelves in single file.

"Have you worked here long?" Laney asked.

"Fifteen years."

"Oh, since it opened."

The woman nodded. "I actually sold the place to Mr. Hanley five years ago. The day-to-day grind of it had gotten to me. I was gone for a month. But I missed it. I asked him if I could come back to work. Now I'm still surrounded by books, but I don't have the headache of billings and acquisitions to deal with."

"That sounds like heaven," Laney said.

The woman stopped at the bottom of a set of stairs, a smile on her face. "I agree. Just follow these stairs to the top. There's only one door."

"Thank you," Jake said.

"Enjoy your book," Laney said.

216

"Oh, I intend to," the woman replied before taking off back down the narrow aisle.

Laney followed Jake up the stairs wondering what her own retirement would look like. *Can I retire?* she wondered. Was there some sort of cutoff point for the ring bearer, or was it a lifetime appointment? She had the sinking feeling it was the latter.

But she had no time to dwell on that as Jake stepped onto the landing at the top of the stairs. "Ready?"

Laney nodded.

Jake knocked on the door.

"Come in," a deep male voice called.

Jake opened the door. Abe Hanley stood up from his desk. "Are you the people from Chandler?"

Jake nodded and made the introductions. Abe walked around the desk with his hand extended. "It's a pleasure to meet you. I'm Abe Hanley."

Laney had to admit, he was not what she'd been expecting. In his DMV photo and the bookstore's website, he'd been slim, muscular, with dark hair. That hair was now liberally sprayed with gray, and his face was almost puffy with the extra weight he'd put on. His glasses were pressed tightly into the sides of his head as if he needed a larger size. He looked harmless. Laney began to have doubts about how much help he could possibly be.

Abe ushered them over to the couch. "Can I get either of you anything? Coffee? Tea?"

"No, we're fine," Laney said, sitting next to Jake on the couch. Abe took a seat across from them, a small coffee table between them.

"Now, I'm familiar with the Chandler Group, but I must admit I'm confused as to what help I could offer. Unless, of course, you're looking for a book?" Abe asked hopefully.

"No, not a book," Laney said. "We actually wanted to speak with you about your time with the Honu Keiki."

217

"Oh." Abe sat back, a slight shake in his hand. "I—It's been so long."

"Maybe we could just start with some background," Jake began.

Abe shook his head. "I really don't want to turn you away, but I don't like talking about that particular topic."

"We understand, but it's very important. Life and death important."

Abe studied them for a minute before sighing. "All right. What do you want to know?"

"Why don't we start with how you became affiliated with the group?" Laney asked.

"Well, that's easy. I was born a member. My parents both were—are—members."

"How did you come to leave?" Jake asked.

He gave a small, bitter laugh. "Sorry. It's just, that phrasing makes it sound like it was my decision. As if it wasn't the Naacal that had me exiled."

Laney frowned. "The Naacal?"

"They're a council of priests who advise the priestess," Abe said.

Laney opened her mouth to ask a question, but Jake gave a shake of his head. She closed her mouth and waited for Abe to wade through his memories.

His voice took on a wistful quality. "It really was paradise. It was beautiful—big palm trees, bright colorful flowers everywhere, a lagoon to swim in. My childhood was pure joy. The goal is to encourage the individual to be who they are and to respect one another. There was no competition, no pressure to be something you weren't. The only rules as far as I could tell were that you had to be kind to one another. Can you imagine?"

It did sound like paradise. Today, kids in the US seemed to have a ridiculous amount of pressure placed on them from childhood. Kids were supposed to excel in school, sports, extra-curricular. Everyone was supposed to be a stand out in all

218

areas. But how could anyone stand out when everyone excelled? And what happened when you didn't? Even at the Chandler School, Laney had seen students stressing about their futures, their clothes, their weight, and a dozen other issues. And that was before you added in all the social media influences. It was heartbreaking.

"What changed?" Jake asked.

"Well, as I got older, my rose-colored glasses lost their tint. I saw that it was not as perfect as I had imagined, although it was close. The Naacal, the priestess—it all became much stricter, much harsher. I didn't understand why. And then, suddenly, that harshness was aimed at me."

"What happened?" Laney asked.

Abe sighed. He pulled off his glasses, cleaned them on his shirt, then placed them back on again. "Some friends of mine were exiled. I thought the punishment was too harsh. I spoke my mind. And the next thing I knew, I was on a boat myself."

"Did you meet up with your other friends once you were removed?" Laney asked.

Abe shook his head. "I didn't know where they had gone. Exiles are dropped at different locations. And on the island we only use first names. I was given identification when I left, along with the name Hanley. I don't know what names they were given, or even what country they were dropped in."

"That sounds horrible," Laney said.

"It was. But they gave me enough money to start over, to get set up. I enrolled at UCLA and got a degree in literature. With the money, I bought this place when Karen went to sell. It's been a good life, but…" He shrugged.

"But not *as* good," Laney finished for him.

Abe nodded.

"Have you found any other exiles since you left?" Jake asked.

Abe shook his head. "I looked for the first few years, but it was like trying to find a needle in a haystack. Finally, I stopped looking. I realized I needed to look forward, not back. Now I travel the world in search of books and I have a small circle of friends. It's a good life. I'm content."

His words sounded good, but Laney didn't think he was telling the truth. She just wasn't sure if he was lying to them or to himself.

"We have reason to believe that some exiles may be involved in some rather violent killings. Have you heard anything about that?" Jake asked.

Abe's eyes grew large. "Killings? That's not possible. It's against everything we stand for."

"We think the killings might be linked to a purification ritual," Laney said.

"I don't see how," Abe said. "I mean, yes, we did purification rituals. But no one is ever harmed. In fact, it's for the good of the individual that the ritual is performed. Through it, an individual's sins are cleansed. They rejoin the group as if the sins had never occurred. I don't see how death could be part of that ritual. There must be some mistake."

"We've found evidence that ties members of the Honu Keiki group to the crimes."

Abe shook his head. "No. Obviously you don't know our history—"

"You mean the Children of the Law of One?" Jake asked.

Abe looked surprised but relieved. "Yes, exactly. We don't believe in violence. It's just not what we do."

"And you're sure you've never run into any exiles since you left?" Jake asked.

"Unfortunately, no."

Laney glanced at Jake, who shook his head. She stood. "Thank you for your time, Mr. Hanley."

Jake extended a business card. "If you can think of anything else, please give us a call."

"Of course. I'll call you immediately," Abe said, slipping the card into the breast pocket of his shirt.

220

A few minutes later, Laney and Jake were back in the car. Laney pulled on her seat belt as Jake started the car. A light drizzle had begun while they were inside with Abe.

Laney turned to Jake. "What do you think?"

"I think he's hiding something."

Laney was surprised. "Really?"

Jake nodded. "He wasn't as surprised at the murders as he should have been. Hold on a sec." Jake pulled out his phone and dialed. "Hey, Frank." Laney knew Frank was Frank Culkin, a member of Jake's research team. "Can you check Hanley's phone records? See if he makes any phone calls?" He paused. "Okay, thanks."

"I thought he was sincere," Laney said.

Jake smiled. "That's because you always believe the best in people. I tend to take a more cynical approach."

Laney sighed. "He did seem heartbroken about leaving."

"That I agree with. I just don't agree that he hasn't been in contact with any exiles."

"Do you think he has anything to do with these murders?"

"I don't know, but part of me hopes he does, because if he doesn't, I don't know where we go from here."

CHAPTER 53

Malama Island, Hawaii

Noriko smiled as she helped five-year-old Skye place her painting on the shelf.

Skye looked up at her with big eyes. "I can bring it home tomorrow?"

Noriko ran a hand through Skye's hair. "Yes. It will be dry by then."

Skye looked past Noriko and let out a squeal. She ran for Jamal, who had just appeared at the school door. "Jamal!" she cried happily. Jamal picked her up and swung her around.

All Noriko could think was that Hanale would never have the opportunity to do the same with his daughter. But she shoved those feelings down. "She did great today," she said.

"Of course she did." Jamal smiled, holding Skye in his arms. The little girl wrapped her arms around his neck, a giant smile on her face. "Thank you," Jamal said to Noriko.

Noriko held the door open. "You're welcome."

"Bye, Noriko!" Skye called as they headed down the path, waving furiously.

Jamal had to duck to avoid getting hit by an elbow. He lowered Skye to the ground and took her hand. Skye skipped happily next to him.

Noriko watched the two walk hand in hand down the path. She knew that, more often than not, families like Skye's worked. In fact, Noriko wouldn't change her upbringing for anything in the world. But she still couldn't understand why those who wanted to stay with their own child were prevented from doing so. It hadn't always been that way; the priestess had initiated the change only eleven years ago. Before that, it had been the mother's choice.

Noriko felt the weight of the unfairness pressing down on her as she tidied up the classroom. She had just closed the supply cabinet door when she felt dizzy. She reached out a hand to the wall to steady herself.

A vision of a man popped into her mind. He was of average height, with light brown hair and a pear shape. He was walking down a busy street in some city Noriko had never seen. He turned into a parking lot. A man in black slipped out of a car behind him and aimed a weapon.

Noriko gasped, wanting to call out to the man. But there was nothing she could do. Two prongs shot out of the weapon and attached themselves to the brown-haired man. He began to shake, then collapsed to the ground.

The vision shifted. The man was now lying on a stone slab. His eyes were closed. Unmoving. His clothes were soaked and his chest didn't rise. A different man stepped up from behind, a knife in his hand. He raised the knife high... and plunged it into the man's chest.

Noriko screamed and fell to the ground.

The vision disappeared. Once again she was alone in the classroom, crouched on the floor. Her breaths came out in pants. She stayed there for a few minutes until she was sure her shaking legs would not fail her.

She quickly finished tidying up the school, then slipped out the back door. She kept her head down as she made her way to her home. She prayed no one stopped her. With relief, she saw her home ahead. She ran up the path and threw open the door. "Aaliyah?"

No answer. *The Naacal meeting. She's at the temple.*

Noriko stepped out onto the lanai. She sat on a chair and pulled her knees up to her chin. She wasn't sure how long

223

she stayed there, the image playing over and over in her mind. The sun had begun to dip to the horizon.

"Noriko?" Aaliyah called from the front room.

Noriko jerked her head up and wiped at the tears on her cheeks. She stumbled from her chair, nearly turning it over, and hurried into the house. "Aaliyah, thank goodness. I need to speak with you."

Aaliyah frowned. "You're upset. What's wrong?"

"Something horrible."

Aaliyah shook her head as Noriko opened her mouth to explain. "You're too worked up. Breathe with me first."

Noriko was anxious to tell Aaliyah everything, but she knew Aaliyah was right. She needed to calm. She nodded and closed her eyes. She focused on her breathing—the breath coming in, the breath going out. With each successive breath, she felt more calm, more centered.

"Open your eyes, Noriko."

Noriko did, feeling calmer than before.

Aaliyah took Noriko's hand and led her over to the table. "Now, tell me what's happened."

Noriko took strength in Aaliyah's unwavering love. "I believe I have the gift of sight."

Aaliyah paused. Then a smile spread across her face. "That's wonderful. And rare. You are blessed."

Noriko nodded, knowing it was true. Only a few dozen people had developed abilities. Seers were held in high regard for their ability to foretell what was coming. But after her vision, she was not feeling particularly lucky. "It doesn't feel like a blessing. It was so violent."

Concern etched Aaliyah's face. "Tell me."

Noriko recounted what she had seen. Aaliyah's facial expression grew more concerned as Noriko spoke. When Noriko was done, she felt better at being able to share the burden, but guilty for the concern she had caused Aaliyah.

Aaliyah took her hand. "It is right you told me."

"But what should I do? I cannot let this poor man die."

224

Aaliyah studied Noriko for a moment, then she stood and pulled the bolt across the door. She walked around and pulled all the shutters closed, and even closed the doors to the balcony. Noriko couldn't remember ever having those doors shut, except during storms.

"Aaliyah?"

Aaliyah held up her hand and resumed her seat. She studied the tabletop for moment without speaking. Then she raised her eyes to Noriko. "You have been a wonderful blessing for me. I have been privileged to help guide you through this life."

"And I have been doubly blessed with you." Noriko meant it. She couldn't imagine having a more loving person in her life.

Aaliyah gave her a smile. "You know that in Honu we are of two minds. Some of us believe the old ways are the best for our people."

Noriko nodded. It was not discussed openly, but she knew that a schism had been growing within the group. Aaliyah believed in the old way: pacifism, respect for the world, and a Naacal that guided the people. But the rules had become so much stricter lately, and banishments had become more commonplace. People were being sent away for even the mildest infractions. It was unsettling.

And then there was the Guard, and the guns they carried. Never before in the history of the Guard had guns been used.

"What you do not know," Aaliyah said, "is that we have learned that some of those who have left us have found one another in the outside world."

Noriko wondered where Aaliyah was going with this and what it had to do with her vision. She spoke slowly. "Well, it is good that they are not alone."

Aaliyah nodded. "It should have been. But I am not sure it is."

225

"I do not understand what this has to do with my vision. I've never seen the man before. He is not from Malama."

"What about the people who hurt him? Have you seen them before?"

"I—they weren't clear. But you can't think—I mean, it was too horrible."

Aaliyah licked her lips. "We have learned that some of those who have left us may have taken it upon themselves to punish the ones they see as being responsible for the downfall of the larger world. I wonder if your vision is part of that."

Noriko rebelled at the thought. "*Our* people are responsible for what I saw?"

Aaliyah's eyes were troubled. "It's possible."

Noriko gaped, trying to imagine how someone could come to that. "There must be something we can do."

Aaliyah nodded. "With your help, there very well may be. Do you know who this person is? The one who is to be harmed?"

Noriko shook her head. "No. But I can draw his likeness. And I know where they will be. I can draw that as well."

"Good. You do that." Aaliyah stood up. "But let's keep this just between us for right now, all right?"

"Why?"

"It's safer that way."

"What are you going to do?"

"Find some allies."

226

CHAPTER 54

Baltimore, Maryland

Laney opened the front door of Henry's house just as he stepped out of his office. "Hey."

"Hey yourself," Henry replied. "How'd it go?"

"I'm not sure," Laney said. She followed Henry to the kitchen. Henry grabbed a plate of muffins from the counter as Laney took a seat at the table. He placed them in front of her. "Hungry?"

Laney reached for one. "Starving." Using a napkin for a plate, she ate while trying to figure out how everything was connected. They knew someone was attacking companions of the Fallen, and someone was attacking the Fallen themselves. Gerard claimed both attacks were by the same group, but they had no proof of that. They had a link to Honu Keiki, but it was tenuous at best, and it didn't look like Honu Keiki was to going to be helping them out. They needed a break—one simple thing that would make at least part of this insanity clear.

"How'd it go with the bookseller?" Henry asked.

Laney shrugged. "He didn't really tell us much. Just painted a fairytale picture of his childhood."

"What's he like?"

Laney paused, picturing the bookseller. "Lonely. I think he really misses the group. He says he has friends and that he's content, but if given the chance I think he'd go back there in a heartbeat. He says he hasn't been in contact with any other exiles. I believed him, but Jake doesn't."

Henry raised an eyebrow. "And how are you and Jake?"

Laney hesitated. "Actually, it was nice. It was, normal, you know?"

Henry smiled. "Good. Where is he, by the way?"

Laney waved back toward the front door. "He got a call as we were walking in."

Just then Laney heard the front door. Jake appeared in the doorway to the kitchen and took a seat next to Laney. "Ah, muffins." He pulled one over and Laney handed him a napkin to use as a plate.

"Thanks," he said with a grin. He took a bite before speaking. "That was Frank who called. Abe didn't make any calls after we left."

Laney felt her shoulders drop. "So we have nothing."

"Not exactly. Because *Karen* made a call right after we left."

Laney looked up in surprise. "Really?"

"Who's Karen?" Henry asked.

"She's the former owner of Hanley's bookstore," Laney said. "She still works there."

"Who'd she call?" Henry asked.

"A couple from Taiwan—Derek and Maura Katz. I have one of the analysts running a background check on them right now." Jake's phone beeped. "And that should be them." He scrolled through the message, then looked up. "Maura and Derek Katz were members of Honu Keiki before being exiled ten years ago."

"Son of a bitch. He lied," Laney said, feeling indignant. "I believed him."

Henry laughed. "After everything, I love that you're still surprised when people are dishonest."

"It's just—I felt bad for the guy." She let out a breath. *Goddamn it.* "So what do we know about them?"

228

Jake scrolled through the information on his phone. "Maura and Derek Katz became residents of Taiwan eight years ago and had one daughter. She was killed in the tsunami in Japan when they were on vacation."

"Oh my God," Laney said. The tsunami that had hit Japan had resulted in nearly twenty thousand deaths. Two hundred and thirty thousand people were still displaced. "That's horrible."

That kind of loss—what did it do to a parent? Laney couldn't imagine it. She was having enough trouble dealing with Max being gone, and he was still alive, just out of reach. The idea of losing him permanently... She sucked in a breath. Even the idea of it was too painful to visit for more than a second or two.

"Well, the good thing is now we have a direction," Jake said.

Henry nodded. "I'll pull a handful of analysts. I'll make sure we find everything there is to know about the Katzes."

Laney only nodded. She was still thinking about what the loss of a child could do to someone. Would it be enough to push them to murder?

Her phone buzzed, and she looked at it with a frown.

"What is it?" Henry asked.

"An email marked urgent—for the ring bearer. But I don't recognize the sender." It was sent from a TOR account, which meant someone wanted to keep their identity under wraps.

Laney immediately dialed one of the people in the IT department. "Hey, Cathy, I just got an email. Can you check and make sure there are no viruses or anything attached?"

"Yup, give me a second," Cathy said.

Laney drummed her fingers on the table while she waited. Finally Cathy got back on the line. "You're clear, Laney. There is an attachment, but there are no viruses attached that I can see."

"Okay, thanks."

Laney hung up. *Well, here goes nothing.* She opened the email.

Dear Ring Bearer,

You do not know me, but I hope you receive this email in the intent with which it was sent—to help. I have attached a picture of a man who I believe will be the next target of the group you are seeking. I could not think of any other way to help him. I hope you can find him in time.

Laney frowned and opened the attachment. It contained photos of several drawings; they appeared to have been done with colored pencil, by someone with a skilled hand.

In the first drawing, a man with brown hair and light green eyes stared back at her. She clicked on the next picture; the same man was walking down a street. The next drawing showed him in a parking lot. In the final shot he was on a stone slab.

She felt her jaw fall open. "You guys need to see this."

"What is it?" Jake asked.

"I think it's a chance."

CHAPTER 55

By what Laney could only describe as a small miracle, they had been able to find the man in the picture. In the first drawing, there was an emblem for a company on his shirt. They were able to trace it back to a plumbing company, Knight Brothers, based outside Charlotte, North Carolina. A quick search of his employer's computer had revealed a name: Brian Hansen, age thirty-eight. Brian was married with one child on the way and had been with Knight Brothers for nearly twenty years.

Laney and Jen had immediately hopped on a plane. Now they sat in a car across from the plumbing headquarters. They had been trailing Brian all day, but all they knew so far was that he was not a Fallen or nephilim, and he really liked donuts.

Jen stretched her back. "You know, there's a reason I never became a cop. Stakeouts are boring."

Laney laughed. "Yes they are."

Brian stepped out of the Knight Brothers offices. He was of medium height and carried a lot of weight around his stomach—no doubt due to his donut habit. The brown coveralls he was wearing did nothing to help his pear shape.

Jen nudged her chin toward him. "Heads up—here comes our friend."

Brian headed down the street to the right. His wife worked at a diner a few blocks in that direction.

"Let's go," Laney said, getting out of the car.

"You go. I'll drive ahead to the parking lot from the drawing."

Laney nodded. They had already scoped out the landmarks they'd seen in the drawings. The parking lot was only three blocks away, right on the way to Brian's wife's diner.

Laney fell in step behind Brian. She had her ring on, but she wasn't sensing anything. She scanned the street, but no one was paying any particular attention to Brian.

When Brian reached the parking lot, he turned in. Laney quickly picked up her pace so as to close the distance between them. She scanned the parking lot, but still didn't see anyone. Where were they?

Just then, Brian stepped past a dark minivan, and a man climbed out behind him. Not a Fallen.

Laney ran up. "Hey."

The man turned. A ski mask hid his face, and a Taser was in his hand. Laney slammed her foot into the man's groin. His knees went weak, and as his hands reached for his groin, the Taser dropped to the ground. She grabbed him by the back of the head and slammed his face into her knee. Then, still holding onto the back of his head, she slammed him into the van and wrenched his arm behind him.

Brian Hanson had turned and watched the whole thing, his jaw hanging open.

"Mr. Hanson, my name is Agent McPhearson," Laney said. "I'm going to need to speak with you."

Brian's head bobbed up and down. "Uh, okay."

Jen came hustling up with another ski-masked man in tow. "You good?"

"I'm good. Let's get these guys—"

A dark-paneled van wheeled into the parking lot and the side door slid open.

232

"Gun!" Jen yelled.

Laney threw her guy to the ground, vaulted over him, and tackled Brian as bullets sprayed the cars around them. Jen leapt on top of the two of them.

The van peeled off, bumping over the curve as it swung wildly into traffic.

Jen rolled to her feet and ran for the street.

Laney pulled on Brian's arm. "Brian? Are you all right? Are you hurt?"

Brian sat up, his cheek scraped, his head swerving from side to side. "Um , I—"

"Are you hurt?" Laney repeated.

"No. Not hurt."

Jen returned and nodded toward the two men on the ground. "I can't say the same for these two."

In a glance, Laney could tell the two attackers were gone. "Did you get any van info?"

Jen shook her head. "No. Sorry."

"Damn it."

"Um… those guys were after you, right?" Brian asked.

Laney helped him up. "No. They were after you."

Brian's mouth fell open. "But—but, I'm nobody."

Jen glanced at the bullet holes in the cars surrounding them. "Apparently somebody disagrees."

CHAPTER 56

Taipei City, Taiwan

Maura put the phone down with a frown. Two people from the Chandler Group had questioned Abe, and not long after, two women from the same group had interrupted their abduction of Hansen.

She made her way to the study, sat at her computer, and ran a few searches, looking for any links to the Chandler Group. A few minutes later she had her answer: Sheila Lachowski. There had been a number of contacts between the group and the family. Sheila had even visited the school a few times.

Derek walked in and kissed her on the forehead. "Everything okay?"

Maura shook her head. "I'm not sure. Two members of the Chandler Group visited Abe, and then they interrupted the Hansen operation. I think they're looking into us."

"They interrupted an operation? When?"

"Just now."

"Why would we be on their radar?"

Maura pointed to the screen. "Sheila Lachowski was connected to them."

Derek frowned. "Is this going to be a problem?"

"I don't know. Can you see what you can find on The Chandler School for Children? I'll look up Delaney

McPhearson and Jake Rogan—they're the two that spoke with Abe. Hopefully they're just fishing."

An hour later, Maura's concern had grown into worry. She looked up from her screen. "You ready to talk?"

Derek nodded, looking a little pale himself. "Yeah."

Maura turned to face him. "Delaney McPhearson, Jake Rogan, and Henry Chandler are tangentially related to a number of high-profile events. And the kids that they saved in the Grand Canyon—something is definitely off there. I think they might be Fallen."

Derek nodded. "I think you're right. The school brochure mentions that the children are 'gifted.'"

Maura's anger began to grow. "They're helping them. They're *teaching* them."

"Maybe they're also Fallen."

Maura simmered. "And now they're on our trail."

"I'm afraid it may be worse than that." Derek flipped his screen around for Maura to see. "I checked the social media sites of a couple of students."

Pictures of teenagers, all smiles, filled the screen. Maura curled her lips. Arrogance—hubris. Not even concerned with the evil they'd brought into the world.

"Look in the background," Derek said. "Here," he pointed, "and here."

Maura stared. "Is that a leopard?"

Derek nodded. "A Javan leopard."

"It looks huge." Maura wondered if that was just trick of the camera angle, because the leopard wasn't the focus of the shots, just caught in the background.

"It *is* huge," Derek said, his voice grim. He pulled up a third shot, and this time he zoomed in on the leopard. A young boy with dark glasses stood next to the giant cat. She was seated, and her head was level was his. "This boy is Danny Wartowski," Derek said. "He's a genius. There've been a number of articles on him. He's the unofficial son of Henry Chandler. But that's unimportant. What *is* important is that because of that publicity we know he's five foot ten. And sitting, this cat is almost his size."

Maura's mouth dropped open. "That's not natural."

"No, it's not."

They had heard rumors that the Fallen had been tampering with nature, twisting it to meet their depraved vision. But to see proof of it—it was chilling. And to use a leopard—the guardians of the Holy Mother. "There is no end to their depravity."

"What should we do?" Derek asked.

Maura stared at the abomination on the screen, then shook herself. "First, tell Abe to go to ground. It's not safe for him."

"I already did."

"Good. We need to learn all we can about the Chandler Group and their involvement with the Fallen," Maura paused, her gaze returning to the nightmare on the screen, "but I also want to know about that cat. Where it came from, what it is, and most importantly, if there are any others."

Derek nodded. "I agree. This type of depravity cannot be allowed to exist."

Maura's gaze flicked back to her own screen—to the picture of McPhearson, Rogan, and Chandler. "No, it can't."

CHAPTER 57

Malama Island, Hawaii

The group meditation finished with the usual words: "Be well. Be peaceful." Aaliyah smiled and nodded to her neighbors, but inside she was strung tight. Working her way through the crowd, many of whom stayed to chat, she found Noriko.

Noriko's pale green eyes caught Aaliyah's gaze across the space. Aaliyah smiled and nodded toward the path that led back to their home. Noriko excused herself and joined Aaliyah on the path, linking her arm through hers. "So, are you ready to tell me what's so important about this meeting?"

Aaliyah looked around, but no one was near enough to overhear them. "Please keep your voice down."

It had been twenty-four hours since Noriko had told Aaliyah about her vision. Aaliyah had contacted the ring bearer with the information; she hadn't been able to think of any other way to help him. But since she'd taken that step, she'd felt like there was a ticking clock over her, counting down the time to a disaster. And she had learned long ago not to ignore such feelings.

In times past, they would have gone to the priestess. But Aaliyah was not sure the current priestess could be trusted to do the right thing. Her heart nearly broke at that thought. Instead, she had called a meeting with her most trusted friends to see if they had any ideas.

Noriko lowered her voice. "Sorry, but I don't understand the secrecy. Does this have to do with my vision?"

Aaliyah sighed. Secrets were not something that happened on Malama. *At least they didn't used to be.* She squeezed Noriko's arm. "Yes—but also something more. You must keep this quiet. Can you do that for me?"

Noriko wrapped her arm around Aaliyah's. "If you think that's best, of course."

Aaliyah once again thanked the Mother for providing her with such an exceptional young woman.

Ahead she saw one lantern lit outside Kai's home. *Good.* That was the signal that everything was all right. "Noriko, there are things you will hear tonight that may shock you. I ask that you trust that I know what I am doing and that I always follows the way of our people."

Noriko narrowed her eyes. "I know that, Aaliyah. But what will shock me?"

Aaliyah opened her mouth to answer, but then closed it as she saw two people enter Kai's home. "You will learn soon enough. Come on."

Aaliyah ushered Noriko inside. Kai's house was similar to Aaliyah and Noriko's, except that the exterior of his was white. Kai had lived on his own since his son, Masu, moved out two years ago. Masu had become a member of the Guard. In fact, it seemed that everyone who was beginning to question the priestess had a member of the family in the Guard or in another position that placed them close to the priestess. Aaliyah didn't think that was a coincidence. And she worried the same fate may be in store for Noriko when her ability became common knowledge.

Inside Kai's small foyer, two women Aaliyah had been friends with since childhood stood talking quietly. Aaliyah nodded to them but didn't stop. She ushered Noriko down the small hallway and into the kitchen, which was open to the family room. A dozen people sat scattered through both rooms, most of them Aaliyah's age.

238

Noriko looked wary, but as her eyes moved from one familiar face to another, her nervousness seemed to reduce.

Aaliyah squeezed her hand and nodded to the couch along the back wall. "Why don't you go take a seat?"

Noriko nodded, but Aaliyah could see some of her nervousness return. She squeezed Noriko's arm. "It will be all right."

Noriko searched her face before giving an abrupt nod and turning for the couch.

Aaliyah moved over to the dark-haired man standing by the doors. "Is everyone here?" she asked.

Kai nodded. "Yes. A few couldn't make it, but I will speak with them personally afterwards."

She lowered her voice. "Did Hanale get away all right?" Kai had smuggled Hanale off the island this morning.

"He was reunited with his family."

Aaliyah smiled. "Okay. I guess then we need to get started."

Kai looked into her eyes. "You've got this."

Looking back at him, Aaliyah could feel his strength and support. And she realized that somewhere in the past few years, while the priestess had been changing things, her own feelings for Kai had changed as well: from friendship to something more. She wasn't sure if they had shifted for him as well, but once all of this calmed down, she planned on finding out.

"We're doing the right thing, aren't we?" Aaliyah asked.

Kai nodded. "You know this is how we are supposed to be. The priestess is our leader, but if she is not holding to the old ways, it is up to *us* to hold to them. The laws of this world don't mean much compared to the laws of our souls."

"You are right. As always."

"And I never get tired of hearing you admit that."

She laughed. "Well, you may have to return for a lifetime or two to reduce your ego."

He smiled, his brown eyes twinkling. "As long as you return with me."

The scrape of a chair reminded Aaliyah that they weren't alone. With an encouraging nod from Kai, she turned to face the group. "Thank you all for coming tonight. A development has occurred that you need to be aware of." She paused. There was no easy way to say this. "We have been contacted about murders that some on the outside believe may have been committed by some of our exiles."

There was a collective gasp in the room, followed by a burst of questions. Aaliyah held up her hand. "I will tell you everything I know, and then we can discuss what should be done."

Aaliyah told them about the phone call and the murders. The crowd looked more horrified the longer she spoke. "Now, I'm sure you are wondering why they contacted us." Aaliyah paused. "I took the liberty of gathering more details on the murders. This may be difficult for you to hear but I think it is important that you know."

Aaliyah searched Noriko's face and noted that it had grown paler. There was nothing she could do about that. Because of Noriko's visions, she had even more need to know about what was going on than anyone else in the room. When the knowledge of her ability became known, she would catch the eye of the priestess. And Aaliyah needed her to be prepared.

"The victims are killed on an altar. They are drained of blood, and their heart is removed, then burned. But their death is the result of water being poured endlessly into their throat."

The room stirred, and Aaliyah could see that more than one person recognized the description.

"It is a return of the old ways," murmured Babette, who was sitting at the table. "The ritual of the moon and the sun."

Aaliyah nodded. "So it would appear."

240

The older members of the group looked concerned, but the younger members just looked confused. "The ritual of the moon and the sun—the end and the beginning—is from our dark times," Aaliyah explained, feeling the weight of the words.

"But that's just a myth," someone called out.

Kai shook his head. "No. When the motherland broke up, some of our people turned to brutal methods to deal with the changes in the earth. It was paganism, it was against God, but they were desperate. They believed that if they offered enough, the earth would calm, and all would be right."

"Our ancestors could almost be forgiven their ignorance," Aaliyah added. "But whoever was behind these new sacrifices is not ignorant."

Seymour, who was sitting next to Noriko, spoke up. "But you do not think... You do not think it is *our* people, do you?"

Aaliyah's gaze swept the room before she nodded. "I believe it may be, yes."

Her answer was like a thunderclap. Everyone began speaking at once.

Aaliyah held up her hand for silence. After a few moments, everyone returned their attention to her. "I cannot say for sure it is our people, but because of the nature of the murders, who else could it be? Who would know of the ritual? We need to be sure."

"But why would they do this?" a voice called out.

Kai nodded at Aaliyah, and she took comfort in his gaze. "We know the first great end came when the world became selfish and cruel," she began. "At that time, a small group of the Children took it upon themselves to wipe out the cruel ones, to try and turn back the tide. I believe the same reasoning is at work now. Some believe that if they can remove the evildoers, the world can be saved."

"But that's crazy," someone said.

Aaliyah gave the group a small smile. "We have been raised on the belief that the Fallen are the source of all evil. And the world is becoming more dangerous."

"But is it the Fallen that are being killed?" Babette asked.

Aaliyah shook her head. "No. It is their associates, their intimates."

"But then it is not like the olden times. It is different."

Aaliyah paused again, knowing that everyone in the room wanted her to be wrong. Aaliyah wanted to be wrong herself. But she knew she wasn't. "I do not think so."

"But why?" Babette asked.

Aaliyah exchanged a glanced with Kai. He gave her a nod. "It was the ring bearer who was asking about the murders," Aaliyah said.

A gasp went across the room. But Noriko only looked confused, as did a few of the other younger members.

Aaliyah spoke quietly. "The ring bearer is the one individual given the power to fight back the Fallen. When she is called, it means the world has reached a critical point. And she *is* involved, which means we *are* at that point. We need to act."

"But the ring bearer is even more than that," Kai said. "She is the guardian of the Great Mother. She is her agent here on earth. If this woman is indeed the ring bearer, then it is our duty to help her."

Aaliyah looked across the faces in front of her. The older members looked shocked. They had been raised on the stories of the Great Mother and her agent of good. But none had believed she'd appear during their lifetimes.

The younger members just looked confused. When the priestess was appointed fourteen years ago, she had decided that the ring bearer should not be emphasized as much in the children's teaching. She said the violence of her role would be disconcerting for the children. Aaliyah had thought the decision unwise, but she could not fault the priestess's logic. The tales

242

of the ring bearer's deeds were indeed bloody. But now, Aaliyah wondered if there might have been another reason for the priestess's suggestion.

"What about the high priestess? What does she think?" someone asked.

Aaliyah swallowed, knowing her next words could mean her exile or worse. "The priestess does not recognize the signs. It is up to us."

A man stepped into the room from the hallway. He must have arrived late. Aaliyah's heart clenched. *Enzo.*

Enzo's gaze scanned the room before settling on Aaliyah. "We are the descendants of the first people—the keepers of the old ways, of the true way. But the true way does not involve violence in any form. If others engage in violence, we should let them. It is no stain on us to allow others to make their own choices."

Kai spoke quietly. "Perhaps we are wrong in that. Allowing others to do harm when there is a chance to do good—where is the rightness in that? Is that who we truly are? People who turn a blind eye?"

Enzo shook his head. "The outside world has set themselves up for this fall. The priestess tells us of how they have destroyed this world. How they continue to do so to line their own pockets."

Aaliyah knew she was on shaky ground here. One wrong word and this house of cards would tumble. "The priestess is right. There *are* those who line their pockets. But there are also those who struggle to do the right thing—who *fight* to do the right thing." She paused. "And one of those people is the ring bearer."

"The ring bearer has contacted *us* about these murders," Kai stressed. "She is asking for our help."

"And what has the priestess said?" Enzo demanded.

"She has turned them down," Aaliyah said.

"Why?" Enzo asked.

243

"Why does not matter. We must do the right thing here. We must help—"

"Does she know it is the ring bearer who has asked?" Enzo demanded.

Aaliyah hesitated. "I do not know."

Enzo straightened his shoulders with a smile. "Well, then that is the answer. We will inform the priestess that it is the ring bearer asking for our help, and she will do the right thing."

"I am not sure—"

Enzo's gaze locked on her. "Are you suggesting we engage in an action without the blessing of the priestess?"

Aaliyah stared back at him, fear for all those in this room snapping at her heels. If someone was to be held responsible, she would make sure it was her and her alone. "Of course not, brother Enzo. You are right to point out this course of action."

He smiled. "I will speak with her myself."

Aaliyah agreed with a nod of her head. "Thank you." *Oh, God help us all.*

CHAPTER 58

Baltimore, Maryland

A hand touched Laney's shoulder. "Laney," Henry said softly.

Laney's head jolted upright and she blinked rapidly. "What?"

"Sorry," Jen said, placing a cup of coffee on the table in front of her. "Have you been here all night?"

Laney wiped her eyes. "Yeah."

Yesterday, she and Jen had gotten Brian squared away with some SIA agents who took him and his wife into protective custody. While Laney was glad she had saved Brian, she would have been happier if she could find something that linked him to the Katzes—or to anyone else. Laney had shown Brian pictures of the Katzes and Abe Hanley, but he didn't recognize them. Neither Brian nor his wife had any idea about any Fallen or nephilim that they had come in contact with. And as for the two attackers who had been killed, they weren't in the system, which meant it was going to take a little longer to learn their identities.

Laney and Jen had made their way back to Baltimore, and after a quick bite to eat, Laney had sat down in Henry's office to find something, anything that could link the Katzes to the murders. She had come up with nothing, and she had fallen asleep at Henry's conference table.

Laney pulled the coffee mug toward her. "You are a goddess."

"I do try," Jen said. "So what did you find out about the Katzes?"

"Believe it or not, they're bloggers," Laney said.

"Really?" Henry said, taking a seat next to her.

Laney nodded. "They have an environmental blog. It's pretty doom and gloom."

"Like what?" Jen asked, sitting on the arm of Henry's chair.

"Hold on a sec." Laney brought up the Katzes' website and clicked on a post that had caught her attention earlier. "This entry is about the two-degree benchmark that the international community has agreed on for avoiding horrific climate change."

Henry and Jen leaned forward to read.

Two degrees is all that stands between us and dangerous human interference in the climate that will be the point of no return. In the last one hundred years, we have raised the climate by .75 degrees. And each year, we pour more dangerous gases into the air, speeding up that process. Without immediate changes to how we live, we will doom parts of the planet.

"That's a little strong," Henry said, sitting back.

"Maybe," Jen said. "But it's also accurate. As the planet heats up, we're already seeing a milder version of what the future holds. Storms will grow more intense. Drought will spread, as will wildfires. Winters will be snowier. Summers will be dryer."

Laney nodded to her screen. "According to this, we'll see a fifteen percent reduction in crops across the world, which means famine. And then there's the mega droughts."

"Mega droughts?" Jen asked.

"According to NASA, it may already be too late to avoid them," Laney said. "The drought the west coast is currently experiencing? It's nothing compared to what's

246

coming. And it will encompass almost the entire western half of the United States. It will be like the Dust Bowl of the 1930s. But where that lasted ten years, this will last thirty, maybe even forty years. And there will be no food and very little water in the western half of the United States during that time."

"Well *that's* terrifying," Henry said.

"What's that?" Jen pointed to a blog entry titled "The Stupidity of Negative Emissions."

Laney clicked on the post. She had done her own research after reading the Katzes' blog, and this topic had been more than a little terrifying. "It's criticizing the idea that we can somehow fix the problem of carbon dioxide in the atmosphere after we've crossed the threshold by rapidly reducing our emissions after the fact. And again, I agree with these guys. If we can't reduce emissions before we hit the threshold, it seems pretty stupid to assume we can reduce emissions dramatically afterwards."

"You sound like you support them," Henry said.

"I support taking better care of the planet," Laney clarified. "That's pretty much a no-brainer at this point. I'm just having trouble trying to figure out how these guys went from passionate environmentalists to ritualistic killers."

Laney scrolled through older blog posts—on vanishing rain forests, polluted oceans, and cancer spikes. All were topics that environmentalists across the board viewed as critical.

"Anything on Lemuria?"

Laney shook her head as she continued to scan. "No, nothing." She paused and backtracked to a title. "But there is one on Easter Island."

"What does it say?"

"It's one of their first posts. They talk about how it was the last refuge of an ancient race of people. How this great kingdom was reduced to nothing due to the tempestuous whims of Mother Nature. But then it talks of Easter Island's violent history. How these proud people were destroyed by other people's greed. That Easter Island is an example of what happens to the good people in the world. And how we're creating the conditions to destroy the world with our inaction."

She scrolled through the post until she reached the end. "The last line reads, 'Remember the lessons of Easter Island. Or prepare to repeat them.'"

"Not exactly a manifesto, but a little troubling," Jen said.

Jake walked in holding his own mug of coffee. "Hey. I see I'm late to the party." He took a seat next to Laney.

"Not really a party. More of a depressing reality check about the state of the planet," Laney said.

"Well, I have more depressing news: Abe Hanley has disappeared."

"What?" Jen said.

"Yep. I had an operative following him, but Hanley gave him the slip this morning on the Metro."

"What about Maura and Derek Katz?" Laney asked.

"Bad news there too. The closest operative the SIA had was in China," Jake said. "He flew to Taiwan immediately, and I just got a call from him. He went to the Katzes' home, but by the time he arrived, they were already in the wind. Turns out they flew out of Taiwan last night and arrived in France this morning."

Laney groaned. "Meaning they could be anywhere in Europe right now."

Jake nodded. "Yes. I have their names and faces in the system, so if they show up anywhere, we'll get a hit. I've also asked for their passport history, so we can if their travel history matches up with any of the murders."

"Damn it," Laney said. *She* wanted to hit something. "They could grab someone anywhere in the world. We don't even know what country they're in."

"So what do we do?" Jen asked.

"We try," Jake said.

Laney looked up. "Why does that not make me feel good?"

248

She clicked over to the "about" page on the Katzes' blog. A picture of the couple was posted in the top right. "It's hard to believe these people are behind such gruesome murders. They look... nice."

Jen looked over her shoulder. "Yeah. Nothing screams serial killers."

"No. Nothing screams crazy cult leaders either. I mean, these guys just don't seem like the bad guys. Neither has a criminal record."

"Hold on," Jake said as his phone beeped. "I just got their passport record." He turned to the computer under the conference table and brought up the file. "They were in Italy in December last year."

Laney checked the murder dates on the whiteboard. "That matches."

"Portugal in February."

"Match," Jen said.

Jake called off six more locations and dates. All matched.

Laney stared at the whiteboard. Not all of the murders aligned with the Katzes' travel.

"Some of those locations they could have traveled to by train across Europe," Henry said.

Jake nodded. "And they were in the United States during the time of three of the murders, including Sheila's."

Laney put her hand to her mouth as she stared at the photo of Derek and Maura Katz. He had an easy smile, his hand resting on the small of his wife's back. She had her arms wrapped around his waist. Their heads were tilted toward one another.

"We're missing something," Laney murmured.

"There have been killer couples before."

Laney nodded. "I know. But this doesn't feel like that. Those murders tend to be about power or jealousy—there's no overarching goal. I mean, look at Paul Bernardo and Karla Homolka from Canada. Back in 1991, Paula drugged her fifteen-year-old sister, presenting her virginity to Paul as a wedding present. Then they videotaped both of them raping her. The poor girl died, choking on vomit, but no one originally knew Paul and Karla were involved. They went on to kill and rape two other teenage girls before they were caught."

"Well, that's ridiculously disturbing," Jen said.

"Yeah, but with couples, that's kind of a typical story," Laney said.

"So is that what you think is happening here?" Henry asked.

"No. There's nothing sexual in any of these crime scenes, although power plays a role." Laney shook her head. "I don't know. It just doesn't feel like those murders."

"Well, we don't actually know what they were like at Honu Keiki," Jen said. "It's possible one or both have had violent incidents. I mean, that could even be the reason they were exiled."

"You contacted Taiwan Law Enforcement, right?" Henry asked.

Jake nodded. "No arrests, no complaints. Quiet citizens. But aren't most serial killers described as quiet?"

Laney shrugged. "Actually, they're normally described as quiet in that weird, socially awkward or off-step kind of way. These guys don't seem to be that. So I just can't quite see why they're doing it."

"Maybe their daughter's death pushed them over the edge," Jen suggested.

Laney nodded. "Possibly. But why target the companions? Or the Fallen? And how? Besides the basic issue of finding the victims—and let's just assume there's some psychic thing at work there—it costs a lot of money to travel like that. Where are they getting that money from? Are they financing this? Or is someone else?"

"They're not doing this alone," Jake said.

"No," Laney said, her hopelessness growing. "There's a network of them. There has to be."

Jen's voice was somber. "Which means we're not just trying to stop two or three people. We need to stop much more."

CHAPTER 59

Taipei, Taiwan

Maura sat at her computer and typed in a message: The Chandler Group is looking into us.

She had debated whether or not to make contact. She had never initiated it before, but this was too important. She and Derek had spent the night looking into the cat, and what they had found made their blood run.

She knew she should be more concerned about having drawn the Chandler Group's attention, but she just could not get the image of that leopard out of her mind. It was a complete violation of the laws of nature. Its existence was proof that humanity had strayed so far from the proper path that they would never be able to get back, even if they had all the time in the world.

Which, of course, they didn't. In fact, they had very little time left.

She waited, not knowing how much time it might take for a response to appear, but knowing it might be a long wait. But after only a minute, a return message appeared. She frowned. That was awfully fast.

We know.

Maura hesitated. There is more. We think they may be helping the Fallen.

What makes you think that?

Maura thought of all they had learned about the Chandler Group, and about Jake Rogan, Henry Chandler, and Delaney McPhearson in particular. It was too much to write in a message.

Many things, but perhaps a picture will help. She sent the picture they had found of the giant cat.

What is this?

It's a Javan leopard. But it's not normal. They have done something to it. Changed it. I have found other cats like this one. Big game hunters have killed them, usually in sport hunts.

Someone is creating them.

Maura nodded as she typed. That is our thought as well.

The screen remained blank for two minutes before the next message appeared. *Leave the Chandler Group to us. But find whoever is creating the animals. I believe the animals will be a perfect final sacrifice.*

Maura smiled. Thank you.

CHAPTER 60

Malama Island, Hawaii

Enzo was as good as his word. The priestess called a meeting right after the morning meditation.

The priestess eyed Aaliyah as she entered the Council room. Aaliyah gave her a deep bow before taking her seat next to Kai. Vanessa stood next to the priestess, her anger obvious from her rigid stance and hard glare.

Aaliyah did not glance over at Enzo. Under the table, Kai found her hand and gave it a squeeze.

"We have received some disturbing news," the priestess said, her eyes traveling from one member of the Naacal to the next. "Some of our exiles may be involved in a series of murders."

There was an uncomfortable silence in the room. The priestess raised an eyebrow. "I see you have all been informed." She was silent for a moment longer before she pinned Aaliyah with her gaze. "It is good that you have followed up on this matter. If we had ignored a call from the ring bearer…" The priestess shook her head. "That would have been a true tragedy."

"Are we sure it is our people?" Enzo asked.

"The ring bearer seems to think so," the priestess said.

"Are we sure she's even the ring bearer though?" Enzo asked.

The priestess beamed. "An excellent question, Enzo. Aaliyah, why do you believe she is the ring bearer?"

Aaliyah frowned. "She wears the ring."

"On her hand?" the priestess asked, her eyes calculating.

Aaliyah paused, trying to figure out the priestess's angle. "No, on a chain around her neck."

"Hmm. So we cannot say for *sure* she is in fact the ring bearer," the priestess said.

Aaliyah opened her mouth, but Kai put a warning hand on her thigh. Aaliyah shook her head. "No, priestess, I cannot say for certain she is the ring bearer. But if she is, and we ignore her request..." Aaliyah left the statement unfinished.

The priestess looked back at her, an eyebrow raised. Aaliyah had the distinct impression she was playing a game whose rules she was completely ignorant of.

"I could speak with her," Aaliyah said. "And get to the truth of the matter."

The priestess waved away her words. "Perhaps, but there is a reason we keep ourselves away from the rest of the world. Even a conversation can lead to influence that takes us from the path. Besides, people lie. We need a way to verify her identity that does not put us at risk or allow her to deceive us."

"How?" Enzo asked.

The priestess seemed to mull over Enzo's question, but Aaliyah had the feeling it was all an act. *What is she doing?*

"A test," the priestess finally said. "If she passes, she is the ring bearer. If she doesn't, then we do not need to concern ourselves with this."

Aaliyah did not like the look on the priestess's face or the look on Vanessa's face behind her. They both looked too happy with the idea. But Aaliyah couldn't come up with an alternative suggestion.

"All in favor?" the priestess asked. Everyone raised their hands. Kai and Aaliyah were the last.

"Good. I will have Vanessa arrange the test immediately."

Vanessa looked directly at Aaliyah, a smile slowly spreading across her face. And Aaliyah had the distinct impression the ring bearer was about to step into a world of trouble.

CHAPTER 61

Baltimore, Maryland

Lou pushed open the door to the courtyard. Across the space, Cleo picked up her head from inside her enclosure. "There is no better time," Lou argued.

Rolly held up his hands. "Hey, preaching to the choir. We have a couple days off from classes to study, so I completely agree. It's not me you need to convince."

Lou knew he was right. She, Danny, Zach, and Rolly had all agreed that finding more modified leopards was the priority, and that as soon as there was a chance to go out west, they would take it. But Danny had been dragging his feet. And Lou was done waiting. She was going to figure out a way to go, one way or the other.

Lou walked over to the enclosure, and Cleo stepped up to her. Lou reached between the bars and ran a hand through the big cat's fur. "Hi, girl."

Behind them, the door to the courtyard opened, and Danny and Moxy stepped through. Moxy sprinted to the enclosure and began racing up and down beside it, as usual.

Lou stepped back to let them race without her as an obstacle. She looked at Danny. They had all agreed to find the animals, but Danny had been coming up with one excuse after another as to why they shouldn't go. Lou opened her mouth to once again to try and convince him that they needed to go and find the animals before they told Laney and Henry anything.

But Danny spoke first. "I'm ready to go," he said. He held out his phone.

With a frown, Lou grabbed it. On screen was a picture of a man who was easily four hundred pounds. He sat in a chair, a rifle nestled in his arms. At his feet were a black leopard and a smaller cub. Blood stained the cats' faces.

Lou gasped.

"That's Mark Hanover. He had two leopards brought to his compound, where he killed them."

"That guy couldn't outrun an ant," Rolly growled.

"He didn't have to," Danny said. "They brought the leopards in and drugged them. He sat on his back porch and waited until they stumbled into view. The whole kill is on video. The cats could barely stand before he shot them."

Lou's blood began to boil. "How the hell is that a sport?"

Danny looked at Lou with unshed tears in his eyes. "I'm sorry. We should have gone sooner. If we had, maybe these two would still be alive."

"But you're ready now?" Lou asked.

Danny nodded. "Yes, I'm ready."

"Okay then," Rolly said. "We're going to need to figure a way off campus. They're not just going to let us walk out of here." Ever since the latest threat, the security had been incredible. Lou was pretty sure inmates had more freedom than they did.

"Don't worry. I've figured out a way," Danny said.

Rolly threw an arm around each of them, hugging them into his side. "Oh, this is going to fun."

258

CHAPTER 62

Henry held the phone out to her. "Laney? It's the Baltimore Police Department."

Laney looked up in surprise. "For me?"

"What did you do?" Jen demanded.

Laney put up her hands with a smile. "Nothing, I swear." She took the phone from Henry. "Hello?"

"Dr. McPhearson, this is Sergeant Kevin O'Malley. I tried to reach you on your cell phone but didn't get an answer."

Laney pulled her cell out and looked at it. "Oh, sorry. I must have turned the volume off. What can I do for you?"

"We have a situation down here that we could use your help with."

"Okay, what's going on?"

"A man has taken six people hostage at a coffee shop on Bennett Place. And he's demanding to see you."

"Me? Who is it?"

"His name is Charles Garner. I'm sending you his DMV picture. Do you know him?"

Laney clicked over and opened the photo. The man on the screen was about forty, with light brown hair, small eyes, and a big smile. Laney frowned. "I've never seen him before in my life."

"Well, he seems to know you. And he says if you don't arrive here within the hour, he'll kill the hostages."

CHAPTER 63

Laney and Jake pulled to the side of the street, and Jen and Henry pulled in a few spots behind them. Bennett Street was blocked off with yellow police tape, and the police were keeping people back.

"One of the analysts just texted me," Jake said. "There's a live video feed coming out of the coffee shop."

Laney turned to him in surprise. "The coffee shop has security?"

"No, but someone's watching the place."

"So he *is* working for someone else," Laney murmured. They had gone over and over again what the man could possibly want with Laney. It was possible he had a personal grudge against her, but they'd both thought it was more likely he was working for someone else. Laney had a feeling Samyaza may finally have decided to stick someone else's head out. Although why do it this way was beyond her.

"Can you see if they can set the outgoing video on a repeating loop?" Laney asked. "If someone's watching, they want to see me. And I'd rather we didn't let them."

"Already arranged it."

Laney surveyed the street. Sharpshooters that had taken position on rooftops, and a few stray civilians were being escorted behind the barricade. She watched it all with a growing sense of dread. How many innocents were going to lose their lives today?

Her hand on the door, she said, "Okay. Let's get this show on the road."

Jake grabbed her other hand. "Laney."

She looked back at him. He squeezed her hand. "Just be careful and take as few chances as you can, okay?"

She leaned over and kissed him. "You got it."

They stepped out of the car. Henry and Jen joined them. "You sure you don't want me to go in with you?" Jen asked.

"Thanks, but no," Laney said. "He asked for me. Let's do what he says for now. I promise to yell if I need help."

"And I'll come running," Jen promised.

Laney spotted a terrified woman and her young daughter hurrying to get outside the perimeter. The stirrings of fear rumbled in her own stomach. "I'm counting on it."

CHAPTER 64

The coffee urns lined up behind the counter in Java Joe's seemed to be beckoning Charles Garner, known to one and all as Charlie. The smell of coffee made his mouth water. He hadn't had his second cup this morning, and now he was beginning to get a headache. But he couldn't risk stopping to pour himself one.

A refrigerated display case stood next to the counter, holding sandwiches and cakes. Along the other walls were tall built-in refrigerators and shelves with snacks.

And right now, six people sat on the floor in front of those shelves. Only two were men, both in suits. One was in his fifties, the other probably his thirties. The thirty-year-old was trying to look strong, but a sweat had broken out on his forehead. It was the older man, Charlie thought, that he'd have to worry about. He had the eyes of a man who'd seen a lot.

Two of the women were in their twenties, in workout clothes. They sat close to one another, trembling. A third woman was in her late sixties, maybe even early seventies. She kept repeating, "Oh dear, oh dear." The fourth woman was in jeans and a fleece. She glanced between Charlie and the door but made no movement. In fact, she was sitting back, her legs bent. Not a position you'd be in if you planned on breaking into a sprint.

Besides, Charlie knew he'd be able to catch her before she'd taken two steps.

"What do you want with us?" the older man suddenly demanded.

Charlie's gaze flicked over to him. "Nothing. Someone's coming. When they arrive, you can leave."

"Could you just let us go now?" one of the young women asked.

"No!" Charlie barked. The woman cringed, and tears sprang to her eyes. Her friend wrapped her arms around her.

"No," Charlie repeated in a softer tone. "But you'll be free to go when she arrives."

"And none of us will be harmed?" the man asked.

"You'll all be released unharmed." *But I can't say the same for Delaney McPhearson.*

Charlie resumed his pacing, his heart beating heavily in his chest. Delaney McPhearson—he'd never heard the woman's name before this morning. And he still knew nothing about her—except for one simple fact.

He was going to kill her.

CHAPTER 65

Laney pulled on her bulletproof vest and zipped her jacket over it. She closed the back of the SUV.

Henry stepped up next to her. "You ready for this?"

"Well, seeing as I'm still not really sure what 'this' is, I guess."

Henry frowned.

"Hey, none of that. I'll be fine. Come on." Together, Laney and Henry headed to the police divider, Jake and Jen falling in step behind them. They showed their badges to the police officer at the tape.

"Where's O'Malley?" Laney asked the officer.

The officer nudged her chin toward a balding man across the street, who was addressing a group of officers. Laney and the others walked over to him, and Laney pulled out her badge. "I'm Delaney McPhearson."

"You're a fed?" O'Malley asked, his eyes going wide.

"Yeah—with the SIA." At his blank look, she added, "It's a small agency. You've probably never heard of it. So, what do you know?"

O'Malley nodded to his officers, who dispersed. Then he turned to Laney and jerked his head toward Jake, Henry, and Jen. "Who are they?"

"More feds," Laney said. "Garner?"

O'Malley eyed each of them, his eyes growing a little larger at Henry's size, then shrugged. "Okay. Charles Garner, age forty-two, married with two kids. He's an electrician. No priors, just two speeding tickets over a decade old. The guy coaches his son's basketball team."

Laney frowned. Not the typical criminal background. "And what's this all about?"

O'Malley shook his head. "I don't know. He won't say anything except that he will kill the hostages if you don't go in there. We called his house, got no answer. I sent some uniforms by, but no one answered. The kids never made it to school today, and the wife never made it to work."

"Did you search the house?" Jake asked.

O'Malley nodded. "Yeah. But there was nothing. In fact, the place is under renovation. We don't think they're even living there right now."

"So what *are* you thinking?" Henry asked.

"Not sure, but I'm hoping we're not dealing with a family annihilator."

Laney cringed. "Annihilators" were men who one day, seemingly out of the blue, killed their entire family. Motives were a little murky, but the most common seemed to be financial difficulty or marital disruption—and more recently, honor killings had occasionally come into play. There'd been a couple of cases where annihilators were also spree killers, going from place to place killing family members. Laney really hoped that wasn't what they were seeing here. And it didn't seem likely that an annihilator wanted to speak with her, unless he was another long-lost brother.

"Anything from the neighbors?" Jake asked.

"Not really. We spoke with one who said they seemed happy, but that could mean anything. And he admitted he didn't know them well. No one was home at the other houses."

"Nothing about why he wants to speak with Laney?" Henry asked.

O'Malley shook his head. "No. But we just learned about all this just under an hour ago."

"Okay, well, let's see what he has to say," Laney said. "Do you have a line into the coffee shop?"

O'Malley handed her a phone. "Hit one."

Laney did, waiting while the phone rang out.

Someone picked up. "I told you I don't want to speak with you. I only want to speak with Delaney McPhearson." Charlie Garner sounded stressed, worried. But he didn't sound angry.

Interesting, Laney thought. "Mr. Garner, this is Delaney McPhearson."

There was a pause. "You came."

"You asked, and here I am."

"You need to come in here," he said in a rush.

Jake shook his head. Laney kept Jake's gaze. "I understand you want that, Mr. Garner. But I'm going to need something from you first. I'm going to need a guarantee that you will release the hostages once I'm inside."

"Yes, yes. Of course."

"As a show of good faith, how about you send two out right now?"

"And then you'll come in?"

"And then I'll come in."

"Okay." He disconnected the call.

Officers moved in next to the coffee shop. Ten seconds later the front door flew open. An older woman in her seventies came out, helped by a man in his fifties. Officers grabbed them both and pulled them out of the line of fire, toward waiting ambulances.

"This doesn't make any sense," Jake murmured. "He gave up two of his hostages just like that."

"He's not a criminal mastermind," Laney said. "In fact, he sounded scared."

"So what does he want?"

"I guess I'll go find out."

266

CHAPTER 66

Running her thumb over her ring, Laney left the security of the police. She walked slowly toward the coffee shop and raised her hands up. Halfway there she felt the familiar tingle roll over her skin.

She managed to keep walking, but her mind was racing. She wanted to signal to her group, but she didn't know if Garner was watching, and she didn't know how he would react if she turned back. *Oh, I don't like this.* She was walking in blind, and she didn't know whether the Fallen was one of the hostages or the kidnapper. Although her money was certainly on the kidnapper.

Heart pounding, she eased open the door to the coffee shop. She had on her body armor, but she knew that with certain bullets, that protection would be useless, especially at close range. And she also had nothing covering her head, so there was that.

The bell hidden beneath the rug at the front door jangled as she stepped in. Four hostages sat along one wall— three women and one man. None of them looked hurt, but all of them looked terrified.

Laney only spared them a glance. Her focus was on the man standing in the back with his handgun trained on her. He looked just like his driver's license picture except for the sweat on his forehead and the fact that he was shaking. And she was certain now: he was a Fallen.

Laney worked on keeping her voice calm and non-threatening. "Mr. Garner? My name's Delaney McPhearson. I'm here. So how about we let these hostages go?"

Garner nodded, and his gun bobbed up and down, making Laney wince. "Yeah, yeah, okay."

Keeping her eye on the gun, she waved the hostages toward the door. "Everybody out. Now."

The hostages stumbled to their feet. One of the women paused, but Laney said, "Go."

With a nod, the woman followed the others out of the building.

Garner held the gun on Laney. His hand was shaking so hard, Laney worried he'd jerk the trigger. Tears appeared in his eyes. "I'm sorry. I don't have a choice."

"Put the gun down," Laney ordered.

The man started to lower the gun. His eyes grew wild. "No."

"Drop the gun and kick it away from you," Laney said.

The man did as Laney said, although he shook his head disbelievingly the whole time. "How—?" Then he sprinted at Laney so fast she didn't have time to think, only react. As he reached her, Laney dropped onto her back, brought her legs up, and kicked him up and over her. He slammed into a display behind her.

Laney rolled to her feet and put up her hand. "Stop fighting me."

The man strained to move toward her. Tension radiated from him and a tear rolled down his cheek. "Please," he said, "I have to. You don't understand."

"What don't I understand? Why are you doing this?" Laney asked.

"They have my family."

"Who?"

"I don't know. But if I don't kill you, they will kill them."

Laney stared at the man. *What the hell is going on?*

CHAPTER 67

Laney turned the steering wheel sharply around the corner. "You good?"

Jake slammed the magazine into his Glock. "I'm good."

As soon as she had Garner incapacitated, Laney had handed him over to Jen and Henry, quickly explaining about the man's family. The video feed was still on loop, which meant whoever was watching hopefully wouldn't realize what had happened. But they couldn't hope to fool them for long.

Now Laney and Jake were rushing to Garner's sister's home, which was where the family had been staying while their house was under renovation. Jen was behind them, but she'd turn off well before they arrived.

It would just be Laney and Jake. Explaining everything to the police would have taken way too long, and Laney couldn't chance bringing Jen or Henry along, not if one of the people holding Garner's family was a Fallen. They couldn't risk them sensing their approach.

"Are you up for this?" Laney asked.

"Shooting only." Jake grinned. "Well, maybe a few punches."

"Jake," Laney warned.

"Laney, you walked into a hostage situation because there was no choice. There's no choice here either. You can't go in alone, and unless you want to waste time explaining to the police about Fallen angels, I'm your backup."

Laney wanted to object, but she knew he was right.

"Any ideas who grabbed his family to get to you?" Jake asked.

Laney shrugged. "You want a list? But my money's on Samyaza, although I really don't get the play. Why send someone to kill me now? And why this guy? I mean, he's got nothing in his background but a few speeding tickets. He's one of the law-abiding Fallen. You should have seen him—he was terrified. This guy is not a killer, or even much of a fighter. And no offense, but he's going against *me*. Someone a little more seasoned makes more sense."

"So why send him?"

"I don't know. But once we grab these guys in the house, we'll be sure to ask them."

"Are we sure they're even at the house?"

"No, but according to Charlie, that's where they were this morning when this all began. So we have to hope that's where they're waiting it out. After all, it'd be easier than trying to move the family."

"Assuming they kept them alive."

Laney didn't say anything. For now, she *had* to assume the Garner family was still alive.

"The house is on the next block," Jake said.

In the rearview mirror, Laney saw Jen pull over. Jen was instructed to stay out of any Fallen's range, but she would come running if it turned out there were no Fallen, or once the element of surprise was lost.

Laney slowed down and turned the corner.

"Yellow house on the right," Jake said.

Laney pulled over. The street was quiet and lined with cars. The house had a deep porch and a driveway that ran along the side. "Thoughts?"

"Let's make for the car in the drive and hope no bad guys look out the windows," Jake said.

271

"Oh, so we're relying on luck. Excellent. Because that's never failed us."

Jake smiled and Laney could tell that, danger or not, he was enjoying himself. "Porch will be too risky," he said. "We'd be exposed for too long. That window on the side should be the kitchen or dining room. We'll take a look there and then go from there."

Laney nodded. "Okay."

"Let's go."

Laney ran toward the house, Jake at her side. Ducking behind the car in the drive, they paused, but the street remained quiet.

They inched up to the window. Laney peeked in. Two men were in the kitchen, gun holsters strapped across their shoulders with a handgun in each. They could be brothers—same dark hair, tanned complexion, but one wore a blue jacket and the other a black. Laney saw no sign of Charlie's family, but, if these men were here, it was a safe bet that she and Jake were at the right spot. And even better, neither of them was Fallen.

Laney tapped the mike at her throat. "They're not Fallen."

"Got it," Jen replied.

Blue Jacket's phone rang, and he answered it. "What?"

As he listened, his face grew darker. After a few seconds, he snapped the phone off. "Goddamn it. They did something to the tape."

Laney met Jake's gaze.

He nodded. "Go."

Laney sprinted for the front door. As she rushed up the steps, she called on the wind, and it surged past her, blowing the front door open. Breaking glass sounded from the kitchen.

Black Jacket appeared in the hallway, his gun drawn. "What the—"

Laney dove for the floor as a bullet splintered the doorframe. Again she called on the wind. It rushed through the open front door and the man flew into the wall with a scream.

A burst of gunfire sounded from the kitchen.

"Laney!" Jake yelled.

"I'm good," Laney said, getting slowly to her feet. Her side ached, and she knew she was in for a few days of bruises from that little move. "You?"

"Good," Jake called back.

Jen came running through the front door. "The family?"

Laney nodded to the stairs. "Check upstairs. I'll take the first floor."

Jen sprinted up the stairs. Laney grabbed Black Jacket's weapon from the floor, tucked it into her belt, and cast a quick glance around. The first floor contained only the kitchen, the dining room, and a small living room to Laney's right. She headed into the kitchen first.

Blue Jacket was on the floor with a bullet wound in his shoulder. Jake stood just outside the window, his gun trained on the man. As soon as he saw Laney arrive, he disappeared in the direction of the front door.

Laney kicked the gunman's weapon away and grabbed him by the lapels. "Where's the family?" she barked.

His brown eyes widening, the man shook his head. "We weren't—"

"Where?" Laney demanded as Jake entered the kitchen.

The man's eyes rolled back into his head.

Laney let him drop to the ground. "Goddamn it."

"Laney," Jake said.

She turned, and he nudged his chin toward a door off the kitchen. "Basement."

Laney felt her stomach hollow. She got to her feet just as Jen appeared in the kitchen. "No one's upstairs."

"There's a basement," Laney said.

Jen nodded, her face grim. "I'll go first."

Laney took a step toward the basement door. "It's okay, I can—"

"I heal quicker," Jen said.

Laney nodded. "Right, you go first."

Laney pulled open the door and Jen poked her weapon in. It was dark. Jen reached in and flipped the light switch. A single bulb illuminated the old stairs. "God, I hate old basements," Jen muttered.

"Me too," Laney said.

They swept the basement as they made their way down. It was small and filled with old junk. They searched the space, but saw nothing.

Laney stepped past the boiler and spotted stairs going down. "It's got a root cellar," she said. She wound her way down until her feet found a dirt floor surrounded by the cold rock foundation of the house. She shone her flashlight around. "There's nothing—"

Her light flew back to a spot in the corner.

Three bodies—a woman and two boys—lay there on an old rug, hands and feet bound. *Oh no.*

On trembling legs, Laney made her way over, barely conscious of Jen beside her. Laney knelt down and touched the shoulder of the woman. Her eyes flew open.

Laney fell back with a yell, followed by a nervous laugh. She scrambled forward and pulled the tape from the woman's mouth. "It's okay. You're safe."

"My husband—"

"He's safe too."

The woman burst into tears. Laney sliced the woman's restraints with the knife she kept on her belt. "It's okay. You're safe," Laney repeated, but the woman continued to cry.

Jen untied the two boys, who immediately flung themselves at their mother. Laney sat back, watching the family, feeling tears forming in her own eyes. They were all right. But what had any of this been about?

CHAPTER 68

Malama Island, Hawaii

The Naacal and the priestess, along with Vanessa and three guards, watched the scene on the TV. It was a coffee shop in the United States. Six people were huddled against one wall. A man with a gun paced back and forth. Aaliyah frowned as the scene continued. Something was wrong.

Kai leaned down to whisper in her ear. "It's repeating." Aaliyah realized he was right.

When the Naacal had been summoned to the Council room, Aaliyah had thought they were to be told when and where the ring bearer would be tested. She had been aghast to learn that the test had already begun.

The priestess frowned and gestured for Vanessa to lean down. The priestess whispered in Vanessa's ear, then Vanessa nodded and stepped away from the group to make a phone call.

Aaliyah kept her eyes on Vanessa, but she kept her back to the group. After a few moments, she turned and handed her phone to one of the guards. The guard walked over to the TV and began to link the phone and the screen.

Vanessa returned to the priestess's side and whispered something in her ear, then stepped back.

"Something was wrong with the original feed. But we have another link," the priestess said to the Nacaal. "It seems the group we sent has been compromised. The situation has been resolved, but we do not have the full details yet."

Aaliyah clenched her fists. No one had even been told the nature of the test; only Vanessa and the priestess knew that. Aaliyah had hoped to contact the ring bearer to warn her, but there had been no time.

The TV flashed to life again. Now they could see the storefront of a coffee shop called Java Joe's. The image jiggled; it appeared to be a feed from someone's cell phone camera. Whoever was holding the phone walked inside. A few minutes later, a man burst in the door telling everyone to freeze.

"Fast forward," the priestess ordered.

Vanessa did until a woman stepped into the shop. Aaliyah recognized her from the video call and tensed.

"Is that her?" Enzo asked.

"Yes," Vanessa said.

They watched as the woman ordered the man to lower his weapon and then drop it.

On screen, the man cried as he fought her. "They have my family."

"Who?"

"I don't know. But if I don't kill you, they will kill them."

"Okay, that's enough," the priestess ordered.

"What was that about?" Aaliyah asked.

"Nothing," Vanessa said. "He was a Fallen. His family was merely held to ensure his cooperation."

"Are they safe?" Kai asked.

The priestess waved away the concerns. "Of course."

"So she *is* the ring bearer," Aaliyah said quietly.

"Perhaps," the priestess said.

Kai looked up. "She was able to subdue the Fallen without harming him or anyone else. Who else could have done that?"

The priestess shrugged. "It appears she is the ring bearer, but it does not necessarily follow that we should help her. There have been ring bearers in the past who have been unworthy. After all, she let the Fallen live."

Kai frowned. "She showed compassion. That's not a fault."

"Compassion can be an admirable quality," the priestess said. "But in the ring bearer, it's a weakness."

"It's not a weakness. She didn't kill the man because she didn't have to," Aaliyah argued—even as she inwardly warned herself to stop speaking.

"Still, she demonstrates an affinity for the Fallen that is a concern. We have learned that she helps run a school where the students are Fallen and nephilim."

"Perhaps she is hoping to help them make the right choices," Kai said.

"And she saved that man's life after we put it at risk," Aaliyah said, yet again sending her inner sanity into a tizzy.

"Not man—Fallen," Vanessa corrected, her voice hard.

Aaliyah dropped her gaze, realizing she was letting her emotions get away with her. "Yes, of course."

"But that does not change the fact that the murders may very well be our responsibility. And if the ring bearer is trying to stop them, we should help her," Kai argued.

The priestess's gaze focused on Kai; he looked back with humility. Finally the priestess nodded. "Now we have to determine *how* to help. We need to learn more about this situation without raising any suspicions. Aaliyah—perhaps you could take charge of that, seeing as you are so interested in this case."

Aaliyah bowed her head. "Yes, priestess. Thank you for the honor."

"Priestess," Enzo cut in. "I believe *I* may be better suited to speak with the ring bearer. And I am the one who brought this to your attention."

Aaliyah looked up and found the priestess's eyes still on her. "Yes," the priestess said. "But Aaliyah is intimately acquainted with the *risks* such a venture will entail. We stay

277

out of world affairs because they can be so dangerous. And this one may very well be life and death. Isn't that correct, Aaliyah?"

Aaliyah swallowed, hoping she was not hearing a promise in the priestess's words. "Yes, priestess."

CHAPTER 69

Addison, West Virginia

Exhaustion weighed down on Laney as she sat in the SUV next to Jen. And it wasn't physical exhaustion, but emotional. Charles Garner was being held in the SIA facility for at least the night, although there were no plans to charge him. Laney had escorted him personally to the facility, not only because she could control him, but also because she wanted to see if he knew anything that could help them.

But he was as much in the dark as they were. He'd received a call on his cell from his wife's phone. A man he did not know was on the other end, telling him he had taken his wife and sons. His wife was put on the phone to prove the threat. He was then given instructions on what to do and told that if he deviated in any way, his family would be killed. Charlie hadn't even considered going against their instructions. He'd been terrified for his family.

Charlie was an unwitting pawn in someone else's game, and they still didn't know whose.

Jake and Henry were traveling with Charlie's family so they could join him. Right now, what the Garner family needed more than anything was protection.

Jen pulled away from the facility and headed back to the estate. "You okay?"

Laney shook her head. "No."

They drove for a while in silence. Laney pictured the fear in Charlie's face. Then she frowned.

"The kidnappers told Charlie that if he deviated in any way from their instructions, his family would be killed."

Jen grimaced. "Assholes."

"Yeah, but how would they know?"

"The video feed at the coffee place?"

"Yeah, but then they got a phone call. Someone tipped them off." Laney pulled out her phone and dialed.

Detective O'Malley answered. "Dr. McPhearson?"

"Hi, detective. I have just a quick question for you. Did you get a background on all the hostages?"

"Most of them."

"What do you mean?"

"One of them disappeared. We don't have a name or any contact information."

"Which one?"

"The woman in the jeans and fleece."

Laney remembered her; she was the woman who had paused when Laney told the hostages to leave. "Did you find anything unusual in the coffee shop?" she asked.

"No. All the hostages left something inside—bags, phones—"

"Phones? How many?"

"Three."

"Were any recording?"

"Yeah, actually. One."

"Can you check if it's still in evidence?"

"Hold on."

"What's going on?" Jen asked.

"Just playing a hunch."

O'Malley returned to the phone. "Goddamn it—the phone's missing. I have the techs tearing apart the van. We'll find it."

No, I don't think you will. "Thanks, detective."

Laney ended the call and turned to Jen. "One of the hostages recorded the incident. I think she was a plant."

"What?" Jen snapped her head toward Laney before turning her attention back to the road. "Why?"

"I'm guessing as a backup."

"Was it in real time?"

Laney shrugged. "I don't think so. If it was, I doubt the Garner family would still be alive."

"Someone really wanted to see what you could do."

Laney pictured the Garners' terrified faces in the root cellar. "That poor family. They got yanked into this and they have nothing to do with anything. And Charlie knew what he could do but never used his abilities. He says his wife doesn't even know. He's like Xavier—a good man just trying to live his life. Why would someone do this? And why bring it to my attention?"

"Do you think this has anything to do with the Fallen murders or the companion murders?"

Laney shook her head, frustration rolling through her. "If it is, I'm not seeing the connection. Hell, I'm still not even clear on *why* the companion murders are happening."

"Well, I have some news," Jen said, her voice serious.

Laney blew out a breath. "Go ahead."

"While you were getting Garner set up, we got a hit on facial rec with the Katzes."

"Where?"

"They were entering the US over the Canadian border in Seattle."

"Canada? As in where the latest murder was?"

"Yep. They drove over the border under assumed names."

Laney went still. "And now they're here."

"And now they're here," Jen agreed.

"How long ago?"

"About two hours."

Crap. "Any sightings since then?"

"No, but once they're in the country they can move around pretty easily, unless they plan to get on a commercial plane."

Laney slumped down in her seat. "Well, that's just great."

CHAPTER 70

Malama Island, Hawaii

Noriko skipped down the temple steps. She had just completed a test of her abilities, and had passed with flying colors.

"Noriko."

She turned and saw Arrow approaching. Tall with dark hair and eyes, Arrow exuded confidence but not arrogance. He was a year older than Noriko, and she had watched him from afar for years. Everyone, including Noriko, assumed he was destined for the Naacal one day.

"Your gift is very impressive," Arrow said as he caught up with her.

"Thank you. And I have heard of all your great accomplishments."

Arrow smiled. "I wish you well." He passed her and went to join his teacher, who was already at the bottom of the temple steps. Arrow waved at Noriko over his shoulder and she smiled back. But Arrow's teacher only cast a glare in her direction. He had not been happy that his prize student had been outperformed by Noriko.

Aaliyah came up behind her and slipped her arm around Noriko's shoulders. "Let's go."

Noriko frowned as they walked away from the temple. Aaliyah didn't look proud—she looked concerned. "Is something wrong?"

"No, of course not." The wrinkles on Aaliyah's brow faded. "You did wonderful, by the way."

Noriko knew Aaliyah was distracted; she had been ever since the priestess had put her in charge of contacting the ring bearer. Aaliyah had been hesitant to do so, and Noriko, now having read everything Aaliyah had on the history of the ring bearer, could understand why. The woman was larger than life, a true force of nature. Even so, Noriko had never known Aaliyah to be unsure. It was a little disconcerting.

Before Noriko could question her, a vision burst into her mind. She gasped and clutched at Aaliyah's arm as her knees went weak. Images of blood, hate, and fear swam in front of her. She lost all sense of the here and now. When at last her mind began to clear, her heart pounded and she felt lightheaded.

"Noriko! What is it? What's wrong?" Aaliyah knelt on the ground next to Noriko, one arm wrapped around her. Noriko couldn't remember having fallen.

"It was a vision," Noriko stammered. She stared into Aaliyah's concerned eyes. "You need to call the ring bearer."

284

CHAPTER 71

Baltimore, Maryland

Laney's cell phone rang just as she and Jen arrived back at the estate. They'd caught the Chandler helicopter a short distance from the SIA facility.

Jen raised an eyebrow. "You going to get that?"

"No," Laney said, wanting a moment to think. It continued to ring. *Crap.* "Yes."

Laney stopped to answer, and Jen waved and continued on toward the main house.

Swallowing her frustration, Laney spoke. "Hello?"

"Is this Dr. Delaney McPhearson?"

Laney didn't recognize the voice. "Yes. How can I help you?"

"My name is Aaliyah. I am a member of the Naacal on Honu Keiki. I believe you called the other day to discuss a situation that may involve some of our people."

Laney froze. "Yes, yes I did."

"I have been instructed to help you, but I was hoping you would be willing to switch to a videoconference. I need to verify that it is actually Delaney McPhearson I am speaking with."

"Yes, of course. Hold on." Laney quickly switched over to a video call. A few seconds later, a woman in her late forties appeared onscreen. She had dark hair and dark eyes, and a warm cocoa complexion.

"Is that better?" Laney asked.

The woman smiled, and Laney immediately noted she seemed much friendlier than Vanessa had been. "Yes. Thank you."

"You said you had some information on the murders?"

"I may. But first, do *you* know who is perpetrating them?"

"We believe it is a group of people led by a couple named Maura and Derek Katz. Do you know them?"

Aaliyah nodded slowly, a crease developing between her eyes. "Maura and Derek were members. They were exiled over ten years ago."

"Why?"

"I'm afraid I'm not at liberty to tell you that. But I *can* tell you we had no inklings that they were prone to any sort of violence. They were strict adherents to the old ways. It is surprising that they have chosen this path."

"Are you suggesting they aren't the ones calling the shots?"

Aaliyah shook her head. "No, no. I am merely surprised. How can I help?"

"Well, we'd like to find the Katzes, if that's something you can help us with."

Aaliyah nodded. "I am not sure how familiar you are with our group. We have ways of knowing things."

"You mean some of you are psychic."

Aaliyah smiled. "I have been told that people outside of our world are not so easily accepting of such things."

"Were you the one who sent me the pictures?"

"Yes. Were you able to find the man?"

"We got to him in time. He's been put somewhere safe."

Aaliyah closed her eyes. "Thank the Holy Mother. I wasn't sure if you would take the drawings seriously."

286

"I tend to keep an open mind about things. I've had one or two situations that people outside of my world may have trouble believing as well."

"You mean because you are the ring bearer?"

Laney stared at the screen, her jaw falling open. "You know about the ring bearer?"

"We know you are called into service when the world has reached a dangerous point."

Laney didn't know what to say. Finally she shook her head. "Sorry. I just, I'm just not used to people knowing about me. And understanding."

"We know quite a bit. Including about the Fallen."

"Wow. I'm kind of blown away right now." Laney cleared her head. "What did you mean about the world reaching a dangerous point?"

Aaliyah hesitated. "The world has reached this same point many times in the past. Many times, the world survived. But sometimes it didn't—at least, not like it was before."

"The floods."

"Yes. We believe that is part of the reason the ring bearer came into being. To help humanity."

Laney pictured Cain. "Someone told me that these murders are being committed to save the world."

"It's possible. The Fallen and the people who help them have been viewed as the agents of our destruction. Some would say that if they were removed, the world could be saved."

"Do you believe that?"

"No. And the Honu Keiki don't either. The Fallen aren't the only ones who can do evil. Humans... we have a choice. We can be tempted and pushed, but the ultimate choice is ours."

Laney found herself liking Aaliyah. She seemed genuine. Of course, Jake would say she was being too trusting, but Laney's gut suggested otherwise.

"What about the Fallen? Would Derek and Maura be able to kill them?"

Aaliyah's eyes grew large. "Kill Fallen angels? I don't see how. Derek was a fisherman and Maura was a doctor. Neither was trained in fighting."

"Are *any* of the exiled fighters?"

"No. No member of the Guard has been exiled in at least the last twenty years. And before that, the training was rudimentary. I can't see any of them going against a Fallen, at least not successfully."

Laney frowned. Were there two different groups committing these attacks? One aimed at the Fallen and the other at their compound?

"The Fallen are being killed as well?" Aaliyah asked.

"Yes. But like people, not all Fallen are bad."

"Like the man in the coffee shop?"

A chill rolled over Laney. "How do you know about that?"

Aaliyah's jaw dropped, but she tried to cover it. "We hear things," she said quickly.

This time Laney didn't need Jake to tell her that Aaliyah was lying. "Were you the ones watching? Did *you* set this up?"

Aaliyah bit her lip. "I'm sorry. I shouldn't have said anything. Please forget I said that."

Laney wanted to press the point, but she didn't want to risk Aaliyah hanging up, and she could tell the woman was terrified. But why? She pushed down her concerns. *That's a problem for another time.* "Do you know why this is happening? I mean, I don't understand how killing people is going to save the world."

Aaliyah hesitated, and Laney got the impression she was weighing how much she was allowed to share. "In our history, there was a dark period. A time when the very ground we stood on seemed to reject us. Some of our people blamed the Fallen for the difficulties. When possible, people killed

288

them, and if they couldn't, they killed the people the Fallen knew. And then the world quieted. They believed they had saved the world by sacrificing the Fallen and their intimates. It was called the ritual of the moon and the sun—the beginning and the end."

"And after the world quieted, it entered a new beginning."

"Yes. It became a tradition to sacrifice the Fallen and their intimates when the world became troubled. And people believed that an especially large sacrifice was necessary to complete the ritual. The last sacrifice therefore is always multiple sacrifices, not just one. And it has to occur on a solstice."

Laney knew the solstice was an important event in the lives of ancient peoples. Occurring twice a year, the solstice was when the sun reached either its highest or lowest point in reference to the equator. Incredible structures in the ancient world had been built to allow the light to flood the structures only on these dates. Stonehenge in England, the Great Pyramids in Egypt, the Ajanta Caves in India, the Serpent Mound in Ohio, the Mayan city of Tulum, the Newgrange Passage Tomb in Ireland—all were aligned with either the summer or winter solstice, and they were scattered across the world.

Laney's heart began to race. "The next solstice just two days away."

"Yes. But if the murders have only just begun, there is time. The ritual must go on for at least a year, usually closer to two."

"The murders have been going on for almost eighteen months," Laney said quietly.

Aaliyah stared, her mouth hanging open. "I didn't—we didn't know that."

"The murders also appear to be increasing in frequency."

Aaliyah swallowed noticeably. "That is not good. It means they are indeed approaching the last sacrifice."

Laney wasn't sure what to say. A large sacrifice. Already nearly forty victims had been sacrificed. How many would there be in the final sacrifice? "Do you have any idea how many victims we're talking about in the final sacrifice?"

Aaliyah's eyes were troubled.

"Aaliyah?"

"I'm not sure. This might sound a little crazy, but you wouldn't happen to know where there's a pack of leopards, would you?"

Laney went still. "*Black* leopards?"

"Yes. One of our seers had a vision of a group of them being sacrificed."

Laney tried to rein in her fear. *Cleo's fine. She's at the school.* "When was this?"

"The vision happened only a few hours ago. But the seer is not sure where the vision took place."

"What can you tell me?"

"There was a warehouse in the beginning, where the animals were all in crates. And then the scene shifted to outside. All the animals were lying on stone altars. But I do not see how anyone from Honu Keiki could be responsible for this."

"Why not?"

"Cats are revered here, leopards in particular. They were the guardians of the Great Mother. No one from our group, exiled or not, would ever hurt them. It would be a complete violation of our beliefs."

Violation. Laney felt cold. "But if someone were to have genetically modified the leopards?"

"Modified?"

"Changed their DNA, enhanced them, combined their DNA with non-leopard DNA—possibly Fallen DNA?"

Aaliyah's eyes grew wide. "Why would someone do such a thing?"

290

"It doesn't matter. What do you think Derek and Maura would think of that?"

"They'd think like I think—that it's a complete violation of the laws of this world. Leopards are sacred. To change them..." Aaliyah shook her head. "It's unnatural."

"Would they kill the animals?"

Aaliyah's gaze locked onto Laney's. "If they knew they existed, then yes. They would kill them."

CHAPTER 72

Laney stepped onto the back veranda of the main house, her mind whirling. Henry had told her that Lou, Danny, and Rolly were researching Cleo's background. Maybe they had come up with a lead that would lead them to the pack. But even with that slim ray of hope, her fears couldn't be held back. *A large sacrifice and a vision of black leopards.*

Laney imagined Cleo being laid out like Sheila, and she felt lightheaded. Her gut clenched at the idea that Cleo could be in danger, even as she knew that it was a baseless fear. Cleo was fine, she reminded herself. She was at the school. And if anyone moved on Cleo, Laney would be informed immediately. Besides, taking Cleo down would be quite an undertaking, especially with Yoni, Lou, and Rolly around. Still, her reasoning didn't calm her pounding heart or stop the tremors that had worked their way into her hands.

Jen was working on her laptop on a lounge chair. She looked up as Laney sat down next to her with a frown. "What's wrong?"

Laney could hear the tremor in her voice. "We need to see what Danny and the gang came up with in their research on Cleo's background. I'll call Danny; can you call Lou? See what she knows?"

"No problem."

Laney pulled out her phone and dialed Danny. Her call went straight to voicemail. She frowned and called Henry. He answered quickly. "Hey, Lanes."

"Hey. Do you know where Danny is?"

"He's over at the school. He was going to stay there for a few days. Everything all right?"

"Yeah, I just wanted to ask him some questions about their research on Cleo. I'll see if I can track him down over there."

Her next call was to Jim, the analyst she'd originally had looking into Cleo's background. Jim quickly apologized, said he'd been pulled off of Cleo research to work on another project, but that he'd forward her all his files.

As she got off the phone with Jim, Jen set down her own phone. "I can't reach Lou *or* Rolly. Do you have Zach's number?"

Laney shook her head. "He doesn't have a cell." She was beginning to become concerned.

"They wouldn't do anything stupid, would they?"

Laney didn't answer; she just pulled out her phone and called Yoni, telling herself she was being unreasonable. There was nothing to fear. The Katzes were on the other side of the country.

When Yoni answered, Laney quickly explained to him about not being able to reach the teenagers. Yoni promised to track them down and call her back. That made Laney feel a little better. "Yoni will find them," she said to Jen.

Jen didn't look convinced. "Why are we trying to reach them?"

"That call I got? It was from a member of the Honu Keiki. And she believes that the Katzes' next target is going to be a group of black leopards."

Jen's eyes grew wide. "Really?"

"Really. And Danny, Lou, Rolly, and Zach were researching Cleo's background. So I'm hoping they might know where these guys are going to hit."

"And now we can't get in touch with any of the kids."

"Yeah." Laney didn't want to think about that. "Do you mind if I use your computer while I wait for Yoni to call me back? I want to see if we have anything new on Maura, Derek, and Abe."

"Sure." Jen passed her laptop over. "I'm going to grab some files from inside. I'll be right back."

Laney pulled up the files the analysts had compiled. By now, the analysts had become quite confident that Maura and Derek were in contact with over forty other Honu Keiki exiles—and that those exiles lived all over the world. It *was* a network. What they hadn't figured out yet was how they were financing all of this. The Katzes had, like all the exiles, been sent away with a large financial settlement, but that wasn't enough to cover the expenses of a global operation. Someone else was holding the purse strings. But who?

Laney's phone rang and she looked down at it, surprised that almost an hour had passed. "Hey Yoni. Did you find Danny?"

"He's not at the school," Yoni said. "I'm sure of it." His normal exuberance was absent.

Laney stared at the sky, not sure if she should be angry or worried. They'd had the campus on lockdown since they'd learned of the companion murders. No one should have been able to leave. "How is that possible?"

Yoni's voice was a growl. "Well, Danny's a genius, so I'm guessing that played a role."

Laney groaned. "Right. You're sure it was voluntary?"

"Oh yeah. Especially when I tell you who he's with."

Laney closed her eyes. *No. They wouldn't dare.*

"Yup. The fabulous threesome: Danny, Lou, and Rolly."

Laney looked at Jen, who raised an eyebrow. "Hold on a sec, Yoni." She covered the phone. "Danny, Lou, and Rolly have taken a little field trip."

294

Jen went still and then pulled out her own phone. Two seconds later, she was using a tone that promised a world of misery. "Lou Thomas, you call me as soon as you get this." She disconnected the call and looked at Laney. "I'm going to kill them."

"Get in line," Laney said, and then pulled the phone back to her ear. "Any idea where they went?"

"No. They were last seen at breakfast. I tried Dom to see if he knew anything, but he's conducting some sort of experiment and can't be disturbed."

Laney ground her teeth. *Convenient.* "See what you can find. And let us know what you come up with. Jen and I will start the search from here." She ended the call and called one of the analysts. "Sandra, I need you to grab three other analysts and find Danny, Lou, and Rolly. They disappeared from the school."

"But I'm about to—"

"Whatever you guys are working on, hand it off. This is a priority."

"Okay. You got it." Sandra hung up.

"What are we going to tell Henry?" Jen asked.

"The truth."

"You don't think they're in trouble, do you?"

Laney started to shake her head, then stopped. "I don't think they *left* because they were in trouble. But right now, I'd be shocked if they weren't."

Her phone rang, and she answered it with a frown. "Yoni?"

"Uh, I have good news and bad news."

Crap. "Okay. Give me the good."

"I found Zach, and he has the cell phone numbers they should be using. I just texted them to you. You should be able to find them through those."

Laney's phone dinged indicating a text. She quickly forwarded it to Sandra. These are the kids' numbers. Run a trace.

She clicked back to Yoni. "Okay, what's the bad news?"

"Um, I was wrong. It's not just the three of them. It's four."

Laney scrambled to think of who else was close enough to them to join them on whatever this little adventure was. Maybe Zach, but Yoni had just said he was still at the school.

"Who's the fourth?" Laney asked.

"Cleo."

CHAPTER 73

Show Low, Arizona

Lou adjusted the bag on her back as she stepped off the plane and followed Danny down the stairs to the tarmac at the Show Low Regional airport.

Rolly stretched as he followed. "Got to say, I could get used to traveling in private planes."

Lou looked around. They were in the back of the airport and hidden from the other hangars. "Come on, Cleo," she called.

Cleo slunk down the stairs. "You've got five minutes, girl, and then we're taking off."

Cleo seemed to nod before heading for the high grass on the side of the runway.

"I'm still not sure bringing her was the best call," Danny said.

"Well, it seemed like the right thing to do. Besides, wouldn't you want to come along if you were her?"

The Suburban they had reserved stood nearby. Danny had arranged for the car to be dropped off next to the hangar with the keys left inside. It helped that one of them had credit cards with no limit.

Danny nodded at it. "So who's driving?"

"That is *so* me." Rolly opened the driver door and turned the engine on. He popped back out a moment later. "This thing is totally loaded."

"How long a drive is it?" Lou asked.

"Two hours," Danny said, climbing into the back seat. "This is the closest airport." He paused. "We're sure this is the right thing to do? We could just head home."

Lou couldn't miss the hopeful tone in his voice. He'd agreed to come along, but Lou was pretty sure the long plane ride had given him too much time to think of all that could go wrong. And with Danny's brain, that was probably a really long list.

Rolly turned around in the driver's seat. "We're already here—we might as well take a look."

Lou climbed in the back next to Danny. "Yeah. We're just going to see what we can find out. No gunplay. No violence. What can possibly go wrong?"

Rolly put the car in gear and started to pull away. A black shape dashed from the tall grass and leaped in front of the car. Cleo stood there, staring at Rolly, her tail swishing back and forth. Lou gaped, then quickly got out of the car and opened the back.

Cleo walked over, stopped in front of Lou, and stared at her.

Lou ducked her head. "Sorry, Cleo."

Cleo huffed before jumping into the back and curling up.

Lou closed the rear door, then once again climbed into the back seat.

Danny crossed his arms over his chest and glared at her. "So nothing's going to go wrong, huh?"

Lou slumped down in her seat. "Oh, shut up, Danny."

298

CHAPTER 74

Baltimore, Maryland

Laney was just coming down the stairs of her cottage with a bag in her hand when Henry stormed in. "Where are they?"

Jen had driven to downtown Baltimore to get him—he'd been in meetings all day—and had probably broken every speed limit on her way back. Meanwhile, Laney had sprinted to the cottage to pack a quick bag.

"We're not sure," Laney said.

Jake stepped out of the kitchen, his phone in his hand. "Sandra tracked one of Danny's credit cards. He rented a plane."

Laney shook her head. *Normal teenagers run away on foot. Our teenagers run away by private jet.*

"To where?" Henry asked.

"Arizona."

"Where in Arizona?" Jen asked.

"The eastern edge. A place called Show Low."

"Show Low?" Jen asked. "What on earth is in Show Low?"

Jake shrugged "I don't know, but I have more bad news. There's been a report of the Katzes in Utah. They were caught on a street cam."

"The kids are heading to Arizona and the Katzes are one state away. I don't like that coincidence," Jen said.

"Why are they going to Arizona?" Henry demanded.

Laney and Jake exchanged a glance before Laney spoke. Jake had been going through the files on Cleo. "I had one of the analysts looking into Cleo's background earlier," Laney said. "He tracked them to a doctor named Ruggio, who runs a lab called GenDynamics in New Mexico, right on the border of Arizona. It's possible that's the lab where Cleo was created."

"I gave them permission to do research," Henry said. "I should have—"

"No," Jen said. "You are not to blame for this. Giving them permission to do a Google search is not the same as giving them permission to traipse across the country. They knew what you were giving them permission for, and it wasn't this."

"We need to get out there," Laney said.

"Agreed," Jen said.

"Do we know if the Katzes even know about the lab?" Jake asked.

"Officially, no. But if Aaliyah is right, we have to assume they do," Laney said. Her stomach tightened at the idea of Cleo being caught.

Jen gestured to the door. "Well, let's go round everybody up. I'll feel better once we have the kids and felines in cages."

"You mean custody," Henry said.

Jen shook her head. "No, I had it right the first time."

Jake snorted. "Okay. I've got a plane being prepped as we speak. And I called up a security detail."

Laney looked over at him in surprise.

"Oh, please," he said. "Like you running to the rescue is something even a little surprising. As soon as you're ready, we'll head to the airport."

"Jen?" Laney asked.

"I've got my bag in the car."

"I'll stay here," Henry said.

Laney looked up. "Really?"

"If we're wrong and the Katzes aren't out west, someone needs to be on this side of the country to run point. Just bring the kids back."

Laney hugged him. "We will. And it will be all right. I mean, they're all smart kids. They wouldn't do anything *really* stupid."

Jen, Jake, and Henry just stared at her.

Laney groaned. "They're doing something really stupid, aren't they?"

CHAPTER 75

Virden, New Mexico

GenDynamics Laboratories was located outside Virden, New Mexico, population 143. It was set back on five acres and surrounded by fields with little grass and lots of dry earth. The two-story building itself was rectangular, gray, and unimaginative. Even the sign, which they had to strain to find, was boring: simple black and white with "GenDynamics Laboratories" written in block lettering.

Rolly drove around its outside perimeter, which was marked by a fence. "Wow—ritzy," he drawled.

"Don't let the facade fool you. They made over five million last year," Danny said.

"And they *obviously* didn't put it into landscaping," Rolly replied.

Lou shook her head. "Not everybody cares about outward appearances."

"Oh, come on, this place makes a prison look like the Taj Mahal."

Lou ignored the comment, knowing any response would only lead to a protracted discussion of what Rolly would do with the place if given a chance. *I really need to stop him from watching any more HGTV.* "Okay, so according to the blueprints Danny conveniently downloaded from the town clerk, the first floor is offices, and the second is laboratories."

"But I think the basement has probably been renovated for other projects," Danny said.

"Why's that?" Rolly asked.

"Well, if this is where Cleo was created, they'd need a large holding area for the animals. Not to mention somewhere away from the prying eyes of the public."

"So the top two floors are the public face of the company and the sublevels are where all the Frankenstein stuff goes down?" Rolly asked.

"Exactly," Danny said.

"Danny can you get into their security system? Get us a look inside?" Lou asked.

Danny shook his head. "Not from here. The signal doesn't extend beyond the building."

Lou hadn't planned on that. She'd been counting on Danny's abilities to pave the way.

Rolly raised an eyebrow. "You can reroute satellites but you can't hack into some lab's security system? What kind of genius are you?"

Danny blushed.

"Just kidding, Danny. You're still the coolest genius I've ever met." Rolly paused. "Although Dom does have his moments."

Danny turned to Lou. "Okay, so how do we do this?"

"Well, I was thinking we just walk inside and ask for a tour," Lou said.

"You're kidding," Danny said.

"Not exactly. If we get inside, how long do you think it will take you to hack their system?"

"Two minutes. And if I can place a signal booster somewhere inside, we'd then be able to access the system even after we leave."

"That's just what I was thinking," Lou said. "So all we need is a way to keep them entertained while Danny does his thing. Thoughts?"

Rolly grinned. "I have an idea."

CHAPTER 76

Lou pushed through the door into the main lobby of GenDynamics. "I told you this is ridiculous."

Rolly stomped in behind her. "It is not. We're doing this."

Danny followed behind them and took a seat in the lobby area.

The receptionist, a brunette in a blue sweater vest looked up. "Can I help you?" she asked, though it was obvious she was hoping the answer was no.

Rolly strode over to her. "You guys do genetic testing here, right?"

"Yes," she said slowly.

Rolly turned to Lou, who glared back at him. "Told you."

"Whatever," Lou said, looking away. She took in the cameras in the corners of the large open atrium.

Rolly leaned against the counter. "Well, we need a genetic test done. Today."

The receptionist paused. "Uh, we don't take samples here. Samples are sent here from all over the country. You'll have to contact your doctor or another lab."

Rolly threw up his hands. "You guys must have *someone* who can take a sample!"

Lou glanced over at Danny. He shook his head.

The receptionist looked ready to call security. Her hand inched toward the phone. "I'm afraid I'll have to ask you to—"

"I told you I never slept with your brother!" Lou yelled.

The woman's hand paused.

"Yeah? Well then why does Joe Junior have brown eyes like him, huh? Mine are obviously green. Aren't they?" He turned to the receptionist, who nodded.

"*I* have brown eyes," Lou said. "He takes after me."

Rolly's look was incredulous. "Why on earth would he do that when I'm so much prettier?"

Lou rolled her eyes. "Really?"

Rolly turned back to the receptionist. "My eyes are prettier, aren't they?"

"Um, you two really need to leave."

Across the room, Danny stood.

Lou tugged on Rolly's jacket. "Come on. I don't want little Joey staying too long with your mother."

Rolly followed her across the room. "What's wrong with my mother?" he demanded.

"Oh, shut up," Lou said, pushing through the doors.

As soon as they were out of sight, Rolly grinned. "That was fun."

Lou shoved him. "What do you mean you have prettier eyes than me?"

Rolly wrapped an arm around her shoulders. "Yours are pretty. Mine just happen to be prettier."

They climbed into the Suburban and pulled away with Rolly behind the wheel. As soon as they were off the lab's property, Cleo popped her head up from the back.

"So? What's the verdict?" Lou asked.

Danny looked up from his laptop with a grin. "We're in."

While Danny explored the security systems, Rolly picked up some fast food and found a small park. They sat in the parking lot to eat, but as there didn't seem to be anyone around, they took their food and Danny's laptop over to a picnic table and let Cleo disappear into the park.

"She'll be okay, right?" Rolly asked.

"She knows to stay away from anyone," Danny replied. "She just needs to stretch her legs."

Lou watched Cleo disappear into the brush. "All right. Show us what you have."

Danny turned the laptop so the three of them could see it at the same time. "Okay, so I've been through most of their system. They have pretty decent security."

"But nothing you couldn't get past," Rolly said.

"Of course," replied Danny. Lou smiled. Danny might be introverted, but he didn't lack for confidence when it came to his abilities.

"We were right about the labs being in the basement. There are a lot of animals down there."

"Can we see?" Lou asked.

Danny pressed a few keys. Lou and Rolly leaned forward. The image was hard to make out. Lou could tell there were cages, and animals moving inside them, but she couldn't see exactly what type of animals they were.

"Are those dogs?" Rolly asked.

"I think so," Danny said.

"Anything bigger than that?" Lou asked.

Danny flipped to another screen.

"Cows?" Lou said. "Huh. What about leopards?"

"I didn't see any," Danny said. "But if they're young, then it would be hard to see them. I can't see into all the cages."

"What about their files? They must tell you something," Rolly said.

Danny shook his head. "Their files aren't linked to the system. I'm guessing that was deliberate, to keep anyone from doing exactly what we're trying to do."

"So the only way to know what's really going in there is to go take a look?" Rolly asked.

306

"Yeah."

Lou took a bite from a fry. "Then I guess we're going in."

CHAPTER 77

Laney stared out the plane window. Jen was sleeping in the back, as were Jake and most of the team, but Laney couldn't. She had tried all of the cell phone numbers Zach had given them, but the kids must have had them turned off because her calls went right to voicemail. *Or they're avoiding me,* she thought with a growl. She still couldn't believe they'd done this. What were they thinking?

They were going to land in about forty-five minutes, and then it was another two-hour drive to the lab. But Jake had contacted the local police to let them know a contingency of feds would soon be driving through the area at well over the posted speed limit, so Laney was hoping they'd be able to make it there in just over an hour once they hit the ground.

Her thoughts drifted to Honu Keiki. She wasn't sure what to make of the group. They *had* warned them about potential victims, but Laney was also pretty sure they had set up that whole incident in the coffee shop. She couldn't figure out their angle. Jake had suggested it was a test to see what she could do. But why? And Laney had gotten the impression that Aaliyah hadn't been behind that test. So who had? And what did any of that have to do with the companion murders?

Laney's thoughts were going around in circles. Her phone rang, and she snatched it up with a glance at the ID. "Aaliyah?"

Aaliyah's voice came out rushed. "Laney, I'm glad I reached you."

Laney frowned. "What's wrong?"

Aaliyah responded with a question of her own. "Do you have a location?"

"We think so. There's a lab in New Mexico that specializes in animal research. We think some of our teenagers are headed there. It's possible that Maura and Derek Katz may be headed there as well."

"Yes. She had the vision again, but it was different." Aaliyah paused. "These teenagers, they're important to you."

Laney wondered at the conversation change. "I don't know if you've heard of the Chandler School. The children there, they all come from tough backgrounds. Most of them are alone in the world. We hope to provide them with not just a school but a home."

"And you care about them."

Laney thought of Lou, Rolly, and Danny. "Very much—especially these three. They..." She paused. "They've had such a hard life. They've had these horrible circumstances handed to them, and they still do the right thing. They still see the good in the world. How can you not care about people like that? I just need to know they're safe. I mean, I'm probably worried for nothing. Maura and Derek could be anywhere."

Aaliyah was silent.

Laney's heart clutched. "Aaliyah, you haven't said what changed in the vision."

"As you know, the sacrifices don't occur until sunset tomorrow. There's still time."

Laney said nothing, but a cold ball of fear began to develop in her stomach.

"Previously, the seer only saw cats."

The ball of fear grew. "That's changed?"

"Maybe not changed, so much as the picture became bigger."

"It's not just cats, is it?"

309

"No. Now there's a human on one of the altars as well."

CHAPTER 78

Lou, Rolly, and Danny waited until eleven o'clock that night to head back to GenDynamics. They had driven around for a while, but downtown Virden hadn't had much to offer. Danny had finally rented a motel room online. They'd snuck Cleo in and all of them had taken a nap. None of them had slept well the previous night.

Now Lou and Rolly crouched next to the fence of GenDynamics. There was only a skeleton crew on at night. They had been watching the facility for thirty minutes, but had seen no activity. It was time to move.

"We're ready," Lou said into her mike as she pulled her ski mask over her face. Danny had brought a bag full of spy gear. Lou really did feel like she was in a movie.

Danny spoke quietly into her earpiece. "The southwest door will be unguarded in three, two, one."

Lou and Rolly leapt over the fence and sprinted for the door. It unlocked for them as they were almost on it. Lou pulled it open.

"Down the stairs on the right," Danny said.

Lou sprinted toward them and descended as quietly as she could.

"Guard coming. Door on the right," Danny ordered.

Lou slipped through the door, with Rolly right behind her.

Ten seconds later, Danny spoke again. "All clear."

Lou opened the door and hurried down the hall. It ended in a crossing corridor that went a long distance both left and right. Her nervousness spiked. They'd decided to split up. Lou would check out the animals' pens and Rolly would head to the office and download all the files he could.

Rolly grinned at Lou. "Good luck, partner."

"You too." She turned and headed to the right.

CHAPTER 79

Rolly made his way to an office in the back. "Danny, I'm here." He sat at one of the terminals. "What do I do?"

"Insert the flash drive I gave you."

Rolly did. "Done."

"Okay. Open the program on there. It will download everything for you."

"Okay." On the screen in front of Rolly, pages flashed by. Fifteen seconds later, the screen went blank. "Screen's blank," Rolly said.

"You're done. Grab the drive and head out," Danny said.

"Roger." Rolly ejected the flash drive and pocketed it, feeling very much like James Bond.

"How's Lou doing?" Rolly asked.

"She's almost done."

"Okay, am I clear?"

"Yeah." Rolly hurried down the hall, pausing to look into some of the windows as he passed. Cages and cages of animals stared back at him, but none were leopards.

"Someone's coming, Rolly. Door on the left," Danny said.

Rolly stepped into the room. It was an old lab. He inspected a few cages and then reared back. All the animals were dead. There were a few bald cats, some he thought were dogs, mice, snakes. He shuddered. *What the hell is wrong with these people?*

A movement behind him caused him to turn. A small shape huddled by an open cage along the back wall. It let out a little whimper and moved a little closer to Rolly. Rolly squinted and realized it was a small dog.

"Hey there, little guy," Rolly said. The dog shuffled forward. A tumor covered half of its face. Rolly covered his mouth. "Jesus."

The dog, a dachshund, looked up at him with her one good eye. Rolly let the dog sniff his hand, then ran his hand over the dog's face. It leaned into him.

"Rolly we need to go," Lou yelled into his ear.

Rolly's throat felt tight as he pulled back his hand. "Sorry little guy, I have to go."

The dog gave a whimper.

Rolly stood. Danny's voice came over the headset, sounding panicked. "Rolly, you need to go, *now*."

"Okay, okay. I'm coming."

Klaxons rang out through the room.

CHAPTER 80

Lou sprinted down the hallway as the alarm blared. A night janitor taking a stroll had caught her, but at least she'd had a chance to check all the rooms first. She'd seen some wretched cows, bunnies, and chimps. Unfortunately, she hadn't seen any leopards.

These scientists are the real animals, she thought as she rounded the corner. She expected to see Rolly waiting for her impatiently, but the hallway was empty. *Damn it, Rolly. Come on.*

Just then Rolly rounded the corner at the other end of the hall. "About time," Lou said.

"No time for chit-chat. Let's go." Rolly ran right past her and through the door.

Lou took off after him, and together, they raced for the exit. A guard stepped out from a doorway ahead of them, but they didn't slow down. Rolly ducked around him; Lou barreled right over him, and he let out a yell and slammed into the wall. Lou and Rolly kept running, straight out the door and across the property. They heard shouts from behind them as they leapt over the fence, and as soon as their feet hit the ground, they continued their mad sprint.

At their rendezvous point, Danny had the engine running and the doors open. Lou put on a burst of speed and dove into the back seat. Rolly tumbled in behind her.

"Go, go, go!" Lou yelled.

Danny slammed on the gas and tore out of the dirt lot. Behind them, four security guards had just reached the fence, but they were too late. Danny turned onto the highway and headed north.

Rolly's shirt moved and then whimpered.

Lou sat back, her eyes growing wide. "Um, Rolly, your shirt seems upset."

Cleo leaned over from the back and sniffed Rolly's shirt. The hair on her neck stood up. "It's okay, girl," Rolly said.

Another whimper emanated from Rolly's shirt.

"Now, don't get mad," Rolly said.

"What did you do?" Lou demanded.

Rolly pulled a small black and brown dachshund from under his shirt. One of its legs was missing, and when the dog turned toward Lou, she let out a gasp. "Oh my God."

"I couldn't leave her there. They left her in a room to die. Henry's got to know somebody who can help her."

"I can't believe you did that," Lou said. "That dog could have all sorts of diseases."

"There were no bio warnings on the door, and I saw them on some others."

"Rolly, that was really reckless."

Rolly glared. "Really? Because we're not racing around looking for Cleo's siblings, breaking all sorts of laws?"

Lou glared back at him before finally shaking her head. "Fine. But if I get leprosy, you are in so much trouble."

"Fine."

"Hey, one of you guys want to drive so I can go through the files?" Danny asked.

"Don't look at me," Rolly said. "I need to take care of Princess."

Lou rolled her eyes. *Princess. Great.* "Pull over. I'll drive."

"You don't have a license," Danny said.

316

"Neither do you. And FYI, that would be the most minor crime I will have committed tonight. Pull over."

Lou and Danny switched seats. Lou drove in silence. Rolly kept the dog against his chest, and Cleo licked it for a little while before resting her head on Rolly's shoulder.

After fifteen minutes, Danny spoke. "We need to turn around."

"Did you find more leopards?" Rolly asked.

"Maybe. There are notes here about a special project. It's called Project Panthera."

Panthera, the Latin name for leopard, Lou thought. "Where?"

"At another facility. It's called the nursery."

CHAPTER 81

Lou pulled over to the side of the road about two miles from the nursery. The "nursery" was actually another lab, only a few miles from the original one. But according to the files Danny had found, this was where all the most exotic research happened. The building was three stories high and set on large plot of fenced-in land. Security manned the front gate.

"Okay, so what's the plan here? Another Jerry Springer scenario?" Rolly asked.

Lou gave a nervous laugh. "Somehow I don't think that's going to work here. We could just jump the fence, sprint over to the building, and take a peek."

"Yes, that worked so well for us before," Danny grumbled.

"Okay, so one janitor happened to spot me," Lou said.

"And Rolly took a friend," Danny said.

Rolly smiled. "Yes, but Princess was so unhappy in that place. She's much happier with us. Aren't you, baby?" He leaned down to the little dog, who licked him on the cheek.

Lou rolled her eyes. "You realize that dog has been in a mad scientist's lab. You have no idea how many diseases she has. She could be a walking Typhoid Mary."

"Nah, Cleo gave her the seal of approval. She's good," Rolly said.

"Right, well, back to the immediate problem—what's going on in the nursery," Lou said.

"Guys, I think maybe we should call home," Danny said. "We've got enough information. We need to hand it off to Henry and Laney. Get them to come in here and grab everybody."

Lou did feel a little guilty. She'd seen all the missed calls from Jen, Laney, Henry, Jake, even Yoni. She had listened to the last few messages and knew they were on their way here—and that they were not happy.

But they hadn't accomplished anything yet. So far, all they'd done was worry everybody for nothing. They needed something tangible to give them. She shook her head. "We don't know for sure that those leopards are inside the building. We just need one quick peek, and then we'll call in the cavalry and get them out. I mean, if we call right now, all we can say is we *think* they're inside." She met Danny's gaze, and he didn't look away.

"It's dangerous," he said.

Lou nudged Rolly. "Not for the Super Twins."

Rolly frowned. "I thought we were going with the Dynamic Duo?"

"Whatever. The point is, we're not going to be interacting with anyone. We'll hop the fence, scale the building, and take a peek through the skylights. No one will even know we're there," Lou said.

"Why am I not reassured?" Danny muttered.

Rolly clapped him on the shoulder. "Because you have no faith. In ten minutes we'll be in, out, and headed back."

Lou turned to Cleo. "Cleo, you need to stay with Danny."

Rolly coughed and nudged his chin toward the little dachshund staring up at him with worship in her eye.

Lou rolled her eyes. "And Princess."

Danny looked at Lou. "If there's any problem, any at all, I'm calling in help immediately."

319

Lou stood up and dusted off her pants. "No problem. But you don't have to worry. They'll never even know we were here."

CHAPTER 82

Maura reviewed the blueprints for the GenDynamics facility. She was confident they could get in and out without too much trouble. There was security, but they wouldn't be expecting an armed assault. *It will be enough.*

Derek strode into the room. "We have a problem."

"What?"

"Nick called. An alarm was tripped in the basement of GenDynamics."

Nick had been placed at GenDynamics, as part of the janitorial staff, as soon as they learned of their connection to the beasts. He had been assigned to the basement level tonight when two of his colleagues conveniently became "ill."

"What happened? Did he set if off?" Maura asked.

"No. There were two intruders in the basement level."

Maura frowned. "Intruders? Were they caught?"

"They moved too *fast* to be caught. Nick sent me a copy of the security tapes."

He brought the footage up on Maura's laptop and stepped back for her to see. On screen, two individuals stepped into a hallway in ski masks. They went in opposite directions. Derek fast-forwarded, then slowed back down when the alarm was tripped. The intruders could be seen sprinting for the exit, moving faster than any human could run.

"Fallen," Maura whispered.

"Yes. But I don't understand why they were there. If they created the beasts, why sneak in?"

"Maybe they don't like the deal they have with the scientist. Whatever the reason, we need to move quickly."

"The team is ready to go."

"Make sure they know the Fallen may be there. And that they are fair game."

CHAPTER 83

Lou crouched behind a tree and waited for the security guards to walk past. As soon as they looped around the building, she looked over at Rolly, who nodded. Without a sound, they sprinted for the fence and jumped over. Landing in a crouch, they barely paused before racing for the building and taking cover. All was quiet.

"So far, so good," Rolly said. "Although there is a certain sense of déjà vu at work here."

Lou nudged her chin toward the fire escape. "Let's go." She had just started to move toward the ladder when Rolly yanked her back, his hand over her mouth. "Sh."

Lou went still. Then she heard the footsteps too. A door no more than twenty feet away from them swung open, and Lou held her breath. *Please don't look this way.* A man exited and headed straight for the parking lot, not glancing behind him.

Heart pounding, Lou watched him until he disappeared from view. *Maybe I'm really not cut out for this spy stuff.* "Okay. Let's go before someone else shows up."

They sprinted for the fire escape and leapt up to it. Lou cringed when it squeaked under her weight. But they raced up to the roof, so that even if someone came to investigate the sound there'd be nothing to see. Lou rolled onto the roof and crouched low.

The roof was flat with a dozen large skylights strewn across it. They kept low as they made their way over to the nearest one and peered down.

Inside, the building was completely open. A series of catwalks rimmed the space, and several more crossed from one side to the other. A couple of offices were situated at the back of the building, along with shelves of supplies. A lab was set up near the front. Directly below them were at least two dozen cages. And inside each one was a leopard.

Most were black, but Lou could see at least one white and one yellow. The cats were beautiful, even in the dim light, but the cages were too small for them. They had no room to stretch.

"Bastards," Rolly growled.

Lou nodded, but she couldn't speak. All she could think of was Cleo being stuffed into one of those cages. "Come on. Let's get out of here and let everybody know."

"Guys," Danny said through their earpieces. "There are some trucks approaching."

Rolly and Lou quietly crept to the edge of the building. Four sets of headlights rolled through the front gate.

"Probably a late-night delivery," Lou said.

A streak of light raced from the lead truck toward the gate.

The guardhouse exploded in a flash of fire and wood. Three large military trucks sped through the opening.

Lou felt her mouth fall open. "What the hell is going on?"

As the trucks approached the building, men leaned out of the windows, weapons in hand. Two security guards ran out the front door of the building and were quickly mowed down.

The trucks turned the corner of the building and Lou and Rolly ran along the edge of the roof, keeping track of them.

"They have to be going for the cats. What do we do?" Rolly asked.

324

"I don't know." Lou tapped her mike. "Danny? Danny, are you there?"

"Yeah. Are you two okay?"

"Yeah. I need you to call Laney. See where they are. Tell them what's happening."

"I will. What are you to going to do?" Danny asked.

Rolly looked at her and shook his head.

"You're not going in there, right?" Danny asked.

"Not unless we have to."

"Lou—"

"Call Laney." Lou disconnected the transmission.

Below them, the trucks pulled to a stop by the loading dock. Men and women with weapons took up positions around the trucks while other disappeared inside. Lou and Rolly ran to one of the skylights and looked down.

The intruders were headed straight for the crates. Two men leveled their weapons.

"No," Lou cried.

Rolly grabbed her arm. "No. They're tranqs. Look."

Darts, not bullets, flew at the animals, and one by one the animals collapsed.

Lou and Rolly could only watch helplessly as the men began moving the crates to the trucks. They were prepared. They had ten crates up and loaded in about ten minutes.

Two of the gunmen were apparently responsible for guarding the nursery's employees. They rounded up everyone—five men and three women—and held them at gunpoint. Lou did not like how the men kept looking at the hostages. By her count there were eleven gunmen.

A man in a white coat let out a yell as he was dragged in front of the others.

"Where did he come from?" Rolly asked.

One of the gunmen turned and shot him point blank. Lou gasped.

"Goddamn it," Rolly growled.

"Rolly," Lou said. "We have to do something. We have to stop this."

"Lou, they have guns. We have none. It's suicide."

"No. We heal. Those people trapped down there don't. We need to help them."

"But Laney and Jen—"

"Are not here. We are. And those people have run out of time." Lou touched her earpiece. "Danny, Rolly and I are going in."

"But-" Lou turned off her earpiece and looked at Rolly.

Another gunshot rang out from below.

Rolly shook his head, took Lou's hand, and ran for the fire escape. "Do not get me killed."

CHAPTER 84

Laney sat next to Jen as they barreled down the highway toward GenDynamics. By the time their plane had landed, Jordan Witt, Jen's brother, had already landed himself and had taken a team east. Laney and Jen had grabbed the first car they saw, leaving Jake to organize the rest of the troops, who would be a few minutes behind.

They'd just received word about the break-in at Gen Dynamics a few minutes ago.

"I can't believe Lou pulled this," Jen said. "What was she thinking?"

Laney shook her head. "I can't believe it either, but I think *they* think they're helping."

"Right, helping," Jen growled.

Laney's phone rang and she answered it immediately, knowing it was Jake. "We're almost at the facility. Have you—"

"Laney." Danny's voice was filled with panic.

"Danny, where are you? What's going on?" Laney switched to speakerphone.

"The main lab didn't have the cats, but we learned there was another site. Lou and Rolly were just going to peek and make sure the cats were there. They were about to leave when these trucks showed up with all these guys with guns."

"Are you okay?" Laney asked, her heart rate spiking.

Danny took a stuttering breath. "I am, but Lou and Rolly are inside. I don't know what happened. Those trucks just came out of nowhere."

"Tell us where you are," Jen said.

"I've just now texted you the address."

Jen pulled it up and entered it into the car's GPS. "We need to turn around."

Laney slowed only enough to initiate a U-turn. Jen held on to the panic bar, her eyes wide, as two tires left the road.

"Send the address to Jake and Jordan too," Laney said.

"On it."

"How long?" Laney asked.

"We're ten minutes away," Jen said.

"That's going to be too long," Danny said, his voice shaky. "We have to go help them."

"We?" Laney asked.

"Me and Cleo."

"No! Danny, you stay in the car. You hear me?" Laney said, tears springing to her eyes.

"I'm sorry, guys. We just wanted to help."

"Danny!" Jen yelled. But the call had been disconnected.

"Call him back," Laney said, her hands gripping the steering wheel.

Jen fumbled with the keypad, punching the numbers in. The call went unanswered.

Jen's voice trembled when she spoke. "Drive faster, Laney."

CHAPTER 85

Rolly and Lou quickly descended the stairs and started to creep along the side of the nursery opposite the loading dock. "Okay, so what's the plan?" Rolly asked.

"Um..."

"You don't have a plan?" Rolly whispered furiously.

"Yes, of course I do. We sneak in, you get the people out. And I'll distract anyone who happens to swing by."

Rolly glared at her. "That is a lousy plan."

Lou sighed. "Yeah, but it's the only one I've got."

"Hey!" a voice yelled out behind them.

Lou whirled around just as bullets blasted the ground next to them. Rolly grabbed her arm and yanked her forward. They sprinted around the side of the building. But another armed man was waiting for them there.

"Shit," Lou yelled. She grabbed Rolly and dove with him through the nearest window.

"Pretty sure they heard that," Rolly groaned.

"Just stick to the plan. You get the humans. I'll distract the gunmen."

Running footsteps approached. "Hide," Lou said to Rolly. He gave her a glare and ducked behind some crates.

Lou stood where she was, her fists clenched. As soon as the first face came into view, she took off at a run—a human-paced run.

"Stop!" a man yelled, and bullets chewed the ground behind her.

Who would stop? she wondered as she anxiously scanned the room for something she could use to fight them off. Up ahead, she saw a rack loaded with tall canisters of oxygen. She smiled and sprinted toward them—this time at Fallen speed. She turned one canister on its side with the nozzle aimed away from the gunmen. Then she grabbed a wrench from a bench behind her and waited.

As soon as the first man came into view, she slammed the wrench down on the nozzle. The nozzle clanged to the ground and the container took off like a torpedo, with Lou right behind it. The first gunman got slammed in the leg. He went down with a cry. Lou kicked him in the head as she passed. The second one stumbled and took a shot to the groin. Lou landed a solid uppercut.

The third gunman managed to leap out of the tank's way. But before he could bring his weapon up, Lou was on him. She grabbed his gun and slammed it against the wall. He cried out. She kneed him in the groin and brought her other elbow across his jaw. He eyes rolled back in his head and he dropped.

Lou stepped back, breathing hard. She looked around but saw no one else. She smiled. *One for the good guys.*

A bullet slammed into her side. She cried out and dove for the ground as more bullets struck the wall behind her. She army-crawled for the stairs, leaving a trail of blood. She pulled herself up, risking a look behind her. A woman with dark hair strode toward her. Lou ran up the stairs, her wound already healing.

Another man sprinted along the catwalk toward her. Lou jumped onto the long metal bar spanning the entire room balancing like a tightrope walker. Down below, she saw Rolly hustling the lab coats out of the building. Two gunmen lay sprawled behind him.

Bullets hit the catwalk. Lou jumped and lost her balance.

"No!" she yelled, her arms spinning. But it was no use. With a scream, she fell from the catwalk. She managed to roll as she hit and distribute the force as she hit the floor, but it wasn't pretty.

She got to her knees. Four gunmen surrounded her. *Oh shit.*

CHAPTER 86

Lou tensed, ready to run.

"Hey!" Rolly yelled. He appeared from off to the side and flew at one of the men, landing an elbow on the man's jaw. The man did a complete three-sixty with the hit.

Lou reacted quickly; she dove for the knees of the man nearest her. He let out a yell, pulling the trigger, but his gun was trained upward. Lou punched him in the groin, and followed that with a punch to the throat.

Gunfire burst out behind her and Lou whirled around. Rolly shook like he was having a seizure, and bright spots of red burst out across his chest and legs.

"No!" Lou yelled. The dark-haired woman was striding forward, firing non-stop at Lou.

A bullet slammed into Lou's leg, and she stumbled back and dove out of the line of fire. Every time she tried to stick her head out, someone opened fire, forcing her back. The vision of Rolly left her numb.

Then at last everything went quiet. The sound of running footsteps approached, and Lou reared back, ready to attack.

But it was only Danny who appeared around the corner, a gun in his hand. "Lou."

The gun made her eyes go wide, but she didn't take time to ask. "Rolly."

"They put him in a truck," Danny said. "I couldn't get to them."

Lou ran to the loading dock with Danny right behind her. As they arrived at the doorway, the trucks were already pulling away.

"Which truck is Rolly on?" Lou asked.

"I—I don't know. They all look alike."

Just then Lou spotted a familiar black shape sprinting through the darkness outside. *Cleo.* The great cat raced toward one of the trucks, and with a single graceful leap, she cleared the tailgate and landed in the back of the truck. Lou nearly cried with relief.

Until gunfire blared from inside.

The truck stopped.

Lou held her breath, but Cleo didn't reappear. And after a few seconds, the truck started to move again.

Lou took a step forward and Danny latched on to her arm. "Lou, you can't."

"They have Cleo and Rolly."

"You'll be killed."

"I'm not that easy to kill."

"If you go, I go."

Lou looked at Danny; she saw the determination in his eyes. He wouldn't let her go alone. And he would get killed. *I'll get him killed.*

Her heart in her throat, Lou reached up and hugged him. Then she slipped around his back and wrapped her forearm around his throat, cutting off his air. "I'm sorry, Danny. But I need to do this. And I need you to find us."

Danny struggled against her, grabbing at her arm, but she refused to let go. When he stopped struggling, Lou lowered him to the ground. She put her ear to his chest. His heartbeat was strong.

She pulled his watch from his wrist. "I'm sorry," she said. And then she ran after the truck.

CHAPTER 87

The truck was already close to a mile away. Even with all Lou's abilities, it took time to catch up to it. She prayed with every step she took. *Please let them be all right. Please let them be alive.*

Finally, she was close enough. She put on a burst of speed and snagged the tailgate. She pulled her legs up onto the bumper and hung on, listening for any noises inside. It sounded quiet, but with the air rushing by her and the rattling of the truck it was tough to be sure.

Okay. Time to go. Carefully, she peeked over the tailgate. And nearly lost her grip. Rolly and Cleo lay on the floor of the truck bed, both bleeding heavily. Two darts stuck out of each of them. But there was no one else in view.

Lou pulled herself over the tailgate and dropped down next to Rolly. She swallowed down the bile that rose in her throat at the sight of him, and quickly pulled the darts out of his arm and chest. Judging by his wounds, the darts had contained some form of sedative; otherwise he would have healed more by now.

"Rolly," she said quietly. "Rolly, wake up."

"Oh, he's not waking up." A man stepped from behind the crates at the front of the truck. She hadn't seen him. He'd been crouched down. *Waiting for me.*

334

Lou heaved Rolly to his feet, holding him upright as the man opened fire. Pain rolled through her as she shielded Rolly. Bullets slammed into her back. She cried out with pain. Her vision danced, and she knew she was going to lose consciousness.

With the last of her strength, she pushed Rolly to the tailgate. With bullets raking her back and legs, she pushed him over. *Good-bye, Rolly.* He hit the ground with a sickening thump.

And then Lou's legs gave out and she collapsed. Blood bubbled up her throat and into her mouth. The gunman strode toward her. She couldn't move away. It was all she could do to keep breathing.

He stood over her. "Say goodbye." He pulled the trigger over and over again.

Lou tried to scream, but the pain was too much and it was everywhere, all at once. She felt like she was drowning. She tried to grasp her throat, but her arms wouldn't work.

Her vision dimmed. She felt her heart stutter, and then stutter again.

And then she felt it stop.

CHAPTER 88

The ground beneath Rolly felt hard and rocky. He opened his eyes and stared at the star-filled sky.

Pretty, he thought, closing his eyes again. The memories cascaded over him. He cringed as he remembered the onslaught of bullets.

He sat up and looked around. *Where am I?* Way in the distance he could see the lights of the nursery. He frowned. *How'd I get this far out?*

But then his concerns for his friends crowded out his curiosity and he struggled to his feet. He ran back to the facility, gaining strength and speed as he went.

He called into his mike. "Lou? Danny? Where are you guys?"

He got no answer.

He'd told Lou this was a bad plan. What had she been thinking? They weren't a friggin' team of commandos. They were teenagers.

The fence to the nursery was up ahead, and all was quiet. Way too quiet. Rolly's heart began to pound as he crept forward. He scanned the grounds but didn't see anyone. He paused, listening again, but still there was nothing. He walked through the destroyed front gate, made his way to the side of the building, and peered in. Nothing moved.

He hurried on, knowing he needed to find Danny and Lou before the cops arrived. One of the lab coats must have called them by now.

He turned the corner and came across another body—a security guard. The man eyes stared straight up, and his mouth was open in a silent scream. Blood covered his once pale blue shirt.

Rolly swallowed. Poor man. He'd never stood a chance.

Rolly passed three more security guards as he hurried around the building, but what he didn't see was Lou or Danny.

Okay. This is good. Lou got them out of here. They're probably back at the car. I should—

He stopped suddenly, his breath catching as he caught sight of a familiar red jacket on a body sprawled on the ground ahead. "Danny?" he whispered, tears springing to his eyes.

He ran forward and fell to the ground next to an unmoving Danny. "No, Danny, no."

He pulled back Danny's jacket, ran his hands along Danny's legs, and carefully turned him over, but he found no wounds. He sat back with a frown, trying to figure out why Danny wasn't awake.

Danny let out a small groan.

Rolly lunged forward, crouching over him. "Wake up, Danny."

Danny groaned again. His eyelids flicked open and then closed again.

"That's it. Come on, Danny, wake up."

Danny opened his eyes, looking confused before his gaze was able to focus on Rolly. "Rolly?"

Relief poured through Rolly as he helped Danny sit up. "Yup, that's me. All day, every day. You okay? Where are you hurt?"

"I'm not—" Danny grabbed Rolly's shirt. "Lou. She went after Cleo. She went after you. You were in the truck too."

337

"Truck? What truck?" Rolly asked.

Danny looked down the road. Then he looked at his wrist. He smiled. "Thank God. She stole my watch." He scrambled to his feet. "Let's go."

Rolly watched Danny for a moment. "Oh God, Danny's got a head injury."

CHAPTER 89

The last twenty minutes had been excruciating. Laney had tried each of the kids' phones over and over again, with no luck. Finally, Laney's phone beeped. "Danny, we're almost—"

Danny's words were rushed. "You need to head east. They're heading that way. They have Lou and Cleo."

"Lou and Cleo? How—? No, you know what? Never mind." Laney yanked the steering wheel to the left.

Jen was thrown against the door, but she didn't complain as she grabbed Laney's phone and switched it to speaker. "Danny, do you know where they're heading?"

"There's an old highway. It was never completed. They've landed planes there."

Jen grabbed her iPad and quickly brought up a map of the area. "I've got it. We need to tell Jordan and—"

Danny cut her off. "I already called him. They made the turn. They're almost there."

"How do you know where they're heading?" Laney asked.

"Lou stole my watch. I put a tracker in it in case I ever got grabbed. She activated it."

Laney closed her eyes. *Thank you, Lou.*

"And I've got a satellite feed on them. They've loaded at least half the crates," Danny said.

"What can you see?" Jen asked.

"There's a group of people moving the cages from the truck to the—" Danny gave a sharp intake of breath.

"Danny?" Jen asked.

Danny's voice shook. "They—they're carrying a body to the plane as well. I think it's Lou."

Laney's stomach hollowed out. "Danny, she's a Fallen. Even if it is her, she can recover from a lot. Okay? So let's assume she'll be fine until we know otherwise."

Despite her words, all Laney could think of was how she'd found Sheila. She prayed she wouldn't see Lou the same way.

Relief broke through Danny's voice. "Jordan's there! They're there. I see them." Then he went quiet.

"What's happening?" Laney asked, trying to keep the impatience out of her voice.

"There's gunfire. It's hard to tell—"

The next two minutes were tense. Finally, Danny said quietly, "We're too late."

"No, we'll be there any minute," Laney said.

Danny's voice was flat. "The planes took off. They're gone."

CHAPTER 90

Laney bumped over the curb as she pulled onto the unfinished highway. Ahead she could see a few bodies, but when she'd spoken with Jordan, he'd assured her none of their people had been hurt. Her anger began to build as she saw three men on the ground with two Chandler Operatives guarding them.

Laney hopped out of the car and had to keep herself from slamming the door shut behind her. She stormed toward Jordan. She was not losing Cleo or Lou. Loss was not an option. They were still tracking them, but the Katzes had a head start, so if they were going to catch up, they needed to know what their final destination was.

The captives all stared at the ground. Jordan stood with his arms across his chest, his face set. "You guys got this?" he asked Laney. "Because I need to get away from this filth and check on the plane."

"The plane?" Laney asked.

"I called the pilot. He's heading here from Show Low. If those guys can use this as a runway, so can we. It'll be here in about fifteen minutes.

Laney nodded as Jordan walked away. Then she caught Jen's eye. "We need them to tell us where the plane's going."

Jen reached down and yanked one of the prisoners up so that his feet barely touched the ground. "Where are they taking them?"

The man's eyes bulged.

"He won't tell you," another prisoner said, his voice perfectly calm. "None of us will."

With a shock, Laney recognized him: Abe Hanley. The meek bookkeeper had transformed. There was now a hard edge in his voice and a challenge in his eyes.

Laney bared her teeth. "Oh, you'll tell us."

Abe smiled. "No I won't. But I will tell you this: they are the last sacrifice before it begins."

Laney swallowed hard. Twenty leopards and one human—a large sacrifice for the ritual. "Where is the last sacrifice going to take place?" she demanded.

But Abe said nothing. His eyes went wide, and a white foam began to spray from his mouth. His body shook and he fell onto his side. A second later, the other two demonstrated the same behaviors.

Jen dropped the man she was holding and stepping back. "What the hell?"

"No, no, no." Laney yanked Abe's jaw down and thrust her hand inside, yanking out the remnants of a capsule. It was empty. "Goddamn it."

Horror crept over Laney as she stared at the three corpses. "They killed themselves rather than revealing what they knew."

Jen's eyes were large, her skin pale. Her gaze met Laney's, and it was filled with terror and fear. "What are we going to do?"

Laney shook her head. "We wait for the plane. Danny's tracker is still working. We can follow them."

Jen shook her head. "You mean after they've had a forty-minute head start."

Jen walked over to one of the trucks that had transported the cats. Laney followed as Jen flashed a light inside.

Laney gasped. The truck's bed was coated in blood. Footprints had dragged the blood everywhere, but a giant pool still lay in the middle.

342

Laney put her arm around Jen. "We don't know it's her blood."

"Don't we?" Jen asked softly as she walked away.

Laney knew the Fallen could take a lot of damage. She'd seen it time and time again.

But she also knew that that was a *lot* of blood. In fact, it looked like an entire body's worth.

Shoving her fears down, Laney looked around for something to do. She squinted and saw that six crates had been left behind. She walked toward them slowly, both awed and horrified at the young cats lying inside. As she approached, she read no aggression from them, only fear.

She knelt down at the first crate. The cat inside was beautiful—sleek, muscular but still small, with only his large paws indicating how big he would one day grow. A few seconds later, the cat began to stir.

His eyes opened and he emitted a low growl. Laney looked into his eyes. *You have nothing to fear. We won't harm you. We're friends.*

She could feel the animal's distrust. Images of the abuse he and his littermates suffered flew through her mind.

Laney was sickened by it. *I'm sorry. We won't let them hurt you again. You are safe.*

She reached in a hand and hesitated for only a moment before sliding it over the animal's head. *It's all right.*

He went still and then began to relax, closing his eyes with a sigh. *That's right, sleep. Soon we'll have you in your new home.*

Laney went around to the other cages, going through the same calming process with each of them. She felt the eyes of the Chandler operatives on her as she moved from cage to cage, turning the distrustful cats into peaceful kittens.

In the last cage lay the smallest of the cats. It was a gorgeous female cub, pure white with blue eyes. *It's all right. You're safe now.* Laney reached in and laid her hand on the

343

cub's back. The cub began to purr before turning to lick Laney's hand with her little sandpaper tongue.

Laney laughed, running her hand through the cub's pelt. "Cleo's going to love you."

Fear surged in her when she realized Cleo might not even meet this little one. She cleared her throat and stood. *What am I going to do with all you guys?* A zoo was out of the question, as was a nature reserve. At least, until they knew exactly what these cats were capable of.

She heard a car approaching, and turned. An SUV pulled up, and Rolly stepped out. Laney blanched. His shirt and pants were covered in dried blood and bullet holes. *Dear God.*

She walked over to him and pulled him into a hug. "Are you all right?"

He nodded into her shoulder even as a shudder ran through him. Then he pulled back and stared down at Laney, his eyes filled with regret. "I'm sorry," he said.

"No time for that now. *Now* we just focus on getting them back, okay?"

"What do you want me to do?"

"The plane will be here in about ten minutes. We're heading out, but I'd like you to head back to Baltimore with the cats. I'm leaving some operatives with you, and your transport will be here in about an hour."

"You're trying to keep me away from the action."

Laney looked at the holes in his shirt and the blood that had dried there. Her voice was soft. "Yeah, but I think you've been through enough already tonight."

Rolly looked away, blinking back the tears in his eyes. "Lou's my best friend. After everything that happened with my sister and my family, I thought I was on my own and that I would always be on my own. Then I met Lou in that stupid van. And suddenly I wasn't alone anymore."

Laney's heart broke for him. "I know, Rolly. And we'll get her back."

Again a shudder ran through him. "You can't say that for sure."

"No, I can't," she agreed, softly.

Danny had exited the SUV and now walked toward them. There was a small black and brown dog in his arms.

"Who's this?" Laney asked.

Rolly reached for the dog. As he did, Laney got her first look at the dog's face. She sucked in a breath.

Rolly pulled the dog to his chest. "This is Princess. Henry has to know somebody who can help her. I'm keeping her." He glared at Laney, but Laney could see the tremor in him. He was close to losing it.

"Of course," Laney said. "After I talk to Danny, I'll introduce you guys and Princess to the cats. Okay?"

"I'm going to let her stretch her legs." Rolly headed for the side of the road.

"Is he going to be okay?" Danny asked quietly.

"Eventually," Laney said, watching Rolly for a moment before turning back to Danny. "Are *you* okay?"

Danny wouldn't meet her eyes.

Laney put her hand on his shoulder. "Danny?"

He looked back at her, his chin trembling. "I—I shot someone."

Time seemed to stop. Shock and sadness robbed Laney of words.

Danny rushed on as his body began to shake. "I had to. They had Rolly and they were going after Lou. I didn't—"

Laney pulled him into a hug. "It's okay, Danny. You did the right thing. It's okay."

Danny sobbed into her shoulder. Laney took a shuddering breath, her own tears rolling down her cheeks.

At the side of the road, Rolly lost his battle with his fears and crumpled to the ground, his arms wrapped around Princess.

Laney had never wanted any of this craziness to touch them. Danny and Rolly would never be the same after tonight.

345

Her gaze shifted to Jen, who was leaning against Jordan. *None of us will.*

CHAPTER 91

The Chandler plane landed on the abandoned highway and took off again less than ten minutes later. Even though they were back in the air quickly, Laney could feel the gulf that stretched between them and the other plane. *There's no time to waste.*

She took a breath and, unbuckling her seat belt, faced the cabin. "Okay. We'll never overtake them, so we need to figure out where they're heading so we can have a response group waiting. We can contact any operatives we have in the area as well as local police. I suggest we start by identifying all the possible Mu references along the West Coast."

"None of the other sites were Mu related," Jake said.

"Yes, but this sacrifice is different. It's the last one. The site will have to be special. It has to be some place that is important and, more critically, isolated. They're going to be moving at least a dozen cats and"—she stumbled over the word—"Lou. That will take time. We can get there. We just need to plan ahead."

Jen nodded. "I'll start doing the research. I'll call your uncle and Henry. See what they might have."

Laney handed out assignments to everyone else on board. If someone didn't have a background that would help with the search, Laney put them on phone duty to coordinate with the police and airports.

Then, for the next hour, all Laney did was look up possible locations. Every few minutes she'd check the screen where Danny was tracking the position of Lou's plane—and based on its position, she would eliminate one or more possible landing sites.

Eventually they were down to just one more possible place for the plane to land on their current heading. After that, they'd be out over the Pacific.

In disbelief, Laney watched them sail right by the final airfield. No one said a word.

"Laney, they're starting to head south," Danny said quietly.

"South?" Laney looked at the screen and realized Danny was right. And like that, she knew where they were going. The place that had inspired their calling cards. "Easter Island. They have to be heading there."

Danny shook his head. "They won't make it."

"Why not?" Jake asked.

"It's four thousand miles away."

"They'll have to stop to refuel," Laney said, her excitement growing. *Which gives us a chance.*

"Find out where they'll stop," Jen said.

"If they keep on their current course," Danny said, "there's really only one option: Hawaii."

"Jake," Laney said.

He already had his phone out and was dialing. "I'm on it."

Laney clasped her hands together. Jake would contact law enforcement on the islands and give them a heads-up. Some of the tension drained from her chest. "Okay. This is good. We might not get there in time, but the Hawaiian police will be able to handle it." *We've got this.*

348

CHAPTER 92

The priestess leaned back in the tub, enjoying the warmth seeping into her bones. She had taken a day of pleasure—massage, facial, aromatherapy. It had been delightful. And this was the last step: a soothing bath. She slid farther down in the tub, careful to keep her hair, which was piled on top of her head, from getting wet.

Her home was much grander than the rest of the homes on the island. She'd had it built two years after she'd been made priestess. It was larger and more sumptuous, full of neutral colors that showed her off to her best advantage.

She closed her eyes with a sigh. *Heavy is the head that wears the crown.*

She was just drifting off to sleep when noise from the other room disturbed her. She looked up from her bath with a frown. A muffled yelp came from the other room, followed by an angry tone she knew belonged to Vanessa.

A soft knock sounded at her door.

"Priestess?" Vanessa called. "There is a matter of importance you need to see to."

The priestess sighed and drummed her hands on the sides of her tub. *This had better be good.* She stepped out of the water, dried off, and pulled on her robe, tying the belt with a yank. She strode toward the double doors and pulled them open. "What is it?"

Vanessa stood straight, her gaze on the priestess. Next to her, Amil, the priestess's attendant, cowered. There was a red mark across his cheek.

Vanessa bowed. "You have received a message from lotus blossom."

The priestess narrowed her eyes. "When?"

"Three hours ago," Vanessa said.

The priestess whirled on Amil. "What? Why was I not contacted about this?"

"You—you said you did not wish to be disturbed."

The priestess narrowed her eyes. "You idiot. You are dismissed."

"Y-yes, priestess." Amil backed out of the room, and his hasty footsteps could be heard echoing down the hall.

"Have you read the message?" the priestess asked.

"Yes. The Chandler Group contacted the Big Island ahead of the Katzes' plane arriving there. They were attempting to have the local police meet the plane."

"Meet the plane? How did they know where it was landing?"

"I do not know. I would guess they are tracking it somehow."

The priestess turned away and cast her gaze out through the balcony doors. But she was not focused on the stunning garden that had been created for her. Vanessa was right: they were most likely tracking the plane. But how? The conventional way, or did they also have unconventional methods they could tap into?

After all, the ring bearer was involved. Anything was on the table.

"Contact Maura. Let her know she's being tracked. And then find out what the ring bearer knows."

Vanessa raised an eyebrow. "I do not think she will just tell me."

"Perhaps. But she does seem to trust Aaliyah. Have her call. Make sure she knows we are trying to help the ring bearer

350

in her hour of need and that the best way for us to do that is to know everything the ring bearer knows."

CHAPTER 93

"They're landing," Danny's voice called through the cabin.

Laney's head jerked up from her computer screen and her heart began to race. "Where?"

"The Big Island. Um, looks like it's a private airport."

"Jake?"

"Already on it," he said, his phone to his ear as he walked to the back of the plane. "Lieutenant, this is Jake Rogan with the Chandler Group."

Laney tuned out the rest of the conversation. "Danny, how far away is the police station from the airfield?"

"Maybe twenty minutes. I sent a text to Jordan." Jordan was up in the cockpit with Jen.

"Good job." It would be close. But if the police moved quickly, they could get there.

Jake's angry voice cut through the cabin. "A court order? Are you kidding? This is a federal investigation—"

Jake went silent and looked like he was trying hard not to bite off his tongue.

"Fine. I'll get you your damn court order," he growled before ending the call. He quickly redialed.

"Jake?" Laney asked.

"Chief won't move a finger without a court order. He claims he doesn't know us and therefore can't verify we are, in fact, federal agents."

"Well that's—"

"He's stalling, Laney. They must have paid him off. I'll contact the local FBI field office. Have them visit the chief. Matt," he said into the phone. "I need you to get a court order over to an asshole police chief on the Big Island."

Jen came back from the cockpit. "Did Jake reach the police?"

Laney nodded. "But they're not cooperating."

"What? Why?"

"Jake thinks the chief might have been bought off."

"But that means—" Her voice cut off.

Laney nodded. "We're not going to stop them in Hawaii."

CHAPTER 94

The Illyushin had been retrofitted for this particular job. Seven crates and one stretcher had been placed in the back of the plane, chained to the floor. All the seats in the front of the plane had been removed except for one row, with four seats on either side. Nothing about it was comfortable, and the constant droning was torture.

Maura leaned over to Derek. "I'm going to sit up with the pilots for a while."

He nodded and closed his eyes. They were the only two back here. Abe, Hank, and Tyler were supposed to be here too, but they were probably dead now. The other six members of their team were on the other plane.

Maura unstrapped herself and walked carefully to the cockpit. The cats in the back of the plane looked up at her, and a few hissed. *Hiss all you like.*

Her eyes fell on the girl. She'd been strapped to a stretcher, a drip in her arm as a precaution. Her wounds had healed, although it had taken about two hours; Derek thought maybe the sedation had slowed her abilities. Maura curled her lip in distaste, then opened the door to the cockpit.

One of the pilots smiled back at her. "I'm surprised you lasted back there as long as you did. Take a seat."

Maura pulled down a jump seat and sat. The pilot poured her a coffee from a thermos. She took it gratefully.

After the first few sips, she sighed. *So much better.* "Are we on schedule?"

The pilot nodded. "We'll actually be in a little ahead of schedule. We'll be landing in a few minutes."

"Any word from the rest of the group?"

"Everything's set up. They're just waiting for us."

"Good." Balancing her mug on her lap, she pulled out her phone and frowned. She had a new text:

`They are tracking you.`

She read it again, her anger and fear growing. Nothing could stop the ceremony tonight.

"Everything all right?" the pilot asked.

"We're being tracked. Is there anything on the plane that could allow them to do that?"

"No. Even if they had our call sign, they wouldn't be able to track us." He paused. "Maybe there's something in the cargo, something transmitting a signal?"

"Do you have anything that could find it?"

The pilot nodded toward a cabinet. "In there."

Maura opened the cabinet and pulled out a wand like those used at security checkpoints. She handed the pilot the mug. "I'll be right back."

Exiting the cockpit, she nudged Derek's foot with her own.

He opened his eyes. "What's wrong?"

"We're being tracked."

Derek's eyebrows rose. He unbuckled and followed her.

Maura examined the animals in the cages. None of the cats had a collar or tags of any kind. It was possible one had a subcutaneous tag, but she ran the wand over them, and it didn't beep.

She walked over to where the two unexpected guests lay. This larger cat didn't have a collar or a tag either. Obviously she was an older version of the cats from the lab, and her wounds had healed. So in way, it had been advantageous that the animal had been there. Without her, they

355

never would have realized these cats healed the same way the Fallen did. Which meant they would need to be killed the same way the Fallen were.

She ran her wand over this beast too, but again it was quiet.

"Which leaves the girl." The girl lay on a stretcher next to the cat. She was slim and muscular, and wore fitted jeans, a black top, and sneakers. On her wrist was a large silver watch. "The watch," Maura said immediately.

Derek pulled it off her and frowned. "What should I do with it? Should I smash it?"

"No. I have a much better idea."

CHAPTER 95

The plane was taking a long time to refuel. Jen and Laney stared at the little dot on Danny's computer screen. It hadn't moved in thirty minutes.

"Maybe they're switching cargo to another plane," Jen said.

Ten minutes later, the little dot still hadn't moved.

Jake stormed up from the back of the plane. "They're gone."

"What?" Laney pointed to the screen. "No, the plane's still there."

"The agents and police arrived just in time to see them take off."

"The tracker?" Jen asked.

"One of the agents found Danny's watch in the middle of the hangar."

"So we don't know where they went?" Danny asked.

"The agents managed to reach out to some other towers and pilots. They confirm it's heading west out over the Pacific."

Jen frowned. "West? But Easter Island is south."

"Which means they're not going to Easter Island," Jake said quietly.

"So where *are* they going?" Danny asked.

Steeling herself, Laney stood, not giving doubt or fear an opening. "Nothing's changed. We just a need a list of landing locations west of Hawaii. We can cross-reference them with any Mu sites. Let's get back to work."

She met everyone's gaze and got their nods before they turned to their own research. Then Laney re-took her seat and hoped no one noticed the tremor in her hand.

The Chandler jet arrived on Maui twenty minutes later. Jake had arranged for a smaller, faster jet to meet them there. Laney, Jordan, and Jen lost no time transferring to the new jet, and Jordan had them up in the air only a few minutes later. Jake and the rest of the team would follow as soon as the Chandler jet was gassed up.

All in all, Laney thought she was doing a pretty good job of keeping her fears at bay—until Jake called. The Chandler jet was having engine trouble and was going to be delayed. So for the time being, it was up to Laney, Jordan, and Jen to track down the landing site for the Katzes' plane, get there, and stop the ritual.

Laney lowered her phone and stared at the list of possible landing sites. There were dozens of them. *How am I going to find them?*

She closed her eyes and took deep breaths, forcing herself to focus only on the problem at hand and nothing else. *Okay. The last sacrifice for the ritual of the moon and the sun. It has to be important, not just any old place. Not if they're going to all this trouble.* Panic bubbled in her. *I really need a Mu expert.*

Her eyes flew open and she grabbed for her phone. *And I know just the one.*

358

CHAPTER 96

Hurrying down the path, Aaliyah scanned the face of everyone she passed. Where was Noriko? She should have been home an hour ago. It wasn't like her to just not show up. In fact, Aaliyah couldn't ever recall her doing that.

"Aaliyah."

Aaliyah looked up with a frown. Oasu, Kai's nephew and one of the Guard, hurried toward her.

"Have you seen Noriko?" she asked.

He shook his head. "No. I'm sorry. But you're needed in telecommunications. You have a call from the ring bearer."

"Oh," Aaliyah said. "I'll call her—"

"She said it's urgent. She's holding."

Aaliyah hesitated. Something was wrong with Noriko. She knew it in her soul. "I need to find Noriko."

"I'll find her."

Aaliyah searched his face. Finally she nodded. "All right."

She hurried to the telecommunications room in the administrative building. Vanessa was standing in the hallway outside. Aaliyah inclined her head as she moved to pass her. "Vanessa."

Vanessa shot out an arm.

Aaliyah stumbled back with a frown. "What are you doing?"

Vanessa smiled. "The priestess wants to make sure that you convey to the ring bearer our desire to help in any way possible."

"Of course," Aaliyah said.

"And be sure to let the priestess know all the ring bearer knows. We can't do our best to help if we don't have complete information."

Vanessa stepped aside to allow Aaliyah to pass. Aaliyah did so warily. *Help in any way possible?* Alarm bells rang through Aaliyah's mind.

But she didn't have time to focus on the priestess's machinations. As soon as Aaliyah stepped into the office, the technician handed her a phone and left the room.

"Laney? It's Aaliyah."

Laney's words burst across the line sounding more frantic than Aaliyah would have thought possible. "Thank God. I have a problem." Laney hurried on to explain what had occurred over the last few hours. Aaliyah listened in stunned silence. "Now we're trying to figure out where they might be going," Laney finished. She paused. "Aaliyah?"

"Sorry. It's just—wow. That's a lot to take in. You've been through a lot."

"Would it make you feel better if I told you this has been relatively calm compared to my usual week?"

Aaliyah let out a nervous laugh. "No. I think that would worry me even more."

"Sorry. But do you have any idea where they're heading?"

Aaliyah sat back, going through the possibilities. There just seemed to be so many. "The ritual of the moon and the sun always happened at the beginning of the harvest."

"So we're looking for something that relates to food or crops?"

"Maybe..." Aaliyah murmured, her mind racing through the sites west of Hawaii. Then she went still and her eyes grew wide. "The Banaue rice terraces," she blurted out.

"In the Philippines?"

"Yes." Aaliyah pictured the artificially created plateaus in the mountains of Ifuago. "In the ancient world, the terraces could feed thousands upon thousands of people. They was an unrivaled source of food production. Today they still extend over three thousand feet high, even though a large portion of them has been destroyed. There is nothing in modern times that even comes close to their production capability."

"Okay." Both relief and hope tinged Laney's words. "I'll see what airfields their planes can land in."

"Wait. Did you say planes?"

"Yes. There are two planes."

Aaliyah's jaw dropped open and dread coursed through her as another possibility entered her mind. "Oh no."

CHAPTER 97

Aaliyah's reaction terrified Laney. Seconds ago she had believed that maybe, just maybe, they could do this. Now that hope was being yanked away.

"Aaliyah, what is it?"

"I don't think they're going to the rice terraces."

Laney tried to rein in her impatience and fear. "Why?"

"The Philippines is hit with extreme weather regularly. The wet season from June to November is known for typhoons. It's probably why the terraces fell into disrepair."

"Okay," Laney said, trying not to demand that Aaliyah spit it out.

"But there are legends that in the past, storms were held at bay by two islands and the structures there."

"*Two* islands?" Laney closed her eyes. *No.* "What are they?"

"Pohnpei and Lelu Island at Kosrae."

Pohnpei—the Venice of the Pacific. Cain had mentioned it. *Damn it.* "I know Pohnpei. That's where Nan Madol is." Laney pictured the ancient ruin.

And she knew Lelu Island was a smaller version of Nan Madol—the same type of artificial island. The only difference was the scale and the addition of two pyramids.

"The north equatorial current divides up right there between Pohnpei and the island of Kosrae," Aaliyah said. "The miles between are where typhoons are born. And when cold air rushes in, it creates these huge storms. When it comes to storms, these two islands are among the safest places in the Pacific."

Laney paused. Something was scratching at the back of her mind. Something about the two islands and the rice terraces. She thought of Nikola Tesla, and then it hit her. "You're saying these two islands disrupted storms and protected the rice terraces."

"Yes. It's been theorized that the structures on the two islands formed a weather control system. The structures would send electrical currents into the air and disrupt the effect of hurricanes."

"Just like Tesla suggested," Laney murmured. Back in 1900, Tesla made the argument that the earth pulsates with electrical current. This current bounces off the ionosphere and can be used to actually break down storms after they begin. Tesla began creating a tower on the eastern end of Long Island to prove his theory in 1901. He strongly believed that with his electromagnetic tower he could ricochet the earth's current off the atmosphere and stop hurricanes shortly after they began. But his funding was withdrawn in the middle of the project.

"How sure are you that they went there?" Laney asked.

"Very sure—for two reasons. One, Nan Madol was destroyed by floods. The ones caused when the world leaders gathered to discuss the problems of the large animals."

Laney closed her eyes. That was the reason for one of Atlantis's large destructions. "So humans caused its destruction."

"Yes. But it's the second reason that confirms it for me."

Dread filled Laney. "What's that?"

"The name Pohnpei. It means 'on an altar.'"

CHAPTER 98

Maura seethed. All she could picture was all her well-laid plans being dismantled. And all because of some stupid Fallen. She paced up and down the fuselage, her anger growing with each minute that passed. Finally her phone beeped, signaling a new text message. You are not being tracked.

Maura closed her eyes and exhaled heavily.

Derek tapped her shoulder. "We're good?" he asked.

"We're good." She placed her hand on his with a smile. But then her gaze fell on the girl. The girl who had nearly ruined everything.

Maura stormed over to the girl and pulled out her knife, but Derek stepped in the way.

"Why waste your anger? She'll be part of the ritual. Let her death help the world."

"You're right." She smiled. "You always are."

She stepped around Derek and plunged her knife into the girl's back.

Derek let out a yell. "What are you doing?"

Maura wiped her knife on the girl's shirt. "You forget. She's one of them. It won't kill her."

She headed back to the cockpit. *But it does make me feel better.*

CHAPTER 99

As soon as Laney had finished speaking with Aaliyah, she headed to the cockpit and explained Aaliyah's reasoning to Jen and Jordan. Jen grabbed her computer and confirmed that everything Aaliyah had said was true.

Laney then dialed Jake. The Chandler jet was finally in the air and on its way as fast as it could manage. That should have made Laney feel better, but as she hung up the phone, she glanced at the horizon and knew he wouldn't make it to either island before sunset.

"Okay," she said. "We'll have to get to both islands."

Jen looked up from her screen, her face drawn. "The islands are three hundred and forty miles apart."

"Jordan, is there any way we can get to both the islands before sunset?"

Jordan shook his head. "I'm sorry. No."

"What about law enforcement? The islands must have somebody we can call."

"Laney," Jen said, "these islands are not highly developed. Pohnpei has a total population of thirty-five thousand people, and Kosrae has only six thousand. Most residents exist through subsistence farming. The economy is practically non-existent in some parts. Their law enforcement won't be up for this."

"And even if they were," Jordan added, "these guys already bribed their way through Hawaii. There's no doubt they'll have made the same preparations at the two islands."

"There *must* be some place that can send help," Laney said.

"Not in time," Jordan said quietly.

"So what do we do?" Jen asked.

Laney's chest felt heavy. She'd known what they'd have to do ever since Aaliyah mentioned the two islands. "We're going to have to choose."

CHAPTER 100

"Wake up," a woman's voice insisted near Lou's ear.

Lou grimaced against the fog in her brain. *Jen?*

A hand slapped her cheek. "Wake up," the voice ordered.

Gritting her teeth, Lou prepared to wreak damage on whoever had hit her. But she felt so weak. She couldn't remember having ever felt so weak. She couldn't even move her arms or legs. But she could open her eyes, and she stared at the straps that held her down. She frowned. *Am I in a plane?*

A woman in her forties, a woman Lou had never seen before, stood above her. She smiled at Lou, even as Lou's cheek still stung from her slap.

"What do you want?" Lou had meant to demand an answer, but her words came out as a plea.

"I want the world to be free of your influence." The woman smiled again. "And your participation in the ritual will help make up for your transgressions."

"Ritual?" Lou's mind still felt sluggish. "What ritual? Who are you?" Then it all came flooding back to her: the nursery, the cats, the people with guns. And the man in the truck.

"My name is Maura, but that is unimportant. My *job* is what's important."

Lou waited, but the woman seemed content to leave it at that. "Okay, I'll bite. What's your job?"

"I am the one who helps fight against the evil of this world. I am the one who will *save* this world."

Lou thought about Laney as she replied, "Yeah, I'm pretty sure that's someone else's job."

"You are mistaken. *I* am the one chosen to push back the evil. I am the usher of the new age. The progenitor of redemption."

Right, crazy pants. "Okay, good to know. Now, how about you let me go?"

Maura narrowed her eyes. "Arrogant to the end. That will be your kind's downfall. And still, I give you this chance at salvation—a chance you don't even deserve."

"That's okay. I don't need salvation. I'm doing just fine—"

Maura's eyes grew large. "Oh, but you do. Without it, you are doomed for eternity. This is a gift for you, and for mankind."

"Mankind?"

The woman nodded. "At the setting of the sun, we offer a cleansing and sacrifice to show our devotion to the old ways, a reminder that we are truly the repentant ones. And that is how we will avoid the calamity to come."

"Yeah, well, if it's all the same to you, I think I'll pass."

Maura only smiled.

CHAPTER 101

Laney sat in the dark, staring out the window of the plane. They'd decided on Pohnpei. It was larger, and its name had the word "altar" in it—but honestly, it was a coin flip.

She'd been studying the history and layout of both islands. Pohnpei was only 129 square miles and was surrounded by a barrier reef and small islets and swamps. Kosrae was only 42 square miles. Neither had a strong transportation or road infrastructure. Moreover, once they got there, they'd have to contend with searching the aging towers of Nan Madol, separated by canals.

Laney glanced behind her to where Jen sat. Laney had thought she was asleep, but now she too stared out the window.

Laney dropped her head onto her hand, picturing Cleo running with her at the estate or standing guard over the teenagers. It wasn't right. She hadn't lived enough yet. And half of her life had been horrific.

She felt tears burning the backs of her eyes. Lou hadn't had it much better. She had been through so much and still she had held onto her goodness. She'd gone into that nursery to save people, people Laney knew she did not think of highly of. And yet she had risked her life for them.

And now she might lose it.

As much of a logistical nightmare as finding them on Pohnpei was, Laney had to pray that they were on that island. Because if they weren't…

A tear dropped onto her cheek. *Oh God, please let us have chosen correctly.*

CHAPTER 102

Federation of Micronesia

Structures made from tall black rocks surrounded her. Lou blinked her eyes and realized she was no longer on the stretcher or in the plane. After their little chat, Maura had sedated her again.

Now, she was on something much higher and harder. She turned her head and saw six leopards on rock slabs. She couldn't tell if any were Cleo, and none them were moving. At least another dozen people in white robes stood around them in a circle. *This is not good.*

Maura stepped forward. "Oh good, you're awake." She pointed toward the setting sun. "We're about to begin."

Lou's tongue felt swollen. She tried to speak, but nothing came out.

Maura held up a pitcher. "We are the true Naacal—the followers of the old ways. We offer this lasting sacrifice to refresh the world, here at our homeland that we were chased from so long ago."

Lou struggled against the restraints holding her down, but she still had no strength. It was terrifying. She eyed the IV in her arm. If she could just tug that out, she would have a chance.

One of the men stepped up and placed a hand on either side of Lou's head. Lou struggled to turn her face away, but in her current condition, she was no match for his strength.

Another man stepped up to her side, grabbed her jaw, and forced her mouth open.

"Be cleansed and be fulfilled," the priestess intoned. Then she poured the water into Lou's mouth.

Lou choked and struggled to breathe. Her lungs felt like they were on fire. Pain lanced through them and up her throat.

Pinpricks of light exploded in front of her. Darkness began to seep in at the edges. It felt like a lead weight had been placed on her chest, refusing to let her breathe. Lou struggled against the hands that held her head but even her feeble strength was growing weaker.

I'm going to die.

CHAPTER 103

Laney stared out the window of the helicopter at the approaching island. Henry had a friend who was running a rocket company out of the Marshall Islands, and he had loaned them the helicopter. It had been a gamble making the stop, but they reasoned that the Katzes would have to land at the airport on Pohnpei and then traverse the island, which would take time; whereas the chopper would allow Laney and company to go right to Nan Madol.

It had been a frustrating and nerve-wracking trip. For hours, all Laney had had to do to pass the time was second-guess their decision. Now she was desperate to see if they had chosen correctly.

Jordan looked back at Laney and Jen from the pilot's seat. "We're coming up on Pohnpei. How do you want to handle this?"

Laney looked at Jen, who nodded back to her. "Get us over the water as close as you can, and then go find a place to land."

"I take it I will be alone in the chopper at that time," Jordan said dryly.

"You take it correctly," Jen said.

"Now I know why Yoni's bald," Jordan muttered.

"He was bald before he met us," Jen said.

"Just don't get yourselves killed, all right?" Jordan said.

Laney unbuckled her seat belt and removed her headphones. "Why does everybody keep saying that to us?"

Jen already had her hand on the door. Jordan flew around the island and Laney got her first glimpse of Nan Madol. It was a rectangular series of islands contained by a rock wall. Even from the air, it was obviously not a natural formation.

"I've got heat signatures on some of the towers," Jordan said.

Jen opened the door. "Well, here's good then." She jumped.

"Goddamn it, Jen," Jordan yelled.

Laney gasped, but then she shook her head and dove out after her. Concentrating on the air around her, she created a platform to carry her slowly downward. Below her she spied Jen, and saw that her friend she'd miscalculated—she was going to land on the ground, not the water. Laney extended her hand and willed the air around Jen to grab her. Jen's fall slowed, and she touched down gently.

Laney came down only a few seconds later. Laney was closer to the tower and Jen raced toward her. "Thanks," she called as she blurred past.

Laney didn't say anything as she tore off after her.

Ahead of them, a man stepped out of the tower, his eyes on the helicopter. He held a radio to his mouth. Jen slammed into him with her knee, drilling him into the side of the tower. The wall shook with the impact, and the man fell to the ground and lay still.

Laney reached Jen just as a second man stepped from the interior of the basalt structure. Laney spun, catching him with a back kick to the chest, followed by a round kick to the knee and an elbow to the face.

Laney knelt down next to the second man and grabbed his shirt. "Where are the sacrifices?"

374

He smiled through his bloody mouth. Foam sprayed from between his teeth. Laney pushed him away in disgust.

Jen climbed the structure and surveyed the scene. Laney started up after her. "Laney, they're across the canal. It's at least three hundred yards."

Laney reached the top and saw where Jen was looking. Across the water, a wood stage had been built on top of another basalt complex, and a dozen people in robes were gathered there. Six of them stood in a circle around a leopard laid out on a stone slab; each held a long serrated knife in their hands. Behind them, the others stood watching.

"I can't see Lou," Jen said.

"Me either." And Laney also knew they wouldn't be able to get to them in time. It was too far, and they'd be seen as they approached. The water would nullify Jen's speed.

"My turn," Laney said, staring at the sky. The clouds rolled and the wind picked up. A few of the people looked upward as thunder rumbled. Lightning slashed from the sky, hitting the ground on either side of the temple.

Laney breathed deep. *Here we go.*

One bolt after another tore through the robed figures with the knives.

"Holy shit," Jen muttered.

Laney stumbled to the ground, her legs going weak. "Go."

Jen needed no further urging. She leaped from the wall and dove into the water. In seconds, she was on the other side and climbing the wall. Distracted by their downed companions, the rest of the robed figures hadn't even noticed her coming. Jen was practically invisible as she sprinted from person to person—a deadly gust of wind, taking down everything in her path.

Laney pushed to her feet and climbed down the wall, her strength returning. She dove into the water and quickly made her way across. She focused on her movements, one arm up and over, her legs kicking behind her, ignoring the fear building inside her. *Lou and Cleo are here. We just couldn't see them.*

She reached the other shore and pulled herself up. Taking a steeling breath, she began to climb the basalt log structure. It was twenty-five feet tall, but the logs were set up almost as if to make it easy to climb.

Jen met her at the edge, offered Laney her hand, and pulled her up.

Jen's eyes were wide, and her breath came out in gasps. "She's not here. Lou's not here."

Laney's stomach dropped. "Cleo?"

Jen shook her head. "No. All the cats are young. I'm going to call Jordan."

Jen stepped away to make the call, and Laney could see the effort it took her to get a hold of herself. Laney couldn't blame her. She was having trouble holding on to her own emotions. Because if Lou and Cleo weren't here...

She shut down that train of thought right away, turning to focus on the scene around her.

Six of the robed figures had scorch marks on their chest from the lightning. The rest were unconscious. *Well, maybe dead,* Laney thought as she stared at the unnatural angle of one man's neck.

The cats were still strapped to the rock altars. Laney reached out and felt the pulse of the one nearest her. It was beating away. *Just sedated.*

A movement to her right drew her attention. One of the robed figures, a woman with light brown hair, groaned and sat up. She appeared to be only in her twenties.

Laney strode up to her. "Where's the girl?"

The confusion disappeared from the woman's eyes and was replaced with revulsion. "She's an agent of evil."

"She's just a girl."

"She is the reason the world is heading for destruction."

"So you're going to kill her to punish her?"

376

The woman stared at Laney with hatred. "No, to save the world. You don't realize what you've done. We could have stopped it. You have to complete our work."

"Sacrificing people? Are you crazy?"

"If you don't, the world is doomed. You have to kill them. Kill them all."

"Laney!" Jen yelled from below. "The chopper will be here in two minutes."

Laney nodded and turned back to the woman, but already foam dribbled from her mouth. She stared ahead, her eyes unblinking, her chest still.

Laney stumbled back. *What the hell is with these people? Why are they so committed? What do they know? Or think they know?*

She stared at the carnage surrounding her. Lou wasn't here. And neither was Cleo.

She closed her eyes. The emotions she'd been holding back overwhelmed her defenses. She sucked in a breath, and the world swayed for a moment. Her heart threatened to shatter into pieces as she realized what exactly their arrival at this island meant.

I chose wrong.

CHAPTER 104

Laney and Jen wasted no time getting back to the chopper. Jordan hovered and Jen jumped up with her arms wrapped around Laney. They'd had to leave the cats behind, still sedated, but all the cult members were knocked out—either by lightning, head injury, or suicide—and the Chandler Group would be there soon to clean up the mess. Laney was pretty sure a few more cult members would have taken their cyanide pills by then.

Laney couldn't get a grip on these people. *What exactly is their plan? A little blood seeping into the earth and they think what, everything will be all right? Kill some Fallen and people will be good? Humans aren't that simple. We weren't bad because Fallen existed. We made bad choices for all sorts of reasons. This is insanity.*

"How long, Jordan?" Laney asked.

"Thirty minutes, twenty if I fly this thing in the red."

"Fly it in the red," Laney said. "I don't care if it breaks to pieces when we get there. Just get us there."

Jordan gave her an abrupt nod and turned back to the controls.

Jen sat in the back staring out the window at the setting sun, saying nothing.

"We can still make it, Jen."

"The sun's going to set in seven minutes," Jen said, her voice emotionless.

"They could have been delayed. Maybe something went wrong with the chopper or they had trouble getting the cats under control. You know Lou and Cleo. They'd take any opportunity, no matter how small."

Jen nodded. And then the two of them fell into silence. The hum of the chopper surrounded them as they sped through the air. Jordan was pushing as hard as he could manage.

Laney prayed every prayer she knew and then resorted to straight up begging. But it was no use. Five minutes passed, then another five, and then the sun dipped below the horizon. Laney felt as if a hole had been punched through her chest. *Oh God.*

She looked back at Jen, who said nothing, who didn't even move. She just sat, staring out the window at where the sun had disappeared, tears streaming down her cheeks.

CHAPTER 105

Lou could hear the sounds of fighting. A gun fired near her. She struggled to open her eyes. But it was such an effort.

A soft voice spoke nearby. "It's all right. You'll be all right."

Lou forced her eyelids open. Everything was fuzzy, and the dim light wasn't helping. A dark-haired woman stood over her, loosening her ties. "Jen?"

The woman leaned forward, and Lou realized this wasn't Jen. The dark-haired woman was a stranger, close to her own age. "No, my name is Noriko. Your friends will be here soon. But you are safe."

The cobwebs in Lou's brain begin to clear. "Cleo, is Cleo—"

"She's safe too. Cleo?"

Cleo walked up and licked Lou's face. Tears rolled down Lou's cheeks. "Oh, Cleo, I'm so sorry I got you into this."

"Cleo's not mad. You saved her family. She's just glad you are all right."

Lou nodded, knowing that she was right.

"There you go. That's the last of them. They'll be here any minute. Take care, Lou."

"Wait, where are you—" Lou struggled to sit up, but a wave of exhaustion rolled over her and she lay back again. She swallowed down the bile that tried to rise, waited until the world stabilized, then sat up again—slowly this time. The girl was gone. The other cats were still unconscious and strapped to rock slabs. But there were now bodies littering the ground—over a dozen of them, blood staining their white robes.

Lou carefully stepped off her own stone slab. Her knees gave a little wobble as her feet hit the ground. Cleo pressed against her, and Lou wrapped her arms around her. "Thanks."

Lou started to walk through the bodies, stopping at one with dark hair. It was Maura. Her eyes were cold and dead. Lou looked around in confusion. "Cleo, who was that? What happened here?"

It obviously hadn't been anybody with the Chandler Group. So who had come to her rescue?

Her head jerked back to Cleo. "Wait—how did she know you would help her and not hurt her? And how come you let her help you? And me? Who was she?"

Cleo didn't have any answers for her. Not that Lou had expected any. After all, Laney was the only one who—

Lou went still. *Cleo's not mad. You saved her family. She's just glad you're all right.* That's what Noriko had said. But how would she know that?

Cleo licked Lou's cheek.

Lou stared at her. *No one can talk to Cleo except Laney. So how did Noriko do it?*

381

CHAPTER 106

Laney sat hunched forward as the island of Kosrae finally came into view, the full moon giving them some light to see. The sun had gone down eight minutes ago.

She swallowed. *I'm so sorry, Lou.* She pictured Cleo and the trust in her eyes. *I failed you too.*

Jen hadn't said a word since the sun had slipped beneath the horizon. And Laney didn't know what to say to her. Lou had become Jen's little sister.

Lou was so popular at the school. Rolly, Danny, and Zach were all going to be devastated.

Danny—he was never going to forgive himself. He would beat himself up for the rest of his life. *We're all going to share that blame,* Laney thought as the chopper flew over the basalt structures.

Shadows danced in the lights of the chopper, but there was no sign of movement below. Then the lights of the chopper caught on what Laney thought was a body.

She grabbed the high-powered flashlight and shone it down. Two figures in white lay facedown next to the wall of one of the structures.

Without a word, Laney opened the helicopter door and jumped.

"Damn it, Laney," Jordan yelled.

Jen was right behind her. Laney used the wind to soften their landings. She pulled her weapon as soon as she was stable. Jen ran to the bodies and rolled them over. There were bullet wounds in both men's chests.

"Who are they?" Laney asked.

"Not anyone I know." Jen pulled up the sleeve. A tattoo with three lines and a lotus flower was inscribed there.

"Do you think Lou did this?" Jen asked, hope in her voice.

"I don't know," Laney said, looking around.

A vision of Laney standing over the bodies and a kneeling Jen swirled through her mind. Laney whirled around, her heart leaping. *Cleo?*

Cleo stood silhouetted against the moonlight at the top of the wall. And then a young woman with curly hair stepped up next to her.

Laney grabbed Jen's shoulder. "Jen."

Jen turned and gasped. "Lou."

Cleo and Lou jumped down from the wall. Laney and Jen sprinted toward them, Jen quickly outpacing Laney. Cleo ran at Laney, stopping just as she reached her. Laney dropped to her knees in front of her. *Thank God.* Cleo licked Laney's face and nuzzled her head into her chest. Laney wrapped her arms around the big cat, letting her tears fall and then laughing with pure joy that Cleo was here. She was alive. *I love you, girl.*

Laney lifted her head as Jen and Lou approached. Laney released Cleo and wrapped Lou in a tight hug. "I am so glad you're okay."

Lou hugged Laney back just as fiercely. Laney rested her head against Lou's, feeling shaky. She'd almost lost them both. She would never get used to this. Risking her own life was one thing. Not being able to help when other people risked theirs was going to kill her.

Finally, they broke apart. Jen pulled Lou into her side and kissed her forehead. "Don't ever do that again, okay?"

"Okay," Lou said, her voice shaky.

"How are you here?" Laney gestured to the two bodies at the wall. "Did you do this?"

Lou shook her head, and Jen tightened her hold on her. "No. When I came to, I could hear fighting. I thought you guys had arrived."

"Did you see anyone?"

Lou nodded. "A girl. She was maybe a little older than me. At first I thought it was Jen. She freed me. There were people with her, but with the drugs, I couldn't see them. By the time the drugs wore off, they were all gone."

"How'd you find Cleo?" Jen asked.

"I didn't. The girl did. She brought Cleo to me." Lou paused. "Laney, I think she could talk to Cleo."

"What?"

"I swear, she could talk to her."

Laney looked at Cleo. *Cleo, who helped Lou?*

Cleo's yellow eyes seemed to glow in the dim light. *A friend.*

CHAPTER 107

Aaliyah was frantic. It had been hours, and she couldn't find Noriko anywhere. By the time darkness had fallen, she was out of her mind. She, Kai, and Oasu had been searching all over the island. The two men were still out looking, but Aaliyah had come home, needing to check once more if maybe somehow she had missed her.

She opened the door and walked in. "Noriko?" she called out as she walked into their house. Silence echoed back at her. In a daze, she looked around the kitchen feeling helpless. She couldn't think of anywhere else to look. She'd spoken with almost everyone on Malama. She sank into a kitchen chair.

The front door opened and Aaliyah leapt to her feet. "Noriko?"

Noriko appeared in the doorway. Aaliyah let out a cry and ran to her, pulling her into a hug.

"What's happened?" Noriko asked.

"You've been gone. I've been looking for you. No one had seen you. Where have you been?"

Noriko pulled back with a frown. "Didn't the priestess tell you?"

"Tell me what?"

"Vanessa sent me with the Guard on a mission. I was able to use my gift. I helped save a girl."

Aaliyah stared at her in shock. "You weren't on the island?" She had asked Vanessa about Noriko, and Vanessa had said nothing.

Noriko led Aaliyah to the table. She pushed her gently into a chair before taking a seat across from her. "The priestess sent us to help the ring bearer." Noriko sucked in a breath, her face growing pale. "The people who killed all those people. They were there. They were going to sacrifice this girl and these cats. The cats... they were beautiful, but there was something different about them. Anyway, the Guard stopped the sacrifice. It was—" She shuddered, her eyes looking haunted. She took a deep breath. "But I just focused on the cats and the girl. They were safe. That is what matters."

Aaliyah still couldn't wrap her mind around it. "But why would they send you?"

"To help with the cats."

"Did you communicate with them?"

Noriko frowned. "Only one. Somehow she got loose. She stopped a man who was going to hurt me."

"You were alone?"

"Only for a short while. But it was fine."

Fear lanced through Aaliyah. The priestess had ordered her away and then left her alone. "You could have been killed."

Noriko shook her head. "The priestess never would have sent me if there was any danger."

Aaliyah swallowed down her fear. "I'm sure you're right."

"The priestess wants you to call the ring bearer. Let her know we were the ones who helped on Lelu."

"Yes, of course."

Noriko stood and kissed Aaliyah on the cheek. "I'm going to take a shower and then go to bed. I'm exhausted."

Aaliyah watched Noriko disappear down the hall. A short time later she heard the bathroom door close. *The priestess helped the ring bearer.* Aaliyah should feel relieved. She had wanted that.

386

So why didn't she? Why was it that the only thing she felt was... fear?

CHAPTER 108

The sun rose beautifully over the horizon as the priestess opened her shutters. She leaned against the railing of her balcony and breathed deep. She was going to miss this. There was nothing more beautiful than Malama in the morning.

Her breakfast had been set out on the lanai and she sat down to enjoy it.

A few minutes later, Vanessa stood waiting at the entrance. The priestess placed her fork on her plate and waved her in. "I trust the mission went well."

Vanessa bowed, standing across from her. "Yes, priestess."

The priestess had left instructions to not be bothered last night unless there was a problem with the mission. This morning when she awoke, the lack of disturbance had added to the beauty of the day. Her plan was rolling out perfectly.

"How did Noriko do?"

"Well."

The priestess arched an eyebrow. "I was not expecting her to return."

Vanessa glanced down. "It was unavoidable. My man almost had her at one point, but one of the cats came to her rescue."

The priestess raised an eyebrow. "A cat?"

Vanessa nodded.

The priestess waved her hand. "No matter, I suppose. There will be time for that. You're dismissed."

Vanessa turned to go, then turned back. "The Fallen—does that mission stay the same?"

The priestess smiled. "Right up until the end."

"And the ring bearer? What should we do about her?"

"She won't be able to stop us, not in time. Besides, we just helped her out." The priestess picked up her glass of juice and sat back in her chair with a contented smile. "She thinks of us as allies."

And she has no idea what's coming.

CHAPTER 109

Baltimore, Maryland
Two Days Later

Laney sat on her living room floor with Cleo curled up by her side. It had been an exhausting forty-eight hours, but she couldn't sleep. They had rounded up the animals on the islands, and all had been placed in quarantine, where they would stay until they could be brought back into the US.

The animals they'd rescued in Arizona had already been brought back to Baltimore. Henry had arranged for the construction of a temporary facility for them at an old farm, but it wouldn't be ready for a few weeks; until then, they had been able to rent out space at a small zoo.

Laney ran a hand through her friend's pelt, amazed at what she'd learned when she'd read through the files Danny had obtained. Was it possible? Was Cleo's brain more human-like than leopard-like? And were the rest of the animals the same?

No one was sure what exactly the future of those animals would be. The US government had agreed that the Chandler Group could keep them for now, but custody was still a matter of debate. If Dom was right, they were an entirely new species. And figuring out the best way forward was going to take careful thought.

Laney was nowhere near capable of that right now.

She heard the front door open and close, and then Jake appeared in the doorway. He smiled gently. "Hey, you two okay?" he asked.

Laney stifled a yawn. Her body was ready to sleep, but her mind wasn't there yet. "Yeah, but I'm not quite ready to let her out of my sight."

Jake sat on the floor on Laney's other side. "Jen's the same way with Lou. Lou's protesting, but you can tell she wants Jen there too."

Lou had been really shaken up. Rolly, Jen, Zach, and Danny had been attached to her side ever since she got back, and Dom insisted they all stay at his place for a few days. After taking care of herself for so long, Lou seemed shocked to see how important she was in so many people's lives.

But Laney could see the haunted look on her face. Rolly had a similar one. Neither of them was going to be bouncing back from this. Her Uncle Patrick had already arranged for them to speak with some people to help them sort through what had happened—when they were ready.

Laney leaned her head onto Jake's shoulder. "I can't believe we almost lost them. That was too close, Jake."

He leaned over and kissed her forehead. "Yeah, but it's all right now. Don't go visiting the world of what-ifs. It's a cruel place."

Laney nodded, but it was hard. She still shook when she thought about Cleo and Lou on that island. They never would have been able to save them. If not for Noriko and her friends...

"Have you heard anything else from Honu Keiki?" Jake asked.

"No." Aaliyah had called her when they were in the air on the way back to Hawaii. She explained it was the priestess who had sent help to Lelu Island. But Aaliyah had seemed just as in the dark as Laney as to why they hadn't told her they were sending help.

Jake rested his hand on Laney's thigh. "Well, I guess you've made some new friends."

"Yeah," Laney said softly, looking away.

"What's wrong?"

"I don't know. It just doesn't feel right. How did the priestess know to send them to Lelu? They would have had to have left at the same time we left Hawaii—or even earlier. But we didn't even know where we were heading at that point."

Jake frowned. "You think they had something to do with it?"

"Yes." She paused. "No. I don't know. If they did, why take out all of the Katzes' people? I just don't get it."

"Well, they are a secretive group."

"True. I guess I can't expect too much. I should just be happy."

"And yet you're not."

Laney frowned. All the bad guys were dead. Lou, Cleo, and the other cats were safe. It was over, and yet she still felt unsettled. "We know we got all the members of the Katzes' group. Henry's people traced all their correspondence. That threat is gone."

"So what is it?"

"It's something Aaliyah said. She couldn't imagine how Erica and Derek would be able to subdue a Fallen. They weren't trained for anything like that. And you know how difficult it is. So how did they manage it?"

Jake was quiet for a moment. "You think there's still another group out there targeting the Fallen?"

Weariness settled over Laney. "I don't know. I'm probably just grasping at ghosts. We're usually at DEFCON 1, and I guess I haven't quite settled into the idea that it's over."

Jake scooted forward so he could look Laney in the eyes. "You know, Laney, one of the things I've learned is that we can't logic our way out of everything. And sometimes, we need to trust more than words on paper when it comes to figuring things out." He paused. "On the other hand, you did manage to stop the sacrifice."

Laney's head snapped back. The sacrifice. *No.*

"What is it?' Jake asked.

392

Laney spoke each word slowly. "What if we *didn't* stop the sacrifice?"

"But you did. The cats, Lou—they're all safe."

"But blood was still spilled. The blood of the companion killers."

"But that's not—I mean, they weren't sacrifices."

Laney stood up and paced the room. "This whole thing has been weird from the start. In all the situations we've dealt with, at the end, I knew why everything happened the way it did. Even if the reasoning was out there, I understood it. But here? I feel like we still only have half the story."

She stopped and looked at Jake. "The Katzes couldn't take down Fallen. They weren't trained for it. The Honu Keiki left for Lelu before *we* even knew they were going there. And at the end of the day, over two dozen people lost their lives on both of the islands—a nice large sacrifice."

Jake got to his feet and stood in front of her. "You don't think this is over."

A chill crawled over Laney. "No. I think it's just beginning."

Fact or Fiction?

All of the books in the Belial series come from facts I've picked up over the years—facts I string together in a way that, I hope, makes for a good story. So here are some of the areas that might be of interest to you. Some are big components of the story and some just passing details. Facts are placed here in no particular order.

Animal Hybridization Experiments. All experiments in the book are real: breast milk-producing cows, mice with an ear on their back, even the Harvard professor who wants to cross *Homo sapien* and Neanderthal DNA. The only fictitious experiment is the one that created Cleo. So yes, Cleo is the least horrifying experiment mentioned.

As mentioned in *The Belial Search*, there have been experiments that allowed people to create mice with human brains. The mice demonstrated a higher intelligence compared with the mice brain rodents. And the animals were killed afterward.

Family Annihilator. The information on family annihilators is accurate. There are offenders who kill their entire family out of the blue. Almost always the reason involves a perceived loss of control over the members of their family.

Plum Island and the Montauk Monster. The history of Plum Island is accurate. There was a facility on Plum Island in the Long Island Sound. It began researching animal diseases. In the last two decades of its operation, it was the site of more than a few controversies including both the Lyme disease outbreak as well as the West Nile virus outbreak. A number of animals washed up on the shores, including four creatures on Long Island and in Connecticut that were unusual in their appearance. And all four creatures disappeared before they could be grabbed.

Native American Re-Education Schools. Both Canada and the US had re-education schools for Native Americans. The goal of the schools was to make the students less Indian.

Races. Edgar Cayce did say that Lemuria held all of the races and that when it submerged, the races scattered across the globe. He also said that people of African descent went to Mexico, where the Olmec heads were later discovered. One of the other places was also Melanesia. And as a small little note of something I just thought was cool, dark-skinned Melanesians do have a genetic trait of white blond hair. It's incredibly unique.

Lemuria. All of the information about Lemuria in *The Belial Search* comes from real sources on the legendary ancient civilization. There are tons of facts that litter this book, but as a brief review, these are the facts that I used to create the story: Lemuria was an archipelago that stretched across the Pacific; the discussion of the various lands that were found are accurate; and the Lemurians were allegedly pacifists interested in improving the mind over developing material wealth.

Edgar Cayce even supported that view, arguing that there were fewer life readings about former Lemurians because they had less karmic debt. Other individuals besides Cayce have mentioned Lemuria, including James Churchward, who did claim that he was shown ancient texts on the legendary civilization which he spent eight years learning to read. Madame Blavatsky, the theosophist, also discussed Lemuria in *The Secret Doctrine*.

The proof for Lemuria is also accurate. There are indeed two long underwater ridges of land that were above the water prior to the last ice age. The Nazca Ridge and the Sala y Gomez Ridge are located where Lemuria was said to be.

The Yonaguni monuments off the coast of Okinawa are also real. And academics still debate where the structures are man-made or natural.

Project Paperclip and the Stargate Project. Both projects really existed. Through Project Paperclip, the United States provided refuge for Nazi scientists who in turned worked in many areas of high-level research such as biological engineering and the space program. The Stargate Project was a CIA-sponsored project at Stanford that was designed to determine the efficacy of psychic ability.

Nan Madol. Nan Madol is an actual location. As described in *The Belial Search*, it consists of ninety-two artificial islands built on coral reefs back in antiquity. There is an almost identical ruin three miles from Pohnpei on the small island of Lelu. As mentioned in the book, the two islands share the honor of being located where the storms are created, and therefore they are indeed protected from most of the damaging storms that wreak havoc on the Pacific.

The link between Nan Madol and Lemuria was not my creation. It came from the book *The Lost Civilization of Lemuria* by Frank Joseph. In the book, Joseph makes the claim that the two structures worked in tandem to disrupt storms in the Pacific in order to protect the Banaue Rice terraces.

Honu Keiki. The words are real but the group is fictitious, as is the island they lived on. Honu means turtle. And Keiki means child. Other than that, everything, including the island of Malama, is fictitious.

Mummies on the Gobi. I remember reading about the discovery of Caucasian mummies in ancient China, years ago. I have been fascinated by them ever since. Here's a link to one of the articles on the discovery. No one is really sure where they came from. The pictures of the mummies are unreal, especially the one labeled the Beauty of Loulan. She is absolutely beautiful.

Easter Island. All of the information provided in the text on Easter Island is accurate except for anything related to the murders. Easter Island does have a very violent past involving slavers. There are nine hundred Moai statues strewn across the island, and one theory about their use involves electromagnetism. Easter Island was declared an emergency landing site for the space shuttle and therefore the little tiny island does have a very long runway. Tablets were found on Easter Island that were written in a language that bears an uncanny resemblance to the language of both the Cuna Indians of Panama and the writing of the ancient city of Mohenjo Daro.

The Lemurs of Madagascar. The lemurs of Madagascar were named after the large continent that zoologist Phillip Sclater believed once existed in the region. He believed the animals were isolated once this fabled continent sank.

Suffragettes and Native Americans. The United States suffragette movement was in part inspired by the power structure of early Native American groups. Women in those tribes had a more equal role to play in the tribe than is conventionally understood.

Megadroughts and all Environmental Disaster Information. Sadly, all of the information on the state of the environment is accurate. NASA is projecting megadroughts for the western half of the United States, the two percent threshold information is accurate, and scientists have recently suggested that by 2100 parts of the Persian Gulf will be too hot to live in and that winters will be snowier and summers drier.

Honestly, I didn't really have to do much research on the environment. Every time I read the news, there was some new study with dire warnings. We really need to take better care of our planet.

Nikola Tesla, Mark Twain, and Controlling the Weather. Honestly, I think Nikola Tesla is one of the most fascinating people in recent history. He and Mark Twain were in fact friends, and Twain would occasionally swing by his laboratory. Tesla did attempt to build the Wardenclyffe Tower out on Long Island. Part of the goal, beyond providing wireless electricity, was to stop hurricanes before they became too powerful. Scientists today have acknowledged that the idea of disrupting storms is possible and that Tesla may have indeed been right.

Magna Mater. One of the world's oldest religions is called the Magna Mater, the Great Mother. The religion honored a female deity viewed as being the creator and protector of the world. Romans borrowed the religion, adapting it to a god named Cybele. And the Great Mother is alleged to have been a friend to the animals and is pictured with lions and leopards as her guardians.

Where do we go from here?

I keep trying to figure out where this series ends because it has to end, right? All good things and all that. But I haven't quite reached the end of ideas yet. Once I struggle to make a story work, then I'll know it's time. Having said that, there are at least three more books coming in the Belial Series. Hope you stay around for the ride!

The Belial Guard (Summer 2016)
The Belial Warrior (Winter 2016)
Undetermined Name or Publication Date

In the meantime, if you haven't had the chance, pick up a copy of *Hominid* or *Runs Deep*. And I will also have a sci-fi novel coming out this summer as well called A.L.I.V.E.

Keep Reading for an Excerpt from R.D. Brady's *Hominid*

Hominid

Def., any of a family (Hominidae) of erect bipedal primate mammals that includes recent humans together with extinct ancestral and related forms and in some recent classifications the gorilla, chimpanzee, and orangutan
- *Webster's Dictionary, 2015*

"Well now, you'll be amazed when I tell you that I am sure they exist."
Jane Goodall, Animal Rights Activist, NPR Talk of the Nation, September 27, 2002

PROLOGUE

Twenty Years Ago
Rogue River National Park, Oregon

Her heart pounding, eight-year-old Tess Brannick's eyes flew open. She sat up, pulled her dark hair out of her eyes, and strained to listen.

There was nothing. And there should have been something. She and her twin brother were in a tent on the southeastern end of Rogue River National Park. She should hear crickets, owls, animals skittering through the surrounding forest.

But there was only silence.

"What is it?" Pax asked, turning on the lantern. His bright blue eyes reflected his fear.

Even though they were twins, and separated by only four minutes, Tess had always been the big sister looking out for Pax. Tonight was no different.

She was shaking inside, but she tried to keep her voice calm. "It's nothing. Go back to sleep."

A snarl sounded from somewhere outside the tent, followed by a series of yells—her dad.

Pax latched on to her hand.

Before the trip, Tess and Pax had begged their dad to let them sleep in their own tent. He'd finally relented. Now Tess really wished he hadn't.

"Tess?" Pax asked.

A shotgun blast sounded from close by. Tess jumped. "Get out of your bag," she hissed. They both squirmed out of

401

their sleeping bags, and Tess wrapped her arms around her brother.

When the tent flap flew open, they both screamed.

Their dad rushed in, his shotgun cradled in his arms. Gene Brannick was always calm and ready for a laugh. But now, his blue eyes were deadly serious, and no smile crossed his lips. As he crouched down in front of the twins, Tess could smell his sweat.

"I need you two to run for the ranger's station," he said. "Do you remember where it is?"

Tess was terrified, more than she'd ever been in her life, but one look at Pax's face told her she had to be the brave one. She swallowed down the fear. "Dad, what's going on?"

He shot a glance over his shoulder before answering. His hands shook, and so did his voice. "Mountain lions," he said. "You need to go."

"But Dad, they shouldn't be here," Tess said.

While other kids read comics, Tess read everything she could find on animals. She knew lions shouldn't be out this far, and that even if they were, they stayed far away from people.

"There's been a drought," her dad said. "It must have driven them farther out than before. I never should have brought you here." He stared back at her, his eyes larger than she'd ever seen them. "There's too many of them, Tess. You need to run."

Too many of them? Tess knew that shouldn't happen either. Lions were solitary creatures, unless they were young males.

Her dad placed a trembling kiss on each of their foreheads. Then he pulled them to their feet and pushed them from the tent. "Go."

A crashing sounded from the trees to their right. Her dad pulled his weapon to his shoulder. "Get to the ranger station. Now! Run! And don't look back!" he yelled.

A shadow slunk from the trees, and her father pulled the trigger.

The noise spurred Tess into action. She grabbed Pax's hand and ran. Behind her she heard footsteps. Then another shotgun blast sounded. And the footfalls went silent but a scream split the night air.

Pax stumbled. "Dad!"

Tess grabbed him by the shoulders and pulled him to his feet even as tears ran down her cheeks. "You have to get up," she cried, tears clogging her throat. "We have to run."

A crashing sounded in the trees behind them.

Tess grabbed her brother's hand. "Run, Pax! Run!"

They sprinted through the forest side by side, leaping over downed trees and small bushes.

Footfalls sounded behind them, and then more joined in. Tess's heart threatened to burst out of her chest, but she didn't dare slow, not even to look behind her.

Movement to her left drew her eyes. In the trees, a shadow was moving alongside them. As Tess glanced over, the shadow burst into a shaft of moonlight.

That's not a mountain lion, Tess thought. Whatever it was, it had dark fur and incredible height. Tess was overcome by panic. She sprinted ahead, pulling Pax behind her.

They didn't see the gully until it was too late. They stepped off into nothingness, and with screams they dropped, rolling to the ground below.

Pain shot through Tess's ankle, but she got to her feet. Pax was holding his shoulder. He threw his good arm around Tess and they hobbled across the narrow creek.

On the other side, a wall of dirt and rock blocked their way. Tess pushed Pax toward it. "Go. Climb."

"No. I'm not leaving you."

A roar behind them ended the argument. They both turned. Two lions, both skinny, their ribs showing, slunk across the creek. The lions appeared to be in no rush; this was an easy kill.

Tess's breaths came out in pants. Pax moved closer to her, his shoulder brushing hers.

"I love you, Tess," he whispered. She gripped his hand and squeezed.

The lions stalked closer. They were smaller than adults. *Probably young males.* Tess knew that male mountain lions were kicked out of their home after a year, and that they sometimes banded together. She'd felt pity when she'd first learned that. But now, she felt no pity—only fear. Because even though they were young, they would have no problem overpowering her and Pax.

A shadow cut away from the forest behind the lions and moved down to the creek. Tess jumped. *Oh God, there's another one.*

The cats whirled around. The shadow fell over them with a scream that shook Tess to her core. Before Tess could understand what was happening, one cat went flying through the air, screeching. It slammed into a tree and fell to the ground, still.

Something wet splashed on Tess's face. She reached up and wiped at it. Her fingers came away dark. Blood.

She dropped to the ground, her arms wrapped protectively around Pax.

The shadow grabbed the second lion and broke its back across its knee. Then it ripped the big cat in two.

"No, no, no, no," Pax moaned.

The shadow paused. It stood in darkness, but Tess was sure it was looking right at her. She could only make out its shape— like a man, but huge. Wider, taller. She squinted. Hairier.

Pax moaned again. The creature watched them for a moment longer, then disappeared back up the side of the gully and into the trees.

Tess and Pax stayed where they were, staring at the spot where the creature had disappeared.

"It ripped that lion apart," she whispered, not even recognizing her own voice.

Next to her, Pax only shook harder.

Tess stared into the trees, her arms still wrapped around her brother. She wasn't sure who was shaking harder, her or him.

"Tess?" Pax whispered.

But Tess couldn't answer him. Her entire focus was on the spot where she'd last seen the creature. The creature who had saved them. She pictured its height and bulk. Her eyes were drawn to the carnage it had left behind.

What kind of animal could do that?

CHAPTER 1

Beauford, California
Today

T ess slowed the ATV to a stop at the end of the path. Tall sugar pines with heavy evergreen leaves and long cones surrounded her. In the distance, the dense forest rose and fell over hilltops. It was seven a.m., and she took in a breath, inhaling the early forest air with a smile.

She was at the northeast edge of Klamath National Forest—1.7 million acres of forest that straddled the California and Oregon border. The area was covered with a variety of trees—from Douglas firs and other pines to oak and madrone hardwoods. It was a densely packed forest—with more than five hundred trees per acre in some areas—and teeming with wildlife, from simple squirrels and chipmunks to more elusive animals such as foxes or even bobcats.

Tess's camp was a forty-minute hike from here, but this was as far as the ATV could manage. She grabbed her pack from the back as she climbed off.

Taking a drink of water, she looked around, getting a feel for the forest. It was quiet, which she expected. Her ATV had made enough noise to chase away all but the hardiest of creatures.

She pulled her rifle from the back of the ATV. Checking that it was loaded—even though she knew she'd loaded it earlier this morning—she looped it around her shoulder, just in case in she ran into one of the hardier creatures. Bears, mountain lions, even wolverines lived in this natural safe zone. Tess respected nature enough to know that she could never be perfectly safe here.

She started to walk the trail. It was a familiar path, but there was still always something new to see. She smiled. *Best commute in the world.* She made quick time, but she didn't rush. Rushing, even on a well-known trail, was inviting injury. And besides, it's not like she had a meeting.

She knew people would probably think she was nuts to spend so much time in the woods. And to be honest, she wasn't entirely convinced she wasn't, but being out here... it did something to her. It gave her a sense of peace that the craziness of the real world couldn't.

It didn't take long for the animal sounds to return. Birds flew by overhead. Squirrels and the occasional rabbit skittered ahead of her. Every once in a while, Tess had even come across an elk in the more wide-open areas of the park. Today, an endangered spotted owl watched her from a branch twenty feet up. Above, a bald eagle sailed through the sky. *Yup—nothing better.*

For a year now, she had been making this hour-and-a-half trek into the woods, every Monday through Friday. She stayed overnight at least a few nights a month. She tried to avoid more than that. Her friends and family were worried enough about her without her living out here.

But her escape to the wild wasn't some carefree lark. It was part of a very carefully laid out plan. A tingle of excitement ran through her as she wondered what today could bring.

Up ahead, she spotted one of her field cameras. She'd placed it six feet up the tree—at five foot six, she couldn't place it much higher. She pulled it down, swapped out the memory card, and replaced the battery. She doubted she had anything special on the card, though; her subject was decidedly camera shy.

She continued on up the trail. She paused at a boulder where the path forked. To the right was her camp. She had chosen the spot for several reasons. One, it was in a very secluded portion of the park. In fact, she had never run into another human out here in the year she had been using the spot. Two, it was only a short walk from a small lake, which meant plenty of wildlife was nearby. Three, there was a clearing not too far away, so if she ever needed emergency help, there was a place for a rescue chopper to land. And four, it was a pretty spot.

But most importantly, it wasn't far from where she'd found her first footprint.

She turned left, away from the camp. The path continued over a rise and then down again. At the bottom of the hill, she stopped.

The food bag had been suspended above the trail, but now it lay on the ground, empty. She'd placed over seven pounds of food in there on Friday.

She looked around carefully, staying on the edge of the trail so as not to disturb the area. *Come on, old friend. Show me something.* She walked slowly around, seeing nothing, her hopes dimming. But then, to one side, she saw an impression. A footprint.

Kneeling next to it, Tess could make out the five long toes. The second and third toe were both bigger than the big toe, a condition known as Morton's foot. The print could easily have been mistaken for a human footprint if not for two things: the toes were disproportionately long, and the foot itself was much longer and wider than any human foot.

The animal was flatfooted, Tess noted—the print was uniform in depth—and must be very heavy, as the impression was three inches deep.

Placing her pack on the grass off the path, Tess pulled out a can of aerosol hairspray and sprayed the track. While it dried, she pulled out her white gypsum cement mix and added water. After a little stirring, it was ready. She carefully poured the plaster into the footprint.

It would take about twenty minutes to set, give or take, so while she waited she inspected the rest of the area. She found only one other print—a shallow heel mark—a short distance away. She cast that as well.

"You were careful," she murmured. She thought he had probably stayed as much off the path as possible, limiting the chance for footprints. She carefully inspected the ground around the path, but the vegetation made it too difficult to find any traces left behind. She hoped that maybe a piece of hair had gotten caught in the burrs she had glued to the tree, but no—her little traps were empty.

She headed back to the original cast. She tested it, and smiled when she met resistance. Carefully prying it from the ground, she lifted it up and gently wiped away some excess mud. She pulled out her water bottle and poured it over the underside, cleaning off the rest of the dirt. Finally, she blotted the cast with the towel she always kept in her pack.

Returning the water and towel to her pack, she took a breath, trying to calm herself and act like the scientist her degrees said she was. She needed to look at it objectively. It was possible it was just a bear footprint. She knew that when two bear footprints overlapped, they could be mistaken for her quarry.

But when she inspected the underside of the cast, she saw no sign of an overlap. Whatever had created this print was a single creature.

She looked next for the one mark she hoped she'd find.

And there it was. On the ball of the foot was an old scar that had healed over, making a jagged line.

Tess put the cast down, pulled her tape measure out of her bag, and measured the cast. She confirmed what she already knew: the widest part of the foot was eight inches, and from toe to heel, it was sixteen inches.

Tess smiled.

"Hello, bigfoot."

Click here to go to *Hominid* on Amazon.com

ABOUT THE AUTHOR

R.D. Brady is a criminologist who lives in upstate New York. When she's not writing, she can be found studying Jeet Kune Do, reading, or trying to find more hours in the day.

For more information on R.D., her upcoming publications, or what she's currently reading, check out her blog: http://desperateforagoodbook.com. There's a sign-up on her website if you are interested in being notified about upcoming publications or on her Amazon Authro Page. Or send her an email (rdbradywriter@gmail.com). She'd love to hear from you.